Praise for SYCAMORE

"With *Sycamore*, Ian Rogers delivers a serpentine narrative involving missing people, mobsters, rogue intelligence agents, and monsters that refuse to stay dead. Private investigator Felix Renn is a masterful creation—arch, world-weary, clever and tenacious. Fans of Jim Butcher and Richard Kadrey will be enthralled with the world of the Black Lands."

—NICK CUTTER, author of *The Troop* and *The Queen*

"Indomitable PI Felix Renn is back for another case and I'm delighted to follow him once again into the fray. Rogers' writing is pure gold."

—LAIRD BARRON, author of *Not a Speck of Light (Stories)*

"If Carl Kolchak had a grandson, his name would be Felix Renn. Readers who know Renn from his appearances in Ian Rogers' eerie Black Land stories will be glad to see him back in this bullet-quick killshot of a novel, and readers who haven't met Rogers' supernatural detective yet are in for a real treat. Slot this one on your bookshelf while you can grab it—smart money says it's the first of many!"

—NORMAN PARTRIDGE, author of *Dark Harvest*

SYCAMORE

SYCAMORE

IAN ROGERS

CEMETERY DANCE PUBLICATIONS

Baltimore
2024

Cemetery Dance Publications
132B Industry Lane, Unit #7
Forest Hill, MD 21050
www.cemeterydance.com

Trade Paperback Edition

ISBN:
978-1-58767-990-2

For Kathryn,
my light in the darkness

"Hello darkness, my old friend."
— Simon & Garfunkel

CHAPTER 1

I WAS RIGHT in the middle of getting my ass chewed out when the phone rang. Sandra was the one doing the chewing, and she kept right on going without missing a beat or taking a breath — or answering the phone, for that matter, even though it was her job.

I wanted to ask her to hold on a minute so I could answer it myself, but I was nervous about interrupting her. Sandra scared me a bit. She was my assistant, but she was also my ex-wife. Not my smartest move, perhaps, but we had history, some of it pretty good, and even though our marriage was over, we had discovered we weren't quite done with each other yet. Some people thought I was crazy to have her work for me. Some days I agreed with them.

"You're a snake," Sandra said, stabbing a finger at me. "A *cheap* snake. And that's the worst kind, Felix."

I was sitting with my feet up on the corner of my desk. Sandra was standing with her hands on her hips in the doorway to the outer office. She was almost as tall as me, about five-ten, with cool gray eyes, sharp features, and short ash blonde hair. I considered telling her she was beautiful when she was angry, then decided I liked my testicles right where they were.

The current topic of discussion was money — an unpopular subject when we were married, and one that still managed to rear its ugly head from time to time since our divorce.

Sandra said I wasn't paying her enough and wanted a raise. I told her I couldn't afford it. She said I could. We went back and forth like that for a while, then I did something stupid. Occupational hazard, you could say

— not as a private investigator, but as an ex-husband. I told her I could maybe afford to give her a raise, but only if I could write it off as alimony on my taxes. I'd meant it as a joke, but like most of the witticisms in my repertoire, Sandra didn't find it funny.

She replied that if we were going to go down that road, then she should have been paid a salary for the seven years we were married. She further stated that she should have also received an asshole bonus for lasting that long. Even though we'd been divorced for two years, we slipped into the old argument like a comfortable pair of pants.

Sandra crossed her arms and said, "You know what your problem is, Felix?"

"Too much handsome in one body?"

"You don't appreciate me. You didn't when we were married and you don't now. I do so much around here and you don't even care. I type your reports, I send out your invoices, and I keep your office clean because you're too much of a slob to do it yourself. I reorganized your entire filing system." She made a derisive sound. "Reorganized, hell. You didn't even *have* a system until I came along. I do *all* of your computer shit because you don't even know how to turn one on. Big surprise there — you've always had trouble turning things on."

Ouch.

"I sort the mail, I pay the bills. I cook for you, I clean—"

"Whoa, whoa. Hold on." I raised my hands in a halting gesture. "I think you travelled back in time there for a moment."

Sandra stared at me in seething silence.

"And to be fair, Dee, you never cooked or cleaned even when we were married. If you recall, I was the one who did all that stuff."

It was true, but it was clearly the wrong thing to say. Maybe because I'd brought up the past. Maybe because I'd used her old nickname. Probably both.

It didn't matter. Sandra continued to glare at me and the phone continued to ring. Neither of us made a move to answer it.

"I'd like to pay you more," I said. "I really would. But the money just isn't there. I'm doing the best I can, D... Sandra. Most private investigators can't even afford to have an assistant."

The truth was I could barely afford her. Sandra had started working for me shortly after the divorce. She needed the work and I needed the help. The past couple of years had marked the strangest, most dangerous period in my life, and hiring my ex-wife was the least of it. The funny thing was, when we weren't arguing with each other, about money, or the barely-healed wound that was our marriage, we actually made a pretty good team. Which further confirmed to me that on some level, we still needed each other. Not for love or money, but for some other reason neither of us could put into words. Most days we got along fine. This just happened to be one of the other days.

Sandra said, "*Well?*" and I realized I'd zoned out for a moment while she'd been speaking.

"Uh, what was the question again?"

Sandra shook her head in weary frustration. "You're a real asshole, Felix."

"Listen, I'll do what I can, okay? I'll take a look at the books and see if I can figure something out."

"*You'll* look at the books?" Sandra snapped. "You can barely add. *I'm* the one who does your taxes every year."

I spread my hands. "Then you should know I don't have the money to give you a raise."

Sandra frowned and I thought that was the end of it. Problem solved. Okay, not solved, but put off for the time being. Then she hit me where she knew it would hurt.

"You need to take on more cases."

"I take plenty of…"

"More of *those* cases."

"You know PIs don't get hazard pay, right?"

"I'd like to pay my rent this month, Felix. And I'd like to eat, too."

I looked down at my hands folded in my lap. "Let's get back to work, okay?"

Sandra didn't say anything.

I glanced over at the ringing phone. "You can start right now."

Sandra said, "Ohhh," really drawing it out. I was impressed with the amount of sarcasm she was able to inject into that one little word. "You want me to answer the phone? Is that what you'd like? Okay, let me get that for you."

She came over, picked up the phone, cradle and all, and threw it at my head.

Fortunately I have the reflexes of a cat. Makes sense since I was named after one.

I leaped out of my chair. The phone struck the wall behind me and clattered to the floor.

"It's for you," Sandra said sweetly, then turned and walked out of the room.

I let out a deep sigh as I reached over to pick up the phone.

Nick and Nora Charles, we were not.

CHAPTER 2

"FELIX RENN'S HOUSE of Pancakes, how may I serve you?"

There was silence on the other end of the line, and for a moment I thought Sandra had broken the phone when she heaved it at me. Then, a female voice said, "Hello? Is this Felix Renn?"

"None other."

"The private investigator?"

"The very one."

"Oh." Like Sandra, the caller managed to pack a lot of emotion into that one word. In Sandra's case it had been sarcasm. This time it was the unmistakable sound of disappointment.

"How can I help you?"

"I was wondering if I could speak with you. About some work. A... case." She sighed. "I'm sorry, I've never done anything like this before."

"That's okay," I said. "What's your name?"

"Susan," she said. "Susan Weaver. I'm calling about my husband. He's missing."

"Have you notified the police?"

"The police know," she said in a dismissive way. "But frankly I don't have much faith in them."

"It might be better if we talked about this in person. Could you come by my office?"

"I live in Sycamore, Mr. Renn. And I have a daughter. She's... It's very difficult for me to get down to the city right now. Would you mind coming here?"

"Sure," I said. Sycamore. The name rang a distant bell, but I couldn't make the connection. "It'll take me a couple of hours to get out there."

"That's okay," she said. I could hear the relief in her voice. "I'll be waiting for you."

I jotted down her address and said I'd see her in a little while.

After hanging up the phone (and placing it back on the corner of my desk), I took out my road atlas and looked up Sycamore. Seeing it on the map didn't help me understand why it sounded familiar. Located north of the city, it was one of those small towns that people passed through on their way up to cottage country in the Muskokas. I'd probably driven through it myself and never given it a second thought. But the name still nibbled at my mind.

I went over to the door to the outer office and peeked out. Sandra was sitting at her desk, looking at something on her computer monitor.

"Hey, Dee, it looks like we may have a case. Do you think you could rustle me up some directions?"

Sandra didn't say anything. Something was up and I knew right away it didn't have anything to do with me. The silent treatment was never her style.

I came up behind her and looked over her shoulder. Normally she hated that, but her attention was so focused on the screen she didn't even notice I was there.

She was on the CNN website watching video of a breaking news report. They were showing aerial footage of a park in a city I didn't immediately recognize. Then the view swung around to a stadium in the background that I knew was Fenway. The super at the bottom of the screen said:

NEW PORTAL APPEARS IN BOSTON.

CHAPTER 3

"IT'S LIKE A bad joke."

Sandra looked over her shoulder at me. "What?"

I gestured at the screen. "New portal *appears* in Boston? Portals are invisible, everyone knows that."

"That's all you have to say? You're nitpicking over a stupid word while something like this is happening?"

"It's lazy journalism," I muttered, looking down at my feet.

Sandra shook her head and went back to watching the news coverage.

CNN had switched from aerial footage to a ground crew stationed outside of a police cordon. The camera panned across a long row of cops in full riot gear. Behind them a line of sawhorses and bright yellow police tape blocked off the entrance to a park. Although the discovery of a new portal was usually cause for fear and panic, a large crowd of rubberneckers had formed on the street. Several hands held smartphones, raised high over the tops of everyone's heads so they could shoot video of their own.

"I guess this means Boston's going to lose its 'portal free' status," Sandra said.

"The tourism board won't be happy about that."

Sandra turned her head and glared at me.

"How many portals have been found?" I asked.

"Just one," Sandra said. "So far."

"One's enough. Where is it?"

"Victory Gardens?"

"That's in the Fens."

Sandra looked at me.

"It's a park near Fenway." I pointed at the screen. "The Red Sox fans are gonna be pissed."

"You're one to talk about bad jokes, Felix."

I held up the slip of paper with Susan Weaver's address. "Can you Google me some directions?"

Sandra swivelled around in her seat to face me fully. "You can't ignore this." I stared back at her. *Wanna bet?*

After a long moment of tense silence, Sandra snapped the paper out of my hand, opened another web browser, and printed out my directions.

"It's work, Dee. Work equals money, money equals a raise. Remember?"

Sandra slapped the printout into my hand, swivelled back around, and resumed watching the ongoing live coverage of doom and gloom.

I had grabbed my coat off the hook and was halfway out the door when she spoke again.

"This is the world we live in, Felix." Her voice was low but firm. "The Black Lands, the portals — you can't run from them. None of us can. It's part of your life; it's part of all of our lives. But it's more for you. It's also your job."

I stood in the doorway, one hand on the knob, the other clutching the directions to Sycamore.

"Not today," I muttered.

I PICKED up my car from the underground garage on Bloor Street and headed north on Yonge. It was a little after ten on a Thursday morning and traffic wasn't too bad.

Near the intersection with Lawrence Avenue, I drove past a tall plywood barrier surrounding the site for a new condominium. A common enough sight in Toronto, only this one had been under construction for about four years. That was when the workers who had been digging out the foundation had discovered the portal. No one knew how long it had been there, lying underground like a forgotten bomb from some long-ago war, but it didn't matter. The portal was here now and it wasn't going anywhere. The government swooped in and took over the site; they built a facility around the portal to contain and monitor it, and erected a twelve-foot-tall security fence to keep people out. The plywood barrier from the construction job remained, along with a sign, now old and faded, advertising *Midtown Luxury Condos! Your home in the city, your gateway to a luxurious new world!* A poor choice of phrasing, in retrospect, although no one could have known what the workers would dig up. Still, I'm glad I wasn't an investor on that one.

I got on the 401, took it east to the 400, then headed north. It was a nice drive once you cleared the city. Even though I'd spent most of my adult life in Toronto, I was born and raised in a small town. As a child, on trips to the city, I always enjoyed staring out the passenger window and watching the way the landscape of trees and lakes and farmer's fields would phase into the sprawl of the suburbs, then the bigger, industrial buildings of the manufacturing sector, and finally the full-blown grandeur of skyscrapers and office towers. It was like entering another world without even realizing it. I still enjoyed living in the city, but on occasions like this, where I found myself taking the opposite journey to the one I'd taken as a child, the feeling I often experienced was relief.

I turned on the radio, which was set to an oldies station. Leslie Gore was singing that it was her party and she'd cry if she wanted to. There were probably a lot of people crying in Boston right now. People crying everywhere. It didn't matter where the portals showed up, they affected everyone.

The song ended and the news came on. The top story was Boston. It was the only story, it seemed, squeezing out sports and the weather. I changed the channel. More Boston. I changed it again and got a talk-radio program talking about... Boston.

You can't ignore this, Sandra had said.

She was right, as she so often was.

It wasn't that I didn't care about what was happening in Boston. It was more that I tried to avoid the daily news as much as possible, especially when it was about the Black Lands. I found it was best for my mental well-being to ignore the hysterical highs and the depressing lows that seemed to make up the majority of current events. The downside was that it left me out of touch with the world at large, but for the most part I was okay with that.

Over the past few years I had managed to carve out a small life for myself, and in that life I'd been able to assert an equally small measure of control.

This control wasn't total — it wiggled and wobbled at times, and sometimes it was almost pulled out from under me — but I protected it fiercely.

Some people spent their whole life trying to figure out why bad things happened in the world. Since there was no answer to that question — or because they couldn't accept the fact that bad things sometimes *just happened* — many of these people ended up going to their graves with confused expressions on their faces. I decided a long time ago that that would never be me.

It wasn't about apathy. It was about control. That's what it always came back to. You can't save the whole planet, so why bother trying? Save the people around you instead. That was part of the reason I became a PI. It was about helping some people, but not everyone. It was about maintaining small measures of control. For me it was the only way to live in this world. The only way to survive.

I reached for the dial again, then hesitated. This was not control, I told myself. This was, in actuality, the lead-up to a total and complete loss of control.

I may have been afraid of the Black Lands and the portals — anyone who said they weren't was either a liar or a fool — but I decided I could sit here in my car and listen to a radio show about them.

I put my hand back on the wheel and settled in as the host did what every journalist seemed to do when a new portal was discovered. He went back in time. Back to the beginning of the nightmare.

Back to the arrival of the portals.

IT STARTED over seventy years ago, although some people (myself included) believe it actually began much earlier than that.

On December 5, 1945, five U.S. Navy bombers, designated Flight 19, left Fort Lauderdale to complete a training exercise off the Florida coast. When they failed to return, a massive search effort was carried out. Neither the planes nor the crews of Flight 19 were ever found, but something else was discovered.

Another world.

A dark dimension lying right next-door to our own.

The Black Lands.

That's what they called it, those first explorers who went off in search of missing planes and instead found a sunless realm, a place of forever night that was filled with all manner of supernatural creatures — some of them straight out of our oldest myths and folklore, others that not even the most demented human mind could conceive.

It was a discovery that changed the world. Hundreds of portals, all of them invisible to the naked eye, had instantaneously appeared in the area where the Navy planes had vanished. Flight 19 was the first casualty of the Black Lands, but it wouldn't be the last.

Months later, when it became clear the portals weren't going anywhere, the powers that be decided that drastic measures must be taken. A massive section of the Atlantic Ocean encompassing nearly two million square miles was declared off-limits to all travel, business and recreational. All shipping routes and flight paths were altered to avoid the area, which over time came to be known as the Bermuda Triangle.

Policing a border of this size, especially on water, was virtually impossible, but those who disobeyed the warnings and entered the Triangle ended up discovering that this was the sort of place that policed itself. After a few years passed and more planes and ships vanished without a trace, the rest of the world began to smarten up and give the area a wide, wide berth.

Even though the loss of Flight 19 had been a terrible tragedy, and the arrival of the portals an unexpected and unsettling event, the world might have been able to move on if things had ended there.

But then another portal showed up.

On land.

IT WAS in a farmer's field outside Orrin, Kansas.

The farmer who owned the field discovered the portal by accident when he happened to drive his tractor through it. Much like Flight 19, neither the farmer nor his tractor were ever recovered, and it took several days for investigators to figure out what had happened.

By then, seven people were dead. Not by passing through the portal, but by something that had crossed over from the other side.

Eventually the authorities were able to kill the creature. A werewolf, or what is more commonly known these days as a shifter. I've seen pictures of it in history books.

In the aftermath, the government was at a loss for what to do with a dimensional rift on American soil. They ended up doing the only thing they could think of.

They put a fence up around it. Then they tried to move on.

When the second portal appeared four months later, in the heart of downtown Prague, the world began to realize they had a very serious problem on their hands.

IN THE United States, the President declared a state of national emergency. Several other countries followed suit as portals started popping up all over the planet.

Theologians and tabloid newspapers said we were living in the End Times. The governments of the world did all they could to maintain order, but they were fighting against a tide of panic and hysteria that threatened to wash over the entire planet. Suicides went up for a while, economic markets went down, but when no apocalypse came, things slowly returned to normal. Or at least a new semblance of normal.

The United States and Canada decided to confront this threat together. In much the same way NORAD monitored the airspace over the two nations, the Paranormal Intelligence Agency was tasked with studying and supervising the portals that showed up on land. Their mandate also included the investigation of supernatural phenomena and the elimination of Black Lands entities.

To this day, no one knows exactly how many portals there are. Some countries, like Russia and North Korea, not only claim to have none, but have stated that the portals and the Black Lands are nothing more than a campaign of fear and intimidation created by the West.

Despite their denials, the portals keep coming.

No one knows why they came or how to close them.

No one knows what will happen one day if, or when, they end up covering the entire planet.

Theories abound. Take your pick.

I TURNED off the radio and drove on in silence. I'd heard enough for one day. Or at least that's what I told myself. If only there was a switch to shut off the thoughts in my head.

Like everyone in my generation, I was born in the shadow of the Black Lands. It's hard for me to imagine what the world was like before the portals. A world where parents could tell their kids that monsters didn't exist. It must've been nice.

The government tries to assuage our fears by saying that you're more likely to be struck by lightning than to encounter a supernatural creature from the Black Lands. I managed to avoid any such encounters for most of my life.

Then I was struck by lightning.

Again and again and again.

It started a couple years back when I was hired to work a case that started out normal, and then, through no fault of my own, brought me into contact with a couple of Black Lands entities. I should have been killed, but I wasn't. I attributed this to luck rather than any skill on my part, but that didn't stop me from acquiring a reputation as someone who could make your paranormal problems go away. A kind of supernatural *Spenser: for Hire.*

Since then, I've had run-ins with vampires, shifters, possessors, and even a couple of spooky black-eyed kids who had a thing for bodily dismemberment. Not exactly what I signed up for when I got my private license, but it's a living. At least until it gets me killed.

So you might be able to understand why a simple missing person case was looking pretty good to me right then. A case with no supernatural elements whatsoever. It would almost be like a vacation.

Still, I guess I should have known better.

The best laid plans of monsters and men, eh?

CHAPTER 4

I WAS IN Sycamore by noon. The welcome sign said it had a population of thirty thousand. Entering the town was like approaching a planet surrounded by an asteroid field. The outer ring was made up of older houses on big lots, widely spaced from one another. Then I passed through a new development where the homes were bigger and built closer together. Several of them had Halloween decorations: cardboard ghosts in the windows, cotton cobwebs strung up in the trees, those orange leaf bags that look like giant jack-o'-lanterns. I cruised past the usual assortment of schools, parks, and churches, then into a modest-sized downtown section built around a square with tall trees, walking paths, and a fountain in the center. All of the buildings were old but well maintained. The businesses were an assortment of trendy-looking shops and upscale boutiques, alongside shops of the mom-and-pop variety that looked like they'd been there for fifty years or more. There wasn't a chain or big-box store in sight.

Like a lot of small towns, Sycamore had the timeless quality of a place that had been forgotten by the rest of the world, and the people who lived here probably liked it that way. I'd grown up in a place similar to this, so even though I'd never been to Sycamore before, in a strange way it was like coming home.

My directions took me across to the far side of town and then out of it again. I was starting to think that either Sandra or Google had messed up when I arrived at my destination — a large fieldstone house set back from the road on an immaculately maintained lawn.

I turned into the dirt driveway and parked under an enormous tree. A few other trees of equal size stood around the yard like sentinels. I wondered if any of them were sycamores. They might have been. I didn't know my trees very well.

I climbed out of my car and was immediately overwhelmed by the strong smells of fresh-cut grass and clean country air. I stood there for a few moments, breathing in those heady scents and taking in the sight of all that green.

The Weaver residence was the sort of rustic place one would expect to find in the English countryside rather than small-town Ontario. It had a solidity that modern houses didn't possess. Maybe it was the heavy grey stone from which it had been constructed, or maybe it was just the way the house seemed to stand alone against the wild, untamed nature that surrounded it. Small shrubs ran along the front and sides of the house like a short green skirt. A detached two-storey garage was covered completely in ivy and looked like a giant Chia Pet.

I walked up a flagstone path to the front door. Standing on the small porch, I became aware of a low, rhythmic creaking sound. I glanced around but couldn't find the source. I knocked on the heavy oaken door and waited.

A few moments later, the door was opened by a tall, slender woman in a dark sweater and jeans. She had pale skin, dark eyes, and chestnut hair that fell limply to her shoulders. Her mouth, small and pursed, closed even tighter when she saw me.

"Mrs. Weaver?" I said.

She gave a small nod.

I held out my hand. "I'm Felix Renn."

She looked at my hand like she'd never seen one before, then raised her eyes back to mine.

"You called me?" I said, prompting her.

She twisted her hands together and continued to stare at me without saying anything. I started to wonder if she really had called me. Maybe I had the wrong house. Maybe I was supposed to see another Susan Weaver in Sycamore.

As the silence continued to stretch out, I heard that low creaking sound again. It wasn't coming from inside the house. It was coming from somewhere outside. I was about to ask her about it when she said, "Yes, I called you."

She reached out and clutched my hand in both of hers, shaking it and pulling me into the house at the same time. "Please come in."

I let her drag me into a small, dark foyer. The air inside was cool and pleasant, with a hint of spices that I associated with fresh baking and well-stocked pantries.

"You *are* Susan Weaver?" I said.

The woman nodded, her dark eyes almost invisible in the murk of the house.

"I'm afraid I'm going to need that back," I said, looking down at her two hands still wrapped around my own.

"I'm sorry," she said, dropping my hand like it was hot. "I'm… I'm…" She gave her head a frustrated shake. "I don't know what I am."

"It's okay," I said. "Why don't we sit down and talk?"

Susan Weaver gave a distracted nod and led me through an archway into a living room that was as dark as the foyer. Heavy curtains covered the windows, blocking out the sunlight. There was an overhead fixture and a few lamps scattered around the room, but she made no move to turn any of them on. It was like she wanted to exist in her own private world of darkness.

I sat down on a comfy-looking couch while Susan Weaver perched on the edge of a green leather wingback chair like a bird on a telephone wire. I tried to put her at ease with a friendly smile, worried that a sudden move or a loud sound might send her flying away.

I folded my hands in my lap and said, "So?"

Susan didn't say anything.

"You mentioned on the phone that your husband is missing."

She dropped her eyes from mine and gave a small nod.

"When did he go missing?"

She looked off into the corner. "About a month ago."

"Have you contacted the police?"

Another nod.

"You filled out a missing-persons report?"

"Yes."

I felt like I was conducting a job interview with someone who not only didn't want the job, but didn't want to be here at all.

"Well, Mrs. Weaver," I said, "can you tell me if the police gave you any indication that your husband left under his own power, or if they believe foul play was involved?"

Susan seemed to visibly deflate, as if my question had punched a hole in her fragile façade and let all her air out. Her shoulders slumped and head lolled so far forward I thought it was going to slide right off and land in her lap. She remained like that for a long moment, like a puppet with its strings cut, then she raised her head again, straightened her shoulders, and took in a deep, steadying breath.

"My husband is dead, Mr. Renn." Her dark eyes blazed at me. "I need you to find his body."

CHAPTER 5

I LEANED BACK in my seat and let her words sink in. Or tried to. They didn't so much sink as bob around on the surface of my mind.

One thing was clear to me now, though. Something I should've noticed when Susan Weaver first opened the door. Something I should've seen on her face. Her dark eyes and pale skin, the tight lines around her mouth. Susan Weaver wasn't worried about her husband. She was long past worry. She was already mourning him.

"Why do you think your husband is dead, Mrs. Weaver?"

"I *know* he's dead," she said. "The police found blood in his car."

"That doesn't mean…"

"Too much blood," she blurted. "Too much to have lost and survived."

"That still doesn't necessarily mean he's dead."

I was trying to reassure her, but my words seemed to have the opposite effect. Her eyes clenched shut and tears squeezed out of them. She made no attempt to wipe them away as they slid down her cheeks. Her hands were curled into tight fists in her lap. Her body thrummed as if a strong current was running through it.

"He's dead," Susan said in an emphatic voice that brooked no argument. "I know it. I just want you to find his… I want you to find him and bring him home."

"Mrs. Weaver…" I began.

"Susan."

"Susan, I've found people before, but I've never been asked to look for someone who's... deceased."

"Does that mean you can't do it?" There was a challenging note in her voice.

"No, I'm just saying it's new territory for me."

"This is new territory for all of us," Susan said obscurely.

"Us?"

"Me and my daughter." Her gaze drifted. "Her name is Rachel."

"How old is she?"

"Eight," Susan said. She made a vague gesture, like she wasn't sure, or that it wasn't important. "I don't know how to talk to her about any of this."

Eight seemed old enough to understand that her father was missing and presumed dead. But then again, what did I know. I didn't have any kids. "I'm afraid I don't follow."

Susan gave me a long, assessing look. "You really don't know."

"Know what?"

Susan kept staring at me, like she was waiting to see if I was kidding.

"About the murders," she said. "The murders here in Sycamore."

I REALIZED, much too late, that wearing an expression of complete and total befuddlement is probably not the look a private investigator should go for. Especially when said PI is currently being considered for a job.

Susan was looking at me with wide, incredulous eyes. "Are you telling me the news hasn't reached Toronto?"

"It may have," I said. "I really don't pay much attention to the news."

"So you know nothing about the murders," Susan said. It wasn't phrased as a question, but then it didn't need to be. The answer was pretty clear on my face.

"How many have there been?" I asked.

Susan stared at me for another long, drawn-out moment. "Six," she said.

I nodded like it was all coming back to me. Which, in a way, it was. "When we spoke on the phone, you said you lived in Sycamore. I recognized the name but didn't know why. I recall hearing something about it." I wondered if my explanation sounded as lame to her as it did to me.

"Does that mean you'll help me?"

"Are you sure you still want me to?"

Susan raised her hands, palms up, then let them flop back into her lap. "I'll take whatever help I can get right now."

That stung, but I deserved it.

"Let's start at the beginning," I said. "What's your husband's name?"

"Douglas," Susan said. "Doug."

"How long have you been married?"

Susan thought about it, then said: "Thirteen years." She paused. "It would've been fourteen next month."

"Where does he work?"

"We own a garden store here in town."

I nodded. "I noticed your yard as I drove up. It looks like something out of a painting. I guess it helps when there's not one but two green thumbs in the family. The trees are particularly impressive. I don't think I've ever seen any that big before. Are they sycamores?"

"Those are oak trees," Susan said. "Century-old oaks." Her gaze drifted past my shoulder to the window that looked out on the front yard. "They were part of the reason Doug wanted to buy this house. He loved trees." She paused, maybe because she caught herself using the past tense. "You won't find any sycamores around here. Not anymore."

"So the name of the town is just false advertising, then."

I smiled and Susan gave me a small one in return.

"The name is a bit misleading," she said. "There were sycamores here when the town was originally settled, but they've long since died off from one disease or another. Every few years the city council talks about bringing them back, but they've never gotten around to doing it. There hasn't been a sycamore in these parts for fifty years or more." She shrugged. "I guess they decided to keep the name, anyway."

"Probably saves money on replacing all the signs and tourism brochures."

Susan gave me another smile, a bit wider this time, showing a little teeth. "There isn't much tourism here, Mr. Renn. Sycamore is one of those places people pass through on their way somewhere else."

"Call me Felix," I said. "Are you and your husband both from here?"

"Yes," Susan said. "We met in junior year at Sycamore High."

"High school sweethearts?"

"Yes," she said, smiling broadly now. It was bright enough to push back some of the darkness in the room.

"I didn't think they actually existed."

"They do," she said. "Doug was captain of the football team and I was a cheerleader."

"You're kidding me."

"No lie." There was a photo album sitting on a corner of the coffee table. Susan pulled it into her lap, flipped a few pages, then handed it over to me.

I looked at a double-page spread of colour 3x5 prints, several of them showing a tall, broad-shouldered kid with soft eyes and a shy grin. He was wearing a football uniform in many of the photos, but he didn't seem comfortable in it. In most of the shots he was slouching, with his head hanging down, like he was embarrassed by his size.

"Doug was athletic," Susan said, "but he wasn't the stereotypical jock. He was very smart, very sensitive. I think the only reason he played football was because he was big and strong and his father pushed him into it. Doug was a very agreeable person. He always wanted to help people, wanted them to like him." She wrinkled her nose. "I, on the other hand, was a lousy cheerleader. I ended up breaking my leg at the second football game of the season."

"I didn't realize cheerleading was so dangerous."

"It is when you fall off the top of a human pyramid."

"Ouch."

Susan nodded. Her eyes had gone misty and distant as she looked into the past. "I was off the squad with my leg in a cast for six weeks. That's when I noticed Doug. When I was cheering, he was just another player on the field, but after I broke my leg he was suddenly everywhere. Picking up my homework for me. Opening doors for me at school. Carrying my lunch tray in the cafeteria."

"My keen detective skills tell me he liked you."

"Doug was a lot of things, but subtle wasn't one of them." Susan fidgeted with the wedding band on her ring finger, turning it around and around. "He was spending so much time with me he started missing football practices. Then he missed a couple of games and the coach kicked him off the team. His father was furious, but Doug didn't care. Neither did I. I guess we were too busy falling in love."

"That's a nice story," I said.

Susan nodded and wiped at her eyes.

"Can you tell me about the day he went missing?"

Susan's brow darkened like a storm cloud had drifted over her head. Back to reality. She cleared her throat.

"It happened last month, on September twentieth. Doug went to the store that morning while I stayed home with Rachel. She was having one of her bad days." She saw the confused look on my face. "Rachel has... emotional problems, and a learning disability." She looked at her hands twisting in her lap and made them stop. "We have a live-in nurse, but it was a two-person job that day, so I ended up staying home. Doug was usually home by five-thirty, but that day he didn't show up. I tried calling him on his cell phone, but he didn't answer. I waited a few more hours and when he still didn't come home, I called the police."

I nodded for her to continue.

"They found his truck the next morning. It was parked down by the lake. It was..." She swallowed and her throat made a dry clicking sound. "There was blood all over the interior. So much blood that he couldn't have survived."

"The police said that?"

She closed her eyes and nodded.

"You said there were other murders. Was Doug the first?"

"No," Susan said. "He was the third. And there have been three more since."

"In the past month?"

Susan nodded.

"That's..." The word I was looking for was *incredible*, but the really incredible part was that I hadn't heard anything about it. I suppose that's what happened when you made a point of ignoring current events. I felt bad about it now, as if my attempt to inoculate myself against the toxic daily news cycle had somehow made me an accessory to it.

"Have the police arrested anyone?"

Susan shook her head.

"Do you know if they have any suspects?"

"I don't know."

"Have they told you anything?"

She shook her head again.

I slumped back in my seat. The entire situation was mind-boggling. I didn't know what to ask her next.

"You mentioned a nurse," I said. "She lives here at the house?"

"Above the garage," Susan said. "There's a small apartment up there."

"The police spoke to her, too?"

"Yes," Susan said. "She was with me all day. She couldn't tell them anything. Neither of us could."

"What's her name?"

"Nancy."

"And your daughter is Rachel?"

Susan gave me a funny look, and I raised my hands defensively. "I'm not making a list of suspects. I'm just trying to keep track of everyone."

She sat up straighter. "Does that mean you'll take the case?"

"To be perfectly honest, I don't know if there's even a case to take. If the police believe your husband was murdered and his body was... well, *removed from the scene*, then I'm not sure what I can do to help find it that they aren't already doing."

Susan leaned forward with her hands folded tightly together. "Please," she said. "Just say you'll try."

I sighed and rubbed the back of my neck. I tried to pull my eyes away from the sad, tormented woman with the tears drying to a cracked glaze on her cheeks, but I couldn't. It was like her gaze had locked me in with a tractor beam. The more I stared into those dark eyes the more I found myself seeing the teenage girl she used to be. The cheerleader with the broken leg who had fallen in love with the sensitive jock. Married young, started a business together in their home town, then had a daughter. I could almost picture her, too. Eight years old, with her father's soft eyes and her mother's chestnut hair, and damaged now in some way that may or may not show on the surface. A girl who had lost her father, and maybe didn't have the mental capacity to understand and process that loss. A family of three that had been violently subtracted by one. The picture was clear in my head even though I didn't know these people. But even if I didn't know them, I knew about their need. The need for answers. The need for resolution. For closure. No matter how much pain it might bring. Because the pain of not knowing was worse.

The local police had their hands full with a serial killer. They almost certainly didn't have the resources to look for a body that could have been buried anywhere, or burned, or weighed down and dumped in the lake. They were probably more concerned with making sure no one else ended up dead. That was their priority now. So what was mine?

"I'll try," I said. "But I'll tell you up front, I don't know if I'll be able to find him. I've never done anything like this before, and frankly I'm not even sure where to start. I promise to do my best, but with a case like this one that's about all I *can* promise."

"That's all I want," Susan said. She spoke quickly, like she was worried I might change my mind. "I just want someone to try. It feels like everyone else has given up on him."

"I have one condition," I said.

A look of dread appeared in her eyes. "Yes?"

"I'll spend a few days on this — a week, tops — but if I don't feel like I'm getting anywhere, then I'll have to drop the case. I'm not going to take your money if I feel I can't help you."

Susan gave a slow, solemn nod of her head. "Okay."

We discussed payment in an absent sort of way. I told Susan my daily rate, plus reasonable expenses, and she readily accepted. As I stood up to leave, I asked her the question I always dreaded asking but in this case was genuinely curious to hear the answer.

"How did you find me?"

Susan blinked and said, "The police haven't been much help, so I thought I'd look into hiring a private detective. I didn't know where to look for one, so I Googled it." She blushed. "I realize how silly that sounds, but it isn't the sort of thing you'd find here in Sycamore. I read some articles about you online and they mentioned you were in Toronto, so I looked up your number and called you." She hesitated. "How long have you been a private investigator?"

"Eight years," I said. "I mentored under another investigator named Madeline Ferine. She showed me the ropes until I got my own licence."

"You live in Toronto?"

"That's right."

"Were you born there?"

"No. I'm from a little town named Dover."

"Do you get back there often?"

"I try not to," I said. "And if your next question is about my measurements, I'm afraid I'll have to ask for a nurse to be present."

Susan made a strange face. Maybe she was allergic to dumb jokes. I decided to switch tracks.

"If you researched me, then you know the cases I work tend to involve the Black Lands."

Susan nodded. "I heard they found a portal in Boston. It's been on the news all morning." A look of uncertainty came into her eyes. "You do take other cases, though, don't you? Normal ones?"

This case was far from normal, but I understood what she meant.

"Yes," I said. "And I'll do everything I can to find your husband."

CHAPTER 6

I REGRETTED THE words the moment they left my mouth. I hadn't promised Susan Weaver that I would find her husband, but it felt like I had. A light had come into her eyes when I agreed to take the case. Like I was already well on my way to finding her husband's body. I didn't want to douse that light, but I felt like it was only a matter of time. I could hear the voice of Madeline Ferine chastising me in my head: *Don't make promises, Felix. Make contracts. If you want to make promises, go fall in love.*

I had tried falling in love, but the results had been mixed. I suppose I made a better PI than a husband. Speaking of which, I had to call Sandra and tell her I was employed again. That would make her happy. At the very least, it would keep her from yelling at me for a few days.

I was reaching into my pocket for my cell phone when I heard the creaking sound again.

I went around the right side of the house where the dirt driveway led to the detached garage. Nothing there. I walked back across the lawn to the other side of the house and saw another of those massive trees — one of the century-old oaks Susan Weaver had mentioned. A swing hung from one of its thick branches, and sitting on the wooden seat was a small girl in a grey jacket, her blue-jeaned legs dragging listlessly through the trimmed grass beneath her. An older woman in her late fifties or early sixties stood a short distance away, smoking a cigarette while she watched the girl.

The scene looked like a Norman Rockwell painting — *Young Girl with Nurse*, it might've been called.

I must have made some sound without realizing it because the woman's head suddenly turned in my direction. She didn't seem surprised to see me. She took the cigarette out of her mouth and tapped some ash on the ground. I gave her a small wave and she responded with a curt nod. She turned back to the girl, said something to her that I couldn't hear, then came over to me.

"Hi there," I said, extending my hand. "I'm Felix Renn."

The woman's grip was dry and strong. She had the hard, country-scrubbed face of a farmer, with nets of wrinkles around her pale blue eyes. There were furrows in her cheeks and laugh lines bracketing her mouth. Her silver hair was cut short in a bob. In her Blue Jays warmup jacket and grey track pants, she looked less like a nurse than a grizzled gym teacher who had no patience for wimps and took a sadistic pleasure in dodgeball.

"I'm Nancy Sloane," she said. "Or Nurse Nancy." She shrugged. "Whichever you prefer."

"I'll go with plain old Nancy if that's okay."

"That's me," she said. "Nancy, Plain and Old."

I flushed. "I'm sorry. I didn't mean..."

She held up a halting hand. "I'm just pulling your chain. Besides, Nurse Nancy makes me sound like a porn star, which I most definitely am not. Not even when I had a body that didn't look like a wrinkled-up prune." She leaned her head back and looked at me through slitted eyes. "So you're the private detective."

"I know Sycamore is a small town, but I didn't think news travelled *that* fast."

"It's not that small," Nancy said. "Susan told me you were coming. Don't think I've ever met a real private eye before."

"I hope I don't disappoint."

Nancy gave me a quick up-and-down look. "No fedora, but I guess you'll do."

As we stood there, smiling at each other in companionable silence, I became aware that the creaking sound was gone.

The girl had stopped her lackadaisical swinging and was looking over at us. At me. She had her mother's dark eyes, only they were bigger and shinier, like a doll's eyes. Her mouth trembled, like she was about to start crying. It took me a moment to figure out she was trying to smile. I felt a dull pang in my chest.

"What is it?" Nancy said.

I turned to her. "What?"

"You got a strange look on your face just then. Are you all right?"

"I… yes. She just reminded me of someone."

"Your daughter?"

I shook my head. "Just someone I used to know." I waggled my fingers at Rachel. "Hello there," I said, raising my voice. "How are you doing today?"

The girl stared at me for a few long seconds, then resumed her listless swinging.

I turned back to Nancy. "Is it my lack of charm?"

"She's on the spectrum."

"Autism?"

Nancy nodded. "About a quarter of those diagnosed are non-verbal. Rachel talks, just not very much, and not very often."

"The strong silent type," I said. "Nothing wrong with that."

"Nope," Nancy said. "People talk too much as it is. You learn more by listening."

"Her mother said she has emotional problems and a learning disability."

"That just sounds better than saying she has a neurodevelopment disorder. Autism isn't a learning disability, but it can affect learning. Rachel's a smart kid — most on the spectrum are. She just wasn't made for the typical school classroom."

"So you're her nurse and her tutor?"

Nancy took a drag off her cigarette. "I'm a jack of all trades." She frowned. "Well… two trades. Mostly I'm another set of hands for the Weavers."

"How long have you been working with Rachel?"

"About six months. She had a rough go with school last year — trouble focusing, not participating in class, talking less and less. Her parents were worried she wasn't going be ready for the next grade in September, so they took her to a doctor and had her tested. She was diagnosed with autism and they hired me to help her."

"Susan said you live here."

Nancy pointed across the yard at the apartment above the garage. *"Mi casa."*

"Is it normal for parents with an autistic child to have live-in help?"

Nancy arched an eyebrow at me. "We in the mental health care profession don't use the N-word."

"Right," I said. "Sorry."

Nancy waved it away. "To answer your question, no, they don't usually employ full-time help, much less live-in care. But if you've got the money…" She spread her hands, the one holding the cigarette dragging a small contrail of smoke through the air.

"The Weavers are well-off?"

"They've got their own business, and I get the impression it does quite well. But it's not really any of my business," she added with a certain emphasis that said it wasn't any of mine, either.

"What do you think about Doug Weaver's disappearance?"

"I think it sucks," Nancy said bluntly. She dropped her cigarette on the ground and heeled it out. "Doug was a really nice guy. The folks who can afford private help, they're usually the type who never have anything to do with their kids. It's like they see them as damaged goods that they can't return to the store, so their only solution is to pay someone else to feed them and school them and tuck them in at night. Doug wasn't like that. He asked questions, he did his own research, and he was always involved with the work I was doing with Rachel. He cared, and Rachel could tell he cared. Lots of kids on the spectrum have trouble expressing their feelings, but that doesn't mean they don't have any. That's an assumption lots of people make, that these kids are nothing more than human robots. But that's not the case. They have issues, that's all."

"And who doesn't have issues?"

"Exactly." Nancy looked over at Rachel. "I do worry what this whole situation has done to the progress we've made. Kids tend to keep their thoughts and feelings to themselves. Kids on the spectrum can be even harder to read."

"What does she know about her father?"

"She knows he's missing, but she doesn't know any of the details."

"What do *you* think?" I asked.

"He's dead," Nancy said. "He has to be. At least I hope he is."

I thought I'd misheard her. "You hope he is?"

"Beats the alternative," Nancy said. Before I could ask what she meant by that, she said, "Can I ask you something? Kind of off-topic, might be a little personal."

"Okay."

"How much do you get paid?"

"Depends on the job."

"You get a lot of jobs like this?"

"No," I admitted.

"You got an hourly rate?"

"I do."

"You work a regular eight-hour day?"

"Not usually. PIs tend to keep odd hours."

"Who keeps track of them?"

"I do."

"So when you bill your client they have to take your word that you worked the hours you said you did?"

"I can assure you, I'm as honest as the day is long."

"It's October," Nancy said. "The days are getting shorter."

"My rates go up after daylight saving time."

She laughed at that, a loud, rusty caw that I found strangely endearing.

"I bet you're one of those guys who always has a comeback. Sorry to pry. I was just curious. I've never met a PI before."

"I'm not going to take advantage of Mrs. Weaver, if that's what you're worried about."

Nancy held up her hand. "I meant no offense. Suze has had a rough go of it lately, and it's going to get worse before it gets any better. If it ever does get better. I guess it's in my nature to be protective." She glanced over at Rachel, swaying slowly on the swing. "I should get back to work. It was nice talking to you."

I watched as Nancy walked back over and resumed her spot next to Rachel. She leaned down and whispered something in the girl's ear. Rachel turned her head and looked at me. I gave her another wave, and this time she raised her hand, splayed her fingers wide, and held it there.

Nancy gave me a thumbs-up. Progress!

I tipped her a salute and walked back to my car.

CHAPTER 7

I HEADED BACK to town in search of a motel. I hadn't seen one on the drive in, but I figure there must be a Motel 6 or a bed-and-breakfast that catered to the visiting PI. I could've used my phone to Google one in the area, but I decided to take the opportunity to cruise around and get a feel for the place.

After passing through the downtown section, I started doing wider and wider circles outward, first through the suburban neighbourhoods, and then the more rural areas along the outskirts. I saw a few more residences with Halloween decorations, but not many. Perhaps the locals weren't feeling the festive spirit with a human monster stalking the town.

I didn't see any lodgings, but I did happen upon the Weavers' garden store. I pulled over to the side of the road so I could take a closer look at it.

It was a large three-storey Victorian with a wide wraparound porch, lots of gingerbread trim, and a slate roof. The house sat by itself on an empty stretch of land with no other businesses around. A wooden sign hanging on hooks from the porch eave said THE GREENER SIDE.

There was a gravel parking lot on the right side of the property, with a wooden footbridge crossing over a burbling creek that led to the house. There were several cars in the lot, and I wondered who was working in the store if Doug Weaver was missing and presumed dead, and Susan was at home.

I turned around and drove back into town. I pulled into one of the slant parking spaces in front of the main square and sat there looking through the windshield at the walking paths and wooden benches and the big fountain in the center. Less than an hour on the job and I was already feeling dejected. If I couldn't find a place to stay in this town, what chance did I have of finding Doug Weaver's body?

I'd been hired to find missing people before, and I was usually able to locate them, but I'd never been asked to find someone who was dead. On the one hand, a dead person should be easier to find since they weren't making any efforts to conceal their whereabouts. On the other hand, a body could be hidden anywhere.

I got out of the car and started walking along one of the paths, deep in thought. There was no one around and the only sound was the whisper of a low breeze and the dry rustle of leaves scuttling across the pavement. There were plenty of trees, but if Susan Weaver was right, none of them were sycamores. I went around the fountain (turned off and drained for the season) and looked across the street at a pair of buildings that couldn't have been more different from each other.

The one on the left was Sycamore's town hall — an imposing Romanesque building of weathered sandstone that looked like the sort of place where witches were sentenced to burn in days of yore. The building on the right, Sycamore's local cop shop, was a much more modern, if less interesting, structure of concrete and chrome, with tinted windows and a large parking lot next to it. I made a mental note to stop by there later on, then turned south and started walking in the direction of the lake.

I soon departed the downtown area and entered a dingier part of town. The houses were shabbier, the lawns scruffier, the bars rougher. There was a strip club called Cupcakes that, from the full parking lot, seemed to be doing a brisk business. I wondered if this was the extent of culture in Sycamore, then decided I was probably being cynical.

By the time I reached the small marina at the edge of town, my stomach was growling to remind me I had skipped lunch. I stood for a moment looking at the boats parked in their slips, then turned around and headed back to my car. I took a different route in the hope of finding a restaurant along the way, but the few places I saw didn't look particularly appealing.

I came back to the town square from the other side of where I'd parked my car, and saw a large redbrick building that looked bright and welcoming. It was the local library.

I stepped through the glass doors into a reception area with a circular information kiosk. A woman stood inside the kiosk, hunched over a computer. She was wearing a grey knit sweater over a white blouse, and a plaid ankle-length skirt. Her red hair was tied back in a sensible bun, and there was a pair of horn-rimmed glasses propped on top of her head. She looked like she was in her late twenties or early thirties, but the outfit made her seem much older. Like she had sent away for the librarian hobby kit.

She looked up as I approached and gave me a warm smile. "Good afternoon," she said. "Can I help you?"

Staring into her clear blue eyes, I found myself momentarily speechless. I suddenly couldn't remember why I had come in here, and found myself asking, "Does Sycamore have a local paper?"

"Of course," she said. "The *Observer*. It comes out Tuesdays and Fridays. We keep a couple weeks' worth in the periodicals section." She pointed to an area in the far corner with leather couches and chairs that looked like the lobby of an upscale apartment building. "For anything older than that, you can access the newspaper archives online." She gestured to a double row of study carrels, each one outfitted with a computer workstation.

I thanked her and went over to one of the study carrels. I plopped down in the seat and saw the web browser was already open to the website of the *Sycamore Observer*. I clicked on the link for back issues and was given the option of searching by keyword or browsing the issues by month and year. They had digitized copies of the *Observer* going all the way back to 1922, although I was pretty sure I didn't need to go back that far.

I wanted to start by looking up articles on the first murder, but sitting there I realized I'd never asked Susan Weaver when the murders had begun. She said her husband had been the third victim, and that he had gone missing on September 20th. His truck was found the following day, which was a Thursday. So I clicked the link for that Friday's edition of the *Observer*.

The front page of the newspaper appeared on the screen. The headline read DISAPPEARANCE OF LOCAL MAN PROMPTS NEW FEARS. A black-and-white photo showed a Ford Ranger pickup parked at the dead-end of a dirt lane with a wide view of the lake in the background. Another shot showed a couple of evidence techs in full regalia — goggles, masks, and white garbage-bag suits — peering into the truck through the driver's side window.

I'd seen crime scene photos before, as well as autopsy shots, and despite their grim and sometimes graphic nature, I always found the candid photos in newspapers and magazines to be much more unsettling. Police photos were cold and clinical, almost scientific in their depiction of dead or wounded human beings. Newspaper photos, on the other hand — be it a gutshot Lee Harvey Oswald or a cluster of Martin Luther King's aides standing and pointing on a motel balcony — seemed to capture something more. An element of real life that was even more haunting for all its apparent banality. And like the most horrific images, it was hard to look at them, and sometimes even harder to look away.

This was the frame of mind I was in when I felt a hand touch my shoulder.

I didn't scream, but it was close. I snapped upright in my seat like I'd received an electric shock, kicking my legs out at the same time and striking the chair of the study carrel on the other side of mine. The chair tipped over and struck the floor with a hollow bang that seemed very loud in the library's cavernous silence.

The hand was quickly withdrawn. I turned and watched as it flew up to cover the mouth of the red-haired librarian standing behind me, looking completely mortified.

"I am *so* sorry," she said, her voice muffled slightly by her hand.

"No harm." I tried to smile while my heart slammed against the inner wall of my chest.

She lowered her hand, started to reach out to me again, then decided against it. "I was just coming over to see if you needed any help."

"That depends," I said. "Is there a defibrillator on the premises?"

"I'm really sorry. It gets so quiet around here, sometimes I think I've lost my hearing. I feel like screaming or cranking the radio loud just so I know I haven't gone deaf."

"Don't take this the wrong way, but if you can't handle the silence, then you might be in the wrong profession."

"I love books," she said with an easy shrug, "and love demands sacrifice."

"So do Satanists, but they never call you the next day."

She gave me a slant-eyed look, and for a moment I thought I might have offended her, either as a librarian or possibly as a Satanist. But then I saw the upward curve at the corner of her mouth. It wasn't a full-on smile, more of a probationary one.

"This is the part where I'm supposed to say, 'You're not from around here, are you?'"

"And I'm supposed to say, 'Geez, is it that obvious?'"

"Maybe a little," she said. "I've got a good eye for these things. Are you from Toronto?"

I looked down at myself. "Can you smell the city on me?"

"You smell like coffee and aftershave," she said in a quick, offhand way, and continued her examination. "You don't look like a tourist. Or a salesman. But you're definitely not a townie."

"I could be."

She shook her head. "The only ones who wear suits and ties around here are the city councillors and the people who work at the bank. And none of them ever come in here," she added pointedly.

"Are you a townie?" I asked.

"No," she said. "I'm adopted." She glanced past my shoulder at the computer screen. "Do you have a predilection for murder?"

"I'm interested in local news," I said.

She nodded slowly. "I see. Well, that is definitely the news around here lately. Are you a reporter?"

"No."

"I didn't think so. We don't get many of them in here, either, but they're definitely around."

"You've seen them?"

"Oh sure," she said. "Lots of out-of-towners have been coming around since the murders started. The usual assortment of media types and rubberneckers."

"Rubberneckers?"

"True-crime buffs, mostly. But crimes of this nature also draw in their share of lookie-loos and weirdoes."

"You speak from experience?"

"In this town?" the librarian said, eyebrows raised sceptically. "Absolutely not. But I read a lot."

"When did the murders start?"

"This past spring," she said. "April or May. I can't recall exactly when." She nodded at the computer. "It'll be in the newspaper archives. There was another one in August, and then four more in the past month or so." She shook her head in disbelief. "I never imagined something like that could happen around here. It's almost like it isn't even real." She frowned. "I mean, I know it's real, but most of the time it's like being in the eye of a hurricane. All of this chaos and carnage is happening all around you, but where you're standing everything seems calm and normal. I get up in the morning, I come to work, then I go home at the end of the day — and all the while there's a serial killer on the loose."

"How's the town dealing with it?"

"People are scared, as you'd expect. But I think what they feel more is frustration. They don't know what's happening, and the police haven't exactly been forthcoming with information. Aristotle said that nature abhors a vacuum. Fear can be dealt with, sometimes even ignored, but people abhor a mystery."

"And having a serial killer stalking the town probably isn't good for tourism," I pointed out.

The librarian shrugged. "Sycamore isn't much of a tourist town, not even in the summer months, but these days you won't see anyone out on the streets after seven or so. Part of that is the curfew, I guess. I heard a rumour that..." She stopped in mid-sentence, perhaps remembering that she was talking to a relative stranger. "I guess I should probably keep my mouth shut. Especially around an outsider," she added with a wry grin that was only half joking.

"I'm not an outsider," I said. "Not exactly."

She crossed her arms. "What are you, then?"

I let out a deep sigh and hung my head like I'd been caught doing something naughty. It gave me a few seconds to think up a reply.

"Let's just say that I have a healthy, non-threatening interest in the murders."

The librarian gave me a long, probing look. I could almost feel invisible fingers touching my face, looking for a crack in my façade that would tell her I was lying. Eventually, she nodded her head and said, "I think I understand."

"You do?"

"You're a writer."

I raised my shoulders and spread my hands in a look that said *You've got me!*

"Have I read anything of yours?" she asked.

"No," I said. That much was true.

"What's your name?"

"Felix," I said, and extended my hand. "Felix Renn. This is my first book. Assuming I can get it published."

"I'm sure you won't have any problem there," she said. "Murder is always a big seller. Especially when it's real." She shook my hand. "I'm Anne."

"Of Green Gables?"

She rolled her eyes and touched her hair. "My parents are big book nerds." She looked around the library. "I guess it runs in the family."

CHAPTER 8

AFTER I'D FINISHED embarrassing myself and telling lies I'd probably regret later on, I thanked Anne for her time and headed out. With me I took a bunch of articles on the murders I'd printed out. A little light reading before bed. Which reminded me…

As I was walking back to my car, I realized I had forgotten to ask for directions to a motel. Another great moment in detective history. Raymond Chandler would be proud.

A combination of male pride and general laziness prevented me from going back to the library. Instead, I started the car and resumed my wandering tour of Sycamore.

Thirty minutes later, I was rewarded by either blind luck or the simple process of elimination.

The Lakeview Inn was a single-storey cinder block building that had been painted various shades of blue, presumably to resemble a lake, with white trim to resemble waves. It was near the lake, that much could be said for it. The view, on the other hand, didn't amount to much. The windows of the dozen or so rooms looked out on the parking lot, then the road, then a screen of pine trees, and beyond that, the lake. A more accurate name would've been the Lake Adjacent Inn, but that probably wouldn't have looked as good on the sign.

I went into the office and got a room. The old man behind the counter gave me a key attached to a green plastic fob shaped like a fish. "You're in

Number Twelve," he said, scratching one of his hollow, unshaven cheeks. "Right at the end. Nice and quiet."

I went outside and stood there for a little while, breathing in the crisp autumn air. It was almost pleasant, if you could ignore the undertone of dead fish and diesel fumes wafting over from the marina. I hadn't packed a bag or brought anything I needed for an extended stay in town. I should have gone back to Toronto and returned to Sycamore in the morning, but it was a two-hour drive back to the city, and I wasn't ready to leave just yet. Sycamore was still making its first impression on me and I didn't want to break the moment.

I walked along the cracked concrete walkway in front of the motel, swinging the key on its fish fob. When I got to room 12, I stopped for a brief moment, then kept walking past where the motel ended. The ground sloped down to a trash-filled culvert, then rose again on the other side. There was another screen of pine trees, like the ones blocking the view of the lake, and through them I could make out something big and bright on the other side.

I duck-walked down the embankment, jumped across the culvert, and climbed up the other side. I pushed my way through the trees, holding my hands up in front of me so the branches wouldn't whip back into my face. When I reached the far side, I stood there staring with my mouth hanging open in dumb surprise.

There was a UFO in the clearing.

It was sitting on top of a diner, and my first thought was, *That's a lousy parking job.* Then I realized it was a theme restaurant. The flying saucer was ringed with coloured lights, and the words THE STAR STOP were written across the gleaming silver hull in swooping red neon.

I remembered that I was starving and went inside.

The place was empty except for a couple of fishermen sitting at the counter, one of them telling a story with elaborate hand gestures. A waitress came out of the back and told me to sit wherever I wanted. She was wearing a lime-green uniform that would probably make me go blind if I stared at it too long.

I slid into a booth and drummed my fingers on the tabletop until the waitress came over. Her nametag said JODIE. She slapped a laminated menu in front of me.

"Nice place," I said. "Take me to your diner."

"Never heard that one before," she said in a dry, bored tone. "You want coffee?"

"Constantly." I tapped the menu without opening it. "You got a bacon cheeseburger in this joint?"

"It's called a Galactic Burger," she said.

"Of course it is. Can I get that with fries?"

"Sure." She didn't bother to write it down. She probably had a good memory. Better than some PIs, I was willing to bet.

"What do you call the fries here?"

"They're just fries," she said, and went away.

My food arrived promptly. Everything smelled of great greasy goodness, and it tasted even better. I looked around while I ate. The UFO décor didn't appear to extend beyond the flying saucer on the roof. From the inside, it looked like your typical greasy spoon diner. Booths upholstered in red vinyl, formica tables with tubular aluminum chairs, and lots of brightly polished chrome. It probably hadn't changed much in fifty years except they'd taken out the jukebox and the waitresses no longer wore roller-skates.

As I was finishing up, Jodie the waitress came over and leaned against the side of the booth. She had a coffee pot in one hand and a question in her eyes. "You staying over at the Lakeview?"

I wiped my hands on a paper napkin. "Are you psychic?"

"Nope, just observant. I saw you walk over." She nodded at the row of side windows that looked out on the motel. "I thought you were going to fall in that sewage ditch. I've seen it happen. I keep telling Burt to put a ramp or something across it."

"It's okay," I said. "I needed the exercise."

"I think that burger cancelled out whatever workout you might've got."

"And then some."

She topped up my coffee. "What brings you to town?"

"I'm a fisherman," I replied.

She smiled and held up her free hand. "Sorry, I'm a waitress. We're nosy by nature."

"That's all right. I'm not really a fisherman."

"You had me going there for a moment."

I sipped my coffee and looked around. "Place seems kinda quiet."

"Yeah," Jodie said in a thoughtful way, as if noticing it for the first time. "The curfew's hurting a lot of businesses."

I looked at my watch. It was a quarter of five, just starting to get dark, but still light enough to see the Lakeview Inn through the trees.

"Isn't that just for the kids?"

"Everyone eighteen and younger," Jodie agreed. "But I guess it's catching."

I recalled what Anne the librarian had said about the empty streets. "I guess so."

"They'll catch the guy soon," Jodie said. I couldn't tell if she was trying to reassure me or herself. "Then things'll go back to normal." She chuffed out a laugh. "As normal as they get around here, anyway."

I was impressed that we had managed to talk about the murders without actually saying the word. "What time is the curfew?" I asked.

"Seven p.m.," Jodie said.

"Until they catch the guy."

"That's right," she said. "I don't know what your plans are in town, but you might want to stay indoors yourself."

"I'm not a kid."

Jodie shrugged. "Neither were any of the folks who were killed."

CHAPTER 9

I GAVE SERIOUS consideration to Jodie's suggestion. Not because I was worried about becoming the serial killer's next victim, but because I didn't have anything else planned for the rest of the evening. At the very least it would give me a chance to read the articles I'd printed at the library.

After paying my bill, I left the diner and walked back to the motel. Once again I stood outside the door to my room with the key in my hand. There was one more stop I needed to make before I settled in for the night.

I got in my car, drove back into town, and parked in the same spot I'd had earlier. Then I walked across the main square to the Sycamore Police Department.

I knew I wouldn't get past the front desk with lies about being a reporter or a crime writer. Not that the truth would get me very far, either. Cops don't tend to like private investigators. Sometimes with good reason. My dealings with the Toronto police had been icy at best. The last thing I needed was to get off on the wrong foot with the local law enforcement.

I walked across the lobby to the main counter where the duty officer was working at a computer. His brow was deeply furrowed in concentration or frustration, or both. He pecked at the keyboard like it was a trap that might spring on him.

Many PIs are former police officers, and they use their old connections on the force to access information that isn't available to the public. I was not an ex-cop and therefore had to get by on my charm and good looks.

"Good afternoon," I said, giving the officer my sixty-kilowatt smile. "How are you doing today?"

The officer's brow smoothed out into a bland expression. "Splendid," he said in a monotone. "How can I help you?"

"I'd like to speak to the person in charge of the investigation into the murders that have been taking place recently."

The officer gave me a long, measuring look. "Do you have some information pertaining to the case?"

"Nope," I said. "Just some questions."

The officer stared at me a while longer, clicked his tongue against his cheek, then said: "May I ask what your interest is?"

"Professional," I said, and showed him my PI licence. It didn't seem to impress him very much, but then it never did, at least not to those in law enforcement.

The officer, whose nametag said BREWER, picked up a phone and punched in an extension number. He turned around and had a short conversation with his back to me. When he was done, he put down the phone and said, "Take a seat. It'll be a little while."

Sure, I thought. In this case, I was fairly certain "little while" actually meant "long while." I'd been in situations like this before, and the power play was always to make the private eye wait, with the hope being that he'll eventually get bored and leave.

I might get bored, but I had no intention of leaving.

Instead, I went over and sat down on the bench that ran along the far wall. I stared at the duty officer, thinking that maybe if I got on his nerves he'd hurry up and get the detective, just to be rid of me. I glared at him for a solid two minutes, but no such luck.

My gaze drifted around the lobby. The walls were a pale, institutional green, a colour that was supposed to be calming, but the longer I waited the less calm I felt. There was a bulletin board next to the main counter, plastered with the usual assortment of "stranger danger" and "see something, say something"-style announcements. *Don't do drugs. Don't drink and drive. Don't be a bully.*

My attention was drawn to an angry red flyer, and I felt my throat clench tight as I read the words on it.

PORTALS! the title screamed in bold black lettering. *Do you think you've found one? If so, DON'T GO NEAR IT. Even if you only THINK you've discovered a portal, notify the proper authorities IMMEDIATELY. Call 911! Or better yet, call the PIA Hotline! $10,000 reward for confirmation of a new portal!*

My thoughts turned immediately to Boston. How was the portal there discovered? Did someone find it and call it in? Did they get the reward or were they—

"Mr. Renn?"

I almost fell off the bench. The pressure on my throat was gone and I could breathe properly. I looked over at the duty officer.

"Detective Sergeant Helton will see you. Come around and I'll show you where his office is."

I stood up on legs that trembled slightly and walked to the end of the counter and through a waist-high gate. Brewer led me down a corridor to a squad room that looked like every other squad room I'd ever seen. Lots of cheap metal desks pushed together, each one buried under a mountain of paperwork. There was a copier in one corner, a kitchenette in another, and glass-walled offices around the perimeter for the senior officers.

Brewer led me over to one of those. He knocked on a door with Helton's name on it. A gruff voice on the other side said something that might've been "Come in" or "Fuck off." Brewer opened the door and walked away without speaking another word. I stepped inside.

Helton was standing behind his desk. He was a tall, rangy man in his early forties. He had a narrow head and sunken cheeks like he was tasting something sour. His black hair was cut short and starting to grey at the sides. He was wearing a pale blue dress shirt, navy pants, and a gold striped tie that had been pulled down a little from his unbuttoned collar. A suit jacket hung off the back of his chair.

"Dan Helton," he said with his hand out.

I shook with him. "Felix Renn. Thank you for seeing me."

"Brewer said you're a private eye. May I see your licence?"

I showed it to him. He took the leather holder out of my hand and looked at it closely. Satisfied, he flipped it closed and handed it back to me. "Have a seat."

I took one of the chairs opposite him and refrained from putting my feet up on his desk.

Helton resumed his own seat and said, "So, what can I do for you today, Mr. Renn?"

"I'd like to talk to you about the murders."

Helton folded his hands and propped them on the edge of his desk. "I'm afraid I can't comment on an open investigation."

I leaned back in my seat and looked around the office. There was a green metal file cabinet in the corner. A university degree and various citations on the wall. A trio of photos on a side table showing Helton and his family, a wife, a young son, and a chocolate Lab. A window in the back wall provided a view of the bracken-choked ravine behind the building.

"I understand the need for discretion," I said. "It's part of the reason why they put the 'private' in private investigator."

"I thought it was because you got paid to take pictures of people's privates."

I smiled indulgently to show I could take a good joke with the best of them.

Helton sighed. "Listen, I'm not trying to bust your balls. I've got enough people in this town asking me about these murders. I don't need a PI from the city sticking his oar in, too."

"I take no offence. You must be putting in a lot of late nights."

Helton grunted. "For all the good it's doing."

"It's that bad?"

"It's not good. People are still being killed, and everyone in town is either scared or pissed off, or both. Not that I blame them. I feel the same way."

"Scared or pissed off?"

"Pissed off when I'm on duty," he said. "I'm scared on my own time."

"It takes a big man to admit when he's scared."

"There's no shame in it," Helton said. "Scared people live longer. It's a well-documented fact. Not that being scared is helping anyone around here." He leaned back in his chair and crossed his arms. "Before all this craziness started, there hadn't been a murder in Sycamore in three years. *Three years.* I know that because I'd just made detective when it happened. There was a fight over at Cupcakes — that's our local strip club. Two guys got in a fight, one hit the other with a pool cue, put the guy in a coma, and he never woke up. The accused went down for manslaughter. It wasn't even an intentional murder, but now, in the past six months, we've had five. *Five.* What would you call that, Mr. Renn?"

I shook my head.

"There's nothing to call it because there's no word for it. Except maybe 'clusterfuck.' Because that's what this situation has been, one great big clusterfuck, and it's sitting right here." He gestured at his lap. "So maybe you can understand that right now I need a PI asking for information like I need a kick in the nuts. So please, if you don't mind, ask your questions, then get the hell out of my office."

"You said five murders. I thought there were six."

"Is that a question?"

I sighed. "Do you have a suspect?"

"Do you have a client?"

I frowned. "That's not the same thing."

"No?" Helton said. A small smile played at the corners of his mouth. "You said you understand about discretion. I don't mind sharing a few details of the case with you, the sort of things the newspapers wouldn't print even if they wanted to, but there's a line I can't cross."

"We want the same thing, Detective."

"Do we?" His voice was thoughtful. "I wonder."

I felt a stab of annoyance at Helton's sudden change in manner, which had gone from a stern seriousness to a kind of sardonic amusement. I leaned back in my seat and crossed my arms.

"Is there something about this you find funny? Maybe you'd like to share it with me."

Helton dropped his hands into his lap. "It's not funny. Not in the least. But it does amuse me somewhat."

"Care to let me in on the joke?"

"It's not a joke. But if it was, it would be on you, Mr. Renn."

"How so?"

Helton leaned his head to the side and stared at me in a speculative way, like he was trying to decide something. "You were hired by Susan Weaver, weren't you?"

I squirmed a little in my seat. "I can't divulge that information."

"You don't need to," Helton said. "She was here a few days ago. Made a bit of a scene. She's been less than impressed with the progress of our investigation and decided to tell me in person. Not that I blame her. I'm none too impressed myself." He let out a tired sigh. "More specifically, Susan wasn't happy with the direction our investigation has taken, and before she left the station she mentioned she was going to hire a private investigator to do what we apparently could not. I know Suze pretty well, we went to high school together, and she was never one to make idle threats. If she says she's going to do something, she'll do it. So I'm not surprised to see you here, Mr. Renn. But that doesn't mean I agree with it."

"I'm not here to cause trouble, Detective."

"Sure. And this is the part where I'm supposed to say we don't need any outside help, especially some nosy shamus from the city. Then I order you to leave town by nightfall or I'll send you out on the end of my boot."

"Something like that," I said. "Only no one says 'shamus' anymore. The current nomenclature is 'peeper' or 'dick'."

"Fact is, I can't order you to do anything, and I wouldn't bother even if I could. This thing has gone way past the point of jurisdictional pissing contests. We've got a task force with homicide detectives from Toronto, half a dozen feds from the RCMP, and a profiler on loan from the FBI. Some small-town cops wouldn't want any outside help, but I'm all for it. Hell, I wish we had more."

"I thought you were in charge of the investigation."

"I am," Helton said. "Nominally. Doesn't look good for the town if we can't take care of our own. But the feds are the ones actually running the show, and I'm fine with that. It's not as if we've got a lot of experience with this sort of thing. Frankly I don't care who catches this fucker as long as it happens sometime soon."

"I don't plan to interfere with your investigation. I just want to find out what happened to Doug Weaver."

Helton's shoulders slumped. I didn't notice it before, but I could see now that he was tired — *drained* was the word that actually came to mind. Like the weight of the entire town was resting on his back. "That's what I figured," he said. "And that's the problem."

"What problem?"

Helton leaned forward and locked eyes with me. "You mentioned six murders, I told you there were five. That's because we've got five bodies. In the case of Doug Weaver, we've got a bloody truck and that's all."

I tried to break his stare, but couldn't tear my eyes away from his.

"Suze didn't hire you to find her husband's body."

I felt a tickle of dread in my stomach.

"She wants you to clear his name."

I opened my mouth, but nothing came out.

"Doug Weaver is our main suspect."

CHAPTER 10

I LEFT THE police station and walked back to my car. As I was sliding in behind the wheel, my cell phone rang. I checked the caller ID and saw it was Sandra.

I pressed the answer button and said, "Felix Renn's Punching Bag Service. I'm afraid I've taken all the abuse I can handle today, but I'm booking appointments for next week and the coming holiday season."

"Hardy-har," Sandra said dryly. "If you're done, I called to say I'm sorry."

She sounded sincere, but in my mind I had a vision of an ant crawling past the hidden lair of a trapdoor spider.

"Uh, thank you?"

"Don't be a jerk, Felix. You know I'm not good at this." She blew a frustrated breath into the mouthpiece. "I was up for a part the other day and I didn't get it. I was pissed off and I guess I took it out on you."

"You could have just told me that," I said. "You always did before."

Once upon a time, Sandra had been a moderately successful actress. She had appeared in about thirty movies and a couple dozen TV shows, often as the wry, wacky, best friend character. She was never a leading lady, but that never seemed to bother her. She got enough steady work to make a living and never had to deal with any of the annoyances that came with full-blown celebrity. After ten years in the business, the jobs started to become fewer and far between, and although they hadn't dried up completely, the roles she was offered these days were the kind of parts given to women whom the industry had decreed were now past their prime. Or as Sandra once put it: *Hollywood isn't fickle. It's fuckle. They say they want strong female actors, but only when it serves their own needs, and then only with women of a certain age. Once you're past your best-before date, it doesn't matter how good an actor you are. They still fuck you over.*

"It was different then," Sandra said. "My career isn't any of your concern anymore."

"That doesn't mean I don't care, Dee. I still want to know."

"Okay," she said. "Noted." She cleared her throat to indicate the subject was closed. "So where are you?"

"I'm still in Sycamore."

"You took the case?"

"Yes," I said. "I just finished speaking with the local law enforcement."

"Does the case have anything to do with the murders?"

I hesitated too long. "Uh, yes."

Sandra was quiet for a moment, then she said, "You don't know about the murders, do you?"

"Sure I do," I said. *Now.*

"You just heard about them, didn't you."

I sighed. I couldn't hide the truth from her any more than she could hide it from me. "Yes," I said.

"Oh, Felix." I could picture her shaking her head. "Read a newspaper once in a while, huh?"

"I read the paper."

"You read the comics."

"And my horoscope."

"The murders have been in the news for over a month. Don't you even watch TV?"

"Rots the brain."

"Same old Felix." Sandra sighed. "So tell me about the job."

"It's a missing person case."

"How is it connected to the murders?"

"Well, the guy I'm looking for is dead."

"What?"

"The woman who hired me wants me to find her husband's body."

"That's a new one on me," Sandra said.

"And me," I said. "I've never looked for a dead body before. I'm not even sure I can do it."

"But you said you'd try."

"It was a moment of weakness. The woman, the client, she looks like she's at her wit's end. Her husband is missing and presumed dead, she's got a daughter with emotional issues, she has a business to run…"

"You felt sorry for her?" Sandra said. "So, what, we're taking on charity cases now?"

"It's not charity," I said. "She's paying me. But yes, I did feel a bit sorry for her."

Sandra didn't say anything. Her silence was rare respect.

"In the meantime," I went on, "there's something you can do for me."

"Oh, goodie."

"I'm trying to bring myself up to speed on the murders," I said. "I went to the library and printed out some articles, but I don't know how much information is there. I want to make sure I have everything I need to know about this case. Especially since the police aren't exactly forthcoming with information."

"Wait a minute," Sandra said. "You went to a library? Not just to use the bathroom?"

"Ha-ha," I said. "I met a librarian. A cute one. Her name's Anne."

"Of Green Gables?"

"I made the same joke."

"Of course you did."

"Anyway, I need you to dig up anything you can on the murders," I said. "I've got a feeling this case is going to get very complicated, very fast."

"Why's that?"

"Well, for starters, the detective in charge of the investigation just told me that our client, Susan Weaver, either neglected to mention or purposely lied to me about a rather pertinent piece of information."

"You said all clients lie about something."

"Yeah, but this is a pretty big detail."

"Do tell."

"It turns out her husband isn't just missing and presumed dead. He's missing and presumed the killer. At least that's what the Sycamore PD thinks."

"That is a bit of a wrinkle."

I leaned back against the seat and closed my eyes. "Maybe I should start watching the news. If I'd known what I was getting into, I could've saved myself the drive."

"You wouldn't have taken the case?" Sandra said.

"I don't know. I'm not so sure it's a good idea. I'm diving right into the middle of a major police investigation."

"When has that ever stopped you?"

"The feds are involved, too."

Sandra went silent again. She had the uncanny ability of reading my mind at the most inopportune times.

"You think he might be guilty," she said.

"I have no opinion on the matter," I said. "At least not yet. But it's definitely something I have to consider."

"Investigating the murders would help you figure that out."

"I didn't come here to catch a serial killer, Dee."

"You don't have to," Sandra said. "If you find the guy's body, then you know he didn't do it."

"Easy as that, huh? You got any thoughts on how I should go about doing that?"

"Buy a shovel."

"I was wise to hire you as my assistant."

"Are you coming back to the city tonight?"

"No," I said. "I got a room at a local motel."

"With the librarian?" Sandra inquired.

"I don't think I'm high-brow enough for her."

"Maybe you can impress her with your knowledge of the Russian writers."

"Right," I said. "Dostoyevsky. Tolstoy. Nabob."

"Nabokov. Nabob is coffee."

"Folgers?"

"Also coffee."

"Nuts. Guess that means I'm sleeping alone tonight."

"I weep for you," Sandra said. "So you'll be back in the morning?"

"Yeah. Will that give you enough time to dig up that info?"

Sandra scoffed. "Please."

She was about to hang up when I asked, "What was the part you were up for?"

Sandra groaned. "You don't want to know."

"Tell me."

"If Bart keeps sending me out on auditions like this, I'm going to seal him in an oil drum and dump him in the lake."

"What was it?"

"It was one of those teen sex comedies that never gets a theatrical release," Sandra said. "The part I was auditioning for didn't even have a name, it was just called 'MILF #2'. Do you know what a MILF is, Felix?"

I said, "Uhh…"

"Oh, shut up," Sandra said, and hung up.

CHAPTER 11

IT WAS DARK by the time I got back to the motel. I checked my watch and saw it was just after seven. The curfew was now in effect. I didn't see anyone on the streets on the drive over, but that might have been as much due to the weather, which was damp and generally miserable, as it was the fear of being the killer's next victim.

I couldn't tell if there was an actual sense of dread in the air. It wasn't something that could be measured like barometric pressure. Still, I thought I felt something. A tingle like what Spider-Man must feel when a bad guy is sneaking up behind him. I couldn't tell if it was a real feeling or something I only imagined because I was now aware of the murders. I couldn't recall feeling anything strange or sinister a few hours ago, when it was light out and I knew nothing of Sycamore's troubles. If there was a dark vibe about this town it was probably one I was projecting onto it myself. Then again, there was a killer on the loose, and I would do well to keep my senses well attuned.

On the plus side, my motel room wasn't as bad as I thought it would be. The carpeting was a hideous orange, but it appeared to have been recently vacuumed. There were two single beds of the non-vibrating variety, with headboards that were bolted to the wall in case one was tempted to steal them. There was a nightstand with a lamp on it and a framed print on the wall of a man riding a tractor across a freshly tilled field. There was a small wooden desk with nothing on it, and an armoire with a flat-screen television inside. A door at the far end of the room was cracked open just enough to reveal a glimpse of a white-tiled bathroom. Still, it wasn't the sort of place you'd want to shine a black light around.

I walked across the room, dropping the printouts onto one of the beds, and pushed the bathroom door all the way open. I turned on the light. The shower curtain was a blue plastic sheet. It was closed.

Some people avoid walking under ladders. Others throw spilled salt over their left shoulder. Me, I've got a thing about shower curtains. It probably had less to do with superstition than the number of horror movies I watched as a kid.

I went over and pulled the shower curtain open. There was nothing on the other side except a porcelain tub with a rust stain around the drain.

I went back to the other room and got to work.

THE FIRST murder took place on April 7th. The victim's name was Robin Endicott. She was a twenty-four-year-old legal secretary who worked at a law firm in Orillia. She lived in Sycamore, on Painter's Bridge Road, in a house that she shared with a roommate named Nora Aitken. Ms. Aitken wasn't the one who reported the murder; she was on vacation with her boyfriend in Scotland at the time. A colleague at the law firm where Endicott worked became concerned when she failed to show up for work two days in a row. Driving out to her house, he found Ms. Endicott's car in the driveway. When no one answered the door, the co-worker checked around the house, discovered a broken window along with splatters of blood on the sill, and immediately called the authorities.

After the police arrived and entered the house, they found a large amount of blood in Robin Endicott's bedroom, but no body. According to the article, Painter's Bridge Road was located on the northern edge of town "where the neighbours are few and far between." This was supposed to explain why no one had heard a young woman being horribly murdered in her own home.

Endicott's body was found in the woods behind her house. She had been buried in a shallow grave. There were no further details mentioned in the article, except that the police requested that anyone with information about Endicott's activities in the days before her death should contact them immediately.

That usually meant they didn't have anything to go on.

I wondered about the roommate, Nora Aitken. She had an alibi for the murder, a good one, and the investigator in me wondered if it was a little too good. It was possible Nora Aitken had hired someone to kill her roommate and alibied herself in Scotland with the boyfriend, but what was the motive? Was Robin always late paying her share of the bills? Did she leave the milk out on the counter? Was she always taking the good parking spot in the driveway?

It was more likely the killer had been stalking Endicott for weeks or months, and when the roommate went on her vacay, he finally saw his opportunity to strike, and took it.

One of the articles included a photo of the house Endicott and Aitken had shared. It was a little bungalow at the end of a gravel drive with dense woods all around it. In real life it probably looked cute and quaint, but in the black-and-white newspaper photo it looked isolated and vulnerable. A crime scene waiting to happen.

I stared at the photo for a long time, my attention turned from the house to the woods surrounding it. The woods where Robin Endicott's body had been found.

Further articles described the ongoing police investigation, the heartbreak and outrage of family and friends, as well as information about the funeral, which was held in Kingston where Endicott was originally from, and the continuing requests from police, sounding more and more desperate, that anyone with information about the case to please contact them.

Every article — from the first one reporting the murder of Robin Endicott, to the one published three months later that summarized the case in lieu of providing any new updates — was front page news. Murder was not a faceless statistic in Sycamore. It wasn't something the town could forget or ignore by simply bumping it to the back of the local paper. It said something about the community that they didn't even try.

The second murder occurred on August 15th, four months after the murder of Robin Endicott. The victim was Paul Lindon, a thirty-one-year-old carpenter who lived on Renfield Road. He was a bachelor and, like Endicott, his disappearance wasn't immediately noted. The coroner determined that Lindon had died on Friday the 15th, but his body wasn't discovered until Sunday the 17th.

It could have taken even longer than that. Lindon was an independent contractor who was between jobs at the time, so no one was expecting him at work. The person who finally noticed his absence was his mother, with whom he had a standing Sunday evening dinner date. "He didn't come every week," Dorothy Lindon told the *Observer*, "but he always called if he wasn't able to make it."

On this particular Sunday, when Mrs. Lindon didn't hear from her son, and when repeated calls to his home line and his cell phone went unanswered, she became concerned.

What followed next was eerily similar to the discovery of Robin Endicott's body. After driving to her son's house — described in the paper as a "fixer-upper that Lindon was renovating himself" — Dorothy Lindon found her son's pickup truck parked in the driveway. There was a picture of the truck in the article, with a corner of the house visible in the background — bare timbers covered in plastic sheeting, from one of the sections Lindon had been working on.

When Dorothy Lindon received no answer at the door, she used the spare key her son had given her to enter the house. What she found inside was a scene much like the one in Robin Endicott's house. The same and yet worse.

There was a great deal of blood — in the bedroom, in the kitchen, and in the large unfinished space at the back of the house. According to the police, a trail of blood led through a slit in the plastic wall cover, across the backyard, and out to another shallow grave in the woods.

Like the house Robin Endicott and Nora Aitken had shared together, Paul Lindon's fixer-upper was located in a rural area outside of town — this one on the eastern side, according to my road atlas. This suggested a possible pattern of behaviour. In both incidents, the killer had chosen victims who lived alone — or who he knew would be alone for a period of time — in an isolated area with a close proximity to the woods. Of course, in any town located outside of the major urban centres, a dwelling that wasn't in the suburbs or the downtown core was in an isolated area, most likely near the woods. Even in a town the size of Sycamore, that was still a lot of ground to cover if you were trying to predict where the killer would strike next.

Unsurprisingly, the newspaper articles didn't provide much in the way of details about the murders themselves. The police were undoubtedly holding back some details in order to weed out the inevitable crackpot confessions.

Based on what I did know, I got the impression the murders were carried out quickly, probably in a matter of minutes. The forced entry into the victims' homes, and the amount of blood found at the scene, suggested the killer wasn't interested in torturing his prey, although he clearly had the time and the privacy to do so. The police would know for certain if the victims had died quickly or if they had been made to suffer.

I wondered if they were bothered by the same thing that irked me.

Both Robin Endicott and Paul Lindon had been buried in shallow graves in the woods behind their respective homes.

I could understand why the killer had done so in Endicott's case. It was, presumably, his first murder, and he had buried the body in order to hide it. But the police had found it, and with apparent ease. So why do it again in Paul Lindon's case, when the woods behind his house would be the first place the police would look?

This brought me to the third murder victim, the husband of my client: Douglas Weaver.

There wasn't much information in the *Observer* articles that I hadn't already learned from Susan.

On September 21st, Doug Weaver, thirty-five years old, co-owner of The Greener Side garden store, was reported missing after he failed to return home the previous evening. Authorities believed he was forcibly taken from his Ford Ranger pickup truck, which was found abandoned near Orchard Park. Blood was found in the vehicle, but there was no mention of the amount, and the police spokesperson refused to speculate as to whether Weaver was dead or alive.

It wasn't until the second article that a link was suggested between Doug Weaver's disappearance and the murders of Robin Endicott and Paul Lindon. I didn't see the connection myself, and the police didn't mention one in the piece, but there was a photo showing uniformed officers searching the wooded area around the park, presumably for a shallow grave. They didn't find one.

That, I realized, was my job.

I TRIED hard not to gloss over the details of the next three murders, but it wasn't easy. It was getting late, and I was weary from all the driving I'd done that day. But that wasn't the main reason for my distraction.

There's an unspoken truth about the act of murder, most clearly conveyed in the way it's portrayed in the media — namely, that the level of desensitization among the public tends to grow in direct proportion to the number of people who have been killed. Simply put: one murder is bad, two is worse, and three is a tragedy, but four, five, six? To the general public, that's all they are — numbers. Oh sure, people get scared, they get concerned, they get outraged, but as the body count continues to rise a strange thing begins to happen. The focus starts to shift away from the victims to the killer. Who is he? Why is he doing these terrible things? When will he be caught? *Will* he be caught? These are the things the public cares about when the murders hit a certain number. Everything else, even the victims, becomes filler.

Even though my own interest in the case was based on one particular victim, I did my best to absorb as much as I could about the three that followed. But, as if proving my theory about the weight and counterweight of body count to press coverage, there weren't that many details to absorb, at least not in the *Observer* articles I had printed out.

The fact that the details of the next three murders were so similar didn't exactly help the victims to stand out as individuals who once had lives of their own with family and friends who cared about them.

The fourth murder took place on September 22nd, only two days after Doug Weaver's disappearance-slash-murder. The victim was a seventeen-year-old girl named Ashley Prendergast. She had taken her dog out for a walk around nine p.m. and never returned home. The police didn't wait twenty-four hours to declare her missing, which was the normal protocol. They went out looking for her that night, and found her body in the early hours of the following morning, in the woods near Monck Road, about a mile from her house. She had not been buried.

Once again I consulted my trusty road atlas and saw that Monck Road was located north of Sycamore, further north than Painter's Bridge Road, where Robin Endicott had lived. On the map it was another thin red line surrounded by a whole lot of greenspace. In short, the perfect hunting grounds for a serial killer.

It was after Ashley Prendergast's murder that the Sycamore Police instituted the curfew. Prendergast was the youngest victim to date, although I'm sure that was only part of it. The bigger reason was probably that there had been four murders in town in less than a year with no apparent end in sight. The police had to do something.

The fifth murder occurred on or around September 29th. The victim, Gill Frye, was a man in his late forties who wasn't reported missing by either family or friends because he apparently had neither. His body might have gone undiscovered for weeks or months if a Boy Scout troop hadn't happened upon it while on a nature hike near Mud Lake. That was on October 1st.

According to the *Observer*, Frye was a recluse who lived in a shack in the woods and came to town every few months to purchase supplies and ammo. An acquaintance who chose to remain anonymous said that Frye had a penchant for jacklighting deer. Authorities figured it was on one such outing that Frye ended up meeting his killer.

The sixth and most recent murder took place two weeks ago on October 9th. The body of Keith Morse, 66, was found on his farm located on Concession Road #4. Morse had lived alone since his wife of forty-seven years died of ovarian cancer the previous winter. Two brothers who worked as farmhands discovered Morse's body on the ground outside the barn when they showed up to work early that morning.

Six murders. The first on April 7th, the last on October 9th. Six murders in six months. It was unbelievable, but I couldn't not believe it. I had the proof spread out before me on the motel bedspread. A timeline of murder chronicled in a series of a small-town newspaper articles. It didn't tell me everything about the case, not even close, but it was a start.

I was tired and my eyes were dry and strained, but I forced myself to go through the articles again, looking for any discrepancies or general weirdness. Anything that stood out or sent up a red flag.

One thing I did notice was that even though there hadn't been a murder since Keith Morse's body was found on October 9th, that hadn't stopped the *Observer* from continuing to publish stories about the case. There was an editorial on the curfew — specifically the general uselessness of it — that pointed out something I had already noted. That with the exception of Ashley Prendergast, none of the victims were young enough that a curfew would have protected them from being murdered. Still, I supposed hindsight was twenty-twenty, and it was better to be safe than sorry.

Another article, published only two days ago, put forth the theory that since there hadn't been a murder in the past couple of weeks, and since the last three murders had taken place well outside the town limits, the killer might be moving on to greener pastures. That seemed like a pretty big assumption to me, but I couldn't blame them for hoping.

At first glance the only similarity I could see among the six killings was that the victims had all been murdered in a town where, according to Detective Helton, murder didn't often occur. But a closer look revealed another connection. The first two killings and the last one had all occurred in the victims' homes, while the fourth and fifth had taken place in or near the woods.

The only one that didn't fit any pattern was Doug Weaver.

He was the only victim to be attacked in his vehicle, and his body was the only one that hadn't been found. Strange? Yes. But was it enough to make him a suspect? The police certainly seemed to think so.

It was possible, even probable, that there were other details that linked the murders, information that the press either wasn't privy to or that they were prohibited from publishing. If the police wouldn't give me that information, maybe I could find someone at the *Observer* who was a bit more cooperative.

I also noted there was a four-month gap between the first and second murders, with the next four taking place over a period of three weeks. This increase in activity suggested the compulsion that was driving the killer may be getting out of control; that the fulfillment he received from committing these brutal acts was diminishing. Like an addict who has to constantly increase the dosage of his drug in order to get high, the killer was compelled to hunt more often in order to sate the hunger inside him.

The only positive thing about serial killers of this type was that they tended to screw themselves in the end. The escalation in both violence and their timetable wasn't sustainable in the long run, and they were often captured due to a stupid mistake on their part. The Son of Sam was done in by a parking ticket.

Again, I came back to the wild card that was Doug Weaver. If the amount of blood found in his truck truly suggested he was dead, then where was his body? The police had scoured Orchard Park, as well as the lakeshore and the surrounding woods, and found nothing. Was it possible that the killer had learned from his first two murders and buried Doug Weaver's body in a more remote location? According to Detective Helton, that was what his wife Susan believed. Or what she hoped. She and I were going to have a talk about that in the morning.

I checked my watch and saw that morning would be here sooner than I thought. I put away the newspaper articles, then washed up, stripped down to my boxers, and climbed into bed.

My head felt heavy with stories of blood and murder. I rolled onto my side and looked at the window with its nonexistent view of the lake. I closed my eyes and tried to shut off my brain.

Sleep came, but not for a long while.

CHAPTER 12

"YOU LIED TO me, Mrs. Weaver."

I wasn't one for dramatic entrances, but I was tired and irritable and didn't have the patience for any more of the runaround. I waited until Susan Weaver had let me into the house before I blasted her. I was standing in the archway between the foyer and the living room, ready to turn on my heel and leave if I didn't like the answers to my next few questions.

Susan was across the room, frozen in the act of sitting on the green leather wingback chair. She remained like that, her upper body tilted slightly forward at the waist, staring at me with a quizzical expression. When she answered the door, she had looked as tired and beaten as she had the day before. My words had wiped all of that away like a wet cloth across a messy chalkboard. Now her face was a blank slate. I waited to see what would show up on it next.

"Lied?" she said. "What do you mean?"

"It's the opposite of telling the truth," I said. "Which is something you should do when you ask someone for help."

She said, "I don't understand," but her eyes were wide and her face was a stark white, as if someone had shined a spotlight on her.

She unfroze and finished lowering herself into the chair. I could actually see the exhaustion dropping back on top of her, slumping her shoulders and draining the energy from her limbs. It seemed I wasn't the only one who'd had a rough night. I wondered if the circles under my eyes were as dark as the ones under hers.

"I don't understand," she said again, in a lower voice this time, as if she was referring to her life in general.

"Neither did I," I said, crossing my arms. "I had to find out from the police."

"I didn't lie about anything," she said. "My husband is missing."

"Yes, but you failed to mention he's also a suspect in the murders. The main suspect, I'm told."

"You spoke to Dan Helton."

"Yes."

Susan nodded in an absent way like she was absorbing this information without actually processing it.

"You should have told me he was a suspect."

"I didn't think you'd help me if you knew."

"You think I'll help you now?"

Susan shook her head dismally and looked down at her hands. "I don't know. I don't know anything anymore. I'm just so tired. So... *fucking*... tired. Too tired to even be afraid." She looked up at me. "Do you know what that's like? To be so exhausted that you don't even have the strength to be scared? I can't feel anything anymore. I just want all of this to be over."

A floorboard creaked behind me, and I turned to see the nurse, Nancy, standing at the foot of the stairs. "Is everything okay?" she asked.

I turned back to Susan as she sprang out of her chair. "Go to hell," she said. "Both of you."

She stormed past me and walked around Nancy on her way up the stairs. She stopped halfway up when she saw Rachel standing at the top. The girl was wearing a nightie with Olaf from *Frozen* on the front. She looked down at her mother with a blank expression.

Susan stared back for an extended moment before throwing up her hands and saying, "I can't! I just can't!"

Then she came back down the stairs, pushing past us on her way down the hallway to the kitchen. A moment later we heard the back door open and then slam shut with a loud bang.

Nancy and I stood there looking at each other awkwardly in the silence that followed. I felt bad for Susan. She told us to go to hell when it was clear she was the one already there.

"Sorry about that," I said to the nurse.

"It's not your fault," Nancy said. "Suze is as fragile as a china cup these days. One little bump and she chips."

"I gave her more than a bump."

"You found out about Doug, huh? The cops think he's the one who killed all those people."

"Susan failed to mention that to me the other day. I don't know why."

"You don't?" Nancy looked at me with genuine surprise. "She was ashamed, of course. Would you have come if she'd told you her husband was a suspect in a bunch of murders?"

"It doesn't seem like she wants my help now."

"You can't help her," Nancy said. "The best thing she can hope for is that you find Doug's body and prove he isn't the killer. If that happens, Susan's still a widow with a kid she has to raise on her own. It's better than Doug turning out to be a serial killer, but still not what anyone would call a happy ending."

"You've been following the case?" I asked.

"Of course," Nancy said. "I'm not kin, but I live here, and I work with their daughter."

"You never mentioned that Doug was their main suspect, either."

"I'd just met you," Nancy said. "I didn't know you." She paused, hesitant. "I still don't."

"Do you think he killed all those people?"

"No," Nancy said without hesitation. "I didn't know him very long, or very well, but he seemed like someone who was happy with his life."

"What do you mean by that?"

Nancy scratched her arm. "Well, I'm no detective, but I don't think people who are happy with their lives tend to become serial killers. But in this messed up world, who the hell knows?" She started to turn away, then gave me a sidelong look. "Still, I'm sure it beats chasing down vampires and werewolves."

I stared at her.

"Sorry," she said, and held up a hand like she was swearing on a bible. "I Googled you."

I closed my eyes and groaned inwardly. "Find anything good?"

SUSAN WAS in the side yard, leaning against the tree with the swing, smoking a cigarette. She glanced at me over her shoulder, then turned around to face me. She held up the cigarette, staring at it with wet, red eyes. "I haven't smoked in seven years."

"I never started," I said.

She held the cigarette out to me, but I shook my head.

"Probably a good idea," she said. "You get a bad habit, you always end up going back to it, no matter how many times you quit."

"I'm sorry for what I said. I didn't mean to be so... harsh."

"I was going to tell you," Susan said. "I swear I was. I just didn't know how."

"It's okay," I said. "Nancy explained it to me."

"Did she?" Susan looked at me thoughtfully. "She's good at that. Nurse Nancy has become quite the little expert on our family."

"She's just trying to help. So am I."

She took a drag off her cigarette and let the smoke waft out of her mouth.

"Does that mean you'll stay on the case?"

"Yes."

"Thank you," she said. "I don't know what I'd do if you left. The police haven't been any help at all."

"When did they start suspecting Doug of committing the murders?"

"I'm not sure. I guess when they didn't find his body."

"Did Helton or anyone else ever speak to you directly about their suspicions?"

"Not at first. When they found his truck... and the blood... they told me to prepare myself for the worst. But later on, when they couldn't find his body, their whole attitude changed. Even the way they spoke to me. They started out all warm and comforting, then suddenly they were asking me all these questions like I was hiding something."

"What kind of questions?"

"Were there any problems in our marriage? How often did Doug and I fight? Did we have any financial troubles? Did I ever have the feeling Doug was keeping something from me?"

"Did the police ever say outright that they thought Doug's disappearance was connected to the murders?"

"I think they just assumed it was," Susan said. "It isn't the sort of thing that happens around here."

"When did you realize the police suspected your husband?"

"I guess it was a few days after they found his truck. Dan and some other police officers came to the house and looked around. They searched our store, too."

"Did they have a warrant?"

"They must have," Susan said, "but I don't remember asking to see one. I thought they were just looking for something that would help them find him."

"Yes, the police can be helpful like that," I said in full sarcasm mode. "In the future, I would advise against letting them into your home or your business unless they have a warrant. Do you have a lawyer?"

She nodded. "Ed Sturrow. He has an office in town."

"Call him and bring him up to speed on everything that's been going on. *Everything.* If the police are pursuing a case against your husband, you'll need to be ready with legal representation."

"Does Dan know you're working for me?"

"I didn't tell him, but he assumed as much. He said you went to see him at the police station."

Susan looked down at the cigarette in her hand, tapped some ash onto the ground. "I shouldn't have done that, but I was upset."

"It's understandable," I said, "but from now on, you should only speak to the police with your lawyer present."

"Won't that make it look like Doug is guilty?"

"The police already think that."

She considered this. "Okay, but..."

I raised my hand. "I know, you think he's dead. And you may be right. But you need to be prepared for the possibility that he isn't. That Doug might be..." I didn't finish the sentence. Susan already knew the rest.

"I know he's dead," Susan said. Her voice thrummed with pain and feeling. "I know it in my heart. But I'll do as you say. I'll call Ed."

"Good, then I'll get back to work."

Susan looked at me full on. "Do you really think you can find him?"

"I don't know," I said. "That's the honest truth. A case like this…" I shook my head. "… all I can do is try."

Susan took another drag off her cigarette. "That's all any of us can do."

CHAPTER 13

SUSAN WASN'T HAPPY when I told her I was going back to the city. I explained that it was too far to commute between Toronto and Sycamore every day, and I needed to pick up a few things for an extended stay in town. She said she understood, but I could tell she was upset. I told her I'd be back later that afternoon and departed.

I had a lot to think about on the drive back. I wondered what information Sandra had been able to dig up on the murders. Even if there was nothing I didn't already know, it would still be good to discuss the case with her. Being married for seven years, Sandra was familiar with my thought processes and knew most of my mental blind spots. She may have worked as my assistant because she needed the job, but over the past two years she had proved to be an integral part of my investigations.

Once I reached the highway, I called her on my cell phone and told her I was on my way back. She said she'd meet me at the office. I told her not to rush. I had to go home first and pack a bag.

After we'd said our good-byes, I turned up the radio and tried to clear my mind. Fat chance. There was a tempest going on in my brain, swirling the facts of the case around like debris caught in a tornado. My head was full of questions, too — chief among them, Was I doing the right thing? Was I staying on this case for the right reasons? Would my involvement make things better for Susan, or worse?

I told myself that helping Susan could only make things better, while quitting would definitely make things worse. She needed help, and no one in

Sycamore was lining up to give her any. Even if I couldn't find her husband's body, maybe I'd be able to dig up some evidence that still managed to prove his innocence.

I was good at finding missing people. Of course, all of them had been alive. Still, I figured the concept was more or less the same. When a person went missing, they left behind clues, sometimes intentionally, sometimes not. Dead people usually left behind a body and a bad smell. The problem was that a dead body was like any other inanimate object. It could be moved, hidden, or destroyed. And therein lay the challenge.

If Doug Weaver was dead, he could be anywhere.

I GOT to my apartment just before noon. I lived on the top floor of a five-storey building north of the Annex. It was clean and quiet and full of young professionals and the sort of hipster couples who drove matching Honda Civics and had herb gardens on their balconies. With the odd hours I kept, I sometimes wondered what the other residents thought I did for a living, then decided I probably didn't want to know.

I threw some clothes into a duffel bag, along with a pair of hiking boots that I'd last worn on a trip to Algonquin Park about ten years ago. I wasn't planning on tromping through the woods with a bloodhound and a shovel, but I decided it was best to do like the Boy Scouts and be prepared.

On my way out the door, I stopped, turned, and looked around at my apartment. It seemed even emptier than usual. I'd had this feeling before, but it never really bothered me. I didn't spend a lot of time here. I was either at the office or out on a case. I came here to sleep, sometimes to eat, and that was about it. The place felt as much like a home as my room at the Lakeview Inn. Lately I'd been hearing noises at night, scratching in the walls that I assumed were mice. I hoped it was mice. There was a horror story, I think it was by Lovecraft, about a guy who hears what he thinks are rats in the walls, but it turns out he's insane and it was all in his head. I think he might have killed some people, too, but I couldn't remember. I thought about getting a cat, to take care of the mice and for some company, but then figured it would be cruel to leave it alone for long stretches of time while I was away.

I owned a snake plant, also known by the much cooler name Saint George's sword, and despite a reputation for being tough and hardy, I was still managing to kill it. Its thick, dark green leaves, with lighter green edges, were gradually closing in on themselves like ancient hands curling inward with arthritis. I only seemed to remember to water it when it was on the verge of full-on death, making its existence like a prolonged torture session, where it was getting only the barest amount of attention in order to stay alive.

Good thing I didn't have kids, huh?

WHEN I stepped into my office, Sandra was in her usual position: hunched over her computer with her eyes glued to the screen.

"Kardashians?" I inquired.

"Boston," Sandra replied.

"Oh, right." I had forgotten about the new portal. Or tried to. "What's happening?"

"They've got the whole park fenced off with barbed wire. Some geek from Homeland Security says they found the portal pretty fast, so they don't think anything crossed over."

"Did they say how they found it?"

"A bunch of homeless people have gone missing over the past few weeks. Apparently the park is a popular hangout for them. The cops were looking into it when one of them stumbled upon the portal."

"Literally?"

Sandra nodded grimly.

"They get him back?"

She shook her head.

"Damn."

She turned away from the computer. "How's Sycamore?"

"Cute. Quaint. But no sycamore trees."

"I know," Sandra said.

"You do?"

"They all died off."

"How do you know that?"

"Wikipedia."

"Oh," I said.

"Now the same thing is happening to the people."

"So it would appear."

Sandra crossed her arms. "Nice to see you finally taking an interest in current events."

"What did you find out?"

Sandra picked up a manila folder bulging with computer printouts. She started to hand it to me, then hesitated. "What do you already know?"

"Six murders," I said. "The killer buried the first two bodies, but hasn't bothered with the rest."

"Except for Doug Weaver," Sandra said, "whose body hasn't been found."

"Right."

"And the police suspect he may be the killer."

I pointed at the folder. "Do they actually say that in any of the articles?"

"Not exactly, but you can read between the lines. They stop short of calling Doug Weaver a person of interest."

"How much interest?" I asked.

"What do you mean?"

I sat down on the corner of her desk. "I'd like to know how strongly the Sycamore police believe he's the killer. Enough that their attention is completely focused on building a case against him, or are they still looking for other suspects?"

"Does it matter?"

"It helps to gauge the amount of resistance I'm going to get from them."

"You're a PI, Felix. They're going to give you a hard time on general principle. This is a high-profile case. They're probably under a lot of pressure to close it, and fast."

"But they don't gain anything by pinning it on the wrong guy. Especially if Doug Weaver's body turns up."

"Or if the killings continue," Sandra said. "The articles mentioned an RCMP task force."

"The only cop I've spoken to so far is a Sycamore detective named Helton."

"If the feds are involved, they're not going to let the local cops make a scapegoat out of Weaver." She considered this for a moment. "Well, probably not."

"They must have legitimate grounds to suspect him. There could be forensic evidence that hasn't been reported in the press that links him to the other murders."

"It's a strange case," Sandra said. "Which is saying something considering the sort of jobs you usually work. Are you sure it was a good idea to take this one?"

"You're the one who said we needed the money."

"Speaking of which," Sandra said. "My availability is going to be a bit spotty this weekend. I've agreed, at Bart's urging, to attend the BloodNGutz convention this weekend."

"Good name. Very classy."

"'Tis the Halloween season," Sandra said dismally. "When all the ghosts and ghouls and horror movie fanboys come out to play."

"I thought you hated those things."

"I do, but I could really use the extra cash."

"I'm sorry it's come to that," I said. "Having to sit at a table all day, signing headshots while your adoring fans fawn all over you."

"It's harder than it sounds, and you know it." She stabbed a finger at me. "Bart wants me to wear that stupid costume but I told him no fucking way."

"Oh right. The one you wore in *Bloodsuckers from Mars.*"

"*Venusian Vampire Vixens,*" Sandra corrected me, reluctantly, through gritted teeth.

"I can't believe a film with a title like that didn't do better at the box office. And no Academy Award nominations. It's a damn outrage."

"It was supposed to be ironically cheesy," Sandra said, defensively. "A throwback to the class sci-fi horror movies from the 1950s, like *The Blob* and *The Thing.* But it ended up being just plain cheesy."

"It still developed a following."

"Yeah," Sandra said. "Lucky me." She blew out a long breath. "Anyway, getting back to you case. Have you given any thought to how you're actually going to do this? I mean, finding a dead body…" She gestured vaguely in the air. "… out there, somewhere, *anywhere.*"

"I appreciate the vote of confidence."

"You're a good detective, Felix. But you've never worked a case like this before."

"I know."

"I'm more concerned that you took this job because you felt sorry for the widow with the disabled daughter."

"I assure you that wasn't the reason."

Sandra stared at me.

"Well, it wasn't the *whole* reason."

"It's a noble thing you're doing," Sandra said, "and if she's a paying client, then so much the better. But what do you know about finding dead bodies? When we were married, you couldn't even find your socks."

"I know that dead bodies don't move as fast as live ones. That should make it easier to find."

Sandra counted off her fingers. "His body could have been buried in the woods, burned to a crisp in a fire pit, dissolved in acid, or weighed down with cinder blocks and dumped in the lake. Or eaten."

"Eaten?"

"Sure," she said. "It's been known to happen."

"I have to try, Dee. Doug Weaver is out there somewhere."

"I know," Sandra said, "but there's a helluva lot of somewheres out there."

I TOOK the folder of printouts into my inner office, sat down at my desk, and started reading.

Sandra had been very thorough. She had printed out articles on the murders from all of the major Canadian newspapers, as well as the ones I'd already found in the *Sycamore Observer*. Most of the information was stuff I already knew, but I went through it all anyway, just to be sure I didn't miss anything.

When I was finished, I was left with only one new piece of information, and it wasn't particularly useful. Last week, a woman in Sycamore had accidentally shot her husband after he came home late from a night of drinking. Keyed up on the news stories about the murders, the woman had mistaken her husband for the killer and shot him in the leg with a deer rifle. The man was going to be fine, his wife wasn't going to be charged, and the police reminded the public that if they believed an intruder was trying to break into their home, they should call 911.

Along with the newspaper articles, Sandra had also provided me with information about the town itself, culled mostly from Wikipedia.

Sycamore is a city located in Central Ontario, Canada, on the north shore of Lake Simcoe, 135 kilometres (84 mi) north of Toronto...

There was even a section on the town's sycamore trees. According to Wikipedia, they had all died from a type of anthracnose, which was a disease caused by fungus. Some nice conversation material to use when I was yakking with the locals at the Star Stop.

My eyes started to glaze over when I got to the part about Igopogo, the lake monster that was alleged to live in Lake Simcoe. It was unlikely that any of this material was going to help my investigation, but I pressed on. It was possible that some minor factoid about the town could turn out to be useful. Although maybe not the stuff about Igopogo.

I had just finished reading the final printout when Sandra appeared in the doorway.

"If you don't leave soon, you're going to get stuck in traffic."

I checked my watch. It was almost two p.m. "Trying to get rid of me?" I said.

"Yes," Sandra said. "Once you leave I can close up and go home."

"You can leave now if you want. There's nothing else for you to do today."

"Thanks, boss."

I tapped the folder. "Thanks for these."

Sandra nodded. "Find anything interesting?"

"Not really. I'm going to have to talk to the Sycamore cops again and try to get them to tell me what they've got on Doug Weaver."

"You think they will?"

"Probably not, but I've got to try."

"Maybe that cute librarian could help you." Sandra batted her eyelashes at me.

"Maybe."

"Drive safe."

"I will."

"And try not to get killed."

"I'll do my best."

WHEN SANDRA was gone, I put the folder in my duffel bag and went over to the closet. I pushed aside the hanging coats and crouched down in front of the small safe set into the back wall. I spun the dial, opened the heavy door, and took out my .357 Ruger revolver in its nylon holster.

I dropped it in my bag and headed out.

CHAPTER 14

I WAS BACK in Sycamore by five o'clock. The town was just as I'd left it — quiet and dismal. I drove to the Lakeview Inn and dropped off my stuff. While I was there, I called Susan to tell her I was back in town. I could hear the relief in her voice when I told her I'd come by to see her the following morning.

Pretty confident for a guy who didn't have any plan whatsoever. I figured my best bet was to treat this case like any other. That meant wandering around, asking questions, and keeping my eyes open.

I started right there in my motel room, pacing back and forth across the orange carpet. *If I was a dead body,* I asked myself, *where would I be?*

Any number of places, was the reply. As Sandra had pointed out, there was a helluva lot of somewheres out there.

Of course, the best way to find Doug Weaver's body would be to ask the person who killed him. Unfortunately I didn't know who that was. I didn't even know if Doug Weaver was actually dead. But since I'd agreed to take the case, I decided to go along with that theory until I was convinced otherwise.

This made me think of something the great wise man Dirty Harry once said: "A man's got to know his limitations."

My limitations in this case were clear. Working by myself, with limited resources, it was very unlikely that I would be able to uncover, much less apprehend, the person responsible for the murders in Sycamore. If the police weren't able to catch him, then what hope did I have?

That left me with the victim. I had to find out everything I could about Doug Weaver and hope that somewhere in there was a clue that would lead me to... well, his dead body.

To further complicate matters, I had to consider the possibility that Doug Weaver might turn out to be the killer. On the surface this would provide a very tidy conclusion to the case — finding Doug Weaver's body and the Sycamore serial killer both at the same time. On the downside, Susan would be devastated by such an outcome.

The truth can hurt. Everyone knows that. And yet it never stops us from looking for it.

AFTER UNPACKING my bag, I drove over to the police station. This time the officer behind the counter was a young female constable named McGrath. I asked her if Detective Helton was in. She asked for my name, and when I told her, she sucked her lower lip and stared at me with wide, excited eyes. I guessed word had gotten around that a Toronto PI was in town. I took a quick look around the lobby but didn't see a red carpet laid out for me.

Constable McGrath led me back to the squad room which was once again empty. I wondered if there were any cops in this town besides the two or three I'd met. I glanced at my watch and saw it was after five. Everyone had probably gone home for the day.

Helton's door was open. McGrath knocked on the jamb to announce me, then walked slowly back to the front, looking back over her shoulder at me the entire way.

Helton was seated at his desk, which was still buried under a drift of paperwork. A man up to his waist in bureaucratic quicksand who couldn't decide if struggling would release him from its grip or only cause him to sink faster.

"You," he said.

"Me," I said, and stepped inside.

I dropped into the chair across from him and put my feet up, knocking a pile of folders onto the floor. I said, "Sorry," and bent down to pick them up.

"Leave them," he said. "Out of sight, out of mind."

I leaned back and folded my hands primly in my lap. "I'd like to ask a favour."

"Why not," Helton said. "Since we know each other so well."

"Think of it as a professional courtesy."

"I owe you that much?"

"You don't owe me a thing," I said. "That's what makes it a favour."

"Go on."

"I'd like to see where Doug Weaver's truck was found."

"It's not a crime scene," Helton said. "Not anymore. Snoop to your heart's content."

"I don't know where it is. The newspaper said the truck was found near Orchard Park. I looked at a map and it's a pretty big place."

"Beach Road," Helton said. "South end of the park. It dead-ends at the lake. That's where we found the truck. You can't miss it."

"I was kind of hoping you could show me."

"You were, huh?"

"In case I had some questions."

Helton grunted. "Maybe you'd like a tour of the park, too. A history lesson on the battle between the Huron and the Iroquois over the fur trade."

"That sounds like a no."

"I don't know what it sounds like. I can't hear you with all this paper-work in the way."

"I'll throw in dinner."

Helton frowned. He looked at his desk, then at his watch, and heaved a big sigh.

"Okay."

WE TOOK my car. I insisted on the grounds that I needed to get to know my way around Sycamore better. Helton didn't like that, not because he wanted to drive, but because it told him I was planning to stick around for a while.

Following his directions I headed south out of town, then east along the lakeshore. We passed a trailer park, a church, and a John Deere dealership, then the road took an abrupt turn landward and we were suddenly driving through dense woodland. Helton said this was all park land, protected by the federal government. We had to drive around the perimeter of the park to reach Beach Road. It was asphalt where we turned onto it, but it changed to dirt by the time we reached the end. I pulled to a stop in front of a line of waist-high wooden posts designed to keep people from driving into the lake, which lay about ten yards away on the other side.

A parking lot ran parallel to the road on the right side — a long, wide expanse of crushed gravel with a couple of oil-drum garbage cans next to a wrought-iron archway with ORCHARD PARK written across it.

The parking lot was empty, and when we stepped out of the car I understood why. In the spring and summer, this would've been a nice place for people to come and toss around a football or have a barbecue. But in the colder months it was little more than a picturesque view best enjoyed from the inside of a car. As if to accentuate this point, a chilled breeze came blowing in off the lake, causing me to huddle deeper into my jacket.

"This is it," Helton said. "We found Doug's truck right over here." He indicated a spot near where I'd parked my car.

"Did someone call it in?"

"No," Helton said. "One of our patrol officers found it. We try to keep an eye on spots like this, especially in the off-season. Kids come down here sometimes to make out, drink, smoke up. Nothing too serious, but we want to make sure they don't trash the place."

"What's the drug scene like in Sycamore?" I didn't really care, but I wanted to keep the conversation going while I wandered around.

"No worse than other towns its size," Helton said. "Some weed, some oxy, a little crystal. The users are mostly adults, unemployed or living on welfare. The kids tend to stick to alcohol. Every year or so one or two get killed drinking and driving, and we visit the schools to give our spiel. Same old, same old."

I looked over at him. "Job made you jaded?"

"I'm indifferent," Helton said. "It is what it is. I can't fix it, but I do what I can to prevent it. And when I can't do that, I help pick up the pieces."

"The officer who found the truck, did he notice the blood?"

"Not at first. He didn't see anyone around, so he thought the truck might've had a flat tire or mechanical trouble, and the driver had left to call for a tow. He took a look inside, thinking someone might be sleeping one off, and that's when he saw the blood."

"Were you on the scene?"

"I was." Helton spoke slowly and succinctly. It was the voice I imagined him using when he was called to testify in court.

"Did you know it was a homicide right away?"

"I didn't," Helton said. "I still don't."

"That's a lot of blood for someone to lose and still be able to walk away."

Helton opened his mouth to say something, then closed it again and lowered his eyes.

"What is it?" I asked.

"We did find blood outside the vehicle. A trail of it led off in that direction."

Helton pointed into the woods beyond the park grounds.

"Did you follow it?"

"There wasn't much to follow," Helton said. "The trail petered out just inside the treeline. We thought Doug might have been injured and stumbled into the woods to escape his attacker. We searched the whole area, with dogs, and couldn't find a thing."

"Susan was told there was enough blood found in the truck to suggest that Doug died as a result of his injuries."

Helton shrugged. "It's just a theory until we find his body."

"Pretty strange way to throw you off his trail if he was the killer, don't you think?"

"I don't pretend to understand the way a serial killer thinks."

"You should," I said. "That's how you'll catch him."

"And I don't need some private dick telling me how to do my job."

I raised my hands in a gesture of peace. "I meant no offense, Detective. I'm just concerned that you may be using this situation as an opportunity to kill two birds with one stone. On the one hand you've got a serial killer in your town, and on the other you have a bloody truck with no body. Wouldn't it be nice if you could tie them both together in a nice pretty package?"

Helton crossed his arms. "Is that what you think we're doing?"

"I don't know. It's just a theory."

"Yeah? Well, I think it stinks."

He uncrossed his arms, and for a moment I thought he was going to take a swing at me. He looked like he wanted to. Instead he turned away and looked out at the lake.

"That's good," I said.

Helton faced me again. "Good? How is that good?"

"It means you still give a shit."

He took a step toward me. "I don't need to prove anything to you. I'm not answerable to you. You don't even live here."

I ignored all that and said, "Do you think Doug Weaver is the killer?"

"It doesn't matter what I think," Helton said.

"Of course it does. You're in charge of the investigation."

"I told you before, the task force is in charge."

"But you're running the task force. Aren't you?"

Helton turned back to the lake.

"You think the feds care what I think? I'm only on the task force because it looks good in the press. Interdepartmental cooperation, they call it. Bullshit is what it is. They need me and the rest of the department because we know the town and we know the people, and that's it. They don't give a good god-damn what I think."

"I do."

"Thanks." Helton shook his head wryly. "That makes me feel better."

"Do they think Doug Weaver is the killer?"

"They think he's a person of interest. And so do I. Beyond that, I can't say."

"Is it because his body hasn't been found? Is that the main reason they suspect him?"

"It's the main reason, but not the only one. According to the profiler we have on loan from the FBI, serial killers tend to follow patterns of behaviour. Not all of them, but enough that you can identify their handiwork. The profiler calls it their 'signature.'"

"Are you telling me that Doug Weaver, former high school football star and owner of the local garden store, fits the profile of a serial killer?"

"He might," Helton said. "That's what they say about these people when they're finally caught. 'It couldn't be him, he seemed like such a nice normal guy.' Right up until they start hauling bodies out of the guy's basement."

"So that's what you think?"

"I don't know!" Helton shouted. "All I do know is that Doug's disappear-ance doesn't make sense in the context of the murders. It's an anomaly. And not just because his body wasn't found — although that's a pretty big red flag."

"Fair enough," I said. "The first two bodies were buried in shallow graves, then Doug's truck is found covered in blood, but there's no body. Then there are three more murders and the killer doesn't conceal the bodies at all. Like he doesn't care anymore if they're found."

"That's about right. And the last three murders occurred in rapid succession, at least compared to the first two."

"Like the killer's in a rush," I said.

"Or a panic," Helton offered.

"Because he's on the run? Is that what the feds think? That Doug Weaver killed those first two people, and when their bodies were found he panicked, faked his own death, and now he's, what, out there in the woods killing anyone he comes upon?"

"That is the working theory, more or less."

"It's crazy."

"So's the person we're looking for."

"And you think that person is Doug Weaver."

"He's a person of interest, like I said."

"But he's the one the feds are focused on."

"That's correct."

"Do the feds know that Susan hired me?"

"They know."

I tried to detect if there was any extra meaning lurking behind those two words, but Helton's poker voice was as good as his poker face.

"I don't suppose they'd be willing to talk to me?"

"I doubt it."

"Could you ask them for me?"

"No."

"What about interdepartmental cooperation?"

"You're not in anyone's department," Helton said. "At least that's what I heard."

My stomach tightened. "You've heard about me?"

"The feds talked about you a bit, but mostly it was stuff I read online."

"Lovely."

"You mostly work cases involving the Black Lands, right? The articles I read made out like you're some sort of monster-hunter-for-hire."

"The press exaggerates. You should know that."

"Fair enough," Helton said. "So what's the truth?"

"The truth?"

"Do you really work Black Lands cases? Have you really killed monsters?"

"You want the truth?" I said. "Yes, I work Black Lands cases. Yes, I've killed monsters. But the work comes to me, okay? I don't seek it out. I don't even want it. I'm like a magnet and the stuff is just drawn to me. As for the monsters I've killed, it was almost always in self-defence, and most of the time I was lucky to make it out alive. I'm not some thrill-seeking media whore."

Helton held up his hands. "Peace, Renn. I'm just trying to figure out why you're here. This is a murder case. There's no monsters here." He paused. "Only the human variety."

"Sometimes they're worse."

"Get real," Helton said.

"Okay, you're right. The Black Lands is worse."

"You heard about Boston?"

"Yeah."

Helton shook his head, and for a brief moment he dropped his poker face and looked at me with an open, almost boyish curiosity. "You ever been there? To the Black Lands?"

"If I had, would I be standing here talking to you?"

"Some people come back," Helton said, but there was doubt in his voice. "Don't they? Accidental Tourists. Isn't that what they call them?"

"It's rare for someone to cross over, and even more rare for them to make it back. Those who do usually wish they didn't. Sometimes they come back different."

Helton nodded. "I heard about that. The Influence. You ever seen anyone like that?"

I didn't respond right away. It didn't matter who I was talking to — man or woman, young or old — the moment they found out I'd had run-ins with supernaturals, they all turned into wide-eyed children, eager for stories about monsters and the dark dimension where they came from. Sometimes I obliged them — talking about my encounters was a form of therapy — but mostly I kept my mouth shut. It wasn't that I was secretive about the whole thing — although I knew that talking too much about it might earn me a visit from the PIA. It was more that talking about those cases was like reliving a near-fatal car accident. The people who wanted all the gory details were like rubberneckers cruising by the scene, sopping up the blood with their eyes without a thought of sympathy for the person trapped inside the twisted wreck. Mostly I hated being asked to remember things that I wanted desperately to forget.

"I'm sorry," Helton said. "I was just wondering why you'd take a case like this compared to the ones you usually work."

"I'm on vacation."

"This is what you do in your off-time?" Helton snorted. "Maybe you should go to an all-inclusive instead."

"I'm not being trite," I said. "I took this case because I wanted to take a break from the Black Lands."

"You can't drive a wooden stake through this problem, Renn."

"Sure you can," I said. "A stake to the heart would take care of a serial killer just fine."

"Is it your sense of humour that's kept you alive this long?"

"I don't know, but it's definitely kept me sane."

"I could use a bit of that," Helton said wearily.

"I just want to find Doug Weaver. Dead or alive. Same as you."

"And if he turns out to be the killer?"

"Then Susan will have to accept that."

Helton shook his head. "Easier said than done."

"Like everything else in life, Detective."

CHAPTER 15

I TOOK HELTON to the Star Stop for dinner. We both had a Galactic Burger with non-UFO-themed french fries. We didn't talk any more about the case. We were done with that topic, at least for now. I tried to make small talk, but everything I said came out forced and phony. It was like Doug Weaver was an invisible presence at our table. I did manage to find out that Helton knew Susan Weaver (she was Susan Ross at the time) because she had tutored him in calculus when they were in high school. He didn't know Doug very well because Doug was a jock and Helton said he didn't travel in those circles. He didn't mention what circles he did travel in, and I didn't ask.

Afterwards, I dropped Helton back at the police station. He said the task force was getting together for a meeting later that evening. I asked if I could sit in and Helton gave me a dead look before climbing out of the car.

Sitting there rebuffed, I tried to think of the next logical step in tracking down either Doug Weaver's dead body or the serial killer who had put him in said state.

When I was a kid and I needed the answer to a question, my mother usually sent me to the library. Amelia Renn was no great lover of books — her reading tastes veered more toward *People* magazine and *TV Guide* — and she didn't set any particular store by the knowledge contained within them. It was, more than anything, a lack of patience on her part. Mom couldn't be bothered to come up with answers, not even wild guesses, to the types of questions that are common to children. *Why is the sky blue? How much water is there in the Atlantic Ocean? Can birds sleep while they're flying?* Sending me off to the library was an easy solution, and it got me out of her hair for a few hours. When I was twelve, my mother didn't want me around the house at all, for reasons that were as fair as they were cruel. At that time in my life, she couldn't have cared less if I was at the library, the convenience store down the road, or on the far side of the moon.

Since I wasn't going to find any answers at the local convenience store or on the moon, that left only one place to go.

THE SYCAMORE public library was as bright and welcoming as it had been on my first visit. And just as empty. Walking toward the information kiosk, I wondered if people simply didn't use libraries anymore. Had electronic books, along with Google and Wikipedia, rendered them obsolete? There was no sign of the red-headed librarian I'd met the other day. I wondered why she would go into this line of work. I mean, besides the obvious love for books. Did she like the quiet, the solitude? Did she enjoy spending time in large cavernous buildings that smelled of yellowing paper and old glue? Had librarians become the lighthouse keepers of the twenty-first century?

That last thought sound like a pretty good line and I considered using it on the librarian. If I could find her.

I went into the main room and strolled past rows of bookshelves to the central area where a number of long tables stood under globe lamps that hung down from the high ceiling. A pair of wrought-iron staircases, one on either side of the room, spiralled up to an upper level with more bookshelves. There was no sound at all except the low clank of a radiator.

I was starting to wonder if maybe the library was closed and someone had forgotten to lock up. Maybe it was a small town thing. You always heard how people don't bother to lock their doors in a place like Sycamore. Maybe they did the same thing at the local library. But then again, probably not. Especially with a serial killer prowling about.

Leaning against one of the tables, I asked myself what I was doing here. Was I really looking for information to help my case, or did I just want to talk to the cute librarian again? Couldn't I do both? I asked myself. What if she wasn't here? Glancing around, it didn't appear as if anyone was working tonight.

I was about to head out and try my luck another day when I heard a shuffling sound at the far end of the room. I went over there and found Anne in the periodicals section, folding newspapers and stacking them in a pile.

I watched her for a few moments, then decided it was creepy to be standing there staring at her like that, so I cleared my throat to announce my presence. This was apparently the wrong thing to do. Anne jerked upright like I'd zapped her with a cattle prod and let out a startled squeak. The newspapers she was holding flew out of her hands and went fluttering to the floor.

I said "Sorry" in a sheepish way, and went over and started picking them up, feeling like a huge dumbass.

"You scared the shit out of me," Anne said. She let out a shaky laugh, but for a moment there was a look in her eye like she wanted to throttle me. I held out the folded newspapers like an offering. She considered them — and me — and eventually decided I wasn't worth the strain on her hands, and took them from me.

"I'm really sorry," I said.

"There's a crazy maniac out there and you scare me like that?" She put her hand on her chest and took a deep breath. "It's a good thing I wasn't armed."

"I didn't know librarians went around packing these days."

"I think I'm gonna start."

"It would help keep out the riffraff."

"I don't need a gun for that," Anne said. "I use my charm."

She tipped her head to the side and fluttered her eyelashes at me. I got the idea that a great many men (and even a few women) would do whatever she said if she looked at them like that. But there was a spark there, too. I'd seen it for a split second when I scared her. A peek behind her professional façade that hinted at... what? A temper? A wild side? I didn't know, but I was curious to find out.

Maybe it was her outfit. Today she was wearing a white blouse with the sleeves rolled up and black slacks that made her legs look like tapered blades. A definite step up from the dowdy prim-and-proper look she had been rocking the other day.

Anne said, "How's the book coming?" and for a moment I didn't know what the hell she was talking about. Had she loaned me a book? Had I taken one out of the library? Then it hit me: I had told her I was a crime writer working on a book about the Sycamore murders. Right. That.

After a long pause in which I waited for my brain to reboot, I said: "That's actually why I stopped by. I have a confession to make. I'm not really a writer."

I expected her to give me a knowing look, like she'd suspected all along, but she didn't. Instead she looked at me with a mixture of suspicion and unease.

"Oh," she said. "Then what are you doing here?"

I took out my private investigator's license and showed it to her. She looked at it, then at me. "Are you for real?"

"Real as houses," I said. "Whatever that means."

"And you're here, what, investigating the murders?"

"Yes."

"Isn't that a job for the police?"

"Usually, yes."

She quirked an eyebrow at me. "So what happened? You got bored one day and decided if the cops couldn't catch the killer, you'd come up and do it yourself?"

"Not quite," I said. "I'm helping someone connected to the case. That's all I can tell you."

"Why are you telling me any of this?"

"Two reasons. Part of my work is procedural — talking to people, finding clues, following leads, that sort of thing. The rest is instinctual — hints, hunches, and following your gut. The other day when I asked for your help with those newspaper articles, I was just following my usual procedure. But now I'm thinking it was also instinctual, because I have a feeling you can help me. The other reason I came by was to apologize for lying to you."

Anne smiled tentatively. "Instinct, huh? You sure it wasn't your conscience?"

"Some days I'm not sure I have one."

"I think you do. Why else would you go into this line of work if not to help people?"

"I kind of fell into the job."

"How so?"

"I was an actor."

Anne's eyes widened. "*What?* Are you serious?"

"I was, at the time. Until I came to a very difficult and very painful conclusion."

"What was that?"

"I wasn't a very good actor. I was terrible, actually."

"So the next natural step was to become a private investigator?"

"Not quite." I felt my neck dampen with perspiration at this sudden turn of events. I was the one who usually asked the questions. And I definitely wasn't used to talking about myself.

"So what happened?" Alice prompted me.

"Well, one of the few auditions I managed to secure was for a television pilot. A pilot is a standalone—"

"I know what a pilot is," Alice said. Her eyes bored into me.

"It was a show about a private investigator. I can't even remember what it was called." That wasn't true; I just didn't want to say it out loud. The show was called *Rex Temple, PI in the Sky*, on account of the fact that Rex, in addition to being a PI, also had his pilot's licence, and if the show was picked up he'd fly his private plane to different exotic locales week to week. "The show's on-set consultant was an actual private investigator named Madeline Ferine."

Anne gave a slow nod. "And she took you under her wing because she saw you had promise as a PI?"

"That, and I really needed the job. Especially since I didn't end up getting the pilot gig."

"How long have you been a private detective?"

"About ten years."

"I don't imagine you would have stuck with it for so long if you weren't good at it."

"Good enough, I suppose."

"But you need my help with this case?"

"It's a strange case."

"It is that," Anne admitted. "But what can I do? I don't know anything about the murders except what they've said about them on the news."

"I don't need your help with the investigation. I need your help with the town. I've been here for two days and everyone I've met is connected to the case in some way. I need to talk to someone who isn't directly involved."

"How is that going to help you?"

"I'm hoping it will give me some perspective. That it'll help me see something I might be missing."

"Don't you have someone you normally talk to about this kind of stuff?"

I did, but I didn't want to tell Anne that the person in question was my ex-wife and we had a tendency to spar more than communicate.

"I don't want to put any pressure on you," I said. "We don't know each other, and the details of this case are pretty grisly and disturbing. But right now I'll take whatever help I can get."

Anne considered it. "I'm curious," she said. "But I'm not sure how much help I'd be to you. I've only lived in Sycamore for a year."

"That's longer than me."

I smiled at her and she smiled back. We might have had a moment right then, but we were interrupted by a loud, haughty voice.

"*Excuse* me, Anne, but if you're done with the periodicals, I have some returns for you to take upstairs."

I turned to see a short, crone-like woman staring at us. She was wearing a faded wool dress with a powder blue shawl draped over her shoulders. With her pinched face and steel-grey hair yanked back in a no-nonsense bun, she looked like the sort of librarian who dispensed corporal punishment for people who talked too loudly in the stacks.

Anne said, "Sure thing, Muriel. Are you heading out soon?"

"Soon enough," she said curtly. "Don't try to rush me."

"I wouldn't dream of it." Anne flashed a smile at her, and the brightness of it seemed to repel the woman like a cross to a vampire. A movie vampire, that is; real vampires weren't bothered by crucifixes. She turned and shuffled away with slow, deliberate steps.

"Why can't she do the returns herself?" I asked Anne when the woman was out of earshot. "Are her legs broken?"

"She doesn't like going up the stairs." Anne nodded at one of the two iron staircases. "They're old and creaky — sort of like her — and she thinks they're going to collapse at any moment. There's an elevator, but it isn't working right now. I don't mind. It's the only place in the whole library where I can get some peace."

"Is she always that pleasant?"

"That's partly my fault. When I first started here, she told me to call her Ms. Russell, and I refused. I told her I wasn't a child and I wouldn't be treated like one. I've been in her bad books ever since." She wrinkled her nose. "Pardon the pun."

"How long until you get a shawl of your own?"

"Not until I'm eighty," Anne said. "It's not like winning the Masters. You have to put in your time."

"Goals are important."

Anne folded her arms across her chest and gave me a narrow look that seemed to put an end to our repartee. "What's your goal?" she asked me. "Catch the killer?"

"I don't know. I guess so. If it comes to that."

"You don't sound that confident."

"Honestly, I don't know if I'm up to the job."

"What makes you say that?"

"What's happening in Sycamore..." I shook my head. "Let's just say it's unfamiliar ground for me."

"Beginner's luck?"

"I'm hoping for some."

"And if it doesn't come?"

"I'll try to make my own."

Anne considered this, then gave a slow nod like she was satisfied by this response. "So what can I do to help? I mean, specifically."

"I'm not sure yet."

"What are you gonna do when you figure it out? Shine a bat signal in the sky? Or maybe a book signal?"

"Actually, I thought I'd just give you a call."

"Are you asking for my phone number?"

"I was thinking we could meet for coffee tomorrow. Maybe by then I'll have an idea how you can help me. Then you can decide if you want to. If you don't, you still get a free coffee."

"Throw in a scone and you've got yourself a deal."

"Done."

We shook on it, a gesture that should have been businesslike but came off as oddly intimate. At least it did for me.

"Are you working tomorrow?" I asked.

"No, it's my day off."

"Then how about we meet in the afternoon. Say around two o'clock? Is there a decent coffee shop in town?"

"There's no Starbucks if that's what you mean. But there's a local place that's very good. Café Domo. It's on Viermont Street. Do you know where that is?"

"I'll find it. Tomorrow at two?"

Anne said, "Okay."

"Great," I said. "It's a date."

"It's an appointment," she corrected.

I nodded.

It was a start.

CHAPTER 16

I DROVE BACK to my room at the Lakeview Inn and spent the next couple of hours going over the newspaper articles again. After my mind was thoroughly refreshed with blood and murder, I decided to go to bed.

I had a dream. In it I was running through a dark city of towering skyscrapers completely devoid of lights with narrow, crooked alleys zigzagging between them. I was sprinting through this midnight maze, huffing out breath like an asthmatic, which only went to show that even in my dreams I was out of shape.

At first I didn't know why I was running, only that I had a powerful compulsion to keep moving. I soon came to understand I was chasing someone.

Whoever it was, they weren't that far ahead of me, but the darkness was nearly absolute, and I kept banging off the brick walls and clipping my shoulders on the corners as I struggled to catch up to him.

Just when I thought I had lost my quarry, I came around a sharp corner at high speed, bounced off the opposite wall, and banged right into him, driving us both to the ground.

Crouching over his prone form, I gripped him by the shoulders and turned him over.

I expected to see my own face, or my mother's, or someone else I knew. That's usually how dreams like these went.

But it was Doug Weaver. I recognized him from the photos Susan had shown me.

Then, as my dream self gawped at him in surprise, a shadow drifted across Doug's face, shrouding it, and when it passed, I was looking at a younger version of him, the teenage football player Susan had fallen in love with. Another shadow passed over him like an ink cloud and I was staring at an old man.

"You're looking for me," he said in a hollow, elderly voice.

"Yes," I said uncertainly.

He cocked his head and became teenage Doug again. "You're not sure?"

I was opening my mouth to reply when a loud alarm came blaring out of the night.

"You'd better decide quick," Doug said. He had reverted back to normal middle-aged Doug. "They're coming."

"Who's coming?" I asked.

Doug shook his head in a disappointed way, like that was the wrong question to ask.

"Who are they coming for? Me or you?"

"That's for me to know and you to find out," Doug said.

"What kind of answer is that?" I asked.

"You're the detective. You figure it out."

The alarm got louder and louder as the dream began to dissolve around me. The sound became more shrill and intermittent until I woke up to a telephone ringing.

I blinked in the darkness, unable to remember where I was. The phone kept ringing — a loud penetrating sound like someone was driving a spike into the middle of my brain. Not my cell phone, I thought fuzzily. It was the room phone on the nightstand.

I reached for the phone and accidentally knocked it onto the floor. Sweeping my legs out from under the blankets, I sat on the edge of the bed and glanced at the clock on the nightstand. It was 3:27 A.M.

Who would be calling me at this hour? I wondered. Who even knew I was here?

I looked down at the phone on the hideous orange carpet. The handset had fallen off the cradle. I picked them both up, placing the cradle back on the nightstand and the handset against my ear. I muttered something that vaguely resembled "Hello."

A female voice said, "Felix. Renn." She put a pause between the two words, as if they didn't go together.

"Yes?"

"Burnside Road. North of Coakley."

At first I thought it was Anne, calling to change the location of our date… er, appointment. But even in my foggy, sleep-addled state I knew it wasn't her. The voice on the phone was younger, higher in pitch.

I said, "What?" and the voice repeated the words in the same clipped, precise manner. Like the robot that recites the phone numbers when you call Information.

"Who is this?"

I didn't expect an answer, and I didn't get one. The caller hung up without saying another word.

I put down the phone and went over to the table where I'd put the stack of newspaper articles. I turned one over to the blank side, picked up a pen, and jotted down the words the caller had said.

Then I went back to bed.

CHAPTER 17

THE NEXT MORNING, I showered, shaved, put on a fresh shirt with yesterday's suit, and was out the door by nine o'clock. After picking up a take-out coffee at the Star Stop, I got in my car and headed over to the Weavers' garden store.

Since I didn't know where to look for Doug Weaver's body, I thought I'd try to find out more about what he was like before he got dead.

I parked in the gravel parking lot and walked across the ornamental foot-bridge to the converted Victorian that housed the store. A bell jingled over my head as I opened the front door. I stepped inside and entered Halloweenland.

I had expected to see an assortment of gardening supplies — pots, planters, bags of fertilizer stacked like sandbags — and all of those things were there, but they were buried beneath an avalanche of Halloween decorations. Shelves were crowded with plastic pumpkins and glow-in-the-dark ghost figurines; cardboard cutouts of witches and skeletons hung in every window; and the ceiling was bedraggled with cotton cobwebs and orange-and-black crepe paper streamers.

I had almost forgotten that Halloween was approaching. You wouldn't have known it to look at this particular town. I couldn't recall seeing a single jack-o'-lantern or inflatable yard ghost on my drive into Sycamore. Maybe the locals already had their fill of scares right now.

As I stood there feeling a bit like Ichabod whatshisname, a couple of young guys came out of the back, each of them carrying a pumpkin. They added them to a pile in the corner, a bright orange pyramid of pumpkins, some with dry clods of dirt still clinging to them.

One of them noticed me, gave me a nod, and said, "Sup." I nodded back.

The wooden floor creaked rustically as I went over to the main counter. Next to the cash register, a small plastic skeleton dressed in a corset and fishnet stockings was belting out a chirpy electronic melody that I barely recognized as "The Time Warp." The thing was either possessed by the devil or had a motor inside because it was doing a slow side-to-side movement that I presumed was supposed to be dancing. It was slightly less annoying than the novelty plastic trout that sang "Do Wah Diddy Diddy," but I was still tempted to draw my gun and put a bullet in it.

The girl behind the counter looked like she would've happily taken a bullet herself. She was in her late teens or early twenties, with lank brown hair, close-set eyes, and the kind of pouty lips that went perfectly with her current mood. She was sitting on a stool, slumped to one side with her head propped on one elbow. She perked up slightly as I approached, like she was surprised to see a customer this early in the morning.

"Let's do the time warp again?" I said.

"And again and again," she said with a wince. "Eight hours a day, every day."

"Maybe someone will buy it."

"It's not for sale," she said. "It's part of the seasonal décor." She rolled her eyes. "I'm not even allowed to turn it off."

"I'm pretty sure the CIA uses a similar device to torture people."

"If they used it on me, I'd tell them anything they wanted to know." The girl closed her eyes and pinched the bridge of her nose. "What can I help you with today?"

"I'm in the market for a cactus. Do you have one that isn't pointy?"

The girl — her nametag said HALEY — raised an eyebrow at me. "Seriously?"

"No," I said. "I'm actually looking for Susan Weaver. Is she around?"

The girl, Haley, said, "She's out back clearing out the greenhouse."

"Does the store close down for the winter?"

"The store stays open," Haley said, "but it's too cold to keep the plants in the greenhouse."

"Makes sense."

"You're the private investigator."

I looked down at myself. "Am I wearing a sign?"

"Sort of. You're wearing a suit, and no one comes in here dressed like that. You look city. And Susan said she'd hired a detective to find Doug."

"She told you that?"

"Sure," Haley said. "We're like family here."

"You knew Doug Weaver?"

"Of course. I work for him."

"How long?"

"A few months."

"What's he like?"

"He's a good guy. Friendly. Polite. He's always been nice to me."

I wondered how much Haley knew about Doug's disappearance and what she actually thought about it. I got a vibe that she was keeping her true feelings from me. Not that I blamed her. I wasn't just a stranger to her; I was a guy hired to come here and dig up dirt — and hopefully a body. There were undoubtedly rumours going around town. Did she think Doug was missing, dead, or a murderer? I noticed that she spoke about him in the present tense, like he was still alive. I found it odd that Susan had told her staff that she had hired a PI to find her husband, but neglected to tell them that she thought he was dead.

I nodded toward the back. "The two guys hauling pumpkins, have they worked here long?"

"About as long as me," Haley said. "We were all hired around the same time to help with the fall rush."

"Can I speak to them about Doug?"

"You could try, but they don't talk much."

"That's not true," I said. "One of them said 'Sup' to me when I came in."

Haley laughed. "That's half of their daily word quota. I'm pretty sure they share the same brain."

"Brothers?"

Haley nodded. "Don and Denny Dunbarton."

"Were you working the day Doug went missing?"

Her smile disappeared so fast it was like I'd slapped it off her face. I had done it on purpose, throwing her a curveball so I could get a genuine response.

"Yes," she said. "Don and Denny were here, too. The police said we were the last ones to see Doug before he disappeared."

"You spoke to the police."

She nodded. "Of course. Not that there was much to tell them. It was a day like any other. Doug was acting normal, like he always did, and he left at his usual time."

"When was that?"

"Five o'clock. We all left around that time. That's when the store closes."

"Did he say anything about stopping somewhere on the way home?"

Haley shook her head. "Not to me."

"What do you think happened to him?"

She lowered her head, like she was giving the question some serious consideration, then she raised her eyes to me and said, "I think he's dead." She hesitated, then bit her lip. "I hate to say it out loud, like it's bad luck or something, but I think it would almost be for the best if he was."

"Why do you say that?"

She shrugged her shoulder. "It's better than being a serial killer."

DON AND Denny Dunbarton didn't have anything more to add than what Haley had already told me. They were the ones who had put up all the Halloween decorations, and that was what they were doing on the day Doug Weaver went missing. They spoke to him only briefly (I got the impression this was the way they spoke with everyone, myself included) and didn't feel he was acting strangely or out of character in any way. I thanked them and headed out the back door.

The area behind the store was much larger than one might expect from looking at the front. The property stretched off a considerable distance, with a medium-sized greenhouse on one side, a pond on the other, and a dirt path that ran between them to a gazebo at the far end. It probably looked better in the spring or summer, when the plants were green and the flowers were full bloom, but even now, in the doldrums of autumn, it was still a space of sedate tranquility.

I could see Susan Weaver through the open door of the greenhouse. She was lifting big bags of topsoil and stacking them in a wheelbarrow. She was wearing a green work jacket over a grey fleece sweater, faded blue jeans, and heavy work boots. The boots looked too large for her, and I wondered if they were Doug's. I stood there watching until the stack of bags was almost as tall as her. She never seemed to tire, either because she was in good shape or because she felt like punishing her body. Maybe both.

I went over and knocked on the open doorway. Susan turned to me with a bag in her arms. "Hi," she said, and dropped the bag on the pile and leaned against it, breathing heavily.

"Want a hand?" I said.

She shook her head and wiped sweat off her forehead with the back of her hand. "I'm done."

"So I'm right on time."

"You get settled in okay?"

"Yeah, I'm over at the Lakeview Inn."

Susan made a face and I shrugged. "It's not pretty, but it has all I need." I glanced around the interior of the greenhouse. "Looks like business is going well." The long tables that ran the length of the building were bare except for a few empty nursery pots.

"We close down the greenhouse in the winter," Susan said.

"The girl in the store mentioned that."

"You spoke to Haley?"

"Yes. You told her about me?"

"Yes." Susan's eyes widened slightly. "Was that okay?"

"Yeah, of course."

"I thought you might want to talk to her, and to Don and Denny. Since they were the last ones to see Doug."

"They said they didn't notice anything unusual that day."

Susan nodded and looked down at the ground. We stood in silence for a few awkward moments, then I pointed at the wheelbarrow and said, "Can I drive that for you?"

"Sure," she said.

I got behind the wheelbarrow, picked it up by the wooden handles, and pushed it through the open doorway. I followed Susan around the side of the store to a metal utility shed. She took out a key to open the padlock on the doors, then pushed them open so I could roll the wheelbarrow inside. Working together it only took a few minutes to unload the bags of topsoil and stack them against the back wall.

"Thanks," Susan said, after she'd locked the shed again.

"Thank *you*," I said. "That's the most exercise I've had in weeks." I hesitated. "It's also the most work I've done for you since you hired me."

"It's only been a couple of days."

"I know, but I feel like I'd be in the same position even if I had a month to look for your husband. To be perfectly frank, I don't know how I'm going to find his... find him."

Susan nodded, more to herself than to me. "Even when things seem hopeless, we keep trying. I think human beings are hardwired that way. I don't know if that's a good thing or a bad thing. I can't tell anymore if I'm determined or just plain stubborn." She looked at me. "Can you?"

"If I could," I said, "I probably would've gone into another line of work."

CHAPTER 18

I DIDN'T LEARN much from my trip to The Greener Side. Haley and the Dunbarton brothers only reiterated what Susan had already told me: That Doug had spent the day at the store, he didn't say or do anything out of the ordinary, and he left at the same time he usually did, at five o'clock when the store closed. When he didn't return home, Susan waited a few hours, then called the police, who didn't find his truck until the early hours of the following morning.

That left me with a block of time between ten to twelve hours in which any number of things could have happened. The two prevailing theories were that Doug had either been murdered in his truck and his body disposed of in some unknown fashion, or that he had planted the blood in his truck to make it appear that he had been murdered, presumably to throw the police off his trail so he could keep on killing people in the town where he was born and raised.

Both theories had their problems, and I was starting to come around to Sandra's way of thinking that my best hope of locating Doug Weaver's body was to find the killer — and hope that he didn't turn out to be Doug Weaver.

I was mulling these thoughts over coffee and a cornbread muffin at Café Domo. It was a trendy little spot with an assortment of quirkily mismatched tables and chairs that looked like they'd been acquired at a garage sale. A half dozen booths ran along one wall and there was a small stage at the back. Behind the main counter, a couple of baristas were working industriously with a variety of hissing, steam-spewing machines.

Anne was supposed to meet me here at two o'clock, and it was already a few minutes past. It wouldn't be the first time I was stood up by an attractive woman, but since she'd told me this wasn't a date, maybe there wasn't the same expectation for promptness.

I sipped my coffee and picked at my muffin and continued to wait.

Anne showed up at a quarter past two. She was wearing a camel's hair topcoat, a tan sweater, and slim black jeans. A plaid scarf hung loosely around her neck. She wore her red hair down today and her cheeks were flushed from the cold autumn air. My heart began to thump heavily in my chest.

"Sorry I'm late," she said.

"No problem," I said, rising out of my chair. "Can I get you a coffee?"

"That's okay, I'll get it."

"But it was supposed to be my treat."

"Sit." She was smiling but her voice held a note of command. I sat.

Anne went to the counter and came back a few moments later with coffee and a blueberry scone. She sat down across from me. "Were you waiting long?"

"No," I said. Then, without realizing I was going to say it: "Did you call me last night?"

Anne froze in the process of removing her scarf. "Uh… not that I'm aware of. I don't think I even have your number."

"Right," I said. "You don't happen to know what's on Burnside Road, north of Coakley?"

Anne looked at me like I was speaking to her in backwards Latin. If this had been a date, this would've been the part where she suddenly had to go home and feed her cat. "Not much, I don't think," she said. "Coakley is in the middle of nowhere. So Burnside Road would be…"

"North of nowhere," I finished.

"Don't take this the wrong way," Anne said, "but did you happen to suffer a head injury since the last time I saw you?"

"I don't think so," I said. "But I was thinking about having my head examined for taking this case."

"Have you come up with a way I can help you?"

"You still want to?"

Anne shrugged. "If I can."

"Do you know where Doug Weaver's body is?"

Anne shook her head. "Nope. Sorry."

"Damn." I took a sip of coffee. "That would've been a *huge* help."

"If he really was murdered, the killer could've dumped his body anywhere."

"I know."

"What does Coakley have to do with it?"

"I'm not sure," I said. "Someone called me last night, I don't know who, and all they said was 'Burnside Road, north of Coakley.'"

Anne leaned forward on her elbows, fingers tented under her chin. "You think it's connected to the murders?"

"I'm not sure. If it was a telemarketer, then they've really got to work on their sales pitch."

"Man or woman?"

I blinked. "What?"

"The caller — was it a man or a woman?"

"A woman."

"Young or old?"

"Uh, younger, I think."

"Did you notice an accent? A lisp? A stutter?"

Anne fired off these questions like she was doing a word association test. I wondered if she had experience with this sort of thing, or if she was just excited to be working on a real murder case.

"I don't remember an accent or a speech impediment. Nothing like that." I gave my head a little shake as if it would jog my memory. "I was sleeping when I got the call, and I was still waking up by the time it was over."

"Hmm." Anne tapped her index fingers against her chin. "Burnside Road. North of Coakley." She pointed at me. "You're thinking of going up there." It wasn't a question.

"Someone wants me there," I said. "And right now it's the closest thing I've got to a lead."

"You think Doug Weaver's body is up there?"

"Maybe," I said. "But that would make things a little too easy, wouldn't it?"

Anne gave an absent nod. "It could be a trap."

"Could be."

"But you're going to go anyway."

"It's my job. And right now I don't have anything else to go on."

"You're working for Susan Weaver?"

"I can't tell you that."

"You kind of did," Anne said. "Who else could you be working for?"

"Do you know her?"

"Not really. I've been to the store. What's it called? The Green Way?"

"The Greener Side," I said.

"Yeah," Anne said. "I bought a ficus from her. For my apartment when I first moved here. She seemed nice enough. Never met her husband."

And now you never will, I thought, but didn't say.

"Have you spoken to the police?" Anne asked.

"I have," I said. "They gave me the impression that Doug Weaver is their prime suspect."

"Then I guess you're both looking for him."

"I guess so. You wanna come with me to Burnside Road tonight?"

"Like a date?"

"I was thinking it would be more like a scavenger hunt."

Anne wrinkled her nose. "For a dead body?"

"Uh…"

"Sounds like fun, but I have plans tonight."

"Okay."

"I've got a date."

Damn.

CHAPTER 19

ANNE AND I arranged to meet again at Café Domo tomorrow. Maybe by then I'd have come up with something she could do to help me. Barring that, I figured she could tell me how her date went.

I didn't usually make a practice of mixing business with pleasure, but since there wasn't much business happening in the case of Doug Weaver's missing body, I decided it wouldn't hurt to make a small exception.

After driving back to the Lakeview Inn, I was headed to my room when a man emerged from the office and came jogging over, one hand waving in the air. "Hey!" he said. "Hold up!"

I recognized him as the old man who had signed me in when I first arrived. "Is there a problem with my credit card?" I asked him.

He came to a stumbling, breathless halt and bent over with his hands planted on his upper thighs. For a moment I thought he was going to collapse and I'd have to perform CPR, but then he caught his breath and straightened up.

"You had… a visitor," he said between gasps of air.

"Who?"

The man shook his head. "Young woman. Didn't leave her name."

"What did she want?"

"She said she was looking for you. I told her I hadn't seen you. She said she'd come back later."

"Okay. Uh, thanks."

The man threw back his scrawny shoulders like he was trying to make himself look bigger than he was. "I wanted to tell you, this isn't that kind of place."

"What kind of place?"

"A place where you can have…" He made a fumbling gesture in the air. "…those type of women in your room."

"What type of women would that be?"

The man squinted at me with small, hard eyes. "You know what I'm talking about," he said. "And I won't have it. Not here."

I looked at the shabby building with its flaking blue paint and thought it was exactly the kind of place one brought 'those type of women.' But I didn't say that. Instead, I said, "I'll keep that in mind."

"Be sure that you do," the man said. "I got a reputation to uphold around here."

Once again I bit my tongue. "Got it," I said, and flipped him a small salute.

I went into my room and sat down in the chair next to the desk. This was the first time I'd been accused of being a john. I wondered what Sandra would think about that.

A better question was, who did I know in town that might be mistaken for a prostitute? The motel owner was old enough that any young woman might have looked like a prostitute to him, especially if he was the type who viewed all youth with suspicion. There was nothing I could do except wait until she came back.

I checked my watch. It was three-thirty. I wanted to check out Burnside Road, but I preferred to do it under cover of darkness. I didn't know what I'd find be getting into out there and my natural tendency was for stealth. That left me with plenty of time to get ready, so I decided to grab a bite next door at the Star Stop.

I'D BEEN eating a lot of burgers lately, so I decided to go with fish and chips. It didn't have a UFO-themed name in the menu, which secretly disappointed me. The waitress was one I hadn't seen before, a bottle-blonde named Lara. I almost asked her if the Lakeview Inn had a lot of prostitution traffic, then decided it was probably a bad idea.

I was just finishing up when the bell over the door rang and a young woman came bursting into the diner. The place was half full and several heads turned to look at her. Mine was one of them. I recognized her as the girl I'd met her at the Greener Side just that morning. She saw me and came over to my booth, sliding into the seat across from me and then hunching forward like she was afraid to be seen… or maybe seen with me.

"Haley?" I said. "Were you the one looking for me at the motel?"

"Yes," she said. "I was waiting for you." She spoke in a low, hushed voice only a couple of degrees above a whisper.

"How did you know where I was staying?"

"Susan told me."

"Is something wrong?" I said. "Is she okay?"

Haley shook her head impatiently. "She's fine. She's… at home. At least I think she is."

It might have been the clipped way she spoke, or maybe it was because I was wide-awake now, but something clicked in my head.

"You called me last night," I said. "You told me to go to Burnside Road, north of Coakley."

Haley didn't say anything. A series of emotions flitted across her face — surprise, denial, apprehension, fear, then a kind of grim acceptance.

"Yes, I did," she said with some reluctance. "I wanted to warn you."

"Warn me about what?" I said. "What's on Burnside Road?"

Haley looked down at her hands which were fidgeting on the table. "I don't know for certain," she said, "but I think it's a grow-op."

That was about the last thing I expected to hear, and it took me a moment to process it. "A grow-op," I said. "You think the Weavers are selling marijuana?"

Haley shook her head, and the motion dislodged tears that had been welling in her eyes, causing them to streak down her cheeks. "I don't know!" she said, her voice rising in a querulous wail. The same heads that had turned before turned again and stared at us. I ignored them and reached over and placed my hand on top of hers.

"It's okay," I said. "Start at the beginning."

"I've only worked at The Greener Side for a few months," Haley said. "The guy who worked there before me was named Dennis. I didn't know him, but he went to high school with my younger brother. He told me Dennis's parents made him quit the job because of the stories that have been going around about the Weavers."

"What stories? You mean about the murders?"

Haley closed her eyes and leaned her head back against the padding of the booth. "No," she said, frustrated. "It doesn't have anything to do with the murders." Her head came forward again and her eyes latched onto mine. "Dennis's parents heard that the Weavers are selling drugs."

"Have you seen proof of this?"

Haley nodded. "A couple of weeks after I started working at the store, I was on the evening shift — we stay open later in the summer — and it was kind of slow, so I decided to clean the office that Doug and Susan use. It was pretty messy, papers all over the place, so I thought I'd organize it for them. I was sorting through some old invoices and noticed one for a large shipment of fertilizer, heat lamps, and some hydroponics equipment." She suddenly looked guilty. "I wasn't being nosy. I wasn't even paying attention to what I was looking at. But that one invoice caught my eye because we don't sell that kind of stuff at the store. The fertilizer, yes, but not the heat lamps or the hydroponics equipment."

"They do run a garden store," I pointed out.

"Sure," Haley said, "but that stuff is like the marijuana grow-op hobby kit. And the shipping address on the invoice wasn't for the store. It was for an address on Burnside Road."

"Do the Weavers own property up there?"

"If they do, they've never mentioned it to me."

"Did you talk to the Weavers about the invoice?"

"No." Haley looked down at her hands. "Susan came in and yelled at me for being in the office. I'd never seen her so angry. I felt like I was lucky not to be fired, so I never said anything about it." She bit her lower lip. "I wouldn't have thought anything of it, but I'd heard rumours about the Weavers. And then when Doug went missing…" She trailed off, as if her thoughts were too dismal and disturbing to finish the sentence.

"You think he was killed over a drug deal or something?"

"I don't know," Haley said. "But I can't stop thinking about that invoice."

I leaned back and thought about everything she'd told me. It completely changed my perspective on the case. Doug and Susan Weaver operating a marijuana grow-op? Doug Weaver killed over a drug deal gone wrong? It was an angle I hadn't considered — one that I'd had no reason to consider — but now that it was laid out before me, I had to admit it made a certain amount of sense. It went some way toward explaining why Doug's disappearance didn't fit in with the rest of the murders. It would also account for Susan's skittish behaviour and her attitude toward the police investigation. Maybe the one really didn't have anything to do with the other.

"Have you told the police any of this?"

"I talked to a detective, but I don't think he believed me."

I wondered if it was Helton she had spoken to. He seemed open-minded, but Haley's story might have been too much for him to believe. I wasn't even sure *I* believed it, but it was at least something I could look into. I'd been in Sycamore for three days now and I was getting tired of spinning my wheels.

"Have you been to Burnside Road?"

Haley looked at me like I'd ask if she'd ever gone skinny-dipping in shark-infested waters. "No," she said. "I don't want to go anywhere near there. I…" She stopped and looked around the diner to make sure no one was eavesdropping. "I thought about quitting my job, but I didn't want to leave Susan while all this stuff was going on. She's been really good to me and it would feel like I was abandoning her. But then I think about what happened to Doug…" She trailed off again. "What if they come after Susan next? Would they come after me or Don and Denny just because we work at the store?" More tears streamed down her cheeks. "I don't know what to do."

I reached across the table and touched her hand again. For the first time since I'd arrived in town, I felt like there was something I could do to help someone.

CHAPTER 20

I WENT BACK to my motel room after I saw Haley off. She was still scared about telling me everything she knew, but I could also see some relief in the way the colour returned to her pale cheeks. She didn't ask me what I was going to do next. She probably felt that the less she knew about that, the better off she would be.

I checked my road atlas and saw that Burnside Road was indeed north of Coakley, which was a small red dot on the map surrounded by a whole lot of green. Seeing how short the road was gave me an idea, and I got out my cell phone and called Jerry Baldwin.

Jerry was a real estate agent in Toronto who only dealt in haunted properties. Houses, condos, warehouses — it didn't matter as long as they had some sort of supernatural allure. The only thing I found more shocking than Jerry's profession was the fact that there was a market for such things.

Jerry answered with a seductive purr. "Talk dirty to me, sexy."

"Is that the way you answer your phone now? It could be bad for business, Jer."

"Aw, I knew it was you."

I wasn't sure if that made it better or worse. "I need a favour."

"Are you on a case?"

"Yes."

"Where are you?"

"Sycamore."

"Where's that?"

"North of the city."

"Cottage country?"

"Not that far north."

"I can be there in an hour."

"It's a two-hour drive."

"I can be there in two hours."

For years Jerry had been bugging me to take him on as my partner. I told him it wasn't going to happen, that this was one Batman who didn't need a Robin. Jerry said that was too bad because he looked real good in a cape and green shorts. Even though I've never taken him up on the offer, the image of Jerry dressed as the Boy Wonder pops into my head every now and again. You could say I'm haunted by it.

"I don't need you to come up here," I said. "What I need is a favour. A land title search on a property."

"I can do that," Jerry said.

"The location is on Burnside Road. It's north of a town called Coakley."

"What's in Coakley?"

"I don't know, Jer. That's why I'm asking you to look it up."

"Right, right."

You had to work hard to keep Jerry focused. He had the attention span of a five-year-old hopped up on Pixy Stix.

"What's the addy?" he asked.

"I don't have an address. The road doesn't look very long on the map, so there shouldn't be that many properties on it. Just check them all."

"Okiedokie."

"How long will it take?"

"Not long. Most of this stuff is online these days."

I checked my watch. It was only a little after five, but the light outside the window was already starting to fade. The sun went down early this time of year. "Can you have it for me in an hour?"

"An hour?" Jerry said, incredulous. "I'll have it for you in ten minutes. What do you want me to do with the other fifty?"

"Come up with a better telephone greeting," I said, and hung up.

❧

TRUE TO his word, Jerry called me back in ten minutes with the information I asked for. There were three plots of purchased land on Burnside Road — two were sold several years ago, but the third had been leased only a few months back. The names on the title document were Douglas and Susan Weaver.

This didn't prove anything in and of itself, but it did lend some credence to Haley's story and the suspicious invoice she'd found. I wouldn't be able to confirm anything else until I went up there.

I changed out of my suit and put on a dark sweatshirt and blue jeans. I swapped my dress shoes for hiking boots and clipped my holstered Ruger onto the back of my belt. I put on my jacket and headed out.

Driving north out of town on Centre Line Road, I tried to picture the Weavers as small-town pot farmers. I supposed they had the skill set for it, as well as the cover of their garden store to purchase the necessary equipment without raising any suspicions, but it was hard to wrap my brain around them actually doing it. On the other hand, I didn't know the Weavers very well — I didn't know Doug at all — so who was I to say what they were capable of? The nurse, Nancy, had implied the Weavers were well-off, and they clearly had enough money to afford full-time care for their daughter. Did they make enough selling flowers and fertilizer to pay for that, or did they have another, secret income stream?

One thing I knew about the pot industry was that the people involved in it came from all walks of life. This was mostly due to the ease with which one could put together a simple grow operation. It didn't require the scientific precision of cooking crystal meth, or the difficulty of importing more exotic drugs that were manufactured elsewhere like cocaine or heroin. All you needed to grow pot was a green thumb.

A drug deal gone wrong could account for Doug's disappearance. It would also explain why the local police were treating Doug more like a suspect than a victim. But if that was the case, then what did Doug Weaver have to do with the other murders? And why would his wife hire me to find his body, since my involvement could threaten to expose their criminal activities?

Maybe Susan thought I wouldn't find anything. Maybe she only hired me as a cover, to make it look like she was a law-abiding citizen who only wanted to find her missing husband. It wasn't outside the realm of possibility, but it still seemed farfetched to me.

It was half past six by the time I passed the green reflectorized sign that said COAKLEY. There was no population number on the sign, and from the look of the place that might have been done on purpose. The last light had bled out of the day, leaving behind a murky purple twilight. Despite that, I could see that Anne was right when she said Coakley was in the middle of nowhere.

I didn't see any houses or commercial buildings, no sign of civilization whatsoever except for a few vacant lots with real estate signs posted on them. There were no streetlights up here, so when I came to a crossroads I had to turn my car on an angle to shine the headlights on the street sign.

Burnside Road.

In addition to the names on the title document, Jerry had been able to find the exact address. 1140 Burnside Road. Since I didn't know which side it was on, I turned left and started cruising slowly along the road, looking for a marker of some kind.

I didn't see any lanes of turnoffs, and when I reached the place where the road ended at a crash barrier with a NO DUMPING sign on it, I did a three-point turn and headed back the way I came.

I passed Centre Line and continued along Burnside Road in the other direction. I was driving very slowly, but there was no danger of slowing up traffic. I hadn't seen a single car since I left Sycamore. As I peered owlishly back and forth through the steadily encroaching murk, I was forced to consider the possibility that coming out here under the cover of night — or at least the cover of early evening — might not have been the best idea.

The car was slewing slightly from side to side as I looked around, and as I turned the wheel to straighten it out, the headlights glinted off a metal sign sticking out of the ground on the left side of the road. I pulled to a stop and climbed out of the car.

There was a chill in the air, a small bite that nipped at my bare hands and the back of my neck. I could smell the faint aroma of pine needles and the stronger scent of mouldering leaves. There was also a hint of wood smoke. Autumn was my favourite season, but the smell of it always made me feel sad for some reason.

I went over to the sign. It was a small rectangular plate with the number 1100 on it. What passed for house numbers on properties that didn't have houses on them, I supposed. I got back in the car and continued along until I saw another marker — 1120. When I reached the one for 1140, I pulled over to the gravel shoulder and got out.

A LENGTH of chain hung between a pair of metal posts, blocking vehicular access to the rutted dirt track that continued ahead, cutting a path through the woods. A small NO TRESPASSING sign dangled below the chain. I doubted there was a private investigator on the planet who had ever heeded such a warning.

I climbed over the chain and started walking along the dirt lane. I didn't mind going ahead on foot. This was supposed to be a stealth mission, after all, and I didn't know who or what might be waiting for me at the other end. It wasn't quite full dark yet, and there was still enough light for me to make out a number of tire tracks on the ground. None of them appeared to be recent, but one set, wide-treaded and deeply embedded in the dirt, belonged to either a large truck or some type of construction vehicle.

I don't know how far I walked — the wall of trees on either side made it difficult to gauge distance — but it must've been at least a hundred yards before the lane opened out into a wide clearing of tall grass. I suppose the allure of such a property was to build your home a fair distance away from the road, both for privacy and the peaceful solitude of living in the middle of the woods. It was also a good place to set up an illegal drug operation.

That was what the building at the far end of the clearing looked like to me. It wasn't a house or a trailer, or even an RV like the one Walter White worked out of. It was a Quonset hut, with rusty corrugated sides, a curved roof, and no windows. Huddled back there against the trees, it looked as suspect as a guy in a raincoat standing at the edge of a playground.

A wide path had been cut through the grass to the Quonset, with more of those larger tire tracks — presumably by the vehicle that had hauled it out here. I followed the path, looking all around for any signs that I was being watched.

The trees around the perimeter of the clearing stood tall and dark, like construction-paper cutouts against a blue velvet background. They seemed to stretch even taller the further I went into the clearing, making me feel more and more like I was fenced in, trapped like a caged animal. A low breeze filtered through the grass, making it sway and whisper. I had the feeling of walking through a crowded party where everyone was talking about me in low, hushed voices.

I reached the Quonset hut and found the front door hanging crookedly from one hinge. It swayed idly in the breeze, making a flat banging sound as it bumped gently against the metal frame. Not exactly the type of top-notch security I expected from a clandestine drug lab in the middle of the woods. I took out my cell phone, turned on the flashlight app, and stepped inside.

The first thing I noticed was that the building didn't have a floor. My light shone across the tall grass of the clearing, except in here it was wilted and flattened down in spots, either from people walking on it, or from the lack of sunlight. There was an odd smell in the air, a chemical stench almost like fertilizer, but sharper, muskier, more like that of an animal. With the door hanging open, I supposed any number of critters could have been using this place as a den.

What it didn't look like it was being used for was growing marijuana. As I walked across the length of the hut, shining my light back and forth, I didn't see any sign of the equipment Haley had described on the invoice. No heat lamps, no bags of fertilizer, no hydroponics system. Except for a shovel leaning against one of the rust-pocked walls, the place was completely empty.

A loud bang caused me to spin around, and my phone went flying out of my sweat-slicked hand like a bar of soap. In the brief flash of light before it landed facedown on the ground, I saw a tall shadow move quickly past the doorway.

I dropped into a crouch, drawing my gun with one hand while I pawed around for my phone with the other. My lungs ached from the breath I was holding in. I found my phone and picked it up as another loud bang reverberated through the ribbed metal walls of the hut.

I aimed the light at the doorway. When the shadow flashed by again, followed by another loud bang, I realized it was only the door. The wind had picked up and blown it open on its broken hinge, slamming it against the side of the Quonset hut.

I turned around and resumed my search. There was another open doorway at the far end of the hut. I started toward it, panning the light back and forth across the ground.

I came to a stop and crouched down next to a spot where the grass had been dug up in a wide patch. Long furrows were carved into the dry dirt, and my first thought was *grave*. I glanced over at the shovel, then back at the ground in front of me, wondering if I was standing on the spot where Doug Weaver had been buried. Had someone brought the Quonset hut out here to mark the site, or possibly cover it up?

I ran my fingers over the dirt. It didn't seem to be loose from digging. It was more like an animal had been scuffing at the ground, the way a dog will work at one particular area where it's tied up.

I figured it still might be worth checking out, so I switched off my phone's flashlight app and snapped a picture of the ground. When the flash went off, I lost my night vision for a brief moment. The wind continued to pick up outside, making a constant rustling sound as it combed through the tall grass. The broken door banged a hollow tattoo against the steel wall.

I resumed walking toward the far end of the building. My head was down as I fiddled with my phone, trying to turn the flashlight app back on, but it didn't seem to be working. I couldn't remember the last time I charged it. My feet carried me forward on auto-pilot as I continued to futz with it.

When I looked up again, I was outside.

I stood on the edge of the clearing, with the trees in front of me. They seemed taller than I remembered. I told myself it was because I'd come out the other end of the Quonset hut and I was closer to them now. But the grass looked different, too. Even though it was full dark now, it seemed to shimmer with a faint silver light, like thousands of long, tapering blades.

The wind was still blowing, and the sound it made in the grass was different, too — a low hissing instead of the rustling I'd heard earlier. The air seemed colder, fresher, and there was a smell, but not like the one I noticed in the hut; this one was wet and earthy, the rich aroma of fertile soil. It should have been a pleasant smell, but for some reason it raised goose bumps on my arms and the back of my neck. My breath quickened and my heart began to slam in my chest.

My body was trying to tell me something, and it took my brain a few seconds to get the message. When it did, the fear became a real thing, crystalizing in my head and freezing all thought. I felt hot and feverish and cold and numb, all at the same time.

I knew what had happened, and I knew what I would see when I turned around.

The Quonset hut was gone.

The field of shimmering silver grass stretched away unimpeded to a distant line of black trees. It didn't look like the clearing I had walked across because it wasn't. I was no longer on the plot of land on Burnside Road.

I wasn't even in my world.

I was in the Black Lands.

CHAPTER 21

I STOPPED BREATHING at some point while I was crossing dimensions and had to remind myself to start again. I sucked in a big gulp of air, held it in for a three-count, then blew it out. I repeated this process until I was breathing normally again. I was hoping it would also help to calm my nerves, which were popping and jumping like water on a hot skillet, but it only seemed to make my fear more intense and focused.

I had come out here expecting to find a marijuana grow-op, maybe even a dead body in a shallow grave. Instead, I stumbled through a portal and found myself in the Black Lands. A place where any number of supernatural creatures could be lying in wait to kill me and eat me, and not necessarily in that order.

My back and shoulders were slicked in a cold sweat, and I felt a deep, paralyzing panic starting to creep in. I tried to hold it back, even though panicking seemed like a perfectly natural response to my current predicament. A vampire could have been stalking me right at this moment; a shifter could have picked up my scent and been heading my way; or one of the trees could suddenly pull up its roots and come shuffling toward me. Any of these scenarios were plausible here. This was the place where nightmares came true.

I had to get back. That was the obvious course of action, but it was also easier said than done. First I had to *find* my way back, and that would be difficult. Portals were invisible. It was part of what made them so dangerous. People who stumbled upon one earned themselves an all-expense-paid trip to the Black Lands, and more often than not those trips ended up being one-way.

Despite being scared, more scared than I'd been in my entire life, I couldn't help looking around at my surroundings and feeling an overwhelming sense of awe. Despite all of my dealings with the creatures from this place, I had never actually been to the Black Lands before. I had come up to the border once and peered across to the other side, but seeing it wasn't the same as being here.

At first glance it looked like an ordinary night scene in the woods, but a closer examination revealed things one wouldn't find in the natural world. The sky was choked with clouds that blocked out the stars, and yet there was a faint luminescence in the air, the same one that gave the grass its soft silver glow. The trees were massive black-trunked monstrosities — freakish mutations that looked like no trees found on earth. Their limbs were bent and twisted like they were clawing at the sky, or trying to fend it away.

Even the darkness itself was different. It seemed more like a presence wrapped around me rather than an absence of light. I could almost feel it, tickling the hairs on the back of my neck, seeping into the pores of my skin, like it wanted to infiltrate my body and fill with its inky blackness.

My senses felt unusually heightened. I could pick out every crenellated line in the bark of the nearest trees. I could smell the fetid water of a nearby swamp. And when a scream came tearing out of the night, I felt it as much as I heard it, like an icepick piercing the delicate flesh of my eardrums.

I spun around, looking for the source of the scream, and that turned out to be a huge mistake. If I was smart, I would have done a complete one-eighty and gone back the way I came, which should have taken me back through the portal. Instead I turned around and around, completely losing my sense of direction. Dimensional travel will do that to you.

I finally forced myself to stop moving. Then I closed my eyes and tried to recall the first thing I saw when I looked up from my phone. *My phone.* That was why it had flaked out on me. Electronics had a tendency to act strangely around portals, if they worked at all. My phone had been trying to warn me, but I was too dense to notice.

Focus, Felix, I told myself. *You can get out of here. You have to.*

I took another deep breath and let it out. Okay, I remembered looking up from my phone and seeing… trees. They were right in front of me and I thought that was strange because they seemed closer than they should have been. I had told myself that was because I came out the other end of the Quonset hut. Only that didn't happen. I never left the hut. I'd left the whole freaking planet.

I turned to face the trees — in what I hoped was the same spot I was in when I first crossed over — then I took a step backward. Then another. And another.

I was still in the field. Still in the Black Lands.

My panic went up a notch and a worm of dread began to squirm around in my belly.

The scream came again. Louder this time, which meant it was closer. It didn't sound like a cry of pain; it sounded more like outrage. Almost like it was the sound of the Black Lands itself, angry at my intrusion into its dark domain. I would have done anything at that moment to rectify the situation and go home. I didn't want to be here anymore than it wanted me here.

Looking around, I told myself I couldn't have wandered that far after I crossed over. The portal had to be close by. All I had to do was stick to this specific area and find it.

"You can do this," I told myself. "You can find it. You *will* find it." The power of positive thinking didn't seem to be working for me. The worm of dread in my stomach had grown into a snake.

I had definitely been facing the trees when I first arrived in the Black Lands, that much I knew for certain. So I put them in front of me and took a couple of steps backward. Nothing. I took a few steps to the right — no joy — then went back to my starting position and took a few steps to the left. Still nothing.

Standing there in the swaying silvery grass, my fear and frustration began to mount in equal measure. I wondered if this was how I was going to die: stuck in another dimension, pacing back and forth like the world's worst line-dancer.

The darkness was starting to bother me, as well. I'd never had any issues with the dark before, and I tried to tell myself it was because the darkness over here was different. Just like the trees and the grass were different. But it was a cold comfort. I could feel the blackness closing in on me from all sides, wrapping around my head like a pair of muscular hands, squeezing the walls of my skull.

I closed my eyes and took a couple more steps to the left, then a couple to the right. I was hoping I would open my eyes and find myself back inside the Quonset hut. No such luck.

I was thinking about tapping my heels together like Dorothy in *The Wizard of* Oz when my right foot came down on air where there should have been ground, and suddenly I was tumbling backward. *This is it!* I thought. *I found it!*

I fell in a hole.

It wasn't very deep, but I still landed hard enough to knock the wind out of me. I lay there for several seconds, gasping for air and staring up at the cloud-choked sky.

I was still in the Black Lands.

I sat up slowly, wincing at the pain in my shoulders and lower back. I could tell right away that the hole wasn't a natural formation. It had been dug out of the ground, about seven feet long, three feet wide, and two or three feet deep, with clearly defined edges. There was about two inches of water at the bottom of the hole that my clothes were soaking up like a sponge. I rolled over, bashed my knee against something hard, and climbed out of the hole.

I was slapping the mud off my coat and the seat of my pants, wondering if the shovel I'd seen in the Quonset hut had been used to dig the hole, when I heard the scream again.

It was definitely closer this time.

I really had to get out of here.

My eyes had adjusted to the preternatural night of the Black Lands, at least enough that I could make out a path of flattened grass leading away from where I'd fallen into the hole. I started following the trail, with a small pulse of hope in my chest. The path took an abrupt right turn, then continued on for a ways until it abruptly ended. The feeling of hope evaporated.

I turned around and started back the way I came, taking slower steps this time and looking closely from side to side.

I saw it. A few stalks of the silvery grass on the right side of the path were bent over but not completely trampled. They were already springing back up from where I had walked on them, which was why I had missed them on my first pass.

I took a steadying breath and started walking in that direction. One step. Two steps. Three. I heard the scream again, followed by the sound of something large and fast crashing through the tall grass. There was another scream, the loudest and closest yet, but it was cut off abruptly in mid-cry as I took another step and found myself standing in the Quonset hut.

I was back.

CHAPTER 22

I CAME FLYING out of the Quonset hut like I'd been shot from a cannon. I sprinted across the clearing and down the dirt lane to the main road. I may have left the portal behind, but whatever had been stalking me in the Black Lands could cross over just as easily as I did. I wasn't out of the woods yet, literally or figuratively.

I stopped at the chain with the no-trespassing sign to catch my breath. Leaning against one of the metal posts, I felt something shift against my back. I reached around under my jacket and touched my gun in its holster. The whole time I'd been in the Black Lands it had never once entered my mind to take it out. Not that it would have mattered. A gun wouldn't have helped me over there. Not unless I used it on myself.

I looked back the way I came, but there was nothing there. Nothing had followed me over.

That should have made me feel better, but it didn't. The fear was still there, like a stain on my skin that I couldn't rub off. I looked at the trees that hemmed the lane and the shadows between them where anything could be hiding, watching, waiting for the right moment to strike. It felt like the darkness itself was watching me.

I took a step back and tripped over the chain. I landed on my back, and that made me think of the hole I'd found in the Black Lands. If Doug Weaver had been buried there, someone must have come back and dug him up again. Only it didn't look like the hole had been dug up. It looked like…

An owl hooted in a nearby tree and my entire body froze. I looked down and saw my hand clutching my chest, like I was having a heart attack. It wasn't a scream, I told myself. It was just an owl. I'm not in the Black Lands. I'm home. Maybe if I kept telling myself that, eventually I'd believe it.

I climbed unsteadily to my feet and stumbled across the road to my car. When I opened the door, the interior light came on and I was overcome by a wave of the sweetest relief. I felt protected by that meager glow, the way it pushed back even the most miniscule part of the darkness. It was like wrapping myself in a warm towel fresh from the dryer. I could feel the cold weight that had been sitting on my shoulders slowly melting away.

I slid behind the wheel and pulled the door shut. The light winked out and the fear came crashing back down again. I let out a small whimper, which startled and disgusted me by turns. I'd never made a sound like that before in my entire life. I wanted to slap my own face and tell myself to stop acting like a baby, but my hands were clinging tightly to the steering wheel and I couldn't make them let go.

It was the darkness, I realized. Not the Black Lands, not the creatures that dwelled over there, not even the idea that one of them might have followed me back through the portal. It was the night itself that frightened me. I could feel it all around me, like a physical presence inside the car, pressing against me like the walls of a torture chamber. I feared the dark with a terror that was as strong as it was strange.

My breath was coming in sharp little gasps and I made an effort to slow it down before I hyperventilated and passed out. The thought of that — of being unconscious and surrounded by all that blackness — was too horrible to contemplate. A thought came to me then, one I'd never considered before: *How could anyone sleep in the dark?* How could they allow their eyes to close when anything could be lurking in the abyss of night? I couldn't understand how I had managed to do it myself all these years. The very thought was madness to me.

"No," I said out loud. "*This* is madness."

The sound of my voice snapped me back to a semblance of rationality.

Something had happened to me in the Black Lands. That was the only explanation I could come up with. I had never been afraid of the dark before, not even as a kid, but since I came back through the portal, I'd somehow developed a paralyzing case of nyctophobia.

"This could be a problem," I said to myself.

I put the key in the ignition — it took me a few tries because my hand was shaking so badly. When I turned on the engine, the glow from the instrument panel made me feel a bit better. But it wasn't enough.

I drove back to Sycamore with the dome light on.

CHAPTER 23

DRIVING BACK TO town, the thought going through my mind was: *Were these trees always so close to the road?*

While it might have seemed absurd to think that the trees had somehow shambled closer to the road, a part of me felt this was an entirely plausible scenario. Because I had seen it before. Blackwoods were a species of sentient tree from the Black Lands, and they could move whenever they wanted to. If one started moving toward you, my advice would be to run as fast as you could in the other direction. Blackwoods weren't very quick, but they were extremely dangerous. Imagine Tolkien's ents, except much less pleasant and with a thirst for blood.

Under normal circumstances it would have been extremely unlikely for there to be blackwood trees in the woods near Sycamore, but seeing as how I'd just come from an undocumented portal in the middle of those same woods, it was entirely possible that a few blackwoods might have crossed over.

All trees look black at night, I told myself. *That doesn't make them blackwoods.*

I repeated those words to myself over and over, and by the time I reached the city limits, I was almost starting to believe them. The street lights might have had something to do with that. Being back in the light — even the artificial, electrically-powered variety — made me feel better. As I headed toward the Lakeview Inn, I felt my breathing slow down, along with my frantic thoughts.

I experienced a brief moment of panic when I pulled into the parking lot and realized I'd have to get out of my car — and go back out into the darkness — in order to reach my motel room. It was only a few feet to the door, but it might as well have been a mile away. I seriously considered sitting in my car until the sun came up, then decided I had to nip this thing in the bud. The more I indulged this newfound fear, the worse it would get. Finally, after taking a series of deep, bracing breaths, I pushed myself out of the car and dashed across the cracked concrete to the door. I had the key in my hand and managed to slip it into the lock on the first try.

Once inside I turned on all the lights, including the television. I peeled off my mud-stained clothes, then stood there in the middle of the room shivering in my underwear, partially from the cold, partially from the sliver of night that I could see peeking between the not-quite-closed curtains. It looked like a narrow black eye staring in at me. I went over and closed the curtains the rest of the way, then sat down on the edge of the bed.

My thoughts turned back to the Quonset hut. It hadn't been put there to conceal the location of Doug Weaver's grave. It was put there to hide the portal. Unless the hole I'd fallen into really was Doug Weaver's grave, in which case the Quonset hut could have been used to hide the portal in order to hide the grave. But that seemed like a lot of work for the killer to go through. He may have buried his first two victims, but the last few bodies he'd left right out in the open.

So what was so special about Doug Weaver?

If that was his grave, then why did the killer bury him in the Black Lands? And why did he dig him up again?

It was possible the portal didn't have anything to do with the Sycamore murders, but I didn't buy it. The two things happening in the same town at the same time would have been one hell of a big coincidence. Still, I supposed it was something I had to consider.

The only thing I knew for certain was that the case I had purposely taken to avoid the Black Lands had ended up dropping me right into the middle of it.

As if on cue, I felt a massive headache coming on. I slumped back onto the bed and pulled the paisley comforter around me like a cocoon. I felt a stab of fear as the darkness enveloped me, and brought the comforter down around my shoulders. I closed my eyes, but the darkness was waiting for me there, too. My heart began to race.

I rolled onto my side and looked at the television. It was set to the Weather Network. A meteorologist in a charcoal suit with a bright green tie was gesturing at the map graphic behind him, moving his hands as he explained that a severe cold front would be coming down from the north, with temperatures dropping to almost freezing the following morning. I closed my eyes and tried to focus on his voice and ignore the darkness. My heart continued to rabbit-hop in my chest.

I'm not afraid of the dark, I thought to myself.

"I'm not afraid of the dark," I told myself.

I didn't fall asleep until the sun started to rise.

I HAD nightmares, a whole series of them, then woke up to another one.

I'd slept the entire day away.

I didn't know that at first. When I emerged from my comforter cocoon and saw the dim light behind the curtains, I thought it was from the rising sun. Then I looked at the clock on the nightstand and saw it was a quarter to six in the p.m. The sun was, in fact, on its way back down.

I let out a small moan and started looking around for my cell phone. I couldn't understand how I had slept for so long. Why hadn't anyone tried to call me? I wasn't such a sound sleeper that I would have slept through my phone (especially with the ring tone set to "My Humps," by the Black Eyed Peas).

I found the phone on the desk and pressed the power button. Nothing happened. The phone had gone with me through the portal, which had a tendency of frying electronic equipment. I got the charger from my overnight bag, plugged it into the phone, then tried the power button again. This time the phone came on. It wasn't fried, the battery was just dead. Probably from using the flashlight app.

I left the phone to charge and went to take a shower. As I stood under the hot spray, I went over the questions I'd asked myself the previous night — about the Quonset hut, the portal, the possible grave, and Doug Weaver. I traced them all back to their source, the person who'd sent me out to Burnside Road in the first place.

Haley. The girl from The Greener Side.

When I got out of the shower, I put on clean clothes and checked my cell phone. It was still powering up, but I saw I'd missed three calls during the day — one from Jerry (probably asking how my night had gone — and if I needed his help), one from Sandra (probably wanting an update on the case), and one from Susan Weaver (probably wondering where the hell I'd been all day). I wasn't ready to talk to any of them. Not yet.

Instead, I called the garden store. A young male voice answered, grunting something that might've been "Greener Side." One of the loquacious Dunbarton brothers.

"This is Felix Renn," I said. "Do you remember who I am? We spoke the other day."

The Dunbarton boy — I couldn't tell if it was Don or Denny — grunted what I assumed was acknowledgement.

"Is Susan there?" I asked.

"No," he said. "We're just closin'."

"Is Haley around?"

"No."

"Is she off today?"

The Dunbarton boy grunted.

"What's her last name?"

There was a pause. "Brennan," he said. "I think."

I had him spell it for me.

"Do you know where she lives?"

"No."

"Do you know her phone number?"

"No."

I sighed. If I was going to question him any further, I'd need a pair of pliers and a blowtorch. I thanked him for his help, then hung up and called Information. I asked if they had a number for a Haley Brennan in Sycamore. They did. I wrote it down and asked if they had an address. They did, and I wrote that down, too.

THE LIGHT was bleeding rapidly out of the sky as I drove to Haley's apartment. I knew I couldn't outrun the approaching night, but that didn't stop my foot from pressing harder against the accelerator. I thought my fear of the dark was a temporary thing, a brief holdover from my trip to the Black Lands. I thought it would be gone by the time I woke up. I was wrong on both counts.

Haley's building was in a part of town that the local chamber of commerce probably didn't advertise in their tourism brochures. It was a dirty, rundown neighbourhood with lots of rough-looking bars and storefronts with metal grillwork over the windows. I would have been nervous about parking my car on the street if it wasn't a piece of crap.

The lobby of Haley's building smelled like old grease and fresh urine. The lock on the inner door was busted, so I let myself in and went up the stairs to the fifth floor. I walked down the corridor and stood in front of the door to Haley's apartment. The numbers above the peephole said 506, only the 6 was missing and someone had written it in with black marker. Classy.

I was wearing my Ruger in its holster, but I didn't take it out. It was still possible that Haley hadn't set me up, and I didn't want her to open the door and see me holding a gun. I wanted answers, but I didn't want to scare her needlessly to get them.

I raised my hand and knocked on the door. There was no answer. I knocked again, then leaned in close, listening for the sound of approaching footsteps, but there was nothing. I was debating knocking for a third time when a voice on the other side of the door said, "Yes?"

"Haley?" I said. "It's Felix Renn. I'd like to speak with you."

There was a pause, then the sound of a deadbolt disengaging and a slide lock coming undone. The door opened a crack and Haley peered out. "Mr. Renn?"

"Yes," I said. "May I come in?"

Haley hesitated, then opened the door the rest of the way.

I stepped inside and took a cursory look around her apartment, which was about all it required. It was a small place and sparsely furnished, with a battered couch, a ratty armchair, and a wooden coffee table that looked like it had been salvaged from the trash. There was no television, no pictures or artwork on the walls, no decoration or personal touches of any kind. Maybe she just moved in. Or maybe she was a minimalist.

I turned to Haley. "I've been out to Burnside Road."

She gave a small nod of acknowledgement, but didn't say anything.

I said, "You seem surprised to see me," even though that wasn't true at all. Haley's expression was as blank as a Greek bust. I was trying to get a reaction out of her, and apparently failing. "Are you surprised I went? Or that I made it back?"

Haley took a slow step away from me, moving deeper into the apartment. Her close-set eyes stared at me with something that might have been curiosity.

I took a step toward her. Haley matched me with another step back.

"Why did you send me out there?" I asked.

"He said you were resourceful," Haley replied.

"Who?" I said. "Doug Weaver?"

Instead of responding, Haley took yet another step back. I didn't think she was afraid of me; in fact, the small smile rising on her face suggested the opposite. I didn't figure out she was luring me in until I heard the low, drawn-out creak of the door swinging shut behind me.

I caught movement out of the corner of my eye and started to turn, but it was too late. A towering shape came at me and a starburst went off in my head. There was a blossom of pain, followed by a jolt of fear as the darkness came rushing in. I dropped to the ground.

The fear followed me all the way down.

CHAPTER 24

I DREAMED OF bees.

They were crawling all over my body, and no matter how hard I tried, I couldn't move a single inch to get them off me. Their collective buzzing was so loud it was almost deafening. I could feel it, too, a nerve-tingling vibration that might have been soothing if I didn't know where it was coming from. I wasn't just wearing a beard of bees, I was wearing an entire mask. I could feel their tiny legs tickling my eyelids, crawling inside the soft shells of my ears, strolling across my trembling lips.

Bee-stung lips, I thought, and repressed a dream-giggle. I didn't want to laugh or do anything that would set them off. Because when you angered one bee, you angered them all.

But the bees weren't angry with me. I felt them moving along my arms and legs, across my chest and under my back. I came to realize the buzzing that at first only *seemed* to infiltrate my entire body was actually coming from inside me.

Peering between their swarming black-and-yellow-striped bodies, I could see holes in my skin. Perfectly-formed hexagonal cells that covered every square inch of my body. The bees moved in and out of them industriously.

That's why they weren't attacking me. They were home.

My body was their hive.

I WOKE up with my mouth open in a soundless scream. For a moment I thought the bees were still on me, crawling over my lips, across my tongue, and down my throat. I hacked and coughed to get them out, telling myself it was just a dream, but my brain didn't believe it. I could still hear their buzzing, could still *feel* their buzzing against the side of my face.

I opened my eyes and saw I wasn't covered in bees. I was lying on the ground and it was moving. No, it was moving *under* the ground. I felt a carpeted floor under my hands, but that didn't make sense. There was no carpeting in Haley's apartment, and even if there had been, there shouldn't have been anything moving underneath it.

I was sprawled out on the floor of a car. A big one, I noticed, as I rolled over onto my back and peered around. I was in the passenger compartment of a limousine. I tried to sit up and a heavy hand fell on my shoulder and eased me back down. A heavy voice that went with the hand said, "Take it easy, pal. You had a helluva fall."

This was greeted with low, ugly laughter. I was able to discern two distinct voices, one male and one female. Three people altogether. I could hear them but couldn't quite make them out. It was dark in the back of the limo and my vision was still blurry from being knocked out. My head felt like it was packed full of sawdust and broken glass. I wondered if I had a concussion. Lying back down seemed like a good idea, so I did that and waited for things to come back into focus. It didn't take long, and when it did, I wished I was unconscious again.

There were plush leather seats at the front and back of the compartment. They smelled spicy, more like cinnamon than leather. Two large men, one of them the heavy-handed comedian, were seated in the backward-facing seats. They were both wearing black suits. The one on the left was holding a sawed-off shotgun with the double-barrels pointed directly at my head.

Sitting by herself on the forward-facing seat was a woman who I was surprised to see wasn't Haley. She was older, in her mid- to late thirties, and beautiful in the way an icicle is beautiful right before it falls off the edge of a roof and plunges into your eye socket. She was dangerous. I could tell that right away, not just because of the way she looked, but because of the way she was looking at me: like I was nothing.

I tried to get up again and the guy with the shotgun slammed it against the back of my poor, battered head. I groaned in pain and fell back onto my ass.

"Let me translate for the shotgun-impaired: sit the fuck down or I'll give you a buckshot facial."

I sat the fuck down and turned to face the woman, who was clearly the one in charge. Like the two goons, she was wearing a suit, but hers was considerably more expensive. It was a rusty red colour, tailored to fit her tall, willowy frame, with cuffs and lapels that looked sharp enough to draw blood. It went well with her hair, which was also red, but not the way Anne the librarian's hair was red. This woman's hair was the bright screaming red of a wildfire. It should have made her look like a clown, but it didn't. Which was probably a good thing because I had the distinct feeling that if I were to laugh at this woman, it would be the last thing I ever did.

I reached around instinctively to the small of my back, but my gun and holster were gone.

"You were disarmed for your own safety," the woman said. She crossed one leg over the other, and I saw she was wearing a pair of black six-inch stilettos.

"The gun was a gift," I said.

"From your ex-wife," the woman said. "When you were still married. She's very attractive. I've seen many of her films."

I stared at her, shocked and confused. I couldn't decide if what she'd said was supposed to be a veiled threat. If it was, the veil was so thick I couldn't see the implied violence behind it.

"Do you love her?" the woman asked me.

"What?" I thought I'd misheard her. Or maybe I really did have a concussion.

"Do you love her?" she repeated.

Again, it was the sort of remark that could be construed as a threat, but the woman didn't say it like that. She sounded like she was merely curious.

"Why are you asking me that?" I said.

"Because I want to know."

"That's none of your business."

The woman shrugged and turned her head to look out the window.

"Where are we going?" I asked.

I didn't expect an answer, but the woman surprised me. She turned to face me and there was something in her eyes — or a lack of something — that told me she was crazy. Completely fucking insane. Her response seemed to confirm this.

"Mars," she said. "We're going to Mars."

CHAPTER 25

THEY TOOK ME to one of the upscale neighbourhoods in Toronto. Rosedale, or possibly Forest Hill. I had been unconscious for a good portion of the ride, and I couldn't see much from my limited vantage point on the floor of the limo.

We drove through a set of open gates and climbed a shrub-lined drive toward a large house. There wasn't a single light on in the entire place, which made it hard to determine how big the place was, but considering the affluence of the area I knew it had to be mansion-sized.

We came to a stop at a side entrance under a portico. One of the goons opened the door and climbed out. The guy with the sawed-off shotgun gestured for me to move, then followed me out. The redhead stepped out last, the click of her heels on the pavement the only sound on this cold autumn night.

The first goon opened the side door and we entered the house in single file.

The interior was as dark as the exterior, and as I crossed the threshold, a wave of fear crashed down on me. My feet abruptly stopped moving, halting me in my tracks.

The guy behind me said, "Move it, fucko," and poked me in the back with his shotgun.

At that moment I would've gladly taken a double-barrelled blast rather than go even one step further into the dark house. I opened my mouth to say something — *How about we turn on some lights, guys?* — but all that came out was a breathless croak.

The guy jabbed me again with the shotgun, harder this time, and I fell forward onto my hands and knees.

"Get up," he said.

"I... can't...." I gasped. My lungs felt constricted and my heart was hammering in my chest.

"You havin' an asthma attack?"

I shook my head.

"Then get up."

The guy reached down with one hand, plucked me off the floor, and set me on my feet. My legs wobbled but I remained upright.

"Walk," he said.

I shook my head and waited for him to hit me with the shotgun again.

He didn't. Instead, he grabbed me by the back of the neck and started walking me forward. My feet slid and bumped along the floor. The darkness enveloped me. Like in the Black Lands, I felt it infiltrate my body and fill me up like poison.

The guy's thumb and fingers pressed hard into the sides of my neck. I could feel the pulse in my arteries sending S.O.S. signals to my brain, for all the good it did. My brain was otherwise engaged.

We followed the first goon down a hallway hung with large paintings in heavy gilt frames. I tried to focus my mind on them — they appeared to be landscapes, bleak ones, but it was hard to tell in the dark.

We came to a set of double doors at the end of the hall. The first goon opened them and the second one puppet-walked me into a long room that was as dark as the rest of the house. I wouldn't have been able to see a thing, but the wall at the far end was a single pane of glass that let in a murky half-light.

In front of the window was a desk, and sitting behind the desk, his features obscured by silhouette, was a man. I was directed to a chair in front of the desk and dropped into it. Then the two goons took up positions behind me, one on either side of the chair, while the redhead flopped down on an angular couch along the side wall.

Closer now, I could see the desk was a slab of gleaming black marble shot through with veins of red. It looked less like a piece of furniture than an altar for sacrificing virgins and small animals. The man sitting behind the desk had a narrow fox-face, the skin as smooth and taut as tanned leather.

His nose was a cherubic nub, his lips a thin blade of shadow. At first glance I thought he was in his early fifties. Then I recalculated and put him in his mid-thirties. Then I decided I couldn't tell how old he was, and that it probably didn't matter. He was wearing a maroon suit with a black shirt and a rust-coloured tie. It was similar enough in design to the one worn by the redhead that they could've posed together in the same catalogue ad. He was a redhead, too, although his hair was a darker auburn shade, a tight cap of Caesar curls that made him look regal and ruthless.

Even though we'd never met before, I knew who he was. In addition to being a snappy dresser, he was one of the most notorious crime figures in Toronto. A suspect in numerous felonies, but never charged, much less indicted, he was one of the bosses in a criminal network that stretched across Canada and the United States.

In a voice as smooth as warm honey, he said, "Thank you for coming, Mr. Renn. It's a pleasure to finally meet you."

"I'm not sure I had much of a choice, Mr. Mars."

The goons chuckled and the red-haired man smiled.

"*Mister* Mars," he said. "They call me that sometimes. I don't mind; it's a sign of respect. But please, it's just Mars." He extended his arm in a formal gesture of presentation to the woman sprawled on the couch. "This is my sister, Vermillion."

I nodded. "Vermillion. That's nice. Is it Dutch?"

Vermillion looked up from examining her fingernails. She stared at me for a long moment, then said, "There's a shadow on you."

I squirmed under her gaze, then managed to tear my eyes away and turn back to Mars. At first I thought they had looked similar because of their suits, but now I could see there was a family resemblance, as well. They had the same small, dark eyes, the same narrow mouths, and the same air of barely-contained madness lurking behind the calm façade of their faces.

"The man behind you with the shotgun is Vito," Mars said. "Of course, his name isn't really Vito — he isn't even Italian — but that's what I call him. I like to indulge in some of the old mafia clichés. You don't mind, do you, Vito?"

The shotgun man said, "No, sir."

"Vito means 'life.' Did you know that?"

I shook my head.

"I thought it was appropriate," Mars said. "You are so full of life, aren't you, Vito?"

"Yes, sir."

It was right then I got the feeling I wouldn't be leaving this room alive.

"My other associate is Barney," Mars said, fluttering his hand dismissively at the second goon. "That's his real name. My indulgence only goes so far." He stared at me pointedly while he said this last. "May I call you Felix?"

I nodded.

"Splendid!" Mars clapped his hands together as if he was genuinely pleased. He looked over at this sister. "Civility. Don't you just love it?"

"It's the basis of any civilization," Vermillion responded. She sounded bored.

Mars turned back to me. "It has recently come to my attention that you have taken on a case in Sycamore. I have certain assets in this town that you are set to expose. Through no fault of your own, I'm sure, but action must be taken nonetheless."

"I didn't know you were involved in the drug trade," I said.

It was pretty lame gambit, so I wasn't surprised when Mars threw back his head and laughed. Taking a cue from their boss, Vito and Barney laughed along with him. Vermillion had gone back to studying her nails.

"No, Felix," Mars said. "I'm not involved in drugs. Some of my partners are, but not me. My interest is, and has always been, in people."

"That's a funny way of putting it."

I regretted the words the moment they left my mouth.

"How so?" Mars put on a curious face. All of his mannerisms were slightly exaggerated, like he was talking to a small child.

I shook my head and looked down at my feet.

"Come now," Mars said. "We're having a nice chat. A nice, *civilized* chat. You can speak freely here."

Famous last words, I thought.

"I told you my interest is in people and you said there was something funny about that." Mars folded his hands on his desk. "Please explain it to me. I do love a good laugh."

I felt sick to my stomach. For the moment my fear of Mars was trumping my fear of the dark. I was tempted to remain silent, but it was something I'd never been good at. It was a problem I could trace all the way back to elementary school when I used to mouth off to the biggest and baddest bullies on the playground. It's less about being brave than I can't keep my mouth shut when someone is feeding me a lot of bullshit. It worked out okay in school because my legs could usually outrun my mouth when the latter got me into hot water. But it wasn't going to help me in this situation. I couldn't outrun a bullet.

"*Fee-lix*," Mars said in a singsong voice, "I'm *waiting*."

I blurted out the words before I could stop myself.

"I know who you are. I've heard about what you do. Human trafficking, prostitution, extortion, murder. Among other things. Yeah, you're a real people person."

Mars stared at me with an amused grin affixed to his face. He stared so long that I thought I'd died and this was the last image I'd seen before Vito used his shotgun to turn my brain into Hamburger Helper. Then Mars blinked and I realized I was still alive.

"You're a very clever man, Felix, and what you say is true. But I still like people. I even like you." He wagged his finger like he was scolding me. "I make it a point to keep an eye out for those who are special. I'm like the person who goes to minor-league baseball games looking for players who might be good enough for the big leagues." He looked over at Vito. "What are they called?"

"Talent scout," Vito said.

"Yes!" Mars clapped his hands again. "That's what I do. I scout for talent."

Something clicked in my head. "Like the serial killer in Sycamore? Is that the asset you're protecting?"

Mars put on a serious face. "I would like to meet that person. He — or she! — has a skill set that is truly impressive. But no, the murders do not interest me. You interest me, Felix."

"I do?"

"Indeed. You say you know about me? Well, I know about you, too." Mars leaned back in his chair and steepled his fingers under his nose. "I know you were born in a town called Dover. I know you're a private investigator, and that you were mentored by Madeline Ferine, a legend in the field, known by friend and enemy alike as Mad Maddy. I know you employ your ex-wife as your assistant and that you have a predilection for supernatural cases." He paused and a narrow grin creeped slowly across his face. "I also know that you had a sister who went missing when she was very young, and that you hold yourself responsible for her disappearance." He turned his head slightly to the side, his eyes still locked on mine, and put on a thoughtful face. "Is that why you became a private investigator? So you could become a finder of lost things?"

I felt my blood pressure rising, along with my anger. I spoke only two words in response, but I felt they adequately summed up my thoughts on the matter.

"Fuck. You."

Something hard and metallic cracked me upside the head. The blow was strong enough to send me tumbling out of my seat. A pair of large hands caught me before I hit the ground and set me back in the chair. I touched the side of my head and winced. I looked over my shoulder at Vito with his shotgun. I supposed I should have been glad he'd only hit me with it instead of emptying both barrels into my face.

Mars shook his head. "I'm sorry about that. My men tend to be a little overprotective. They don't even like to see my feelings get hurt." He pointed at me. "You put on a good act, but I can see how afraid you are. Your wife was a better actor, although not by much. I don't mean to disparage her talent. Most of her work was in horror movies, which don't require much in the way of acting ability. I did some work in show business myself. Did you know that?"

"Is this how you plan to kill me?" I said, "By boring me to death?"

Mars glanced over at Vermillion, and they burst into laughter at the same time. Watching them I was reminded of Alice's exchange with the Cheshire Cat. *But I don't want to go among mad people*, Alice said. To which the Cat had replied: *Oh, you can't help that. We're all mad here.* That's what I was dealing with. Mars and Vermillion. Two shades of red. Two shades of crazy.

I waited for them to finish, then said: "If you didn't bring me here to kill me, then what do you want? Are you trying to keep me away from Sycamore?"

"I wouldn't dream of doing any such thing," Mars said sincerely. "A man's actions are his own. But so are the consequences."

I didn't rise to the bait. The line was so scripted I expected to turn my head and see a studio audience watching us.

"Then what's this all about?"

"An introduction," Mars said. "We wanted to meet you. And now we have."

Something red moved in the corner of my eye. I turned my head and Vermillion was suddenly standing next to me. There was a smile on her face and a syringe in her hand. I didn't like either one. She moved cat-quick, stabbing the needle into the side of my neck.

"Hello," she said. "And goodbye."

CHAPTER 26

I WOKE UP on the couch in my apartment. Early morning sunlight was pouring in through the sliding glass door that let onto the balcony. I was grateful to see that light, but it still hurt my eyes to look at it, so I rolled onto my side away from it, feeling like a vampire. I might even have hissed, but I don't remember.

There were a lot of things I didn't remember — like how I had gotten to my apartment, or where I'd been the previous night. Then I touched my neck and everything came rushing back. The contents of my stomach weren't far behind, and I barely made it down the hall to the bathroom before I was sick.

When I was done, I flushed out my mouth with water and looked at myself in the mirror over the sink. I looked like shit. There were purple bags under my eyes, my cheeks were speckled with stubble, and my hair looked like it was trying to leap off my head in protest. I turned my neck to the side and looked at the spot where Vermillion had jabbed me with the needle. The crazy bitch had knocked me out, kidnapped me, brought me before her crime lord brother, and then drugged me. To top it all off, she put a Band-Aid on the injection spot. A Hello Kitty Band-Aid.

Like I said, crazy.

I took off my clothes and climbed into the shower. I turned on the water as hot as I could take it and washed myself slowly and gently. It hurt everywhere I touched. My body felt like one big bruise. I took special care while washing my hair, being mindful of the large goose egg that Vito had given me when he knocked me out in Haley's apartment.

After I dried off, I popped a couple of ibuprofen and got dressed. I noticed my snake plant was still looking rough, so I gave it some water. Then I brewed a pot of coffee, poured myself a cup, and took it out onto the balcony. I sat on a plastic lawn chair I kept out there and listened to the city waking up. I was still trying to do the same. The coffee helped.

I had to get back to Sycamore. That much was clear. What wasn't clear was how I was going to do that. My car was still up there, parked outside Haley's building (if it hadn't been towed). That meant I had to either get a rental or take the bus. A rental would be faster, but my head was still foggy and I didn't trust myself to drive yet. The bus would be slower, but it would give me time to go over everything that had happened in the past day or so. I had a lot of new information to process, and I still didn't know how it all fit into the disappearance of Doug Weaver.

I thought about calling Sandra and telling her I was back in the city, but that would mean telling her about what happened last night, and I didn't want to worry her. Not because Sandra couldn't handle the stress — she handled more than her share working for me — but because she'd have questions, and I didn't have any answers. That had been the story of this entire case — lots of questions, no answers — and it was time to start changing that.

I had a second cup of coffee before heading out to the bus station. As I was pulling on my jacket, I spotted something on the coffee table that I hadn't noticed before. My Ruger revolver, sitting snugly in its holster.

I took the gun out and looked it over, but it didn't appear to have been messed with. I slid it back into the holster, then stood there holding it in my hand, running my thumb over the rough nylon material.

Mars said he had assets in Sycamore, but he wasn't warning me off the case. What did that mean?

He said he only wanted to meet me.

What did *that* mean?

I didn't know, but I didn't like it. If Mars was involved in this, that made things a hell of a lot more complicated. And dangerous.

I clipped the gun back onto my hip, and that made me feel a bit better, a little more in control.

It wasn't much, but at that point I'd take whatever I could get.

THE BUS smelled like stale sweat and fried food. I took a seat at the front, hoping that being near the door would help to cut the smell. It didn't. This was due largely to the fact that the bus only made two stops — one in Barrie, the other in Orillia — before it finally reached Sycamore.

On the plus side, the smell managed to break through the fog that filled my head and allowed me to focus on the events of the previous evening. My hand drifted up and touched the Band-Aid on my neck. Vermillion. Mars. Who gave their children such weird names? The answer was obvious: Someone as crazy as them.

But their names didn't matter. I was more interested in their intentions, which were still a mystery to me. Why did Vermillion abduct me and take me all the way to Toronto to meet her brother? Was it really just for an intro-duction? In the mafia films that Mars seemed to be a fan of, such meetings always had ulterior motives. The crime boss might ask you for a favour, but it was really a demand. Threats were phrased vaguely or euphemistically. Like Marlon Brando's infamous offer that couldn't be refused.

The thing was, Mars didn't make any threats, vague or otherwise, and he didn't make me any offers, either. So what the hell did he want? He claimed to have no interest in the murders or the serial killer carrying them out — but was that the truth? Could I believe anything he told me? Not necessarily, but then what did he gain by lying to me? Mars said he had assets in Sycamore. Haley was one of them. She worked at The Greener Side, which connected her to the Weavers, and she was the one who said they were drug-growers. But Mars said he wasn't involved in the drug trade, so why did Haley tell me that? To get me up to Burnside Road. So I would find the portal. That had to be the other asset Mars was talking about. But what did he want with it? What would the head of a criminal organization want with a doorway to another dimension?

Lots of ideas came to mind, none of them good.

I WAS back in Sycamore just before noon. The bus dropped me off at the downtown terminal, not too far from the main square where a few people were strolling along the paths, huddled deep into their coats against the wind, which had turned cold and sharp that morning.

I made the trek back to Haley's building to retrieve my car. It was still there, which was the first piece of good news I'd had in a long while. I was glad to see it hadn't been stolen or towed, and was even gladder when it started right away after I climbed in and turned the key. Things were looking up, although I was smart enough not to actually say the words out loud and jinx myself.

I drove back to the Lakeview Inn and parked in front of my room. It was hard to believe that only two nights ago I'd had to race the ten feet from the car to the door because I was afraid that something in the dark would come out and attack me. It should have seemed silly, the way most fears do in the light of day, but it wasn't. Maybe because I knew it would come back the moment the sun went down. Vermillion said there was a shadow on me. Was that what she meant? Could she see the fear inside me, like a stain on my soul? And more importantly, was there any way to get rid of it?

I got out of the car and dug around in my pocket for my room key, the one with the plastic fish fob on it. I pulled it out and was moving it toward the slot in the knob when I noticed the door was open a crack. I put the key back in my pocket and drew my gun.

I thought maybe it was only the maid, but this didn't seem like the sort of place that had daily turn-down service.

I glanced around the parking lot. There was a silver SUV sitting in the far corner, and a couple of cars pulled up to the doors of rooms where the occupants were presumably staying.

I took a deep breath, eased the door open with my foot, and moved quickly inside with my gun raised.

The room had been turned upside down. Papers and clothes were strewn everywhere. The desk and the nightstand were tipped over on their sides, and the bed was stripped down to the mattress, which lay crookedly on the box spring from when someone had searched underneath it. Mars's men had been thorough, although I didn't know what they had been expecting to find. It was a good thing I hadn't been asked to put down a security deposit for the room because I probably wouldn't be getting it back.

I slid my gun back into its holster and started cleaning up. After straightening the mattress on the box spring, I kneeled down to set the nightstand back on its stubby little legs.

While I was crouched there, I heard a low, drawn-out creak — the sound of a door opening slowly on unoiled hinges. A split second later, I felt the unmistakable pressure of a gun muzzle pressing against the back of my head. A voice behind the gun spoke the thought that was going through my mind at that very moment.

"You forgot to check the bathroom."

I closed my eyes and waited to be knocked out again — or maybe they'd just shoot me this time; maybe Mars had been lying about not wanting me dead.

Instead, I felt the gun move away from the back of my head. I opened my eyes and chanced a look over my shoulder. Then I did a double take.

It was Anne. The librarian. Only her friendly good looks had been replaced by the cold expression of a killer. Her eyes were half-lidded, her lips were a thin line, and her hair was pulled back in a fierce ponytail. It was a transformation that was startling both in its simplicity and its effect. She still looked like the woman I'd met a few days ago, the one who'd offered to help me find the person responsible for the murders, and yet at the same time it was like I was looking at a complete stranger.

She'd taken the gun away from my head, but still had it pointed at me. "Go ahead," she said in a voice as cool as her demeanor. "Say something trite."

I looked at her face. I looked at the gun.

"Is this about those overdue library books?"

Nailed it.

MY FIRST thought was that she worked for Mars, that she was another one of his "assets." She had the red hair and the same dark glint in her eye. Maybe she was another one of his siblings. But there was something about her — maybe it was the way she was looking at me like I was a total ass clown — that told me she played for the other team.

"You're a cop," I said.

Anne continued to stare at me, her gun still aimed at my face.

"Tell me why you're here," she said. "Don't lie. I'll know if you do."

"I'm investigating the murders," I said. "Just like I told you."

Anne took a step forward and the muzzle of the gun almost bumped my nose. "I know who you are, Mr. Paranormal PI. There's no supernatural angle to this case. So tell me what you're really doing here."

"That's the truth," I said. "I was hired by the wife of one of the victims." I hesitated. "And as for there being no supernatural angle to this case..."

Anne cocked an eyebrow. "Go on."

"First tell me who you are."

"I'm a federal agent."

"Do you have any identification to back that up?"

Anne nodded at the gun in her hand. "Sure, right here."

"Okay. I'm convinced. Are you part of the RCMP task force?"

Anne stared at me a moment longer, then she seemed to decide something and slid the gun into the holster on her hip. She reached into her inside jacket pocket and took out a black leather ID case. She flipped it open and held it out for me to read.

The case held a badge and a plastic card that identified the woman standing before me as Special Agent Alice Baffle of the Paranormal Intelligence Agency.

"Baffle?" I said. "What kind of name is that?"

Anne — or I guess it was Alice — just kept staring at me.

"PIA," I said. "So you are on the task force."

"I'm undercover. Deep cover."

"But you just said there was no supernatural angle to this case. So why is the Paranormal Intelligence Agency looking into these murders?"

"That's classified."

"I knew you were going to say that." I sat down on the bed. "Seriously, though, what kind of name is Baffle?"

"It's the name of someone who has zero sense of humour and an extremely low tolerance for bullshit."

"So what you're saying is you're not much fun at parties."

Alice shook her head. "I heard you were a wise ass."

"Heard from who?"

"The PIA has a file on you."

"Really? A whole file. I'm touched."

Alice gave me an unreadable look — sizing me up, or sizing me down, I couldn't tell which.

"So I'm going to go out on a limb here and say you're not really a librarian."

"The agency arranged for the job at the library," Alice said. She went over to a chair that was lying on its side, righted it, and sat down. "There's been some chatter that something strange was happening in this area, and they sent me to check it out."

"What sort of chatter?"

"Are you familiar with a government operation called Project Mirror?"

"It sounds familiar," I said. "Wasn't that in the big government document leak a few years back?"

Alice nodded. "Project Mirror is SIGINT — signal intelligence — only with psychics. It was an initiative by the PIA to set up listening stations around the world to monitor paranormal activity. Each one has a team of psychics — telepaths, precogs, remote-viewers — that keep an eye out for supernatural threats. They're pretty good at their job, but psionics isn't an exact science. Even when their intel is correct, it's usually lacking in specifics. A few months ago, one of our psychics said that something was happening — or was about to happen — here in Sycamore."

"You mean the murders."

"That's what I thought at first," Alice said, "but I've been monitoring all of the information coming out of the task force, and I've seen nothing to suggest a supernatural creature is responsible."

"What then?"

"I'm not sure. I was told to come here, lay low, and keep my eyes open. So that's what I've been doing."

"Sounds pretty vague."

Alice shrugged. "The psychic did say one thing that I found odd. He said there was a shadow on this place."

I DIDN'T say anything for a while, and neither did Alice. I was still in shock from what the PIA psychic had told her — a phrase that clearly had no relevance to her — while Alice merely seemed the type who preferred silence. I guess that's why she made such a convincing librarian.

"How long have you been in town?" I asked her.

"A month," she said. "I've been going out of my freaking mind."

"What," I said, "a serial killer stalking the local citizenry isn't exciting enough for you?"

"Like I said, there was no indication that a Black Lands entity was responsible." Alice paused. "Until you showed up."

"Me? I'm just a crime writer working on a book about the murders."

Alice scoffed. "I knew you were lying to me, I just didn't know why. So I had my partner run a check on your name and found out the PIA has a file on you."

"The same file that says I'm a dumb ass."

"A wise ass," Alice corrected me. "Among other things."

"Such as?"

"That you're a private investigator based out of Toronto. That you've had more than a few run-ins with supernaturals and somehow managed to survive them."

She spoke in a tone that was different from the way she'd been speaking to me up till now. A kind of clinical scepticism potentially bordering on respect.

"Maybe I'm just lucky," I said.

"No one is that lucky," Alice said. "You have some skills. I'll give you that."

"So does the task force know you're here in town?"

"Why would they?" Alice said. "I already told you my assignment doesn't have anything to do with the murders."

"I'm not so sure."

"Are you saying the killer is a supernatural creature?"

Alice skewered me with her gaze like a butterfly pinned to a piece of corkboard. There was an intensity in her eyes that made me feel uncomfortable. At first I thought it was excitement, but then I recognized it for what it truly was. Anger bordering on full-on fury.

"No," I said. Then: "Yes." A pause. "I'm not sure."

"I didn't ask for multiple choice," Alice said. "Your client is Susan Weaver?"

"I can't tell you that."

"You pretty much did the other day when you were speaking to Anne the helpful librarian."

"You were very convincing," I said thinly. "For a moment you gave a remarkable impression of a decent human being."

Alice ignored my gibe. "So Weaver hired you to find out what happened to her husband."

"Yes."

"And you're aware he's the prime suspect in the murders?"

"I'm aware."

"His body is the only one that hasn't been found. The police think he staged his own death to throw them off his trail." Alice gave her head a small shake. "Cute theory if this was a movie, but it doesn't happen much in real life."

I nodded.

"So what's your plan?" Alice asked. "Find his body and prove he's not the killer?"

"That was my *initial* plan, but…"

"But you realized a body could be hidden anywhere," Alice said. "Or it could've been destroyed." She drummed her fingers on the arm of the chair, thinking. "No, it would be best to tackle it from the other side. Find the killer and see if it's Doug Weaver."

"That was my thought."

Alice leaned back in her seat and regarded me with a critical eye. "I still don't understand what you're doing here. Isn't this case kind of vanilla for the Paranormal PI?"

"I thought it would be a nice break from the vampires and shifters and black-eyed kids."

"I get it," Alice said. "You dance with the devil enough times, he's bound to step on your foot. This is dangerous work. We're trained for it in the PIA, and the death rate among field agents is still…" She cut herself off and made a dismissive gesture. "Well, it's high."

"I didn't know about the murders when I came up here. I thought this was a simple missing-person case, with no supernatural elements whatsoever. I was wrong on both counts."

Alice shot up out her seat. "You're saying this *is* a Black Lands case?"

"You remember that call I got in the middle of the night? The one telling me to go to Burnside Road?"

Alice nodded.

"Well I went up there and found a vacant lot with a Quonset hut on it."

"Then it wasn't vacant," Alice said.

I stared at her.

"Continue," Alice said.

"I checked it out, but it was empty. Or at least that's what I thought until I stumbled through a portal and ended up in the Black Lands."

Alice blinked at me. "A portal?" she said. "You found a new portal?"

I nodded.

"And you went to the Black Lands?"

I nodded again.

"And you came back alive?"

I nodded for a third time.

Alice stared at me for a long while. I had a hard time reading the look on her face. Partly because she was a difficult person to read. Partly because her face shifted across such a wide spectrum of emotions. One moment she looked like she was afraid for me, the next she looked like she was afraid *of* me.

"What did you see over there?" she asked in a small, firm voice.

"The Black Lands," I said. "It was… dark. I was in a field of silver grass. Surrounded by woods. I fell in a hole."

"A hole?"

"I think it was a grave. I found a shovel in the Quonset hut."

"Was there a body in it?"

"No, but it was the right size. I didn't get the impression someone was going to put in a swimming pool over there."

Alice started to pace around the room. "Okay, so whoever dug the grave knew about the portal. And they probably arranged for the Quonset to be placed there, so they could hide it."

"That's what I was thinking."

"But who would want to cover up the location of an undocumented portal?"

I scratched the back of my head. "Funny you should mention that."

Alice stopped pacing and turned to face me.

"It turns out this case is a lot more complicated than either of us thought."

\(\text{❦}\)

I TOLD Alice how I figured out my late-night caller was Haley, the girl who worked at the Weavers' garden store. I told her about the rumours that Doug and Susan were secretly drug dealers, and that the property on Burnside Road was where they had their marijuana grow-op.

Alice's eyebrow rose higher and higher while I spoke. When I was finished, she said, "You believed her?"

"I didn't *not* believe her," I said, hating the defensive note I heard in my voice. "It wasn't like I had a lot to go on at that point. I didn't see the harm in going up there to check things out."

"So Doug Weaver's murder was what? A drug hit?"

"It would explain why his death was different from the rest of the murders."

"You don't even know for certain that he's dead."

"All signs point that way."

Alice shook her head. "You're putting a lot of faith in some random girl who works in a garden store."

"That's where things get complicated," I said. "Haley doesn't really work for the Weavers. She works for Mars."

Alice's head went back like I'd thrown a punch at her. "Mars?" she said. "As in the Planets?"

"The same."

"What does Mars have to do with any of this?"

"That's the question of the hour," I said. "He told me he's not involved with the murders, but I'm not—"

"Whoa, whoa, hold up a sec." Alice's hands were raised in a halting gesture. "You met with Mars?"

"That's one way of putting it. Another would be to say I was knocked unconscious and carted off to the city to answer some questions for His Royal Mars-ness and his lunatic sister."

"You met Vermillion, too?"

I nodded.

"And you're still alive." Alice spoke in a low tone of awe like she couldn't quite believe it. A trip to the Black Lands one day, a meeting with a notorious crime boss the next. I guess it sounded pretty unbelievable when you looked at it like that.

"What does it all mean?" I asked.

"I'm not sure yet," Alice said. "Mars's involvement changes everything."

"What's he even doing in Toronto? I thought he operated out of New York."

"There was a power shift about a year ago," Alice said. "Mars left the business for a time. He tried his hand in Hollywood, if you can believe that, but it didn't work out, so he came back to the family. Jupiter had already replaced him in New York, so Mars was sent north."

"As punishment?"

"Something like that." Alice looked off into the corner. "I know a bit about being banished."

"What does that mean?"

Alice seemed to realize she'd said too much and shook her head. "Nothing."

"Toronto isn't so bad," I said. "Except in the winter."

"I'm from Florida," Alice said. "I'm not used to these things you people call 'seasons.'"

"You get used to it."

"I won't be here long enough to find out." She paused. "I hope."

"Mars was pretty adamant that he wasn't responsible for the murders. And he said he wasn't involved in the drug business, either. If that's true, then I don't know what his connection is to the Weavers. But there must be something if he has one of his minions working at their garden store."

"It's interesting, that's for sure," Alice said. "I also find it interesting that two people whose work involves the supernatural both happened to end up in this town at the same time."

"Do you believe in coincidence?"

"No," Alice said.

I nodded. Neither did I.

"Is there any way to find out why Mars is involved in all of this?"

Alice appeared to think it over, then said, "I'll see what Diane can dig up."

"Who's Diane?"

"My woman in the chair."

"What?"

"She's my partner."

"Where is she?"

"Boca Sombra."

"Florida? What's she doing there?"

"That's where she lives."

"Why isn't she here?"

"Diane never leaves her house."

"She's, what, agoraphobic?"

"Yes, but she's still a good agent."

"Does she make many arrests from inside her house?"

"You're not even a little bit funny," Alice said. "But you know what is? The kinds of things Diane could do to you with her computer."

"I'll take your word on that." I said. "Sorry."

"Diane gets more done at home than most agents do working in the field. Sometimes I think she's the sane one staying indoors while the rest of us are out here trying to make sense of this messed-up world."

"You may be right about that."

Alice glanced at her watch. "Until I figure out Mars's angle in all of this, there's only one thing I can do right now."

I saw where she was going and I was already shaking my head before she finished speaking.

"I need you to take me to the portal."

"No way," I said. "No fucking way."

"It wasn't a request."

"That's fine," I said, "because I don't work for you. You'll have to wrap me in chains and drag me there."

"That can be arranged."

"You can try," I said. A tremor had slipped into my voice.

Alice stared into my eyes. I'm not sure what she saw in there — that I was dead serious or just dead scared — but after a long, considering moment, she nodded her head slowly.

"Fair enough. But if what you say is true, then I need to get up there and secure the site until I can call in a STAR team."

STAR stood for Supernatural Threat Assessment and Response. It was the PIA version of SWAT.

"I can tell you where it is," I said. "That's the best I can do. I'm sorry."

Alice nodded and I gave her directions to the property on Burnside Road. She was on her way out the door when she stopped and turned back to me.

"We should meet back here later on, say around six o'clock. Does that work for you?"

She seemed pretty confident that she was coming back from Burnside Road. I wasn't so sure that would happen, but I nodded anyway.

Six was fine. There was something I needed to do, too.

CHAPTER 27

I WENT OVER to the window and watched Alice jog across the parking lot to the silver SUV sitting in the corner. She got in and sped away on squealing tires. Woman on a mission. I hoped I'd see her again. Sort of. She was kind of intense, even for a PIA agent.

A PIA agent with an agoraphobic partner.

"It's a strange old world," I said out loud.

After setting the room back in order, I drove across town to Haley's apartment. I banged on her door, but there was no answer. I wasn't expecting her to be in there. I figured she had cleared out the moment she'd been exposed.

The door was locked, so I took out my Swiss Army knife. A friend of mine in the RCMP had modified it for me, so that in addition to its usual collection of useful attachments it also had a number of lock-picking tools. I used a couple of them to pop Haley's door open and slipped inside.

The first thing I did was check behind the door to make sure Vito wasn't waiting to bushwhack me again with his sawed-off shotgun. When I saw it was clear, I started looking around the apartment.

I went through the main living area, the kitchen, the bedroom and bathroom. I even checked the closets. No one was home, and I had the feeling they weren't coming back.

I examined the few pieces of furniture Haley owned, but I didn't find anything under the couch cushions or taped to the underside of the coffee table. The fridge was empty except for some old Chinese food takeout boxes and a couple cans of Diet Coke. All of the kitchen cabinets were empty, but in one of the drawers I found a few packages of plastic utensils, the kind that comes with fast food.

I didn't get the impression that Haley had cleaned the place out. It was probably like this the whole time she was staying here. And how long was that? When I spoke to her at the store, she told me she'd been working there for a few months. That might have been a lie, but the apartment definitely had the look of someone who hadn't been living here as much as squatting.

It struck me that Alice had done much the same thing. She'd come to Sycamore incognito, gotten a job, and laid low while she waited for something to happen. Where was she staying? I wondered. Was her place as bare and impersonal as Haley's? Probably. Both of them were only here on business. I knew Alice's business, sort of, but what was Haley's? Why did Mars send her here? To keep an eye on the Weavers, I assumed, but why? If Mars was telling the truth and he wasn't involved in the murders, then why did he station one of his people in a garden store in small-town Ontario?

Haley told me the Weavers were drug dealers, but that was almost certainly bullshit. Nothing I'd seen about this case suggested anything to do with illegal drugs. Haley had sent me to Burnside Road because she wanted me to find the portal. But why? There was a piece of this I wasn't seeing. Something that connected Mars to the Weavers.

I decided to make that my next stop.

THERE WAS no answer when I knocked on the Weavers' front door. I tried the knob, but it was locked. Same for the back door. The house was dark and buttoned up like the Weavers had gone on vacation. I didn't like it.

I was heading back to my car when I saw a light on in the apartment above the garage. I went up the outside staircase and knocked on the door. A brassy female voice called out: "Come on in!"

I opened the door and stepped into a small entry with a closet to my left and a coat hanging on a hook to my right. Beyond was a long room that made up the main living area. Past it, through an archway, I could see a bedroom with a daybed and a small bathroom.

Nancy was sitting on the floor with Rachel Weaver. The girl was playing with a dollhouse that was almost as big as she was. It was the kind that opened in the middle so you could move your dolls around the inside of the house or reorganize the furniture. At the moment, Rachel was using a piece of Kleenex as a blanket to cover up a pair of figures — a red Power Ranger and a honey-haired Barbie — lying on a bed in one of the upstairs rooms. She didn't look up as I entered, but Nancy did.

"Hello there, Mr. Renn."

"Felix, please."

I went over and sat down on the floor with them. Rachel gave me a sidelong glance and continued to pile Kleenex on top of the two figures, pulling sheet after sheet from a box on the floor next to her.

"Is it bedtime for your dolls?" I asked her.

Rachel gave me the same sidelong look, but didn't say anything.

"You can talk to him," Nancy prompted her. "It's okay." She ran her hand down the back of the girl's shiny, dark hair.

Rachel turned her head toward me, not quite facing me, and said, "They're not dolls." She tapped her finger on them in their miniature bed. "That's Mommy and that's Daddy. They're asleep now. I'm tucking them in." She placed another tissue on the figures, then patted it down gently.

"That's very thoughtful of you," I said.

Rachel narrowed her eyes at me suspiciously.

"She's shy," Nancy said. "Especially around strangers."

"That's okay," I said. "People are always telling me I'm a pretty strange guy."

I put on my friendliest grin and waggled my eyebrows as I said it. Rachel shook her head in a tired way that made her look about thirty years older.

"I was actually looking for Susan," I said to Nancy. "Do you know where she is?"

"At the store, I think," Nancy said. "She hasn't been going in much since…" She looked at Rachel and ran her hand down the girl's hair again. "… since all of this has been going on. I told her it would be good for her to get out of the house. You know, stay busy, keep herself distracted."

"Okay, I'll try there next."

I stood up and started for the door. Nancy stopped me with a hand on my arm as I was stepping out. "Is it…" She looked over her shoulder at Rachel, but the girl had gone back to playing with her dollhouse, positioning a plastic T. rex in the bright yellow kitchen. "Have you found her father?"

"Not yet," I said. "I just wanted to ask Susan a few questions."

"She should be at the store. That's where she said she was going."

"Have you been there?"

"To the store?" Nancy said. "Sure, a few times. Rachel likes to visit her parents at work, and they've got a pond and a gazebo out back that she likes to play in."

"Have you ever spoken to any of the other people who work there?"

Nancy frowned, like she didn't know where I was going with this line of questioning. I wasn't sure either.

"Not really," she said. "They're just kids, I think."

"I know this might sound like a strange question, but did you ever get the impression that the Weavers were hiding something?"

Nancy's frown deepened. "About the store?"

"About anything."

Nancy gave it some thought, then shook her head. "I've been living with the Weavers for six months, and I've never seen anything unusual about them. Not until Doug vanished."

"What do you mean?"

"It's probably nothing," Nancy said, "but since Doug's been gone, Susan has been acting strange. I didn't think anything of it. Her husband is missing, after all, and there are people in town who think..." A little colour came into her cheeks. "Well, you know what they think."

I nodded.

"I just thought she was in shock. Or in mourning. I don't know. I tried to talk to her about it once, but frankly it's not my area of expertise. I figured the best thing I could do was help with Rachel, which I was doing already. The thing is, even when Susan is here she seems a million miles away. I'm really worried about her. And I'm worried about Rachel, too. We've made a lot of progress in the past few months, and I don't want to see that slip away."

"I understand. Since the start of this case I've felt like I walked into a crowded room two seconds after everyone stopped talking. It's like I'm missing something, but I can't tell if it's something I can't find or if it's something that's being purposely kept from me."

"I know how you feel," Nancy said. "Susan is hiding something, but I don't think it's anything about her husband or what happened to him. I think she's hiding her grief, hiding her pain. Maybe it's just the way she is, or maybe it's because she feels like everyone in town is against her. The thing about the mourning process is that one part of it is private, the other part is public. You can cry in bed or in the shower for the one you lost, but you also need to cry with other people — your family, your friends, and all the others who knew him. Susan hasn't been allowed to do that. The town won't let her." She lowered her voice. "I hope he's dead, Mr. Renn. I really do."

"You think there's a chance he isn't?"

"I don't know," Nancy said, "but Susan might."

"Does Susan think that Doug is the killer?"

"No," Nancy said. "But something is eating her up from the inside. I don't know what it is. And to be honest, I'm afraid to ask her."

She turned her head and looked over at Rachel. "I hope to God he's dead."

CHAPTER 28

I LEFT THE Weaver residence and headed over to The Greener Side. On the way there my cell phone started playing "My Humps." I answered it with "Felix Renn, World's Handsomest Detective."

It was Alice. "Where are you?" she asked.

"On my way to the Weavers' store. I need to ask Susan a question or twenty."

"I need to see you right away."

"I'm flattered, Agent Baffle. Truly. But I might be onto something here."

"So am I," Alice said, "and I don't want you screwing it up by tipping our hand too soon."

"*Our* hand?" I said. "I don't remember taking on a partner."

"You didn't. *I* took *you* on."

"You've really got a high opinion of yourself, don't you?"

"I'm at the motel. And I don't like waiting."

She hung up before I could come back with a witty reply.

I thought about continuing on to the garden store just to spite her, but I was curious to hear what she had found. I decided Susan Weaver could wait. I turned the car around and headed for the Lakeview Inn.

WHEN I got there I saw that Alice had let herself into my room — and taken it over. Her coat was draped over a chair, there was an aluminum briefcase and a large duffel bag on the bed, and a laptop was open on the desk.

Alice came out of the bathroom drying her hands on a towel.

"Making yourself comfortable?" I said.

"Trying to," Alice said. "This place is a dump."

"You should see my apartment."

"I'll pass, thanks."

I took off my coat, looked around for a place to put it, then dropped it on the floor. "So how was your day, dear?"

Alice glared at me.

"It's called levity, Agent Baffle."

"Never heard of it."

"It's my way of saying 'I'm glad to see you made it back alive.'"

Alice grunted.

"So," I said. My throat was suddenly dry. "Did you see the portal?"

"Portals are invisible," Alice said.

"You know what I mean. Did you…"

"I found it. Right where you said it would be. I also found the grave you told me about."

I stared at her with my mouth hanging open, utterly speechless. When I was finally able to speak, I had to keep from shouting. "You went *through* the portal? What the hell is the matter with you? Are you insane?"

Alice gave me a look like I was chastising her for crossing the street. "*You* went through it," she said.

"Not on purpose," I said. "I didn't even know it was there!"

"I did," Alice said. "And you know what they say: forewarned is forearmed. I was also armed in the more traditional sense. It was fine," she said with a shrug.

I didn't know how to respond to that, so I just stood there staring at her with my hands clenching and unclenching at my sides. I was seething with outrage at the way she had blithely ignored my warning and went traipsing into another dimension like she was skipping through a field of wildflowers. I wanted to express to her how stupid, how completely irresponsible and reckless her actions were, but the calm expression on her face and the brusque way she dismissed my concerns told me it would have been a waste of time.

"Listen," she said, "I appreciate the concern. I really do. But I can take care of myself."

The funny thing was, I believed her. Mostly it was the way she said it. Not like she was bragging or trying to sound tough. More like she was stating a simple fact.

I suddenly felt very tired. I shuffled over to the bed and dropped onto it. Alice came over and I thought she was going to console me — put her arm around me, maybe give me a playful punch in the arm and tell me to "Hang in there, champ." Instead she opened the aluminum briefcase and took out a couple of plastic evidence bags.

"If it makes you feel better," Alice said, "I didn't stay in the Black Lands for very long. Just long enough to get these."

She tossed one of the bags at me. I barely got a hand up in time to catch it. It was filled with moist black dirt. "What's this?"

"Black Lands soil," Alice said.

"Great," I said, bouncing the bag in my hand. "This is the clue we needed to catch the killer. We've finally got the dirt on him."

Alice frowned. "It's powerful stuff. If you know how to use it."

"Powerful how?"

"That's classified."

"I knew you were going to say that." I passed the bag of dirt back to her. "Maybe you can sell it online. I'm sure there's a market for mementos from another dimension. Even a bag of dirt."

"There is, actually." Alice bounced the bag in her hand. "But this stuff is particularly noteworthy. Take another look."

She passed it back to me and I looked at the bag more closely. I didn't see it right away. I was too busy looking at the soil instead of the stains it was making on the plastic. Most of them were black streaks from the dirt, but there was some redness in there, too.

"Blood," Alice said. "I haven't tested it yet, but I'd bet my life on it."

"You already did," I said, tossing the bag on the bed. "What else have you got?"

Alice passed me the second evidence bag. There was no question about what it contained. It was a gun. A snub-nosed revolver.

"Smith & Wesson Chiefs Special," Alice said. "Thirty-eight caliber. Two-inch barrel." She took the bag from me and turned it around so I could see the red smears on the nickel plating. "There's blood on it, too. See?"

I saw. "So what do you make of all of this?"

Alice put the evidence bags back in the briefcase and closed it. "The grave you found wasn't waiting to be used. Black Lands soil does a lot of things, but it doesn't bleed. Someone was buried there. Someone who'd been murdered. I found the gun in the grave."

I thought back to when I'd fallen in the grave, rolling over and banging my knee against something that I'd thought was a rock.

"Okay," I said. "So the killer shot someone and buried the body along with the murder weapon. Then they came back later and dug the body up again. Presumably because they were worried someone was going to find it." I looked at Alice. "Does that even make sense?"

"No," she said. "For a couple of reasons. One, I'm not convinced the gun was used to murder anyone. It's fully loaded, which isn't proof of anything, but if it was used to commit a murder, then why would the killer bother to reload it if he was only going to throw it away?"

I nodded. That was a good question.

"Two, why would someone go through the trouble of burying a body in a place where no one would probably ever find it, then tell you exactly where it was?"

I nodded again. That was an even better question.

"And why bury it in the Black Lands?" Alice said. "That seems like an unnecessary risk."

You're one to talk, I thought.

"Even riskier," I said, "since they apparently went back and dug it up again."

"There's something else that bothers me even more," Alice said.

"What's that?"

"Whoever did this had to know about the portal. They didn't just happen upon on it while they were looking for a nice secluded place to bury a body."

I considered that. "So the Quonset hut wasn't put there just to cover up the location of the portal. It was put there to hide where the body was buried, too." I frowned. "But where's the body now?"

Alice didn't have an answer for that. She stared off into the corner with an expression I hadn't seen on her face before.

She looked worried.

CHAPTER 29

I WENT INTO the bathroom and splashed water on my face. I looked around for a towel, but Alice had used them all. The two large towels and the smaller hand towel — the one Alice had been wiping her hands on when I came in — were lying on the floor, stained black with dirt. Black Lands dirt, I presumed.

I came back into the main room patting my wet face on the sleeve of my shirt. "You're a bit of a slob, huh?"

Alice grunted. She was sitting at the desk, reading through the newspaper articles I'd printed at the library.

I went over and sat on the bed since Alice was using the only chair in the room. "I still can't believe you just strolled into the Black Lands and did your CSI bit. Weren't you scared of something attacking you over there?"

"Of course I was," Alice said distractedly. "But it's part of the job. I don't have the luxury of being you."

"What the hell is that supposed to mean?" I snapped.

Alice looked up for her reading. "Don't get so hot under the collar. I didn't mean anything by it. I'm just saying that you have a choice as to whether or not you decide to take on a supernatural case. I don't. I'm a federal agent with the PIA. If I see a portal, I have to secure it. If I see a monster, I have to kill it."

I wanted to be offended, but like the outrage I'd felt earlier, Alice had quickly and effortlessly quashed it. I couldn't deny that she had a point, but that didn't mean I had to like it. I decided to change the subject.

"Have you been there before? To the Black Lands?"

Alice grunted and went back to her reading. In the short time I'd known her, I had determined her grunts could mean "yes" or "no," but they usually meant "mind your own business."

A beeping sound came from Alice's laptop. She put down the papers and punched a few keys.

"What's that?" I asked.

Alice turned the laptop around so I could see the screen. "I'd like you to meet my partner." A video chat window was open, but the view was all black.

"Is she... invisible?"

"Not today," said a female voice from the laptop's speakers.

"Diane has a thing about her image being put on... transferred through..." Alice turned to the screen. "How do you put it?"

"Relayed across a digital platform," Diane said. She spoke with the strained patience of one who has had to repeat this information over and over again. "And you'd be concerned too if you knew what someone could do with your name and an electronic image of your face."

"I do know," Alice said exhaustedly. "You tell me all the time. I just don't care."

"You should," Diane said.

"So you're not on Facebook?" I said.

"No."

"Twitter?"

"No."

"LinkedIn?"

"No."

"I guess that means you don't do much online dating."

A small snicker came over the laptop speakers. "Alice, you didn't tell me he was funny."

"He isn't," Alice said. "Can we get back to work?"

"Don't be rude," Diane said. "Remember, we talked about this."

Alice curled her hands into fists and bit her lip.

"You're biting your lip," Diane said. "You can't see me, but I can see you."

Alice unclenched her fists. In a calm voice, she said, "I apologize. Can we get back to work, please?"

I raised a hand to cover the grin that was spreading across my mouth. Alice turned her head and glared at me. *I will murder you with your toothbrush*, that look said.

Our attention was drawn to the laptop screen where a satellite map of Sycamore and the surrounding area now appeared.

"I've plotted the locations of the six murders to date," Diane said. "Numbered sequentially and seen from this perspective, you might notice something of a pattern."

Red pin icons appeared on the screen. The first two were located on the northern edge of town. The third was on the south side, close to the lakeshore. The final three were scattered across the rural area to the northeast of Sycamore. I leaned in close and examined each pin individually, then pulled back to looked at them collectively. I shook my head.

"I see the trees, Diane, but I'm not seeing the forest."

"Funny you should put it that way," Diane said. "Check this out."

On the laptop screen, the first two pins started flashing, and the third pin, the one near the lake, turned from red to blue.

"The flashing pins represent the location of the first two murders. Robin Endicott and Paul Lindon. Both were killed in their respective homes and their bodies buried in the nearby woods. The third pin, the blue one, is where Douglas Weaver was allegedly killed. I say allegedly because his body has yet to be found. Alice told me that's how you came into this case. That you were hired by Douglas Weaver's wife to locate his body."

"That's right."

"The first murder took place on April seventh. The second on August fifteenth — one hundred and thirty days later. Doug Weaver was reported missing thirty-seven days after that on September twentieth. No pattern so far."

"Okay..." I wasn't sure where she was going with this.

"Now watch this," Diane said.

On the screen, the first two pins stopped flashing. The third pin, the blue one showing where Doug Weaver was allegedly killed, remained blue, while the other three red pins, the ones located to the northeast of town, started flashing."

"These are the most recent murders," Diane said. "What can you tell about them just by looking at the map?"

"They were all committed further away from Sycamore," I said.

"Why do you think that is?"

"The first two murders occurred on the edge of town. These three are well beyond the city limits. Maybe the killer is becoming more cautious. Picking his victims where there's even less chance of being caught."

"Okay," Diane said. "But that's not the only thing that makes these murders different from the first two."

On the screen, the three flashing pins changed colour from red to green.

"The fourth victim, Ashley Prendergast, was killed on September twenty-second — two days after Doug Weaver's alleged murder. The fifth victim, Gill Frye, was killed seven days later on September twenty-ninth. The six and final victim — so far — Keith Morse, was killed ten days later on October ninth."

I nodded my head. "So the killer is moving away from Sycamore, but at the same time he's increasing the frequency of his murders."

"That's how it would appear," Diane said. "And there's something else. The first two victims were killed in their homes. The last three were killed *away* from their homes. Ashley Prendergast was out walking her dog. Gill Frye was hunting in the woods. And Keith Morse's body was found outside near his barn. The bodies of the first two victims were buried, but the last three were not. What do you make of that?"

"I don't know," I said, frustrated. I wasn't expecting a pop quiz today. "The killer knows the police are onto him, so maybe he doesn't see the point of burying the bodies anymore. The fact that the murders are now occurring more rapidly suggests that his urge to kill is getting stronger, or he's no longer able to keep himself in check as well as he used to. He probably stalked his first two victims, which is why he felt comfortable attacking them in their homes. The last three he attacked outside. Maybe because he's starting to lose control. Or maybe the thrill of hunting his prey has been replaced by the thrill of the spontaneous kill."

Diane was silent for a long moment. Alice was looking over her shoulder at me, one eyebrow raised slightly.

Finally, Diane said, "Not bad, Felix. Not bad at all."

Alice turned back to face the laptop screen.

"But you're wrong."

"Oh," I said.

Alice snorted.

"It's okay," Diane said. "The task force is currently operating under the same assumptions you are. Their theory is that Douglas Weaver committed the first two murders, then, after realizing the police were onto him, he faked his death and decided to remain in the area in order to kill three more people."

"Doesn't make much sense when you put it like that."

"It does if the killer is psychotic," Alice said. "But none of that matters, because there's one piece of information the task force doesn't have. Something that's come to light only recently, and it changes everything."

"What's that?" I asked.

On the laptop screen, a new pin icon — a gold one — appeared in the middle of the cluster of green pins, the ones that denoted the last three murders.

"What is that…" I leaned forward, squinting at the map to see where the gold pin was located. When I figured it out, a cold tickle of fear went racing down my spine. "Burnside Road. The portal."

"Yes," Diane said. Her voice sounded silky over the laptop speaker, almost thrumming with excitement. "This is what we call a game changer."

I stared at the screen. The first two murders on the northern edge of town. Doug Weaver's murder or disappearance further south near the lakeshore. And the three most recent murders way off in the northeastern corner of the map, loosely grouped around the portal. Looking at those different-coloured pins all together like that, it suddenly hit me.

"Holy shit. There are two killers."

Alice gave a small nod. She stood up and went over to the window.

Diane said, "I fed all the data from the task force into the computer and it came back with a sixty-four-percent probability that the first two murders were committed by a different perpetrator than the last three."

"What about Doug Weaver?"

"Anomaly, the computer said. It needs more information."

"Join the club," I muttered.

"What's even more interesting," Diane went on, "is that the computer said there was a seven-percent probability that the first two murders were committed by a Black Lands entity."

I looked over at Alice. "You said you didn't think there was a supernatural angle to the murders."

"That's the reason why," Alice said, nodding at the laptop. "Seven percent is nothing. Any murder will have some probability that it was committed by a Black Lands entity." She paused. "But then something happened."

"Three more murders."

"Yes," Diane said. "But even then, the computer said there was still only a twenty-four-percent probability that the perpetrator was a supernatural. That's not much of a jump."

"Why did it go up at all?" I asked.

"The first two murders occurred in the victims' homes," Alice said. "Black Lands entities don't usually break into people's houses to kill them. And they definitely don't bother to bury their kills. They're like animals that way. The probability went up after the last three murders because they were all killed outside and the bodies weren't buried."

"But twenty-four percent," I said. "That's still pretty low."

Alice leaned against the wall and folded her arms. "And that's why I still wasn't convinced that something from the Black Lands was responsible."

"But that's where the game changer comes in," Diane said. "The one piece of information the task force — and Alice and I — didn't have. Not until you came along, Felix." She was speaking faster now, really getting into it. "I fed that little tidbit into the computer — the location of a new portal near Burnside Road — and had it run the numbers again." She paused for dramatic effect. "The computer came back with an eighty-eight-percent probability that we're dealing with two different killers, and a ninety-two-percent probability that one of them is a supernatural entity."

"Jesus Christ," I said. "Having a portal in the neighbourhood really changes things."

"Yes," Alice said, "and never for the better."

"Why does the computer think that only one of the killers is from the Black Lands?"

"It's like I told you," Alice said. "The first two murders don't match the other three. Black Lands creatures aren't known for pulling home invasions and then burying the bodies in the backyard. The task force thinks they're dealing with one killer, and that he changed his m.o. because he knows the police are onto him. I think…" — she nodded at the laptop — "*We* think the person responsible for the first two murders is your garden-variety fucked-up human being. A monster, to be sure, but very much from this world. But the other three murders…" Her face turned grim. "… the thing responsible for those might be more up our alley."

"What are you planning to do?" I asked.

"It's been a few weeks since the killer last struck…" Alice said.

"Twenty-two days," Diane interjected.

"… but it's only a matter of time. I don't know what exactly we're dealing with here, but if there's one thing that all Black Lands creatures have in common it's that they'll keep on killing until something or someone stops them. This thing isn't just going to get bored and go home." She pointed to the cluster of icons around the portal on the laptop screen. "It's sticking close to the portal, probably because it's territorial. So that's where I'm going." She turned to face me. "And you're coming with me."

I stared at her. "Me?"

"This is your case, Renn. I wouldn't dream of taking it away from you. Not after all the good work you've done."

"Yes you would," Diane said with a snort.

Alice frowned at the laptop screen. "Okay, I would. But I could use some help on this, and you've proven you can handle yourself when it comes to supernaturals."

I shook my head. "I can't. I'm sorry, Alice, but I just can't do it."

Alice licked her lips. She didn't have a great abundance of patience, and I could see the little she had was eroding quickly.

"Felix," she began slowly, "all of these murders, even the first two, have one thing in common: they all happened at night." She glanced over at the window. "The sun will be down soon…"

"At six-thirteen p.m.," Diane said. "Forty-seven minutes from now."

"… and since I can't predict where this creature will strike next, I have to do the next best thing and wait for it to come back to the portal. I would prefer not to do that alone."

"How do you know it will kill someone tonight?"

"I don't," Alice said. "But it's the only course of action we have."

"I can't go back to the portal." I tried to speak forcefully, but there was a quaver in my voice. "There's no way."

Alice stared at the floor. She exhaled loudly through her nostrils.

"You want to hear the words, is that it? Fine." She spread her arms indulgently. "*I need your help.* Is that what you've been waiting for? You want me to deputize you as an honorary agent? Give you your own badge?"

"*Alice.*"

Diane's voice blasted out of the laptop speakers. It cut a silencing swath across the room, like the stillness following a loud crack of thunder.

Alice glared at the screen, then turned back to me with a look of disgust. She went over to the window and stood there with her arms crossed.

When Diane spoke again, her voice was so faint it was barely audible.

"What happened to you over there, Felix?"

I LOOKED across the room at the laptop sitting on the desk. Even though the chat window was still an empty black square, I could feel Diane watching me. I didn't know what she looked like, but I could picture her eyes, soft and sensitive and encouraging. The eyes of a therapist trying to coax a patient into talking about the thing he doesn't want to talk about. And, like a good therapist, she somehow managed to do that very thing. That difficult, painful thing.

"I don't know what happened to me," I said. "One moment I was walking through the Quonset hut, and the next I was outside. When I figured out I was in the Black Lands, this wave of fear came crashing over me. I'd never experienced anything like it. I've been afraid before, but not like this. The only thing that went through my mind was that I had to get out of there. At some point I became aware that something was stalking me. I didn't know what it was — I never saw it — but I could hear it getting closer and closer. I thought it would kill me and no one would ever find my body or know what happened to me. But that didn't happen. I was able to find the portal and cross back over. Running back my car, I thought every shadow I passed was concealing a monster that would leap out and attack me. It wasn't until I was sitting in the driver's seat with the dome light on that I realized it was much worse than that. It was the dark itself I was scared of. In a way I'd never been scared before. Frayed nerves, cold sweats, borderline paralysis. It's a completely irrational fear, and yet it's there. I keep hoping it'll go away, but it hasn't yet. I'm afraid it never will."

My voice hitched at the end of that last sentence, and when I blinked my eyes my vision doubled, then tripled, like I was looking through a prism. I raised my hand and felt wetness on my cheek. I didn't know when I had started crying.

I scrubbed my face clean and looked up to see that Alice had turned from the window and was now facing me. Her arms hung at her sides and there was a look on her face that wasn't anger, but wasn't quite sympathy, either.

"I think it was the Black Lands that did it," I said, looking down at my hands. "I'm not sure how, but I think it infected me or something."

"Infected," Alice said, "with a fear of the dark."

There was something in her tone, a combination of scepticism and thoughtfulness that caught my attention. I raised my head and saw something I wasn't expecting: Alice with her hand resting on the butt of her holstered pistol.

Wow, I thought. She really doesn't like cowards.

"Could be the Influence," Diane said.

I managed to tear my eyes away from Alice and looked over at the laptop.

"The Influence? Hold on a second." I held up my hands, mostly for Alice's benefit, so she wouldn't bust a cap in my ass. "Isn't that supposed to give you psychic powers or turn you into a mutant or something?"

"Where'd you hear that?" Alice said. "*Info Wars?*"

"I learned about it in school. Like most people."

"The Influence affects everyone differently," Alice said. "If it affects them at all."

"Superpowers don't sound so bad," I said.

"Forget about what your teachers told you," Diane said. "Or what you see in movies or comic books. Psychic abilities are not all they're cracked up to be. Human beings were never meant to have telepathy or telekinesis or pyrokinesis. Exposure to the Black Lands can bring about such abilities, but those who are affected usually end up psychotic, catatonic, or suicidal. The Influence has also been known to cause physical mutations — deformities, growths, tumours. Those who don't immediately die from these 'alterations' end up spending the rest of their lives as inhuman monsters."

"And I thought growing up near power lines was bad."

Alice shook her head.

"Hey, I didn't choose to go in there, okay? I ended up in the Black Lands by accident. What's your excuse?"

"I don't make excuses."

"Tough talk, but that means you were exposed, too."

"It was a calculated risk," Alice said.

"The Influence is real," Diane said, "but it's also very rare. I've never heard of it causing nyctophobia, though." She paused. "But that doesn't mean it couldn't happen. We're talking about the supernatural, after all."

Alice had taken her hand off her gun — which made me feel immensely better — and crossed her arms. "You didn't want to go to the portal in broad daylight, either," she said to me. "So this is more than just being afraid of the dark."

I stared at her in disbelief. "It's a portal, Alice. I try to avoid them whenever possible."

"I told you I can't do that."

"I know. It's your job. I get it. But it's not my job."

Alice took a challenging step toward me. "And how much longer do you think you'll be able to do *your job* if you don't confront this thing. I don't know much about being a PI, but I imagine a large part of the work takes place at night. I don't think a paralyzing fear of the dark is going to be good for business. Do you?"

"Maybe not," I said, "but I don't think going back to the place that did this to me is the kind of therapy I need right now."

"It's *exactly* what you need," Alice said. "If you don't get on top of this thing, it'll control you the rest of your life. I've seen it happen to people, even to other agents. Shit goes down in the field, and even though they make it out alive, they're broken up here." She pointed at her head. "Sometimes they can put themselves back together again, sometimes they can't. Those that make it back do so because they face their demons head-on. You have to own your fear before it owns you. There's no other way to do it."

"If that was supposed to be an inspirational speech, you might want to rethink your delivery. Maybe practice in front of a mirror or something."

I was babbling and trying to look anywhere but at Alice. I thought if I kept it up, eventually she'd get annoyed with me and leave. But when I finally met her eyes, she was looking at me with a mixture of sadness and hurt. The combination didn't quite add up to pity — I'm not sure Alice felt pity for anyone, not even her agoraphobic partner — but it suggested a broader emotional range than I had thought her capable of.

"I know what it's like to be afraid, Felix. I told you before it's part of the job, and I wasn't trying to sound tough when I said it. Fuck tough and fuck courage. Those things only get you so far. To do what I do — what *we* do — you have to be hard. Do you understand? You have to have thick skin, a thick heart, and a thick mind. You have to armour-plate every part of yourself, including your soul, because this work will destroy you if you let it. If you're lucky, it will destroy you all at once. It's the ones who die a little bit over time that suffer. Sometimes they end up turning into monsters themselves. Nietzsche was right about the abyss. We're looking into the Black Lands, and it's looking right back at us. Other people may have the luxury of looking away, but we don't. If the portals keep popping up and we don't find a way to close them, then soon no one will be able to look away. We need to do what we can while we can. And even a hard core loner like me knows I can't do it alone. *You* aren't alone, Felix. I'll watch your back if you watch mine. What do you say?"

I looked down at my hands in my lap. They were trembling. And at some point, my eyes had started leaking again. "What do I say?" I let out a big, fluttery sigh. "I say that's a better speech than your first one. But I'm still not sure."

Alice took another step forward. "I'll protect you, I promise."

"Sure, you're a protector. That's why your partner is two thousand miles away."

Diane laughed. "Wow, he knows you well, Alice. Did you tell him about Bermuda?"

Alice's head snapped around. "Shut it, Diane." Then she turned back to me. "I'm telling the truth. I'll protect you. This needs to be done, and we're the ones who need to do it. Together."

I stood up and went over to the desk. I took a tissue from the box next to the laptop and wiped my eyes. My hands were no longer shaking.

I turned to Alice and said, "Okay. I'll do it." I took another tissue and blew my nose. "I'm sorry. I've never cried in front of a woman before. Not even my ex-wife."

Alice came over and put her hand on my shoulder. I was really seeing a different side of her.

"Felix," she said. "You didn't cry in front of a woman." She nodded her head at the laptop. "You cried in front of two women."

Or maybe not.

CHAPTER 30

AFTER DIANE SIGNED off, Alice said she had a few things she needed to do before this evening's stakeout.

"Let's arrange to meet back here in an hour." She checked her watch, then glanced at the window, where the sunlight was already draining out of the sky. "It'll be full dark by then."

"Great."

"We'll grab a quick bite to eat and then head out. Is that grease pit next door any good?"

I nodded distractedly. I had never felt less like eating.

Alice came over and gripped me tightly by the back of my neck. She looked me straight in the face, her eyes drilling into mine.

"Don't flake out on me now, Felix. We can do this. We *will* do this. That's all it takes. Will."

She gave my cheek a light slap, then was out the door.

I sat on the edge of the bed for a full five minutes after she was gone, trying to find the will that Alice was talking about. I stared at the walls. I stared at the hideous orange carpet. My shoulders sagged like they were being pulled down by invisible weights. My brain felt like an engine that had been flooded from pumping the gas pedal too many times.

I decided I needed to get out of the motel room for a little while. And I knew exactly where I could go. To the place I'd been headed when Alice called me — the Weavers' garden store.

I got there a few minutes past six o'clock, but the place was already closed. I'd missed Susan again. I wondered if she was trying to avoid me, or if I just had lousy timing.

Sitting in the parking lot with the engine running and the interior light on, I thought about my next course of action. I still had some time before I had to meet Alice, but not quite enough to drive all the way back across town to the Weaver residence. If I was late for our rendezvous, Alice would think I had chickened out and gone back to the city. It was a tempting thought, but I couldn't do it. Alice would hunt me down or get Diane to use her computer witchery to destroy my credit rating or something. Also, I didn't want to abandon her. Partly because she needed me, partly because she believed in me, but mostly because I was worried that leaving would have long-term consequences for my nascent fear of the dark.

I was staring through the windshield at the garden store, my thoughts tumbling around like clothes in a dryer, when my phone started pumping out the Black Eyed Peas. Maybe it was time to change that ringtone.

I answered without checking the caller ID, figuring it was Alice, back early from running whatever errands she had to run, and wondering where the hell I was.

"What's the matter, Buttercup? Can't get enough of me?"

There was a pause, then Sandra said, "What the hell, Felix?"

"Sorry, Dee," I said. "I thought you were someone else."

"Who?" Sandra said. She wasn't jealous; she had never been the type, not even when we were married. She was pissed off. "I thought you were working a case, not picking up whores."

"Can't I do both?"

Sandra hung up on me. I sat there staring at my phone.

Was it something I said?

I REMAINED in my car, drumming my fingers on the steering wheel, adjusting the heater, turning the radio on, then off, then back on again. I was killing time, which, ironically, was only making things worse.

I tried to tell myself that I wasn't really afraid of the dark, that I was being affected by some supernaturally-induced form of cognitive dissonance.

It didn't matter. The feelings I was experiencing amounted to the same thing, and kept bringing me back to the same conclusion: fear is fear, and you can't think your way out of it.

I wanted to check out the Weavers' garden store, but I didn't want to get out of the car. Night was descending rapidly; with every passing moment the world was filling up with more and more darkness. I tried to calculate the distance between the car and the front door of the store. How far was it? Thirty yards? Fifty? It might as well have been a mile.

I told myself I could run to the door in a matter of seconds, and the road was far enough outside the city limits that it didn't get much traffic (not a single car had passed in all the time I'd been sitting there), so there wouldn't be anyone around to witness my coward's dash to the store. I went so far as to put my hand on the door handle, but I couldn't pull it open.

I didn't feel so much captured by my fear as contained by it. Like a diver in a shark cage, I knew it was a dangerous to climb out, but I also knew I was only making things worse for myself in the long run if I didn't.

"You chickenshit."

I opened the door and pushed myself out of the car. Then, before I could lose my nerve, I closed the door and pressed my back against it so I wouldn't be tempted to open it and slip back inside. I took a quick breath, let it out, and started across the parking lot. I went over the little footbridge, my shoes clomping loudly on the wooden planks. The creek burbled below, and it sounded like laughter. I kept breathing and kept walking. I was striding forward at a quick pace, but I wasn't running. I was walking briskly, legs pumping, arms swinging. I wasn't running because there was nothing to be afraid of. I told myself that and I almost believed it.

I made it to the porch and climbed the steps to the front door. The sign with THE GREENER SIDE written on it was swinging slightly in the low breeze, making the hooks squeak and squawk. I tried the door, but of course it was locked. I went over and peered in through the big display window, but it was even darker inside than it was out here.

There still hadn't been any cars passing by on the road, but I didn't want to take any chances, so I made my way around to the back of the store. It was even darker back here and I felt my fragile calm begin to crack around the edges. No mantras and no amount of logic were going to help me now. The only thing I had going for me was momentum, and it was fading fast.

Once I reached the back door, I took out my phone and turned on the flashlight app. The light should have made me feel better, but it only made me more aware of the darkness surrounding me. I stuck the phone in my mouth, aimed the light at the lock on the back door, and took out my Swiss Army knife. I selected a tension tool, slid a pick out of the knife's housing, and went to work.

The angle wasn't great, and I wished for a third hand to hold the light properly. As I was dipping my head forward so I could see what I was doing, I felt the phone start to slide out of my mouth. I bit down harder on the plastic housing, and that's when the knife slipped out of my sweaty hand. It made a small clattering sound when it struck the ground. I swore and the phone fell out of my mouth. It landed somewhere in front of me, facedown, and the light went out.

My heart slammed hard against my ribcage. I dropped to my knees and began flailing around on the ground for my phone. My hand touched something hard and I scooped it up. It was a rock, part of a border of similar-sized rocks that outlined a small garden next to the stoop. I dropped it and resumed my search, feeling the fear settle onto my shoulders like a carrion bird digging its talons into my flesh.

I was aware of a sound I was making, a low whimpering that filled me with shame. I couldn't seem to stop it, which only made me more disgusted with myself. Alice was right. What kind of PI could I be if I couldn't work at night?

I forced myself to slow down and search the ground methodically around me, working my way side to side from the door outward. My hand bumped against something I thought was another rock, but it was flat and rectangular. My phone! I picked it up and a spill of light washed over me. The flashlight app was still on and the screen didn't appear to be cracked. I panned it around until I found my Swiss Army knife. I couldn't find the pick, then looked back at the door and saw it was still sticking out of the lock.

With the phone in my mouth again, I went back to work with the tension tool, craning my head around to direct the light at the lock. The darkness was like a presence behind me, peering over my shoulder. Watching me, criticizing me.

You used to be better at this, Felix. You used to be faster. And you really should hurry. Haven't you noticed how dark it's getting? Anything could be lurking out here in the night. Look over there! What's that next to the gazebo? Doesn't it look like someone crouched down over there? Someone or something? Why don't you go over and take a look?

I began to tremble. My hands were greasy with sweat. A bad combination. I dropped the knife again.

The noise it made when it struck the ground seemed even louder than last time. The only thing louder was the bass-beat thumping of my heart. I knew what John Hurt must have felt like in *Alien*.

I swore again and took the phone out of my mouth. I shined it around my feet, found the knife, and jammed it back in my pocket. Then I looked around for the stone I'd found earlier and picked it up. The door had four panes of glass in its upper panel, two on two. I used the stone to smash out the lower right pane, the one closest to the handle, and reached inside to disengage the lock.

Once inside I ran my hand along the wall until I found a bank of switches and flicked the one that turned on the overhead light. I didn't think it would be seen from anyone passing by on the road out front, but at that moment I didn't particularly care.

I stood in the glow of that sixty-watt bulb and felt the fear slowly melt away. The shame remained. I had broken into several buildings and residences over the course of my career as a private snoop. This was the first time I had to smash my way inside. Maddy Ferine would be so disappointed in me. That was okay, I thought. I was pretty disappointed in myself.

But I'd made my bed and now I had to search it for clues.

I HAD twenty minutes before I was supposed to meet Alice. That wasn't nearly enough time to search the entire store; it was barely enough time to search a single room. The fact that I didn't even know what I was looking for didn't help matters, either.

I decided to focus my attention on the small office off the rear hallway. Inside there was a gray steel desk, a wooden swivel chair, a three-drawer file cabinet, and a smaller side desk with an older model PC and printer. A calendar on the wall still showed the month of September, as if the person who used this space had forgotten to change it, or they hadn't been in here for some time.

Next to the calendar was a framed photo of Susan and Doug Weaver standing in front of the store. The couple looked younger and the paint on the house looked newer. My keen detective skills told me it was probably taken when they first opened The Greener Side. The Weavers wore matching smiles and matching denim overalls. Susan had a straw hat cocked back on her head, while Doug was holding a pitchfork. Canadian Gothic.

I sat down in the chair and went through the desk drawers. I found a lot of paperwork and business correspondence related to the running of a garden store, but that was it.

I rolled over to the file cabinet and started searching the drawers. When I was finished, I had learned two things: the Weavers were very organized, and there was no connection between them and the Planets. Not that I really expected to find anything in the form of an incriminating sales invoice or secret communique. The closest I came was in the records for past and present employees. I found old work schedules and pay receipts for everyone who'd ever worked at The Greener Side, including the Dunbarton brothers, but none for Haley.

No surprise there, since she didn't really work for the Weavers. She was a plant whose sole purpose was to keep an eye on the Weavers while they were at work. The irony wasn't lost on me either — Haley working as a plant in a garden store. It was more than an amusing turn of phrase. Some plants were known to infiltrate a new environment and take it over completely. Some of them did it without being noticed until it was too late. Invasive species, they were called. This description could apply to human beings as well.

I checked my watch and saw it was time to go. I gave the Weavers' computer a passing glance, knowing I had neither the time nor the skills to search it properly. Turning it on would've been a major accomplishment for me. I wished Sandra was here, or better yet, Diane. They would've been able to find what I was looking for, assuming there was anything to find.

I turned off the light and went down the hall to the back door with the broken pane. There was no way to fix it or cover my tracks. The first person to show up in the morning, Susan or one of the Dunbarton boys, would know someone had broken in, and it wouldn't take a major leap of deduction to figure out it was me.

That was real amateur hour, Felix.

The sound of Maddy Ferine's voice in my head brought the shame crashing back down on me. But self-pity never helped anyone. Maddy never said that to me, but it sounded like something she would say. It was good advice.

I went out the door and closed it behind me. The darkness was waiting for me. So was the fear.

I ran back to my car and drove to the motel.

CHAPTER 31

ALICE WAS WAITING for me in my room. I wasn't sure how she kept getting in there without a key. I figured the PIA must have taught her how to pick locks. Clearly she was better at it than me.

She was sitting in the room's only chair with her feet up on the desk, watching the Weather Channel. She looked over at me and said, "I thought maybe you'd left."

"A smarter man would have," I said. "But I am not that man."

She turned off the TV and stood up. "We're in luck. Clear skies tonight."

"Awesome," I said.

Alice was wearing a black leather bomber jacket, a dark grey sweater, black jeans, and black hiking boots. The PIA agent dressed in her ninja best. She slapped my arm as she sidled past me out the door.

"Let's grab a bite before we head out. I'm hungry enough to eat the ass out of a dead werewolf."

"Awesome," I said again.

"SO TELL me about Mars," Alice said between bites of her Galactic Burger. She had ordered the full-sized platter with fries and onion rings, a side order of gravy, and a tall chocolate-banana milkshake topped with whipped cream. Alice was about five-ten, maybe 140 pounds, and I wasn't sure where she was putting all the food. Maybe she had a portal instead of a stomach.

I was on my third cup of coffee and I had a plate of fries that I'd barely touched.

"Not much to say," I said.

Alice gestured with her burger. "Tell me what he was like. What did his house look like?"

"Red. Everything was red. His hair, his suit, his office — all different shades of red. His desk was black marble, but it had red veins running through it. The floor…" I shook my head. "I can't remember if it was red carpet or redwood planking… Does it even matter?"

"Guy lives up to his name," Alice said with a shrug. "He and his sister have a thing for red. They don't appear in public too often, but when they do, they're always decked out like hell's high royalty." She took a bite of her burger. "What did you think of *her*?"

"The sister? Mars called her Vermillion."

"It's a shade of red," Alice said.

"My professional opinion is they're a couple of grade-A whack jobs. Which might explain the names. I'm fairly certain they didn't come by them honestly."

"They're an odd pair." Alice put down the remains of her burger and went to work on her onion rings, dipping each one in ketchup and then sliding them into her mouth. "I've had a couple of run-ins with them and I still don't know that much about them."

"They're part of the Planets," I said. "What else is there to know?"

Alice took a sip of her milkshake. "What do you know about the Planets?"

"Not much beyond what they say about them on the news. They're a crime syndicate with, I don't know what you'd call them, *franchises* all over the… well, planet."

"We call them satellites."

"Of course you do." I drank some of my coffee. It was cold. "The main members of the family…"

"System," Alice said. "As in 'solar.'"

"Right. The main members of the *system* operate out of major cities in the United States and Canada."

"That's correct. Mars controls things in Toronto, as you've discovered for yourself. Jupiter runs New York. Neptune is in Miami. Mercury floats between Chicago and Detroit. Venus runs Los Angeles. And Saturn operates out of Seattle."

"What about Pluto and Uranus?"

"Near as we can figure, they don't exist. I guess no one wanted to be named after a dog or an asshole." Alice dipped her last onion ring in ketchup and popped it into her mouth. "Do you know what they all have in common, besides a penchant for celestial nicknames?"

I shook my head.

Alice sat back and gave me a long, scrutinizing look. "This is high-level shit, Felix. I shouldn't be telling you this stuff."

"I can keep a secret, Alice. I may not be a fancy government agent like you, but I know a thing or two about discretion."

She stared at me a moment longer, then gave a small nod. "Fair enough." She cleared her throat and leaned in close. "The Planets is a crime syndicate, that part is true, but their criminal activities almost exclusively involve the Black Lands."

"What does that mean?"

"It means when they put out a hit, sometimes they do it themselves, and sometimes they employ a supernatural creature. Some gangs have attack dogs, the Planets have vampires and werecreatures. Some gangs have enforcers, the Planets have paramentals. Instead of hiding stolen goods in a warehouse, the Planets use portals."

"That's insane!" I said loudly. The waitress behind the counter shot me a disapproving look. In a lower voice, I said, "Why would they do that?"

"Because no one else does," Alice said. "Most of the criminals out there are like the rest of us law-abiding folks — they don't want anything to do with the Black Lands. But for some reason the Planets have embraced it. They see it as a land of opportunity, something they can use and exploit. And since no one else wants a piece of it, they don't even have to share."

"Sure," I said, "but it doesn't seem like it would be worth the risk. It's like setting up a meth lab in a tiger cage. Sure, no one is coming in after you, but you're still in there with the tigers. I just don't see the point."

Alice dragged her finger through the last bit of ketchup on her plate and licked it off. "You said you thought Mars and Vermillion were crazy. That might be all there is to it. Maybe the Planets are just one big fucked-up family. They'd have to be to have done some of the things I've seen and heard about."

"But what do they want with me?" I said. "Up until a couple of days ago, I didn't even know I was on the Planets' radar."

"I'm not sure," Alice said. "But it's definitely a place you don't want to be."

"No shit."

"If it makes you feel better, I'm not entirely convinced they're interested in you. I think it's the portal they want. That falls right in line with what we know about them. They would love to get their hands on a new, undocumented portal before the PIA does."

"But why did they send me right to it? How did they know I wasn't going to call the PIA myself. Hell, they've got a hotline specifically for people who find new portals."

"Maybe they wanted to try it out," Alice said. "Send you through first to make sure it's stable, then let you get killed by something on the other side. No fuss, no muss. Kill two birds with one portal."

"That doesn't make sense," I said. "The grave in the Black Lands proves the portal has already been used. They didn't need to test it. There has to be another reason. And the Weavers are the key to it all. They own the land the portal sits on. The girl, Haley, who works at their garden store actually works for the Planets. These things can't be coincidences. Did you have Diane look into them?"

"I did," Alice said. "She checked all of the Weavers' financial information, both their personal records and those for the store, and she didn't find anything hinky. No evidence that they've been living beyond their means, no evidence of fraud or tax evasion, much less anything major like money laundering. They're clean. At least on paper."

I made a fist and slammed it down on the table, causing my coffee cup to jump, and earning me another reproachful look from the waitress. "There has to be a connection."

"There may be," Alice said, "but right now we've got bigger fish to fry."

I exhaled a deep breath. "Okay."

"Two questions. The sun's down — how do you feel?"

I turned my head and glanced out the window. The lights of the diner made a wall of glare on the glass that made it difficult to see how dark it was outside. But I knew it was there. I could feel it.

"Afraid," I said. "But I'm still going to do this."

"Good," Alice said.

"Second question?"

Alice pointed at my plate. "Are you going to eat those fries?"

WE TOOK Alice's SUV. It was nicer and roomier than my car, and it had a Bluetooth speaker on the dash so we could stay in contact with Diane.

"Sweet ride," I said. "Does it have concealed machine guns?"

"No."

"A flamethrower?"

"No."

"An ejector seat?"

"Keep asking stupid questions and you'll find out."

I nodded and managed to sit quietly for about three minutes.

"Kind of reeks of the undercover federal agent, though, doesn't it?"

Alice glanced over at me. "In what way?"

"Well, it seems a little out of the price range of a small-town librarian."

"And that automatically means I must be an undercover federal agent?"

"I'm just saying some people might have noticed."

"You didn't."

I nodded. "Toush."

"What is that? Are you trying to say touché?"

"Uh, yes. That's how we say it in Canada."

I heard Diane snicker over the speaker.

Alice glared at the dash, then flicked her eyes toward me. "You usually work alone?"

"Yes."

"I can see why."

We had left the lights of Sycamore far behind us and were now driving through the dark woods northeast of town. I was doing okay. My breathing was slow and regular, and there was only a light mist of sweat on the back of my neck. It helped that I wasn't alone. I thought Alice might need directions, but then I remembered she'd already been out this way. Had already been to Burnside Road and gone through the portal. On purpose. It still boggled my mind that she had done that. That someone did this sort of thing for a living. It seemed like a surefire way to *stop* living.

When we reached the four corners that made up the entirety of Coakley, Alice turned right instead of going straight through the intersection. She looked over at me and said, "Short cut."

Goodie, I thought. Just what I wanted: to get there faster.

We drove past a grey stone church with a slate roof, tall stained-glass windows, and an oddly whimsical sign out front, the kind where you can change the letters every week to welcome the Sunday parishioners. The current message said: A LONG TIME AGO IN A GALILEE FAR FAR AWAY. I read it to Diane and she laughed. Alice shook her head at us. "Nerds."

"Doesn't the fact that you get the joke also make you a nerd?"

"Nope," she said.

No one spoke another word until we were on Burnside Road and Alice was turning into the little dirt lane that led to the Quonset hut. The first thing I noticed was that the chain was gone.

"I removed it," Alice said. "I didn't want it to get in our way in case we have to make a fast getaway."

"Good thinking," I said. My stomach started to churn.

When we reached the end of the dirt lane, Alice swung the SUV around the edge of the clearing and pointed it across the field so that the headlights shined on the long metal exterior of the Quonset hut. It was a good spot to sit and wait. From this position we could see both doors on either end of the building, as well as the open field of tall grass around it.

Alice turned off the ignition and the headlights died. My stomach now felt like a pit of bubbling lava.

"Don't you want to leave the lights on," I said in an offhand way, trying to sound casual. "It'd be easier to spot something coming or going from the portal."

"I don't want to spook it," Alice said. "Whatever *it* might be, the one thing they have in common is they're all nocturnal."

"You seriously think the killer is something from the Black Lands?"

"It makes sense," Diane said from the dashboard speaker. "Serial murder in this part of the province is virtually unheard of. And it would explain why the task force is no closer to catching the killer than they were after the first murder."

"Because it keeps returning to the portal," I said.

"That's right. The thing to remember about supernaturals is that most of them don't want to be in our world any more than we want to be in theirs. Alice was right about them being territorial. If a Black Lands entity is the one responsible for these murders, the portal is the logical place to look for it."

I ran my hand through my hair. "I hate to say it, but I've got a bad feeling about this."

Alice let out an annoyed breath. "Christ, Felix, am I going to have to hold your hand the entire night? You said you were up for this."

"I am," I snapped. "I said I'd back you up, and I will. I was speaking more to the plan itself. I don't like the idea of waiting here for this thing to come out of the portal — or worse, for it to come back *after* it's killed someone else. Isn't that like locking the barn door after the horse has gotten out… and, you know, killed someone?"

"We don't have much choice," Alice said.

"She's right," Diane said. "Even though I managed to plot the general area of the creature's hunting ground, we're talking about a very large section of land. Most of it is woods, but there are a number of residences, as well. Forty-two, to be exact."

"And we don't have the time or the resources to monitor them all," Alice added.

"If it makes you feel better," Diane said, "I'm monitoring the local police-band communications as well as any incoming 911 calls for this area. If anything happens, we'll know about it."

"Okay," I said. It did make me feel better, but only a little.

Alice took off her seatbelt and opened her door. "I want to walk the perimeter and check inside the Quonset hut before we settle in."

I looked over and she was giving me a look that it took me a second to translate.

"You want me to come with you."

Alice raised her voice. "Diane, we're going to be offline for the next fifteen to twenty. Call me on my Specter if you need me."

"Ten-four," Diane said.

I climbed out of the SUV and went around to the back. Alice opened the hatch on the rear storage compartment. Inside were a couple of large metal cases with combination locks.

"I meant to ask you before," she said. "What are you packing?"

I raised my jacket and showed her my gun in its hip holster.

Alice gave an approving nod. "Ruger three fifty-seven. Not bad. Except when you have to reload. Takes time, even with a speedloader. When you're dealing with supernatural creatures, every second counts."

She spun the dials on the locks and raised the lids. Inside the one on the left were four semi-automatic pistols — two Glocks, a Browning nine millimeter, and a Sig Sauer P226. The guns weren't sitting in felt-lined cut-outs or on a bed of convoluted foam. They were just lying in the case like Alice had simply dumped them in there.

Alice took the Sig and slipped it into the waistband at the small of her back. Then she reached into the other case, which was longer and narrower, and took out a Remington tactical shotgun with a pistol grip stock. She gestured with the barrel at the three remaining pistols.

"You want to borrow one of mine?"

I said I was good, although compared to Alice's arsenal, it felt like I was armed with a water pistol.

"I've also got a Kevlar vest if you want it."

"Are you wearing one?"

"Not tonight. It slows me down."

I nodded.

"Besides, most supernaturals aren't packing heat. And if they do attack you, they tend to go for the throat or the extremities. A Kevlar vest usually isn't much help."

"That's good to know," I said dryly.

Alice took two boxes of shells out of the long case. She loaded the shotgun with red shells from one box, then opened the other, dumped out some blue shells, and stuffed them in her jacket pocket.

"What are those?" I asked, nodding at the blue shells.

"Double-aught silver shot," Alice said. "In case this thing turns out to be a werecreature. I've also got silver bullets for the Sig. Silver-coated, actually, with silver nitrate mixed in with the gun powder. The PIA used to use silver-jacketed bullets, because they've got better muzzle velocity, but since they tend not to expand on contact, it ends up resulting in less damage. These rounds" — she took the Sig out and popped the magazine so I could see the silver cartridges lined up snugly inside — "are silver-coated nine-millimeter hollow points. Jacketed rounds will go right through a werecreature, which kind of defeats the purpose of shooting them with silver. A hollow point round, on the other hand, mushrooms when it strikes a soft target. It causes greater tissue damage, and more importantly, it keeps the silver in the creature's body, which is what actually kills it."

I nodded. Silver bullets were all the rage among gun collectors and people who took home protection to extreme lengths.

"You packing any silver?" Alice asked.

I shook my head. "I wasn't expecting to run into any were-critters tonight."

"Neither am I," Alice said. She closed the hatch and leaned against it with the shotgun cradled in her arms. "I don't know if this thing will turn out to be a shifter or not, but when it comes to silver bullets, I prefer to have them and not need them, than to need them and not have them."

On that note, we started walking along the edge of the clearing. Alice took the treeline side while I kept pace beside her. She held the shotgun loosely with the barrel pointed at the ground while her eyes scanned the trees. It was full dark and we didn't have flashlights, so I wasn't sure how much she could actually see. Every now and then she would stop abruptly in her tracks and stare into the shadow-choked depths of the woods. I would stop with her, one hand resting on the butt of my gun, waiting to see if something was going to happen. But nothing did, and we resumed walking.

When we reached the far side of the clearing, we did a slow circle around the Quonset hut, like two satellites orbiting a planet, then I hung back a bit while Alice moved toward the door with the busted hinge. After taking a quick look inside the building, she took one hand off the shotgun, grabbed the top of the door, and ripped it off its remaining hinge with a shriek of tortured metal.

That done, Alice raised the shotgun, seated the stock into the hollow of her shoulder, and stepped inside. I trotted up to the open doorway and watched as she moved across the length of the building. There were no lights inside and the only thing I could see was the slightly less dark rectangle which marked the other doorway at the far end.

For a moment, I thought Alice meant to go through the portal. If she did, she'd be making that journey alone. I had already signed on for more than I wanted to tonight. There was a line I wouldn't cross, and it was about thirty feet in front of me, even if I couldn't see it.

But Alice didn't cross over. She went about three-quarters of the way across the length of the Quonset, then turned around and came back.

"Okay," she said. "This area is as secure as we can make it. Let's get out of here."

Back in the SUV, Diane said: "Hey, you guys are still alive. That's awesome."

"My partner exaggerates," Alice said to me. "I would never put you in danger..."

"Ahem!" Diane interrupted.

"... unless it was absolutely necessary," Alice finished. She shot a glaring look at the dashboard speaker before turning back to me. "Being here is a risk, you know that and I know that, but it's also the right play. Our only play, really. If this thing turns out to be a creature from the Black Lands, the local cops won't be able to handle it."

"But we can?" I said.

"We have experience in these matters. That means we're better equipped to deal with them."

"I don't find that terribly reassuring." I pointed at her. "And if you tell me again that it's part of the job, then I'm outta here."

Alice gave a small shrug. "Well..."

"Go easy on him," Diane said.

"Mind your own business."

"Tell that to your other partners, Alice. Oh wait, you can't!"

My head swivelled back and forth between Alice and the dashboard speaker like I was watching a particularly intense tennis match. "What does that mean? What's she talking about?"

"Shut *up*, Diane."

"That's why I'm fifteen hundred miles away!" Diane shouted.

"You never leave your house!" Alice shot back.

"It's safer that way!"

Alice looked like she was about to say something more, maybe something worse, but instead she pressed her lips together and punched a button on the dash to terminate the connection.

WE SAT there in a silence that grew exponentially more uncomfortable the longer it went on. Eventually I said, "So how many partners have you had?"

Alice stared out the windshield without saying anything.

"Does this have something to do with whatever happened in Bermuda?"

Alice shook her head, but she looked more tired than angry. "You don't even know what you're talking about."

"I'm just saying we can talk about it if you want to. We could be sitting here all night."

"I appreciate the thought, but I think I'll pass."

I looked over at her. "You're not big on talking, huh?"

"No."

"Is that why you've gone through so many partners?"

Alice didn't say anything.

"Is that why your current partner is an agoraphobe who lives in Florida?"

"We fit each other well." Alice glanced at the dashboard screen. "Most of the time."

"So what was that about, then?"

Alice was silent for so long I didn't think she was going to answer me. Then she began to speak.

"Diane worries. Not so much about me, but about what happens to those around me. Collateral damage, I guess you'd call it. She thinks I take the work too seriously. 'Obsessed' is the word she likes to use. 'Committed' is what I prefer to call it. Diane does good work, and she knows more about the Black Lands than anyone else in the agency, but it's all theoretical to her. It's one of the disadvantages of never leaving her house." She raised her hand at the Quonset hut, or rather the portal inside it. "Take these creatures, for instance. Diane calls them 'supernaturals' or 'Black Lands entities.' That's how I may describe them in my own reports, but to me they're nothing but monsters. That's it. They're walking, stalking nightmares. I don't want to tame them or teach them or find out what makes them tick. I just want to wipe them out."

"It's not just commitment to duty, though, is it?" I said. "You didn't join the PIA because you wanted to defend your country. You really hate them, don't you?"

Alice's eyes hardened and her voice took on a dreamy, faraway tone. "I do hate them. I don't deny that. I've never denied it."

"What happened? Did they do something to you?"

Alice shook her head like she was snapping herself out of a daze. Her eyes remained focused on the Quonset hut. I could feel her looking through its corrugated steel walls to the portal inside, and through it to the Black Lands beyond.

"Not to me," she said in the same softly distant voice. "To someone else. Someone who doesn't exist anymore."

I could tell I wasn't going to get anything more from her on that subject, so I decided to switch tracks. "Is that why we're out here alone?"

That got Alice's attention. She looked at me with a flicker of wariness in her eyes. "What do you mean?"

"I assume you've heard about the portal in Boston."

"Of course."

"It was discovered the morning I left for Sycamore. The police had only just found it, but the whole area was already cordoned off. This portal" — I nodded through the windshield at the Quonset hut — "isn't across the street from a place like Fenway Park, but I still figured the PIA would've locked it down by now. But so far, nothing. No barriers, no barbwire fence, no STAR team keeping watch. Not even a no-trespassing sign. It's almost like you didn't even call them." I was watching her as I spoke, looking for some sort of reaction, but her face was a blank slate. "That got me thinking about things — like, for one, what am I even doing here? I'm not a PIA agent, and from my own experiences with the agency, they don't like taking help from outsiders, much less ask for it. And yet here I am. Which makes me think this isn't about me. It's about you. So I feel like I have to ask the question: are you on the outs with the agency?"

Alice continued to stare at me for a long moment. Then she said, "Do you know what a floater is?"

I shook my head.

"A floater is an agent with no fixed job assignment. They work out of one field office for a few months, maybe a year, then they're moved to another one." She turned her head away from me and stared out the side window. "I'm a loner, always have been, and I work for an organization that prides itself on unity and teamwork. Yes, I've had a few partners, and yes, some of them have been... injured in the line of duty, but I never hurt them, and I never put them in harm's way. I was just..."

"A loner."

"Over time I developed a reputation as someone who wasn't a 'team player,' which in the agency is synonymous with 'dangerous.' Eventually no one wanted to work with me, which was fine because I didn't want to work with them. I just wanted to *work*. The agency was ready to kick me out, and they would have if not for one teensy little problem."

"What's that?"

Alice turned and locked eyes with me. "I'm very, very good at what I do."

"And you're modest, too."

"The PIA has no use for a lone wolf, but they also didn't want to get rid of one of their best monster hunters. So we made a compromise."

"Diane."

Alice nodded. "They gave me a partner who didn't work in the field — an agent who didn't even leave her own house. Someone who wouldn't get hurt working with me because..."

"She wouldn't really be *with* you," I finished.

"Yes," Alice said. "And since Diane has her own anti-social issues, it worked out for her, as well. She didn't have to leave the security of her home, or engage in close personal contact with someone — which for her is almost as bad as the agoraphobia. I was happy, Diane was happy, and the agency was... well, as happy as it ever gets." She lowered her eyes and a deep sigh came up out of her chest. "But my reputation as a loose cannon continues to follow me around. The agency's solution was to make me a floater. No one wants me around on a permanent basis, but they're totally fine with letting me make a special guest appearance every now and then. Especially if I can clear some of their cases and kill some monsters at the same time." She paused. "I think they're secretly hoping I get killed on one of these little tours of duty, then their Alice Baffle problem will solve itself. Diane keeps me grounded, though, and I like to think I do the same for her. And..." She paused again, a look of reluctance, possibly embarrassment, coming into her eyes. "... she keeps me alive. Most of the time we get along fine, but every now and then we grate against each other, and..." She gestured at the silent dashboard speaker.

"I'm sure Diane is a great agent," I said, "but what do you do when you need someone to back you up? When you need someone to literally watch your back?"

"Between GPS and satellite imaging, Diane is able to watch more than just my back."

"I guess when you put it like that."

"No offense, Felix, but after reading your file and then hearing about everything you've been through here in Sycamore, I'm surprised you're still alive."

"No offense to *you*," I said, "but your bedside manner kind of sucks."

"I speak plainly and honestly. Sometimes I can be brutally honest. I admit that, but I don't apologize for it."

"The truth hurts, is that it?" I gave her an assessing look. "With you, I bet it leaves scars."

"Maybe you're just too sensitive," Alice offered.

"Maybe," I said. "But I don't apologize for it."

Alice snorted with amusement. "Fair enough." She looked back at the Bluetooth speaker. "Diane and I are a good team. We respect each other's…"

"Weirdness?"

"Idiosyncrasies."

"So you were stationed at the Toronto field office when you got the tip about Sycamore?"

Alice nodded.

"That still doesn't explain why you haven't called a STAR team to secure the portal."

"Above all else, the PIA relies on discretion. If it gets out that a new portal has been discovered *and* a supernatural creature is on the loose, one that's responsible for a series of murders, that would reflect poorly on the agency."

"Pardon my French, but fuck the agency. There are people dying here. That's helluva lot more important than besmirching the good name of the Paranormal Intelligence Agency."

"It's not about giving the PIA a bad name," Alice said patiently. "It's about maintaining the illusion of security. People believe the PIA exists to protect them from the Black Lands. If they stop believing that, it could cause widespread panic."

"Then make the call and get them up here," I said impatiently.

"I can't," Alice said. "Not until I know for certain that something from the Black Lands is responsible for the murders."

"But we know it's a monster. You said…"

"The *computer* said," Alice overrode me. "No one has actually seen it. The only proof we have is some statistical data. We need real evidence to back it up. Diane agrees with me on this."

"Shouldn't we get back in touch with her, then. She said she's keeping an eye on the local police band. What if they get a call…"

"She can reach us if she needs to."

Alice reached into her inside coat pocket and took out a smartphone. At least I thought that's what it was. I'd never seen one quite like it before. It looked like a small, flat piece of obsidian.

"Swanky," I said. "Is it Japanese?"

"Custom PIA tech. Diane helped design it."

"That girl," I said. "Is there anything she can't do?"

"Leave her house."

"Good point." I held out my hand. "Can I look at it?"

"No."

We sat in silence for what seemed like a long time but was probably only a minute or two. Alice continued to stare out the windshield, her eyes fixed on the Quonset hut like she was worried it was going to grow legs and run away.

"So," I said, "do you want to tell me about what happened in Bermuda?"

"No."

"Does it have something to do with the Triangle?"

Alice looked at me. "You really don't understand the meaning of 'comfortable silence,' do you?"

I was opening my mouth to say something clever and amusing when Alice's phone rang, a high-pitched trill that sounded like the mating call of a mutant locust. She glanced at the screen and said, "It's her." She pressed a button on the dash that transferred the call to the speaker.

"Hey," Diane said.

"Hey," Alice said.

"Sorry," Diane said.

"Me, too," Alice said.

I beamed. "This is beautiful."

"Shut up," Alice snapped at me.

"I just meant that…"

Now my phone rang. Or rather it started pumping out the chorus of "My Humps." Which only increased the intensity of Alice's nuclear glare.

I held up my hand. "I know, I know. I'm going to change it."

"Who is it?" Diane said. "Do you have a partner, too, Felix?"

"Sort of," I said.

I answered the call. "Hey Sandra, what's up?"

"I'm sorry I hung up on you earlier," she said. "I hadn't heard from you in a couple days and I thought something might have happened."

"I'm alive," I said. "For now."

"What does *that* mean?" Sandra said. "What's wrong?"

"Nothing's wrong," I said. "Things are... good."

I glanced over at Alice. She gave me a warning look. "Don't mention me."

"Who's that?" Sandra said.

"Nothing," I said. "It was... the wind."

Alice lowered her head in disgust. Diane snickered.

"That doesn't sound like the wind. That sounds like a woman. Is it the librarian?"

"Actually, she's not a librarian. She's..."

"I said don't mention me," Alice hissed.

"She sounds bossy," Sandra said.

"Yeah, I guess I've got a type."

Alice said, "Fuck you" at the same time Sandra said, "Don't be an asshole, Felix." Diane was openly laughing now.

"How many women do you have over there?" Sandra said. "Who's that laughing?"

"That's Diane," I said. "I don't think Alice knows how to laugh."

Alice stared daggers at me while Diane continued to laugh.

"Who's Diane?" Sandra said. "One of your whores?"

"I don't call my whores by name. I have a complicated numbering system based on..."

"Save it, Felix. I called to apologize, but now I take it back."

"Dee, it isn't like that."

I glanced over at Alice. The daggers in her eyes had turned into cruise missiles. She gave a small, deadly shake of her head. *Don't do it.*

With the phone in one hand, I raised the other in a helpless gesture.

"The librarian I told you about? She's actually a federal agent working undercover here in Sycamore."

I pressed the speaker button on the phone and set it on the center console. "Dee, I'd like you to meet Agent Waffle of the PIA."

"*Baffle*," Alice growled.

"Nice to meet you," Diane said from the dash screen. "I'm Diane, Alice's partner."

"She works remotely," I said to Sandra. "Just like you, Dee."

Alice frowned at me. "Why do you keep calling her that?"

"Sandra Dee," Diane answered for me. "Isn't that right, Felix?"

I nodded, then realized Diane couldn't see that. "That's right," I said.

"I loved her," Diane said in a dreamy voice. "*Gidget.* 1959. Pretty much responsible for the start of the whole surfing culture in the United States."

"Yeah," Sandra said, "but I looked better in a bikini. No offense to the late Ms. Dee."

Diane made a loud gasping sound that caused Alice and I both to wince.

"That's right! You're Sandra Clifton," she said. "I read Felix's file, but I must have glossed over the part where he was married to a movie star."

"*Used* to be married," Sandra corrected her. "And I was never a star. What did you say your name was again?"

"Diane," she said, barely containing her glee. "I'm a *huge* fan. I've seen all of your movies."

Sandra said, "I feel so sorry for you," and Diane giggled like a schoolgirl. "But I'd rather be talking to you than some of broomheads I've met today."

"Where are you?" I said. Then I remembered. "Oh, you're at the horror convention."

"Which one?" Diane asked.

"BloodNGutz," Sandra said, with a tired sigh. "My agent insisted I come out to meet my adoring fans, and sign autographs and pose for pictures."

"Are you wearing the outfit?" I asked.

"What outfit?" Diane said.

"I'm pleading the fifth on that one, Felix. And if you bring it up again, I will kill you, chop you up into bite-size morsels, and feed you to my fish."

"I hate to break this up," Alice said, "but we've got a lot of work to do."

"Please, Alice," Diane said, "this woman is horror-movie royalty. Like in *Starry Night*, when you used the child's telescope to…"

"Diane," Alice said.

"Is it true that you're one of the only survivors of *The Iowa Barn Experience*? That movie was so scary I couldn't even…"

"Diane."

Listening to them go back and forth, I was reminded of when Sandra and I were married and the times she was approached in public by an overeager fan — usually a pale-skinned, avid-eyed neckbeard in a black T-shirt — who would stand there blubbering and gushing and staring at her like she was a steak sandwich. It was impressive to see the way Sandra's celebrity had such an effect on people, but it was also kind of unsettling. Sometimes even scary.

"It's okay," Sandra said. "My scream queen days were already long behind me by the time I married Felix. After that the only time I did any screaming was when he took off his clothes."

Diane laughed and even Alice let out a small snort.

"Okay!" I said. "Like Alice said, we got a lot of work to do. Good-bye!"

"Okay," Sandra said. "Try not to get killed. And bring back some money."

"It's like I'm still married," I said, and disconnected the call.

Alice said, "That was entertaining."

"I know," I said. "I almost saw you smile. Did it hurt?"

"Sandra Clifton," Diane said, her voice still breathy with awe. "I can't believe it. I…" She trailed off.

Alice stared at the speaker. "What is it, Diane?"

"Hold a sec," she said.

Alice shot me a questioning look. I shrugged. We looked across the clearing at the Quonset hut, but nothing was happening out there.

"Okay," Diane said. "I've got an incoming 911 call. And there's chatter on the local police band."

Alice started the engine. "Where?"

Diane gave us an address on Concession Road 8. "It's six miles away from your current location. That's well within the area of the last three murders. This could be our man."

"A man if we're lucky," Alice said, and dropped her foot on the gas pedal.

CHAPTER 32

THE SUV BLASTED down the dirt lane to the main road. Diane transferred the directions to the onboard GPS and a map appeared on the dashboard screen. A cheery electronic female voice said, "In fifteen meters, turn left onto Burnside Road."

Alice said, "Shut her up, Diane."

Diane said, "Check," and the computer voice shut up.

Alice made the turn onto Burnside Road, jerking the wheel hard enough to make the tires squeal and to slam me into the side of the door.

"Hold on," Alice said.

"Thanks," I said, rubbing my shoulder.

"Diane, tell me about the call."

"Report of an intruder at a residence," Diane said. Over the speaker we could hear the sound of her fingers tapping on a keyboard. "Dispatcher says the call was disconnected before she could get any more information." More tapping. "Attempts to reach the caller by phone have so far been unsuccessful."

I looked over at Alice urgently.

"I know, I know," she said, pressing the gas pedal all the way to the floor.

She flew through an intersection, ignoring the stop sign, and popped on the SUV's high beams.

"Keep your eyes open."

The road was unfolding before us in a blazing trail of light, but the view out the side windows was pure darkness with only the vague outline of fields and trees flashing by. "For what?" I said.

"Anything that doesn't look human."

Alice made a sharp turn onto a gravel road. She hit the gas again and we launched forward with the sound of tiny rocks rattling off the undercarriage. We passed a few houses on either side of the road, tiny oases of light amid all that impenetrable blackness.

"You're on Concession Road 8," Diane said in a voice eerily like the GPS robot. "You'll reach your destination in five hundred metres. Last house on the left. Two-two-one-four."

The SUV ploughed on through the night. Alice had a white-knuckled grip on the steering wheel. The glow from the instrument panel turned her face into a mask of harsh contrasts and jagged shadows. She was leaning forward as far as her seatbelt would allow, as if she thought it would make us go faster.

We passed a house on the left, then nothing for a while, then a house on the right. Out here in the country they were spaced far apart. I wondered if anyone else on the street knew what was happening at their neighbour's house. I wondered if—

Alice braked hard and snapped the wheel to the left. The SUV lumbered around, gravel crunching under its tires, then straightened out as she turned into a long rutted drive, almost clipping a mailbox on a wooden post.

"You're there," Diane said. "Be careful, Alice. You, too, Felix."

A small white bungalow materialized out of the night. There was a bright red F-150 parked next to it. At first I thought it was an emergency vehicle of some kind and that the cops had beaten us here. Then I saw it was just an ordinary pickup truck. We were on our own.

"Shouldn't we wait for the cops," I said. "You know, for backup?"

Alice reached into the back seat and picked up her shotgun. "You're my backup." She pushed the door open and hopped out. "Stay behind me."

I wondered if staying in the car would count as "behind her," then decided it was time to quit screwing around and face this thing. I grabbed hold of the door handle and pulled. There was a click as the latch released, then I stayed like that for a few seconds, gripping the handle and staring out the window. Alice was already on the front porch, banging on the door.

I let out a shaky breath and pushed the car door open. A blast of the night air came rushing inside, wrapping around me and penetrating through my coat to sink icy fishhooks into my flesh. I tried to slide out my seat, but I couldn't move. For a moment I thought the fishhooks were real and they were holding me in place, then I realized my seatbelt was still fastened. I slapped at the button with a numb hand until it released and the belt slid back into its housing. My entire body was cold and tight. My scalp felt two sizes too small and the skin on my arms and back was pebbled in gooseflesh. Fearflesh.

No, I told myself. *Don't think of it as fearflesh. It's armour.* My *armour. It will protect me against the night. Darkness is simply the absence of light. So basically I'm afraid of something that isn't even there. Fear is just the absence of courage. So get rid of the fear and let courage take its place.*

I didn't know where the words were coming from. It sounded like the rah-rah-go-team-go bullshit that Alice had tried to pump me up with earlier. Whatever it was, it seemed to work…at least a little bit. I felt a tingling in the tips of my fingers that sparked me into motion. I pushed myself out of my seat, swung the door closed, and started toward the house.

Alice was speaking to a tall, narrow-chested man who kept looking back over his shoulder as if he were an actor asking for lines from someone standing off-stage. He had one hand on the edge of the door like he was ready to slam it shut on a moment's notice. As I got closer, I saw his face was a pale stricken mask with wide fearful eyes that were rolling around wildly in their sockets. There was blood on his hands, still fresh enough to leave bright marks on the wooden doorframe.

The conversation ended just as I reached the porch. Alice said, "Come on," and headed off around the side of the house. I started to follow her, casting one final look at the man in the doorway. He leaned out to watch us go, opening the door wider and allowing me a quick glimpse inside his house.

I saw a woman crouched at the end of a hallway, her arms wrapped around a small girl in orange pajamas. Something was wrong with the girl's face. There were black marks on her cheeks like streaks of mud, and dark circles around her eyes like she was sporting a pair of shiners. I didn't see any blood on her, but the girl was sobbing uncontrollably, her small body quaking in her mother's arms.

I caught up with Alice in the backyard, a small island of trimmed grass surrounded by a sea of wild, untamed woods. Alice was crouched next to a tall elm with a series of narrow boards nailed to the trunk, ascending to a wooden fort built high up in the branches. A Canadian flag hung in one of the windows as a makeshift curtain.

Everything stood out in perfect clarity thanks to a security light on the back of the house. It was so bright that it felt like I was walking out onto a stage. The light was great for my nyctophobia, although it made the woods beyond its reach seem that much darker.

I went over to Alice and saw she wasn't crouching because she was trying to get the lay of the land or using the tree as cover. She was examining the body of a dead dog.

I couldn't tell what kind it was. I'm not great with dogs, but in this case it wouldn't have made a difference because it was no longer identifiable as anything that had once been living. In the harsh glow of the security light, all I could see was blood, fur, and mangled meat.

Alice touched the dog's head and said something too low for me to hear. Then she stood up with the stock of the shotgun resting on her hip. "They heard the dog barking and came out to investigate. Then they heard it screaming and saw…"

"Saw what?" I said. "Was it a man or a monster?"

"They didn't say. They're in shock."

I felt a case of that coming on myself. I reached under my jacket and took out my gun. The weight of it in my hand made me feel a bit better.

My eyes roved the trees, back and forth, trying to penetrate the darkness between them. I looked over at Alice and saw she was doing the same thing. Something intangible, some feeling or sense of intuition, seemed to pass between us.

"It's still here," Alice said. "I can feel it."

I nodded. I felt it, too.

Alice headed off to the left side of the yard. I stood and watched her go. "You're not going to tell me to wait here, are you?"

"No," she said. "Check the treeline on your side and we'll meet over there at the far end. Stay in the yard. Stay in the light."

She didn't need to tell me twice. I raised my gun in both hands and went off toward the right side of the yard, where the reach of the security light ended at a cluster of low bushes. There were dead leaves all over the ground; the rain of the past few days had turned them into a pasty mulch that squelched under my shoes.

I came up next to the bushes, then started walking along the edge of the yard, moving in a slow, sideways fashion so that I could keep my gun trained on the woods, while making sure I didn't trip over my own feet. I shot a quick look over my shoulder. Alice was on the other side of the yard, swivelling her shotgun back and forth as she peered into the trees. As I approached the back corner of the yard, I began to feel like this was a waste of time. Either the creature had already accomplished what it came here to do — killing the dog — or the security light had spooked it before it could break into the house and attack the people inside. Both scenarios ended with the creature heading for the hills. Or the portal. I turned back to Alice to suggest we should head back to Burnside Road.

She was gone.

I took a few steps to the side so I could see around the big elm tree, but she was really gone. The yard was empty except for the dead dog lying on the ground. I whisper-shouted, *"Alice."*

I looked back at the house, but the security light was so bright I couldn't tell if anyone was watching us from the windows. Where were the police? I wondered. Shouldn't they be here by now?

I desperately wanted to run back to the car. I wanted to call Diane and ask her what I should do. But I already knew what to do. I was here. I had forced myself to come out into the night. I told Alice I would back her up. I couldn't run out on her now.

I crossed the yard, giving the dead dog a wide berth, to the place where I'd last seen Alice.

I called out her name again, a little louder this time, but there was still no response.

I heard a rustling behind me and spun around, gun raised. The bushes at the back of the yard were moving, but I couldn't tell if it was from the wind or from… something else.

"Alice," I hissed.

I started over that way. Every step felt heavier than the last, like I was struggling through thick invisible mud. A cold sensation began to move up through my legs, spreading through my groin and filling my stomach with a chilly queasiness.

It was the fear coming back, trying to lock me up, trying to paralyze me, as if it knew I was moving away from the light. I tried to imagine Alice's presence next to me, calming me, reassuring me, telling me the dark was nothing to be afraid of. It was the things *in* the dark you had to watch out for. I raised my gun out and let it draw me forward like a dowsing rod.

I reached the spot where I'd seen the bushes moving. They were still now. I continued forward to the place where the glow from the security light ended. It was like standing at the end of the high board and looking down into deep, dark waters. I took a deep, bracing breath and stepped out of the light.

I WAS moving through the dark woods and it was okay. I was leaving the light further and further behind me and that was okay, too. I was tempted to turn around and look at it, reassure myself that it was still there, but I knew if I did that I'd blow out my night vision, and it was the only thing I had going for me now. Alice would be next to invisible in her all-black ensemble, but I was hoping to catch a glimpse of her red hair as I pushed through the scratchy branches and stepped around the thick tree trunks. But I saw nothing, nothing.

I heard a sound — not a rustle or a snap or any of the sounds one associates with disturbed nature. It was a low thump. Like something dropping on the ground. Nothing too heavy, or it would've been louder, but big enough to be heard. The trees messed with the acoustics, so I couldn't tell exactly where it came from, but I was pretty sure it wasn't behind me.

Another thump. Definitely not behind me.

There were two trees in front of me, one dead, the other alive. The dead one, a tall pine that had lost all its needles, leaned against the live one, a thick-trunked maple that had dropped most of its leaves. I stepped through the triangular gap between them, swinging my gun first to the left to cover the space behind the maple. No one there. Then to the left—

Someone was standing behind the pine tree.

I thought it might be Alice, and in that split second of hesitation the figure came rushing at me. It didn't make a sound as it crossed the small space between us, which only made it that much more startling. It was as if the darkness itself had taken on form and attacked me. I was bringing my gun around when it crashed into me. I pulled the trigger reflexively, but the shot went high. Then the ground slammed me in the back, and a flare went off in my head to go with the muzzle flash that dazzled my eyes.

I'm dead, I thought. Then: *No, I'm not. Dead people don't hurt this much.*

The shape towered over me. It didn't move, didn't even seem to breathe. A disembodied shadow cut out from the greater darkness of the night.

I tried to call out to Alice, but the body-slam to the ground had knocked the air out of me and all that came out was a thin tea-kettle whistle.

Hoisting myself up on my elbows, I began a slow, clumsy backward crab-crawl away from the shape.

It followed me with a slow, steady gait. Man or monster, I still couldn't tell what it was. My vision was a lava lamp of shifting white and black blobs.

My hand came down in a fibrous mass that felt like a tangle of dried worms. Roots from the dead pine, I realized. I went around it, and the shape followed.

Then two things happened, almost simultaneously.

First, I made it out of the woods and into the glow of the security light.

Second, my vision cleared and I could see what was standing over me.

It was a human being. Which should have made me feel better, but it didn't.

It was Doug Weaver.

CHAPTER 33

DOUG HAD SEEN better days. And better nights.

It was a wonder I recognized him at all. If Susan hadn't shown me all those photographs of him, I wouldn't have been able to reconcile her husband with the misshapen figure standing before me.

Doug's clothes were little more than rags — and so was the body underneath them. Whatever had ripped through his chambray workshirt and torn gaping holes in his blue jeans hadn't stopped there. His body was covered in a tic-tac-toe board of lacerations, some of them deep enough that I could see the dull gleam of bone.

Large chunks of flesh had been torn out of his right shoulder and right flank, and his throat had been ripped open to reveal gristly strands of muscle and tendon. His hands hung at his sides like two slabs of mangled meat. The flesh on his fingers dangled in stringy tatters, with jagged tips of bone protruding from the tips like knobby grey claws.

It was hard to assess the full extent of the trauma inflicted upon Doug Weaver's body. In addition to the dried blood and tissue damage, he was absolutely filthy. His face was covered in a mask of dirt and grime; his hair was a fright wig of coils and clocksprings; and the tattered remains of his shirt and pants were plastered with mud and wet leaves. It looked like someone had driven over him a couple of times with a riding lawnmower and then dragged his body through the woods for good measure.

It was no wonder I hadn't seen him until he was right on top of me. He was covered head-to-toe in natural camouflage.

He also smelled. It wasn't the sickly-sweet stench of bodily decay. This was a sharper scent, like a freshly-fertilized field. Ripe, pungent, almost chemical. Not the smell of growing things, or the smell of rotting things, but an odd combination of the two.

The only sign of life I could see in Doug Weaver, besides the fact that he was standing on his own two feet, was a dull red glow in his eyes. A reflection from the glow of the security light or was it something else? Something supernatural?

Lying there on the ground, waiting for him to fall on me with those nubby bone claws, it didn't seem to matter. Nothing seemed to matter. I didn't know if I was in shock or if this was what came from facing my fear, from confronting the literal monster in the dark. I didn't feel scared or much of anything, really. I was either cured or screwed.

I licked my lips and said, "Doug." It came out on a puff of white vapour. "I don't know if you can understand me, but…"

A gunshot rang out, unbelievably loud, cutting off my words and making me piss myself a little. Maybe more than a little.

Doug Weaver went spinning around — from what I first assumed was the impact of the shot. But he kept spinning until he was turned completely away from me, and then went loping off into the night.

Whatever state he was currently in — dead, alive, or somewhere in-between — he was *fast*.

I heard someone smashing through the brush, then Alice was suddenly crouching next to me, her Sig Sauer pointed into the dark woods.

"Did I hit him?" she said. "I can't see a damn thing out here."

"I don't know," I said. "I don't think so."

She looked down at me. "Are you injured?"

I stared at her like she'd spoken to me in Klingon.

"Are you injured?" she asked impatiently.

I looked down at myself, then shook my head.

"Get up," she said, standing up straight and holstering her gun. "We have to go."

I climbed to my feet, slapping dirt and wet leaves off the seat of my pants. "Back to the portal?"

"That's where it'll be headed," Alice said. "We need to get there first."

We dashed across the yard and the island of brightness thrown by the security light. Alice stopped to pick up her shotgun which lay next to the big elm. I almost asked her why she didn't use it to take the shot at Doug. We could have ended things right here and now. Then I remembered shotguns weren't much good at long distances, and she could have ended up hitting me as well.

We came around the side of the house, and the man Alice had spoken to earlier was standing on the porch. "What's happening?" he said. "I heard a shot."

"Get back in your house," Alice said as she climbed into the SUV. "Lock your doors. The police will be here any minute."

"I thought you were the police," the man said.

The little girl was standing behind him, peeking around one of her father's legs. In the light from the open door, I could see the marks on her face were streaks of black and white paint, and the orange pajamas was a tiger costume.

I climbed into the car and said, "What day is it?"

"Tuesday," Alice replied. "The thirty-first."

She started the engine, jerked the transmission into reverse, and peeled away from the house.

"Happy Halloween."

CHAPTER 34

A PAIR OF police cruisers flew past us with their sirens wailing and light bars flashing. They were followed closely by an unmarked Chevy sedan with what looked like Detective Helton behind the wheel, but it went by so fast I couldn't be certain.

There wasn't much traffic on these rural back roads, and I was expecting one or more of the cop cars to slam on their brakes and whip around and come after us. But no one did.

"Why didn't we wait for them?" I asked Alice. "We could've told Helton and the others what's going on. Even if they didn't believe me, they'd certainly believe you."

"Not necessarily."

"Why not? You're a federal agent."

"I'm a black sheep with a badge," Alice said. "And my reputation precedes me." She glanced over at me. "Just like yours."

"Helton is a local cop. He wouldn't know about your reputation."

"You'd be surprised."

Alice reached out and pressed a button on the dash.

"Diane, are you with us?"

"I'm here," she said from the speaker. "What's happening?"

"We made contact but it rabbited," Alice said. "Now we're headed back to the portal to cut it off."

"What was it?" Diane asked.

Alice looked to me for an answer.

"It was… Doug Weaver," I stammered.

"You're sure?" Diane said. "You recognized him?"

"He was filthy and messed up, but it was him."

"Dead or alive?" Alice asked.

"I couldn't tell." I looked over at her. "What are you thinking? Vampire?"
Alice shook her head. "No way."

"Why not?" I said. "He looked… undead. And he was strong. When he
slammed into me it was like getting hit by a truck. And the portal is only
a few miles from his house. How do we know a vampire didn't cross over,
attack him, and infect him?"

"Because Weaver wasn't attacked at home," Alice said. "He was attacked
in his truck, down by the lake. Which is further away from the portal."

"Nine-point-four miles," Diane said. "As the crow flies."

"Are you saying a vampire couldn't cover that distance?"

"Of course they can," Diane said. "But not without leaving a trail of
bodies in their wake."

I had to agree with her on that. Vampires weren't discrete. They were
hungry, bloodthirsty creatures with no thoughts beyond their next meal. The
more I thought about it the more unlikely it seemed that a vampire came out
of the portal on Burnside Road and made it all the way to Orchard Park to
kill Doug Weaver without slaughter a bunch of other people along the way.

"Another thing," Alice said. "There was blood all over the interior of the
truck. Vampires drink blood, they don't spill it. Even in a frenzy, they're not
that wasteful."

I nodded. "And the first two murder victims were buried. Vampires don't
do that, either."

"Exactly," Alice said. "Vampires are spree killers. They're not methodical.
They don't plan out their attacks. The murders in Sycamore have been taking
place over several months. When a vampire outbreak occurs, it happens fast,
and it's usually over in a matter of hours. A day or two tops."

"Vampires have sub-human intelligence," Diane said, "and they're from
a place where it's forever night. When they come to our world, they might
cause some trouble, kill some people, but more often than not they end up
dying before the PIA ever shows up."

"Because of the sun," I said.

Alice nodded. "The smarter ones might be able to find shelter for a day or two, but as Diane said, they're not too bright. They stay out too late one night hunting or someone uncovers their nest during the daylight hours and the sun cooks them. It's the main reason they've never been able to get a foothold in our world and overrun the planet."

"What about a zombie?" I said. "Doug looked pretty dead to me. Could his body have been reanimated?"

"Did you see how fast he took off?" Alice said. "The undead don't move like that. And contrary to what you might've heard, they're not known for attacking people. No, this is something else."

"Contamination?" Diane said.

"That's what I'm thinking," Alice said.

"Contamination?" I said. "You mean the Influence?"

Alice lifted her shoulder in a small shrug. "Sort of."

"Sort of? What the hell kind of answer is that?"

Alice ignored me. "Diane, I think it's time to make the call."

I perked up. "A STAR team?"

"Feel better?" Alice said.

"Yes," I said, easing back into my seat. "Yes, I do."

She turned onto a dirt lane. I hadn't been paying attention and it took me a moment to figure out where we were. Then I saw the Quonset hut.

"We're here," Alice said.

My good feeling evaporated.

CHAPTER 35

AS ALICE WAS maneuvering the SUV into roughly the same spot we'd been during our stakeout, I remembered another detail from my brief encounter with the shambling ghoul formerly known as Doug Weaver.

"His clothes were filthy."

"You're not exactly dressed great yourself," Alice said, glancing over. "I was going to say something earlier…"

"No, I mean he was covered in dirt. It was on his hands, his face, all over his body. And it was fresh."

Alice looked at me expectantly, one hand on the door handle. "So?"

"So if Doug Weaver was killed over a month ago, then why did it look like he was buried only yesterday?"

Alice's gaze drifted away for a moment, then came back to me. "The answer is obvious if you think about it." And with that, she climbed out of the SUV.

I sat there for a few moments, thinking, then looked across the clearing to the Quonset hut. The wind had risen and the grass — an ordinary green rather than the spectral silver of the field on the other side of the portal — was swaying like the waves of a turbulent sea. The stalks were tall enough that Doug Weaver could've been hiding out there if he was crouching down.

I climbed out and went around to the other side of the SUV. Alice had opened the back door and taken out her shotgun.

"He isn't just going back to the Black Lands after every murder," I said. "He's burying himself again each time."

Alice leaned the shotgun against her shoulder. "That would be my guess."

"But why?"

"It doesn't matter. What matters is he's not making it back to the Black Lands tonight. We're gonna stop him before he reaches the portal."

She opened the driver's side door and leaned in far enough to flick on the headlights. The twin beams cut across the clearing and pinned the Quonset hut in a stark white glare.

With the door still open, Alice said, "What's the status on that STAR team, Diane?"

"They're currently awaiting pickup in Toronto. CFB Trenton is scrambling a helicopter to get them to your location as soon as possible. There's nothing I can do about that, I'm afraid. The Toronto field office doesn't have a bird of its own."

"ETA?"

"Thirty-five, forty minutes."

That sounded like a long time, and from the look on Alice's face, I could tell she thought so, too.

Diane must've read the concern in her partner's silence. "They'll still get to you faster than if they came by land."

"Okay," Alice said. "Fine."

From the tone of her voice, I could tell it was anything but fine. But like Diane said, there was nothing to do about it now.

I followed Alice around to the back of the SUV. She opened the hatch and took out a large duffel bag. She tossed it to me and I slung the strap around my shoulder so it hung on the side opposite of the one where my gun rode my hip. Then we headed off across the field with the headlights shining on our backs, drawing our shadows out long and skinny before us.

We went around to the far side of the Quonset hut, where the headlights couldn't reach. Alice scanned the treeline with her inscrutable gaze, then said, "Open the bag."

I did as she asked — or ordered, rather — and found the duffel was full of glow sticks.

"Get crackin'," she said. "I'll cover you."

It took me a second to figure out Alice was making a joke — or at least her version of one. The sticks worked by cracking the glass capsule inside so that a couple of substances mixed and, through a chemical reaction, gave off a bright green glow.

With the strap still looped over my shoulder, I dug into the bag, grabbed a handful of sticks, and started cracking. I tossed the sticks around and the darkness began to fill with a ghostly green luminescence.

Alice used her shotgun to point out where she wanted more light. "Keep them on this side of the treeline," she said. "If you throw them too far, they're no good to us."

When I was done there was still a dozen or so glow sticks in the bag and the dark side of the Quonset hut wasn't so dark anymore.

"What do we do now?" I asked.

Alice nodded at the doorway of the hut. We went over, past the door she'd ripped off its remaining hinge, and peered inside. There was nothing to see; it was even darker in there than it was outside. Alice threw the shotgun to her shoulder and went inside. I followed her and immediately started cracking glow sticks and tossing them around.

"Make sure you get them in the corners," Alice said. "We don't want to give him any place to hide."

As the inside of the hut began to fill with a witchy green light, I noticed Alice had taken a position about halfway down the length of the building. She wasn't panning her shotgun around like she had done outside. She had it pointed at a spot a few feet from the other doorway — right at the invisible portal.

When I was down to my last glow stick, I cracked it and held it up in front of my face, watching the chemicals mix and brighten. It looked like a cartoonish plutonium rod, the kind Homer Simpson was always dropping at the nuclear plant. I gave it a sidearm toss and watched it bounce and roll across the ground, past where Alice was standing… and then disappear.

"If you want that one back, you'll have to go get it yourself."

"Let's wait outside," Alice said. "It's too tight in here. I want to be able to see him coming."

We left the hut and walked across the field to the dirt lane that led back to Burnside Road. We stood there and looked at the Quonset hut, lit up on one side by the SUV's headlights, and on the other by the glow sticks.

Alice stood with her shotgun cradled in her arms, her eyes tracking slowly back and forth like a security camera. She seemed quite at ease, almost serene.

I, on the other hand, was fighting a powerful urge to run to the SUV and haul ass back to the city.

There were three reasons why I didn't. One, I was fairly certain Alice would track me down and staple my balls to a wooden plank and hang them on the wall of her den. Two, even though I had managed to find Doug Weaver, the case couldn't be properly closed until I reported to his wife on his final outcome. And three, perhaps most important of all, I felt like I was finally getting on top of my fear of the dark, and I didn't want to nullify the progress I'd made so far.

The fear wasn't completely gone, but I was able to push it back to a distant corner of my mind, the way the headlights and the glow sticks had pushed back the darkness of the night. I wasn't cured, not by a long shot, but I was starting to be able to manage it. I didn't know if it would ever go away entirely, but there was one thing I did know for certain: leaving now would make the fear come back. It might even make it worse.

So I waited. And then I waited some more. I checked the time, but it didn't mean anything because I couldn't recall how long it had been since Diane had made the call to scramble the STAR team. I figured it had taken about twenty minutes to disperse all of the glow sticks, so that meant we had another twenty minutes or so to wait. Since the STAR team was coming in by chopper, we would hear them before we saw them.

I was about to give myself a mental pat on the back for being so brave when a disturbing thought slid insidiously into my mind. I didn't want to give voice to it, maybe because I didn't want to consider the series of actions that would undoubtedly follow, then found myself blurting it aloud.

"What if we didn't beat him back?"

Alice turned to me and said, "What?"

"What if Doug made it here before we did and he already went back through the portal?"

Alice considered that possibility for about a tenth of a second, then said, "No way. He's not that fast."

"He seemed pretty spry to me."

"Diane said it was six miles to the portal. There's no way he could have…"

"Six miles *by car*," I amended. "If he came straight here, cutting through the woods and fields…"

Alice continued to stare, but I knew she wasn't seeing me anymore. She was seeing possibilities. Horrible possibilities. Her quarry slipping through her fingers. The STAR team showing up only to be told that the monster had gotten away. Having to report this failure to her superiors. The same ones who didn't want her in the agency and were looking for a reason to kick her out.

I saw all this playing out on her face. The doubt and the dread tightening her features — her brow clenching, her eyes sharpening, her mouth narrowing.

I knew what she wanted to do, and I was already shaking my head.

"Forget it, Alice. There's no freaking way."

"We have to cross over," she said. "We can't let him escape."

"Listen to yourself," I said. "If he made it to the Black Lands, then he's already gone. He has a whole other world to hide in over there. We'll never find him."

"If we missed him, then we only just missed him. We still have time to—"

"Get ourselves killed?" I said. "Thanks, but I'll pass on that."

Alice muttered something under her breath that sounded very much like "chickenshit."

I took a step toward her. "Maybe I am, but I'd rather be a chickenshit than someone with a death wish. What's your problem? If he made it back to the Black Lands, why not wait for the STAR team and go over there with some backup? What the hell are you trying to prove?"

Alice gave me a withering look and went marching off toward the Quonset hut.

I RAN back to the SUV and hopped into the driver's seat. "Diane," I said to the dash speaker, "I just thought you should know. Your partner is a fucking lunatic."

"And?" she said.

"And she just went through the portal."

Diane made a clicking sound with her tongue. "That's a problem."

"This is about her bad blood with the agency, isn't it? Because she gets her partners killed."

"Only one of them got killed," Diane said. "And that was really his own fault. Another one got kidnapped, and another broke his leg, but there were no other fatalities."

"Is that supposed to make me feel better?"

"It's supposed to help you understand her better," Diane said. "Alice has one of the highest clearance rates in the agency, and she's eliminated more supernatural entities than almost any other agent. She's just not exactly a people person. She's still learning what it means to be part of a team. The thing you have to understand about Alice is that she'll do anything in her power to eliminate a supernatural. This is more than a job for her. It's a compulsion. An obsession."

"Why?" I said. "Why is she like this?"

"I... I don't know."

"Bullshit. You're supposed to be this master hacker and you're telling me you never took a peek at your partner's personnel file?"

There was such a long moment of silence that I thought Diane had broken the connection. Then she said, "I honestly can't say, Felix. I'm sorry."

Which wasn't the same thing as saying she didn't know. But I decided to ignore it. "How long before the STAR team arrives?" I asked.

"Seventeen minutes."

"Is there anything I can do?"

"You have to go after Alice," Diane said. "You have to back her up."

"She doesn't want me."

"No," Diane said, "but she *needs* you."

I STILL had the empty duffel bag looped around my shoulder. I pulled it off, dropped it on the ground, and took my gun out of its holster.

I went around to the front of the SUV, stood for a moment in the blazing headlights, then started trudging toward the Quonset hut.

At the entrance, I raised my gun in both hands and stepped across the threshold. The building was filled with swampy green light from the glow sticks scattered on the ground. The portal was somewhere up ahead, and since there was no sign of Alice, that meant she had already crossed over.

I inched forward with small steps like I was approaching the edge of a cliff. Only in this case I would never be able to tell where the land fell away. Here I could only guess.

But that wasn't entirely true. Recalling something from when Alice and I were in here earlier, I crouched down and picked up a couple of the glow sticks. I threw the first one ahead of me, but it flew funny out of my hand and went spinning away into the corner. The second one I threw too lightly and it rolled only a few feet across the ground. I picked it up and threw it again, more forcefully this time.

The glow stick flew through the air, bounced on the ground end over end, landed on its side and rolled for a bit, then vanished. Like it had simply blipped out of existence.

It was hard to judge the distance even with the light from the glow sticks, but I determined the portal was about fifteen feet directly in front of me.

I picked up another glow stick and gave it an underhand toss. I followed it with my eyes as it went twirling through the air. It disappeared before it hit the ground.

I walked up to the edge of the portal. I knew where it was. No more glow sticks. No more excuses.

"Do it." I gripped my gun tighter. "You fucking coward. Just do it."

I didn't want this new fear. I never asked for it. The Black Lands had given it to me.

It was time to give it back.

I stepped through.

THE WORLD became dark again.

Of course it wasn't my world, and it was always dark over here. The shift between the lament green glow of the Quonset hut to the pitch darkness of the Black Lands was instantaneous and unspectacular. There was no flash of light, no queasiness or light-headedness, no feeling whatsoever that I had stepped from one dimension into another.

I was back in the field of silver grass. It looked pretty much the same as the last time I was here. Then I glanced down and saw something different, something that took me completely by surprise. Something so unusual and out of place that for a moment I wasn't sure if it was real.

It was an arrow.

It had been drawn in bright orange spray paint on the tramped-down grass right in front of my feet. It was pointed at the spot where I was standing. Or, more specifically, the portal directly behind me.

Alice must have done it. Not now but when she crossed over the first time, after I had told her about the portal. I looked around for her but she was nowhere within my limited range of sight.

Under normal circumstances — which was to say, in the normal world — I would have started calling out her name until she heard me and came running. In the Black Lands, however, this was the fastest way to get myself killed by any supernatural creature that happened to be within earshot.

Instead, I crouched down until only my head and shoulders were above the level of the grass, then I began to make my way forward through the field, hunched over and stomping down the stalks to create a path that would lead me back to the orange arrow and the portal.

I was breathing faster and the smell of the place filled my nostrils, reminding me of the last time I was here. The stagnant swampy smell that was almost like our world, and yet not quite the same. It was a riper scent, like a farmer's field in June, although it was hard to believe anything good could grow in a place that gave birth to blackwood trees and supernatural monsters. Even things from our world were corrupted by this place, as if through some strange version of cross-pollination.

For some reason, my thoughts turned to something Susan had told me when we first met. I'd asked her about the sycamore trees and she said there weren't any in town, not anymore, that they'd died off years ago from disease. But the city council was talking about bringing them back.

I came to a stop at a place where the grass had been pressed down by some recent traffic and was now starting to spring back upright. I continued forward and spotted something off to the right that disturbed the perfect levelness of the grass. I turned in that direction, continuing to leave a trail of flattened grass in my wake.

I pushed through a veil of swaying silver stalks, and there it was.

Doug Weaver's grave. Or his nest. Or both.

The low ebb of fear I was experiencing was replaced with a feeling of deep sadness. It was fitting in a way, seeing as I was standing next to someone's grave. But I wasn't even thinking about Doug Weaver and what had happened to him in this place. I was thinking about Susan. Having to tell her that her husband was dead was bad enough; how would she react when I told he had come back from the dead and was responsible for the murders in town? What would happen when it got out that she was married not just to a serial killer, but to a monster from the Black Lands? It sounded like the sort of thing you saw on a tabloid headline, only in this case it was real. It was real and it was tragic and so utterly unfair that I wanted to cry out at the wrongness of it all. Cry out or just plain cry.

My sadness had turned so abruptly to rage that when the hand touched my shoulder, I ended up doing the former.

I cried out — long and loud — giving vent to all the anger and frustration I'd been holding in since I'd taken on this case.

Another hand clamped over my mouth, but it was too late. The damage was done.

Both hands gripped me by the shoulders and swung me around, and of course it was Alice, and of course she was pissed off. Still holding onto me, she gave me a hard shake and said, "What's wrong with you? Are you trying to get us killed?"

I thought that was pretty rich coming from her, but decided this wasn't the time for ironic observations. I gestured with my gun at the empty grave. "He's not here."

Alice bent down and picked up her shotgun from where she had laid it on the ground. "Brilliant observation, Detective. Did you follow me all the way to another dimension just to tell me that?"

"I came to back you up." The words sounded strange coming out of my mouth.

Alice must have thought so, too, because she looked at me with something like... well, it wasn't admiration, and it was a far, *far* cry from respect, but it was definitely somewhere in the vicinity of appreciation.

She said, "Okay," which was probably as close to "thank you" as she was going to get. Then: "Is the STAR team here?"

"Not yet."

Alice glanced around. "Weaver isn't here. I don't think he beat us back to the portal, after all."

"You really think he'll come back here?"

"This is his home now," Alice said. "This is where he was born. Or reborn."

We stood there for a long moment, contemplating that. Then I said, "Can we get the hell out of here now?"

Alice said, "Fine," and we started back along the path I'd cut through the field. When we came to the orange spray-painted arrow, I pointed at it and said, "Very clever. Wish I'd thought of that."

"This isn't my first rodeo," Alice said.

I made a sweeping gesture at the invisible portal. "After you."

Alice jerked her chin at me. "Ladies first."

I shook my head sadly. "I'm not going to point out that you're using your own gender as an insult."

I stepped through the portal.

Alice came through a second later, bumping into my back.

"What the hell?"

I pointed at the far end of the Quonset hut. Something was crouched in the doorway, bathed in the green light of the glow sticks.

Alice was right. We didn't beat Doug Weaver back to the portal.

He was here.

CHAPTER 36

I DIDN'T FREEZE up. Give me that much credit.

When Doug came charging toward us, I raised my gun and snapped off three quick shots. Alice was yelling something, but her voice was drowned out by the loud reports that were made even louder in the closed confines of the building.

All three shots struck Doug... and affected him not a whit.

They didn't seem to hurt him, and they definitely didn't slow him down. He kept barreling toward us, arms and legs pumping, the remains of his shirt fluttering behind him like a tattered windsock.

Perhaps the most disturbing aspect about him was his face, which was completely expressionless. There was no visible strain from his exertions, no clenched teeth or furrowed brow, and no look of murderous intent in his eerie red eyes. His face was as blank as the walls of the Quonset hut.

I tried to move out of the way, but it was like trying to sidestep a speeding freight-train. I managed to avoid the full impact of Doug's charge, but he still clipped my shoulder hard enough to send me spinning to the ground.

Behind me, Alice let out a squawk that was abruptly cut off, and when I looked around for her, she was nowhere to be found.

As I climbed to my feet, I discovered I'd lost my gun. A quick look at the ground around me showed it wasn't anywhere close by.

Doug was in the far corner, head slumped down like a kid who'd been told to stand there for being bad. He didn't make a sound. He didn't hiss or growl or recite the Oath of Allegiance. I was also pretty sure he wasn't breathing, which only further confirmed that he was now a member of that class of unfortunate individuals known as the Undead. He simply stood there, motionless as a machine that had been shut down for the night.

I should be so lucky.

Another glance around the inside of the building confirmed that Alice was nowhere in sight. If she wasn't here, then there was only one other place she could be. After Doug knocked me over, he must've ploughed right into Alice and knocked her back through the portal.

I would have gone after her. Despite my reluctance to return to the Black Lands yet again, the thought of leaving her over there was less appealing than taking on Doug Weaver all by myself.

I was scrambling back to my feet when Doug turned out of the corner and came toward me, slower this time but no less menacing. His arms were raised before him, his decaying hands clenching in anticipation of choking me to death, or maybe ripping my throat out.

I looked around frantically for my gun, but all I could see were glow sticks, dozens of them scattered all over the ground. I might have been able to find it if I'd been willing to take my eyes off Doug for more than a second, but I knew that would be a bad idea.

With nothing else left to do, I held my hands out in a calming gesture and tried my best to communicate with Undead Doug.

"I don't know if there's anything human left in there, but if there is, this would be a great time to see it."

I wasn't sure what I expected him to do, clomp his foot on the ground twice for yes, or mutter a few fragmentary words like some latter-day Frankenstein's monster. He didn't do either of those things. He just kept coming slowly toward me.

He reached the point between me and the portal, so I didn't have any choice now but to leave Alice to fend for herself in the Black Lands. I wondered why she hadn't immediately come back across. Maybe Doug had hit her harder than me and she was lying over there, stunned or possibly even unconscious.

There was nothing I could do for her now, so I started edging toward the main entrance, shooting quick looks behind me to make sure I didn't step and slip on any of the glow sticks. Doug continued to follow me at his own steady pace, arms stretched out like he was sleepwalking. I strained to hear the sound of helicopter rotors chopping the night sky.

One of the times I looked over my shoulder, I noticed something that gave me a small surge of hope. Not my gun, but something that could still help me. Leaning against the nearby wall was the shovel I'd seen the first time I came out here. I changed course slightly and picked it up, holding it out before me like a sword, feeling both relieved and ridiculous.

When I reached the entrance, I made sure to high-step over the bottom part of the doorway so I didn't trip on it and fall on my ass. I looked toward where the SUV was parked, its headlights still blazing. I estimated my chances of making it inside before Doug was on me and decided it didn't matter even if I did. Alice had the keys, and it would only be a matter of time before Doug smashed his way inside and tore me to pieces the way he'd done to his other victims.

I made a decision then. I'd have to put Doug down myself.

He was the reason I'd come to Sycamore, and in a way he was my responsibility. Susan had asked me to find his body, and I did. But I knew this wasn't what she had intended. Just as I'm sure Doug didn't intend this fate for himself, either. This existence wasn't natural. It was an offense, not just to his life, but to all life. It was an aberration, an abomination — the very antithesis of life. And it had to be destroyed.

I didn't know if I could do it, if such a thing was even possible to someone who was undead, but I had to try. At the very least I had to immobilize him in some way until the STAR team arrived. Gripping the wooden handle of a dirt-encrusted shovel, I thought that might be easier said than done.

As I took another look toward the SUV, a plan began to formulate in my mind. It was not a great plan, or even a good one, but it was better than the no-plan I'd had a second ago. And even if it didn't work it would at least buy me some time.

Working with the little I knew about Black Lands entities, I circled around to the side of the Quonset hut and put my back to the headlights so they wouldn't blind me. I didn't think they'd blind Doug, either, but if he really was a supernatural creature now, he might not like the intense brightness of the SUV's high beams. It wouldn't hurt him, but it might give me the edge I needed to get the drop on him.

I stood at the corner of the building, with my shadow painted in wobbly lines across the corrugated metal wall. I needed Doug to follow me over here, right to this exact spot, so I banged the head of the shovel against the wall a few times, producing a loud clanging sound. The sound of a dinner bell, I hoped, although I didn't know if the new-and-not-so-improved Doug Weaver actually ate any of his victims. Nor did I want to know at that particular moment.

I heard him before I saw him — the low whisper of his legs cutting through the tall grass. Then his head and left arm appeared around the corner. I swung the shovel in an overhand arc, striking him solidly between his neck and shoulder and driving him to the ground. His left knee shot out to support him while his right leg folded like an old lawn chair, leaving him in an awkward kneeling position.

Before he could get up, I hit him again, a horizontal blow this time, twisting from the waist to get all my weight behind it. If I had struck him with the blade side of the shovel, I might have taken his head clean off, but I hit him with the flat head instead, producing a loud *THONK!* and knocking him onto his side.

Doug didn't make a sound the entire time, which on the one hand was kind of unnerving, but on the other made me feel at least a little better about beating an unarmed man with a shovel.

He lay still for several moments, and I thought maybe I'd done it, maybe I'd managed to beat him into submission. All I needed to do now was stand fast until the STAR team arrived and they could take things from here.

Then, moving stiffly, mechanically, Doug extended an arm and propped himself upright. I gripped the shovel and waited. Doug raised his head and peered at me with his red, expressionless eyes. I stared into them, momentarily mesmerized, then clenched my teeth and swung the shovel.

Doug caught it.

I had been aiming for the top of his head, intending to split his skull wide open, when his arm flew up with a speed that, like everything else about him, was completely unnatural. His hand closed around the top of the shaft, and with a sharp snap of his wrist, he broke off the head of the shovel and dropped it to the ground.

I was left holding a short piece of wood with a jagged tip. Doug began to climb ponderously to his feet, moving with a slowness that belied the speed with which he'd caught the shovel. Gripping the broken handle, I decided to find out if he wasn't a vampire after all.

I raised my makeshift stake high over my head and brought it down with all my strength. Doug came rising up at the same time, as if eager to meet this new threat head-on. Or chest-on, since that's where I was aiming. The handle's jagged tip punched through his sternum with a meaty crack and continued through to the spot where I was pretty sure his heart was located. Either I was off-mark or Doug wasn't a vampire, because it didn't have the desired effect of killing him. In fact, it seemed to have no effect whatsoever.

The force of the blow drove Doug back a few steps. He still didn't make any sound and the blank look on his face never changed. The only thing different about him now was that he had a three-foot piece of wood sticking out of his chest.

I didn't know what else to do. I was out of ideas — and weapons. All I could do now was beat a hasty retreat.

And that was when Doug Weaver's preternatural speed returned and his hand whipped out and closed around my throat.

He caught me in mid-breath, shutting off my air so quickly and abruptly that I didn't have the chance to suck in any more. I choked instead and beat at his arm, his chest, his face, all to no effect. It was like being strangled by a statue. His grip was cold as marble and strong as a vice. He tightened his hold and my vision began to dim and darken around the edges.

I clasped onto Doug's arm like it was a chin-up bar and stared into his eyes, looking for pity or understanding or even malice, any human emotion whatsoever, but there was nothing in there, not even the dull red glow I'd seen earlier. His eyes were black pits and I was falling into them. The darkness was overtaking my vision, like ink dumped into a pitcher of water. I felt my strength dissipating along with my air, and my eyes began to flutter rapidly. What happened next I saw in a series of jittery jump-cuts like a poorly edited film.

First: Doug pulling me closer, his other hand raised, finger-bone claws poised.

Then: A flash of movement like a black lightning bolt.

Then: Doug's head snapping to the side.

Then: Doug on the ground, lying on his side, his hand still wrapped around my throat.

Then: A boot descending from above, stepping on Doug's wrist.

And finally: A concussive blast of sound and light, loud enough to obliterate all other sounds, and bright enough to send the darkness overtaking my vision flying back to the corners of my eyes.

As I blinked myself back to proper consciousness, I saw the boot come off Doug's wrist, then plant itself against my side. A powerful kick sent rolling into the tall grass. I ended up on my back, heaving air into my wasted lungs. I reached up to my throat and Doug's hand was still there, just his hand, clasped around neck. I pulled it off and threw it away as I scrambled to my feet.

Alice was standing over Doug Weaver, much as I had done after hitting him with the shovel. She'd had much better results with her shotgun, striking him on the side of the head with the stock, and then blasting his arm off at the elbow.

Now she backed up a few steps as Doug began to rise once more to his feet, using his remaining arm and the stump of the other to push himself up.

Alice called over to me. "You alive?"

I nodded and rubbed my throat. "Is he?" I asked in a gravelly voice.

Alice looked down at Doug, still struggling to get up. "I'm not sure what he is," she said in a ruminative voice.

Then she racked the slide on her shotgun and shot him in the chest at a distance of about five feet. The blast lifted him off his feet and sent him flying backwards. He landed flat on his back, arms and legs spread wide, crushing the grass beneath him in a star shape that made me think of snow angels.

Alice took a step forward, shotgun balanced on her hip, and looked down at Doug.

"Huh."

I came up beside her. "Huh what?"

"He's not bleeding."

"Should he be?"

"I'm not sure. When we figured out the killer was probably a monster, I thought we were dealing with a possessor — a demonic entity that had taken over Weaver's body."

"They tend to take better care of their hosts, don't they?"

Alice nodded. "Which made me think maybe he really was a vampire. Only he wouldn't have taken off running just because I shot at him." She jerked her chin at the figure lying prone on the ground. "And vampires bleed."

"So what is he?"

"It was the dirt that got me thinking," Alice said. "The dirt and the…"

Doug bolted upright like a rake left in the grass that someone had stepped on. The front of his shirt was ripped to shreds from Alice's shotgun blast, and the skin underneath was black and pockmarked with buckshot. He started to get up.

"Give me a break," Alice said. "This guy's like the undead Energizer Bunny."

She racked the shotgun and fired, hitting him in the chest again and sending him back down like a target in a carnival shooting gallery.

Alice turned and tossed me the shotgun. I wasn't expecting it but managed to catch it without blowing my head off.

"If he gets up again, give him another dose. There are two shells left in the breech."

"Where are you going?" I yelled as Alice trotted over to the SUV. I saw the rear hatch come up, then I turned my attention back to Doug. He was still lying on the ground. The shotgun blasts had stunned him for a few moments, but didn't seem to cause any actual damage. I glanced over at the severed hand that had been wrapped around my throat a few moments ago. I half-expected to see it crawling through the grass toward me, but it wasn't moving at all. I looked back at Doug and he was sitting up now. I called out, "Alice!"

"Be there in a sec!" she called back like I was only summoning her to dinner.

Doug was climbing awkwardly to his feet. Behind me, I heard the click of the SUV hatch closing and the sound of Alice cutting back through the field toward me. I turned to her and my mouth fell open.

She was carrying an ax.

"Hit him again," she said.

I was still staring at the ax. "What are you doing with that?"

"Hit him again," she repeated. "Or I can do it and you can chop off his head."

"Chop off his *what?*"

Alice blew out an impatient breath and dropped the ax on the ground. She took the shotgun from me and fired into Doug's chest for a third time. He dropped back down. Alice gave me back the shotgun, shoving it into my not-exactly-waiting arms, and picked up the ax again.

She went over to Doug and looked down at him. "He's not coming back from this, Felix. There's nothing to do now but put him down for good." She gripped the ax tightly in both hands and raised it high over her head.

"May he rest in peace."

She swung.

CHAPTER 37

WE HAD ALMOST finished wrapping Doug's body in a plastic tarpaulin when we heard the sound of the helicopter coming in.

I looked down at the body while Alice watched the sky. I didn't bother to ask if the decapitation was necessary. It clearly was. Doug didn't get up again after Alice had taken off his head. It had required a few chops with the ax, but I couldn't bring myself to watch after the first one. When she was finished, Alice had tucked Doug's head under his arm like he was carrying a basketball, then went to get the tarp from the back of the SUV.

I was trying to decide if I had failed him and his wife when Alice spoke. "Seems anticlimactic, doesn't it?"

I looked over at her. "What?"

She nodded at Doug in his plastic cocoon. "You come up against something from the Black Lands, the very essence of the supernatural, and you can't reconcile it with anything else you know. You try to make sense of it, but it's like moving a piece of furniture through a door that won't fit. It doesn't matter how much you turn it, or how hard you push on it, it just won't go. You start to think maybe it isn't supposed to fit. Not in your mind. Not in our world. Some feel the need to think of it as something else, like 'evil,' because that makes sense to them. If there's good in the world, then there must be evil, right?" She shook her head. "But there's no evil here. There's just a man who got caught up in forces bigger than him. Forces he couldn't control any more than you or I could if we were in his place. Forces that ended up controlling him. Whatever he became, whatever the Black

Lands turned him into, it wasn't his fault. But he had to be stopped, and we were the ones who had to do it."

"If that's your version of a pep talk, I think you need to work on it."

"I just don't want you to carry any of this afterward."

"This isn't my first rodeo either, Alice. I've killed supernatural creatures before. Just not like this."

Alice gave me a look like she was trying to understand what I meant. Which was fine since I was doing the same thing.

The only way I could explain it was that the monsters I'd killed before had all come from the Black Lands, and there were never any doubts, much less any guilt, about what I was doing when I dispatched them. This wasn't even the first time I'd killed a monster that used to be human, although I did find that harder to reconcile. Maybe even more so in this case since the monster in question was the husband of a client.

The appearance of the helicopter over the tops of the trees allowed me to put these thoughts away, at least for the time being. But I knew I'd come back to them sooner rather than later. There was something else that troubled me on a whole other level, one I couldn't quite reach yet.

The helicopter was a big camo-green Chinook. The propwash from its tandem rotors whipped the tall grass around like an angry green sea as it descended. It landed on the far side of the field, away from the Quonset hut and Alice's SUV. The rear loading ramp lowered to the ground and half a dozen men came rushing out in single file. Alice went over to meet them. I followed.

The men wore black hard-shell body armour, steel helmets, and night-vision goggles. STAR was printed in stark white letters across the front of their ballistic vests. They each carried an MP5 submachine gun that they pointed at various parts of the surrounding woods as they took up positions around the clearing. One of the men approached us, flipping up his goggles as he came over. He looked like all the others, anonymous in his STAR uniform, except for his eyes, which were an icy blue.

"I'm Lieutenant Markowitz," he said. "You Agent Baffle?"

"That's right." Alice gave him a quick flash of her ID, then turned and pointed at the plastic-wrapped bundle. "We've got one supernatural, dead and bagged and ready for transpo back to Toronto."

Markowitz turned his head and gave a shrill whistle. Heads turned and he stabbed his finger at two of his men, then pointed at Doug Weaver's body. The officers came trotting over and picked it up, one man taking the feet, the other the head — or the end that used to have a head — and carried it aboard the helicopter, double time.

I stood by and listened while Alice told Markowitz about the portal in the Quonset hut. He gave a terse nod, then walked off a bit, speaking to someone on his headset.

After the two officers came back out of the helicopter and resumed their positions, Alice said, "Let's go for a ride."

"A ride?" I said. "What about them?" I pointed at the STAR team scattered around the field.

"They're going to stay and keep an eye on the portal."

Markowitz came back over. "HQ says the containment crew is on its way. ETA is about two hours. There just the one portal?"

"One is enough," I said.

Markowitz nodded. "Truth." He gave Alice a comradely slap on the shoulder. "You better get going, agent. They're expecting you."

Alice nodded and turned to me expectantly.

"Why do I get the feeling this trip is nonnegotiable?"

"We both had direct physical contact with an unknown supernatural entity," Alice said. "We need to be quarantined and debriefed. Standard SOP."

I sighed and followed her aboard the helicopter. The ramp closed behind us with a whine of pistons as we sat on the bench seats along the side of the cargo hold. A red light came on over our heads, filling the compartment with a bloody glow. Doug Weaver's plastic-wrapped body was strapped down to the bench across from us.

The helicopter started to rise. I looked out one of the circular windows and saw two of the STAR officers walking around the far side of the Quonset hut, where I'd thrown the glow sticks. Then the helicopter banked away and all I could see were the tops of the dark trees flashing by below.

I turned to Alice and said, "I really need to see Susan Weaver. I have to tell her what happened to her husband."

"Do you *know* what happened to her husband?"

I frowned at her. "You know what I mean."

Alice took out her smartphone and looked at the screen. "You can tell her later. After the lab boys confirm we're not going to turn into undead ghouls with a hankering for bodily dismemberment."

"What about this containment crew?" I said. "What are they going to do?"

"They'll assess the portal and install the proper security measures."

She spoke like she was reciting from the official PIA handbook.

"You're talking about a fence, right?"

Alice raised her head and looked at me. "Yes, Felix. A fence."

"Or maybe a concrete wall," I said. "Some barbed wire, some armed guards. Just like they're doing in Boston, right?"

"That's right," Alice said. "If you've got a better idea, I'm sure the rest of the world would love to hear it."

I didn't say anything. I didn't have a better idea, but that didn't mean I had to like the one we were stuck with.

Alice turned her attention back to her phone, then said, "Oh," and dug into one of her coat pockets. She came out with a gun. My gun.

"I found this in the Quonset hut after Weaver knocked me through the portal."

"Thanks." I took the gun from her and put it back in my holster.

We didn't speak again for the rest of the flight. I glanced over at one point and saw Alice was texting with Diane. I took out my own phone so I could call Sandra and tell her I had made it through the evening without getting killed, but the battery was dead. Again.

When we reached the city, one of the pilots came back to tell us that the Chinook was too big to land on the helipad of the PIA's downtown office building. They would be dropping us off at the old Canadian Forces base in Downsview. The base had been decommissioned years ago, but still maintained a small military presence. Alice grunted and went back to texting her partner.

After we landed and the loading ramp was lowered, a pair of men in combat fatigues came aboard with a stretcher. They removed the straps that bound Doug Weaver's body to the bench seat, then attached different straps that bound him to the stretcher, and wheeled him off the helicopter.

Alice and I followed them outside. The night was cool and brisk, and the tarmac was wet from a recent rainfall. It hadn't been raining in Sycamore, and the contrast of the different weather conditions, combined with having just left the dark woods for the bright lights of the city, left me feeling disoriented and a little dizzy. Or maybe those were symptoms that I was going to turn into an undead ghoul with a hankering for bodily dismemberment.

The army men rolled the stretcher to a blocky vehicle that looked like a cross between an ambulance and an armoured car. One of the men opened the rear doors, while the other folded the legs of the stretcher and slid it inside. Alice and I hopped in behind them, pulling the doors shut behind us, and we were off.

It was a thirty-minute drive to the PIA building. Alice was back on her smartphone, while the army guys sat in stony-faced silence on the other side of the compartment. The gentle thrum of the moving vehicle caused the last of the night's adrenaline to drain out of me. A heavy exhaustion settled in its place, drawing my shoulders down into a slump, and causing my eyelids to drift shut.

I didn't sleep, but I dozed. My mind was too full of frantic thoughts to allow for a proper rest. I went back over my encounter with Doug Weaver. It wasn't overstating things to call it a near-death experience. I could still feel his hand around my throat — the dry peeling flakes of skin, the sharp nubs of his finger-bones. I reached up and touched my neck, wondering if there were black bruises imprinted there in the shape of Doug's grip. Coming that close to death should have occupied all of my thoughts, but I found myself more concerned about my upcoming conversation with Susan Weaver. I tried to formulate in my head what I was going to say, then decided that was probably a bad idea. I didn't want my words to sound scripted or insincere. I needed to be honest and clear when I explained that her husband had been transformed into a supernatural creature, and he was responsible for a series of murders. Oh, and he's also dead. For good this time.

I peered through the rectangular portal into the driver's compartment and watched as we turned onto a ramp and descended into an underground parking garage. We drove past thick concrete pillars with the overhead fluorescent lights bouncing off the windshield in a strobing pattern.

The vehicle came to a stop, and a moment later the rear doors opened and three figures in bright yellow hazmat suits were standing there. Two of them hauled the stretcher out while the third stood by and watched. The army guys sat motionless like a couple of robots that had shut down for the night.

When the stretcher was offloaded, Alice and I hopped out. The two hazmat guys rushed the stretcher toward a freight elevator with its doors standing open.

"What's with the germ suits?"

"Just a precaution," Alice said.

She didn't seem worried, so I tried not to be, either. It didn't work.

The third hazmat man approached us. "Agent Baffle," he said, his voice coming out tinny and hollow through the speaker in his suit's faceplate. "Good to see you in one piece." He turned to me and his helmeted head bobbed back like he was doing a double take. "Felix Renn," he said, with some surprise.

Alice raised an eyebrow at me.

I peered through the hazmat suit's faceplate at the person inside. It was a man in his late fifties or early sixties. His weathered face was etched with lines like a contour map — wavy stress lines across his forehead, crow's-feet at the corners of his eyes, and laugh lines bracketing his mouth. It was a face I recognized.

"Dr. Kovac," I said, shaking his gloved hand. "It's been a while."

Alice said, "What, are you guys in the same bowling league or something?"

"Mr. Renn and I go back a few years," Kovac said. "He's like you, Alice. A magnet for supernatural trouble. And a survivor."

I nodded at his hazmat suit. "This is how you were dressed the first time we met."

"That's right," Kovac said. "The ash angels."

Alice looked back and forth between us. "What the hell is an ash angel?"

"It's a long, sad story," Kovac said. A forlorn look appeared briefly on his face, there and gone, then he clapped his gloved hands together. "But you'll have plenty of time to hear about that later." He swept a hand toward a regular-sized elevator behind him. "Shall we?"

I looked over at Alice. "What happens now?"

"Tests," she said. "Lots and lots of tests."

OVER THE next four hours, I was subjected to every medical test known to man, and a few others that I was pretty sure Kovac and the other PIA doctors had made up on the spot because they were, in reality, nothing more than a bunch of cold, clinical sadists with medical degrees.

I was poked, prodded, fingered, fondled, scoped, scooped, and scanned. They looked inside my eyes, my ears, my nose, and my mouth. They checked my blood pressure, my heart rate, my respiration. They tested my vision, my hearing, and my reflexes. They hooked me up to an EKG and an EEG, and recorded the results. They gave me a CT scan, a PET scan, an MRI, and an fMRI. They took half a dozen vials of blood and gave me two injections, one I was told was a general antibiotic, the other they wouldn't say ("classified"). They asked for a urine sample, which I provided, and a stool sample, which I didn't, or rather couldn't because the entire hours-long process had scared me utterly and completely shitless.

When it was finally over, I was given some blue medical scrubs to wear, and was escorted by armed guard to an austere little room with a stainless-steel sink and toilet, and a single bunk with a pillow on top of a pile of neatly folded linen.

I was so tired I didn't even bother to make up the bed. I simply flopped down on the wafer-thin mattress and fell immediately to sleep.

I DREAMED.

No chase through a dark city this time, no body covered in bees. I dreamed I was sleeping. Once again it was a lucid dream, and I took it as a sign of how exhausted I was. There could be no more deeper symbolism than that. Sometimes a cigar was just a cigar, and a rose was a rose was a rose. If you dream that you're sleeping, well then, it probably just means you're really, *really* tired.

As I slept in my dream, I wondered if it was possible for someone to dream within a dream, and if so, how would one be able to tell? I decided it probably didn't matter and rolled over in my dream-sleep and reached down to pull up my dream-covers.

My hand closed around a fistful of dirt.

It was moist and squelched between my fingers like gritty Play-Doh. I opened my dream-eyes and saw I was buried in dirt right up to my neck. I was lying on my side in a shallow grave. I looked around frantically, but all

I could see was tall silver grass swaying like hundreds of razor-sharp blades, contemplating whether or not to swing down and slice me to ribbons.

Just as I managed to struggle into a sitting position, I heard a sound, a frantic whispering like dozens of gossiping voices. The stalks next to me parted and Alice emerged. She was holding a shovel, the same one from the Quonset hut that I'd used to beat on Doug Weaver.

Alice slung the shovel against her shoulder as she looked down at me. She shook her head and made a tsking sound.

"Shouldn't be out of bed," she said in a scolding voice. "Better tuck you back in."

Before I had a chance to react, the shovel came swinging down in a savage arc. The dirt-clotted head smacked into my chest, slamming me back to the ground and driving all the air out of my lungs.

I lay on my side gasping as the dream-pain spread out from the point of impact, up into my shoulders and down to my stomach where it swirled into a greasy ball of nausea.

Then a clod of dirt landed on my arm. Followed by another. And another. Alice was reburying me. She whistled while she worked, tossing a shovelful of dirt onto my chest, then another on my head. I shook it off, but she replaced it with another scoop. She kept shoveling and she kept whistling. Just before she covered me completely, I finally recognized the tune.

It was "My Humps," by the Black Eyed Peas.

I WOKE up to the song playing on my phone. My dream had bled over into reality. Or reality had bled into my dream. Either way, I really had to change that ringtone.

Then it hit me. My phone. It had been taken from me the night before, along with my clothes, my blood, and a whole lot of my dignity.

The dignity was still gone, but my clothes and my phone had been returned to me. They were in a neat pile on the floor next to my cot. And they'd even charged the battery! I didn't spend a lot of time trying to figure out how someone had managed to drop them off without waking me up. I had been so exhausted that Kovac and his team could have come in and run a bunch more of their tests and I probably would have slept right through them.

I checked the caller ID. It was Sandra.

"Hey Dee."

"You're alive," Sandra said. She sounded surprised.

"I am. And with a clean bill of health, too. Courtesy of the PIA."

"Where have you been? I've been trying to reach you all morning."

I checked my watch and saw it was almost noon. I'd been more tired than I thought.

"What happened?" Sandra demanded.

I told her. Starting with the 911 call that brought Alice and I face-to-rotting-face with Doug Weaver, who was dead-but-not-dead, but who was now dead-dead. To the arrival of the STAR team, the helicopter ride back to the city, and finally, the perfect capper to the evening, my starring role as Felix the Human Pin Cushion.

"Are you okay?" Sandra asked.

"I'm as good as can be expected. I had more hands inside me last night than the entire cast of the Muppets."

"Ew, Felix."

"Sorry. I felt like I had about ten years' worth of physicals in one night. I want a hot bath and a stiff drink, and not necessarily in that order."

I told her I'd call her later, after I got back to Sycamore and spoke to Susan Weaver. I still wasn't sure what I was going to say to her, but I'd have the two-hour drive back to come up with something.

After I ended the call, the door to my room opened and Alice stuck her head inside. "You decent?"

"As decent as I get."

"Get dressed," she said. "I've got a surprise for you."

"I had more than enough surprises last night."

"Look at it as a reward for torture served," Alice said, and closed the door.

I started getting dressed.

CHAPTER 38

MY SURPRISE-SLASH-REWARD WAS being allowed to sit in on Doug Weaver's autopsy. In lieu of donning hazmat suits of our own, Alice and I watched the proceedings through a long double-paned window in an adjoining room that bore the nose-stinging smell of antiseptic.

Dr. Kovac was the one performing the autopsy, with another PIA scientist assisting him. The two men shuffled around the room in their hazmat suits like a couple of balloon people.

Doug Weaver's body lay on a stainless-steel table equipped with a scale, a hose, and a sink. We'd watched as Kovac and his assistant washed the dirt off the body, then collected all of the sludgy material in a series of yellow plastic biohazard containers. Now the assistant was rolling over a wheeled tray of autopsy tools so Kovac could begin the procedure.

Alice leaned toward me and said, "All of our tests came back negative. We're clean as far as supernatural infections go. Your blood did test positive for a couple of STDs, but that's *your* business. Kovac said you should lay off the hookers."

I looked at her in surprise. "I thought you didn't have a sense of humour."

Alice shrugged. "You bring it out in me."

"Lucky me." I nodded at the scene on the other side of the glass. "If there's no infection, then what's with the germ suits?"

"Always best to play it safe."

"I've never liked those things. They remind me of the government assholes who came to take E.T."

"Yeah," Alice said, with a small, wistful grin. "I used to watch that one all the time when I was a kid." She sighed. "Never thought I'd grow up to become one of those government assholes."

"You ever meet any aliens?"

Alice turned and looked me straight in the eye. "You really want to know?"

I stared back at her and felt a sudden chill that had nothing to do with the air-conditioning. "Not really."

There was a squawk of electronic static, then Kovac's voice came through a speaker in the wall above the viewing window. "We've cleaned the entire body, but as you can see there are some black marks remaining — mainly on the face and neck, but also on the hands and forearms."

"Where the skin was exposed," Alice said. The room was miked so Kovac and his assistant could hear us, too.

"That's correct," Kovac said. He gestured at some dark spots on Doug Weaver's cheeks and forehead that looked like scabs. "These appear to be contact burns. Presumably from exposure to sunlight."

"Like a vampire?" I turned to Alice. "But he wasn't a vampire."

"Vampires have the most extreme reaction to sunlight," Alice said, "but many different Black Lands species are allergic to it, in one way or another."

"Huh," I said. You learned something new every day.

"He must have been caught out in the daylight at some point," Kovac mused. "The wounds are fairly minor, which suggests he had a place to hide until the sun went down."

"We found a disturbed grave in the Black Lands," Alice said. "Right on the other side of a portal in the woods outside Sycamore. We think he went back there at the end of every night."

"The subject returning to his grave might be more than just territorial behaviour," Kovac said. "It could be a trace memory from his previous life — or rather, where he ended up in death. A psychological waypoint of sorts. A place he associates with the last thing he recalled when he was human. Or the first thing he recalled when he became..." He gestured with his gloved hand at Weaver's body. "There could also be a physiological component. The subject might *need* to return to the grave in order to hibernate, or possibly to regenerate whatever paranormal power source resulted in his initial reanimation. Lord knows, we've seen it before."

I leaned forward. "You have?" I turned to Alice. "Have you?"

Alice didn't say anything. On the other side of the glass, Kovac patted one of the biohazard canisters. "Black Lands soil is very powerful and very unstable," he said. "We still don't completely understand how it works. You're familiar with the Influence?"

"Yes," I said. "It's like supernatural radiation."

Kovac beamed through his faceplate. "Well put, Felix. Supernatural radiation. I like that!" He turned back to Doug Weaver's body. "What most people don't know about the Influence is that it comes from all aspects of the Black Lands. It's in the air, the water, and the ground."

Alice said, "The Sycamore police found soil samples at the crime scenes of the three most recent murders. My guess is that it'll match the stuff that Doug Weaver was buried in."

I gave Alice an annoyed look. "You never told me that."

"It's classified," she said. "Or I forgot. Whatever."

I turned back to Kovac. "I've never heard anything about Black Lands soil being used to reanimate the dead."

"It's not common knowledge," Kovac said. "And it's certainly not something the PIA advertises. Are you aware that it's against the law to take anything from the Black Lands and bring it back to our world?"

I nodded. "It's similar to the laws against bringing flora and fauna into other countries. It's to keep invasive species from spreading into foreign environments."

"Correct. You may be aware that there is an ongoing threat of blackwood trees trying to spread their seed into our world. They grow like weeds over here, although they are much more dangerous and destructive than your garden-variety dandelion. Excuse the bad pun." He chuckled dryly. "The wording of the Black Lands law is purposely vague. It doesn't specifically mention what materials are prohibited in our world, and for a very important reason."

"Because you don't want to create a black market for the stuff."

"Precisely. Only the market for Black Lands soil already exists. After the portals began appearing back in the 1940s, it didn't take long for people to figure out its power and its worth."

"Maybe that's why Mars was operating in Sycamore," I said. "He said he wasn't responsible for the murders and he wasn't involved in the drug trade.

He might've been telling the truth. Maybe his interest in the portal was because it provided him access to Black Lands soil."

"It's possible," Alice said, sound unsure. "But the portal and the soil are too connected to Doug Weaver and the murders for it to be a coincidence. There's no way his hands are clean on that score."

She was right, but it planted the seed of an idea in my mind.

"You might be surprised to know," Alice went on, "that our own government has been trying to find a positive use for it, as well."

"Not really," I said. "But what kind of positive use can there be for reanimating the dead?"

Kovac looked down at the floor, while Alice scratched the back of her head.

"Seriously, what possible use could there be for a reanimated corpse?"

"Slave labour mostly," Alice said. "The kind of jobs that living people don't want."

"How can that possibly be legal?"

"The dead don't have any rights, Felix."

"Okay," I said, "but most dead people have living relatives who wouldn't stand for that sort of treatment."

"You might be surprised how many people would sign up a deceased family member for something like that if the price was right. I mean, it's not like selling your daughter to white slavers. It doesn't even fall under human trafficking laws because the undead aren't considered human — at least not by the legal definition of the word. Besides, people donate their bodies to science all the time. This isn't much different."

I stared at her, aghast. "Are you saying this is actually happening?"

"It *did* happen," Alice said. "Past tense. There was a pilot project in Florida about a year ago — the Working Dead Initiative — but it didn't go anywhere. You could say it died on the vine."

I looked through the glass at Kovac. "But you said you've seen this before."

Kovac steepled his gloved hands together. "I should amend my previous statement to say we've seen something *similar* to this."

"What does that mean?"

"It means that despite your description of the subject — Mr. Weaver — and my initial examination, which seems to confirm that he was once in a state that we refer to, unscientifically, as 'undead,' the behaviour that you and

Agent Baffle suspect the subject of engaging in — namely, attacking and killing live human beings, and mutilating their bodies — is not the behaviour normally associated with this type of supernatural entity."

Alice turned to me. "Basically he's saying that zombies are nonviolent and have little to no brain capacity beyond the ability to follow simple verbal instructions. They're not serial killers. Or any other type of killer, for that matter."

"Correct," Kovac said. "In my thirty-three years with the agency, I have never seen or heard any report of an undead human attacking someone. They don't crave human flesh or brains like some people believe." He turned back to the body and pointed to the wounds on the shoulder and the side of the torso, the slashes across the chest, the hunk of flesh missing from the throat. "These might have something to do with the subject's unusual behaviour."

"How so?" Alice said.

"Perhaps the reason Mr. Weaver was a violent undead being was because he was the victim of a violent death. That is a very simplistic theory, of course, and not supported by any science. But then, there could be something to it. I have found on many occasions that those who ignored Occam's razor are the ones who invariably get cut by it."

"Do you have any idea what caused those wounds?" I asked.

"I'm not sure," Kovac said. "Assuming it was something from the Black Lands, we might never know. Our knowledge base of supernatural fauna is infinitesimal compared to the number of creatures about which we know next to nothing. I will of course attempt to match the claw and bite patterns to any known supernaturals in our database, but I can't promise we'll find a match. Having said that, these wounds may be the key to this particular mystery. Mr. Weaver may have been reanimated after his body was interred in the Black Lands, but there was something else, some catalyst, that must explain his proclivity for murder and mutilation." He paused. "It's worth pointing out that Mr. Weaver didn't bury himself. Find the one who did and you may find the catalyst."

I DIDN'T bother to stick around for the rest of the autopsy. I left the antiseptic-smelling room and started down a brightly-lit hallway in search of an elevator. Alice came jogging after me.

"Felix! Hold up!"

"I can't stay here," I said. "I have to get back to Sycamore."

Alice grabbed my arm and turned me around to face her. She didn't say anything right away, just stared into my eyes like she was reading the thought that was ticker-taping through my brain.

"You know what the catalyst is, don't you?"

I started to turn away, but she grabbed my arm again and swung me back around. "What are you going to do?"

"I'm going to see my client," I said. "I have to tell her that her husband is dead. Again."

"I'll go with you."

"No," I said firmly. "I need to do this on my own."

Alice's face tightened. "You're not gonna give me a bunch of that a-man's-gotta-do-what-a-man's-gotta-do crap, are you? Because what a man usually ends up doing is getting his stupid ass killed."

I said, "That's not going to happen," but I could tell she still wasn't convinced. "You're a loner, Alice. I get it. I am, too, most of the time. So you should understand more than anyone why I need to do this."

Alice's face softened a bit, but she still didn't look happy about it.

I turned away, and this time she didn't stop me.

I was halfway down the hallway when I stopped myself and turned back to her.

"My car is still in Sycamore. Can I borrow one of yours, or some money for the bus?"

CHAPTER 39

APPARENTLY THE PIA had strict rules about letting outsiders use vehicles from their motor pool, so I ended up taking the bus. Again. Don't let anyone tell you that private detectives don't travel in style.

I didn't really mind. There was an odd symmetry to returning to Sycamore this way, just as I had done after my impromptu meeting with Mars and Vermillion. I had more information about my case now than I did back then, but far from all the answers. I still didn't know how the Planets fit into all of this. Maybe all Mars wanted was the portal on Burnside Road, and he really had no interest in the murders, much less who, or what, was committing them.

But if that was true, then why was Haley working at the Weavers' garden store? She'd claimed they were drug dealers, but she only told me that to get me to Burnside Road, presumably to get rid of me. And when that didn't work, I was taken and brought before Mars. But again I asked the question: why? For what purpose?

Mars knew a lot about my past — things even Sandra didn't know — and he claimed he only wanted to meet me. Which still didn't explain his interest. Or his intentions.

I was still surprised that Alice was letting me go back to Sycamore by myself. Maybe she was doing me a favour by letting me finish this on my own. Or maybe she didn't see any percentage in putting her own ass on the line for something that didn't concern her. That seemed like the more plausible explanation to me. With the monster dead and the portal on its way to being secured, Alice didn't really have any stake in what was going on in Sycamore.

But I still did.

THE BUS dropped me off at the downtown terminal. The day was overcast, the sky upholstered in thick grey clouds that looked like dirty cotton batting. The smell of wet leaves hung heavy in the air. I wandered over to the main square where a few people were walking the paths and sitting on the benches, everyone enjoying one of the last tolerably cool days of autumn. I stood at the edge of the square and watched them, wondering if they knew the horror of the past few months was over. I'd checked the news headlines on my phone on the bus ride up. There had been nothing about last night's excitement. Nothing about the portal. Nothing about Alice and I and our brawl with the undead Doug Weaver. Nothing about a STAR team arriving by helicopter. Still, I wondered if the town knew, on some deeper, unconscious level, that the nightmare was over.

It was only a matter of time before they found out. The PIA might have been keeping a lid on things for now, but there was no way they could keep them secret forever. People would eventually find out about the portal, just like they did with the one in Boston. And they'd find out about Doug Weaver — what he was and what he had done. I needed to make sure Susan Weaver heard it from me first.

I walked along the pavement. The trees were bare and the square seemed smaller as a result. There were only a few leaves on the ground; the rest had been blown away by the wind or washed away by the rain. That familiar fall sadness rose in me again. I'm sure a psychiatrist could have come up with some reasons for that, even without digging too deeply into the topsoil of my psyche, but there were some things a person didn't want to know about themselves. And some things they wanted to forget.

It was a longer walk to pick up my car than the last time I'd bussed back to town. That time my car had been parked in front of Haley's building; this time it was all the way back at the motel. It took about forty-five minutes to walk there, and when I checked the time on my phone, I saw it was almost five o'clock. I'd slept the morning away, then spent part of the afternoon as a guest of the PIA. The bus ride had eaten up another couple of hours, and now here it was, coming on toward evening again, the last light of day fading out like a dimmer switch was being slowly turned down.

I used my key to enter my room, then packed my bags and checked out. I wasn't coming back.

I put my bags in the car and headed out. I passed the Star Stop with its flying saucer parked on the roof. Maybe I could hitch a ride to another planet, one where things made sense. Did such a place exist? Probably not.

I went the long way around town so that I could drive past The Greener Side. The store was closed, and something about the way it looked — the dark windows, the empty flower boxes, the general huddled-down look of the place — told me it wouldn't be open again until the following spring. Maybe not ever.

I pulled the car over to the side of the road and put it into park. What the hell was I doing? I had taken the bus when I could have rented a car. I had gone strolling around downtown, then walked all the way back to the motel, when I could have taken a cab. And now I was cruising around town like I was on a sightseeing tour. Why? Why fucking why?

Because I was trying to put off the inevitable, was the answer.

And now I'd put it off so long it was starting to get dark. Great, Felix. Nice work.

My only consolation was that the fear wasn't creeping in with its usual nerve-numbing paralysis. It was still there, but it wasn't keeping me from what I needed to do.

I put the car in drive and continued on to the Weaver residence. I almost expected to find it as dark and abandoned-looking as the garden store. Expected and hoped, I'm a little ashamed to say, because that would've let me off the hook. But there was a single light burning on the first floor, and another in the apartment above the garage.

I turned into the driveway and pulled up next to the same tree I'd parked under the first time I was here. I got out of the car and walked up the flag-stone path to the front door. I knocked and stood there shifting my weight from one foot to the other. I looked down and saw a jack-o'-lantern on the stoop. I was fairly certain it hadn't been there before, then remembered it had been Halloween the previous night. The Weavers probably didn't get many trick-or-treaters out this way, but they probably went through the motions for their daughter. Of course there was no "they" anymore. It was just Susan now.

I didn't want to think about that, but I was forced to while I waited for someone to answer the door. I decided to think about pumpkins instead. I wondered if this one had come from the garden store, from the stack the Dunbarton boys had been making when I first met them. Pumpkins were such innocent, harmless things until they were gutted out and carved into frightening shapes. Sort of like Doug Weaver.

Oh Christ, why wouldn't someone answer the door?

I reached out and turned the knob. It was open.

I stepped into the dark foyer. The light I saw from outside was coming from the living room. I followed it like a moth, hoping I wouldn't get burned. Or maybe I wanted to. Maybe I deserved to be burned.

The light came from the floor lamp in the corner of the room. Susan Weaver was sitting in the wingback chair next to it. At least I thought it was her. I had to stare for a really long time until I was sure.

She appeared to have aged about five years in the few days since I'd last seen her. She was even paler than before, like she'd spent years living in a cave, and it seemed to have extended to her hair, turning its former rich chestnut to a drab dishwater brown. Her clothes hung strangely on her slight frame, like she was swimming in them instead of wearing them. Her red-rimmed eyes seemed to look at me and through me at the same time.

"Mr. Renn," she said in a small, remote voice.

"Felix," I said automatically.

"What are you doing here?"

"I work for you. Remember?"

"Yes," she said. "Yes, of course I do."

"May I come in?"

I was already in, but still felt the need for formalities.

She gestured to the couch and I sat down. I noticed there was a cut-glass tumbler on a small table to her left. She picked it up, gazed at the inch or so of amber liquid in it, then took a small sip.

"Would you like a scotch?"

"No," I said, "but I would like the answers to a few questions."

"There are no answers here," she said. "We're all out!" She waved the glass and some scotch sloshed over the side.

She was drunk. Drunk and scared. I decided to change my approach.

"I know you're going through an extremely difficult time. I can help you. If you'll let me."

"There's no help here, either," Susan said. "No answers and no help. There hasn't been any since…"

"Since you murdered your husband?"

I don't know where the words came from, they just came blurting out. But now that they'd been spoken, I realized it was something I'd been thinking for some time now. There had been a blind spot in this case since the very beginning, something I wasn't seeing, or something I refused to see. But I knew it was there; I could feel it picking at me like an itch I couldn't scratch. So I took a shot in the dark. And from the look on Susan's face, I seemed to have hit the mark.

My words had the effect of a one-two punch — the first one startling her and causing her head to snap back, the second one sobering her up, at least a little, her eyes widening and clearing at the same time.

"I… I didn't murder Doug," Susan said. "I… loved him." She was having trouble speaking, as if the words kept getting struck in her throat. "I could never murder him. I… I couldn't."

I didn't say anything. I was so used to hearing lies and denials that on the rare occasion when I heard the truth, it tended to halt me in my tracks. And Susan Weaver was telling the truth. But there was something else. Something she wasn't telling me. I hadn't struck the mark, after all, but I wasn't far off.

Clearly I'd missed a step somewhere, and while I was backtracking in my mind to find it, Susan rose from her chair with a suddenness that flash-froze all the thoughts in my head.

I leaped to my feet with my gun drawn and pointed at her.

Susan ignored me and went over to a dry bar in a nook between two windows. She picked up a crystal decanter, removed the stopper, and splashed some scotch into her glass. She cut her eyes at me and said, "That won't help you, Mr. Renn."

"Against who?" I said. "You?"

Susan turned to face me. "I told you, I didn't kill my husband." She took a gulp of scotch, winced at the burn, and went back to her chair.

"If you didn't do it, then who did?"

Susan looked at me like I was simple. Which was a fair assessment since that was how I was feeling at that particular moment.

"You really don't know."

I tried to read the emotion behind her words, but I couldn't tell if she was mocking me or pitying me.

"It was Rachel," she said, and tossed back the rest of her drink. "Rachel did it."

I stared at her for a long time, feeling even more lost than I'd been a moment ago. Rachel? I thought. Who the hell was Rachel?

Susan shook her head at my befuddlement. I didn't blame her. She'd hired a private detective to find some answers for her, and it appeared she hadn't got her money's worth. Maybe she was right. Maybe there were no answers.

She placed the tumbler on the side table, then pushed it with the tips of her fingers until it slid off the edge. It shattered on the floor with a brittle crash.

"My daughter," she said. "My daughter killed him."

CHAPTER 40

I HAD THAT feeling again, like I'd missed a step. Or seven. I holstered my gun and sat back down on the couch.

"Rachel?" I said. "You're telling me an eight-year-old girl killed your husband? Her own father?"

Susan closed her eyes and put a hand to her head like she had a migraine. I knew the feeling.

"No… She's not…"

"She's not what?" I snapped. "What are you talking about? What the hell is going on here?"

"This wasn't supposed to happen!" Susan shouted.

We both fell silent. I suddenly wished I'd taken that drink offer.

"This wasn't supposed to happen," Susan repeated, softer this time.

"What *was* supposed to happen?"

Susan turned her head and looked off to the side. I thought she was staring at the decanter of scotch, eager for another refill, but she was actually looking out one of the windows.

"I was told to hire you," she said. "I was told to bring you to Sycamore."

"Told by who?"

Susan's head swivelled back in my direction.

"Nancy," she said. "The nurse."

I stood up and went over to the window. I looked to where Susan had been staring: the light in the apartment above the garage.

"Is she up there with Rachel?"

Susan nodded.

"And I take it she's not really a nurse?"

Susan laughed at that — a dry, bitter snort completely devoid of humour.

"No one is who they say they are around here."

She got up, went back to the bar, and poured herself a fresh drink in a new glass.

Then she began to talk.

IT STARTED back in April, on the first day of the month.

"April Fools' Day," Susan said, and gave another mirthless chuckle. "Only we were the fools. We just didn't know it yet."

"We who?" I asked.

"Doug and I," Susan replied. "That was the day Rachel went missing. Doug was at the store and I was at home. Rachel went outside to play, and after some time, an hour, maybe two, I realized I hadn't seen her for a while. I went out to look for her, thinking she was playing a April Fools prank on me. I looked all over the yard, in the garage, and the woods out back, but I couldn't find her anywhere. I started out calling her name, telling her the joke was over, that it was time to come out. Then I was screaming so loudly one of our neighbours who lives almost a mile away came over to see what was wrong. That's when I called the police."

I felt an unpleasant tingle of déjà vu, like a cold, greasy hand caressing the back of my neck. "But you found her, right?"

"Doug showed up at the same time as the police. We searched everywhere, but there was no sign of her. The police put out a BOLO. That stands for…"

"Be on the lookout," I said. "I know. Why didn't they issue an Amber Alert?"

"We wanted them to, but they said they only do that if they think she was abducted. At the time it looked like she'd only wandered off." She took a sip of scotch. "The police organized a search. Rachel had only been missing a few hours, but they managed to get about a hundred volunteers out looking for her. They spread out from our house in groups, searching the woods and swamps and…" She gestured with her glass. "…everywhere."

Not everywhere, I thought.

"They didn't find her that night," Susan said. "And when the police said they were calling off the search until morning, I suddenly knew what it was like to go crazy." Her eyes became shiny with tears. "It's the complete and total loss of control. When a situation drifts so far out of your hands that your brain simply stops working. I couldn't think, I couldn't speak, I couldn't even feel. I was completely numb. I felt lost. Even more lost than Rachel. She was out there, somewhere, but for me it was like I'd ceased to exist. Doug tried to be strong. He said it was going to be okay, that they were going to find her. But I could tell deep down he knew the same thing I did. She was gone and she was never coming back."

"But you did find her," I said. "Didn't you?"

Susan sniffled and wiped her eyes with the back of her hand. "The volunteers were back out searching the woods the following morning, but it was a cop driving around in his cruiser who found her. She was just walking along the side of a road a few miles from our house."

"Burnside Road?"

Susan nodded. "A police cruiser pulled up to the house, and I knew it was bad news. I was so angry at Doug. I wanted to scream at him and tell him he was a liar, that it wasn't going to be okay. Rachel was dead and it was my fault, *my* fault, because I was the one who'd lost her. Then the police officer opened the passenger door and Rachel came bouncing out. I thought I was still crazy, that I was hallucinating, then she ran into me and wrapped her arms around me and I knew she was real. She kept saying 'It's me! It's me!' over and over, like she knew I didn't believe this was really happening. I had never felt such relief in my entire life. I held her and held her until Doug pulled her away and then she latched onto him."

"Was she okay?"

"She seemed to be. Her clothes were dirty and her hair was a mess, but she didn't appear to have a mark on her. We took her into the kitchen and got her something to eat. She was hungry and thirsty. She said she hadn't eaten anything since the other day. The chief of police was there and he asked Rachel where she'd been. She said she had been playing on the tree swing when she remembered it was April Fools' Day and decided to play a prank on me by making me think she had disappeared." Susan gave a bitter snort. "She did a good job of that. She hid behind a tree on the edge of the woods behind our house and waited for me to come looking for her. When I didn't show up right away, she went deeper into the woods, and then deeper still. Apparently she got so frustrated that I hadn't come looking for her — that I had ruined her April Fools' prank — that she decided to keep going. She ended up walking miles away to the vacant lot on Burnside Road."

"She found the portal, didn't she?"

Susan nodded and tears coursed down her cheeks. She didn't bother to wipe them away.

"She said she tried to come home, but it got dark really fast and she didn't know where she was. She said the sun went away and it didn't come back. So she laid down in the grass and went to sleep because she thought that would make it come back. But when she woke up the sun was still gone. She said she started walking again, and after a while the sun came back, just like that. She walked a bit longer and came to the road. She was walking along it when the policeman found her."

I said, "That's incredible," with words coming out in a rush of breath. I'd been holding my breath without realizing it. "She went to the Black Lands and made it back alive. Did you have any idea at the time?"

"No," Susan said, lowering her eyes. "But when Rachel saw how much I was crying, she gave me a flower. She said she'd found it when the sun went away. It looked like night-blooming jasmine, but it was red instead of white, and the smell it gave off wasn't like jasmine. It was a spicy scent, almost like cinnamon. Doug and I both studied horticulture in school, and neither of us could identify that flower. But we had Rachel back, so we didn't give it much thought." She paused. "Not then."

"RACHEL WAS different after she came back."

Susan paused to take a fortifying drink of scotch. "She used to talk a lot, like most girls her age, but now she was quiet and distant. Doug said it was just shock, but I knew right away that something was wrong. Rachel seemed... off. Different, somehow. I couldn't put my finger on it. The first few days after she came home, we barred her from leaving the house. I was so paranoid about losing her again. I thought Rachel would be upset about that, being forced to stay inside all day, but she didn't care. She didn't seem to care about anything. She would respond if you asked her something, but only in one- or two-word replies. Mostly she sat at one of the back windows and looked out at the woods.

"Then one morning, we came downstairs and found the front door wide open. The first thing I thought was that Rachel was gone again, but when we checked her room, she was fast asleep in bed. Doug went to check on her, and when he pulled back the covers, we saw her nightie was covered in mud and grass stains and her feet were dirty. We woke her up and asked if she'd been outside. She admitted she had, and when we asked her why, she just shrugged and told us she had to go out. She said she needed to hunt.

I wanted to ask what she meant by *hunt*, but Susan ploughed ahead, the story spilling out of her as if the words were venom and she needed to get them out of her body as quickly as possible.

"We told her not to do it again, but the next morning we woke up and the front door was open again. There was no lock on Rachel's bedroom door, so that night Doug put a chair in front of it to keep her from getting out. The next morning the front door was closed and the chair was still propped under the doorknob, but when we went into her room to check on her, Rachel's nightie was filthy again. And her window was open. There's no tree outside her window, and it's a two-storey drop to the ground. We couldn't understand it. Even if she went out the window and managed to land without breaking her leg, how the hell did she get back inside?

"Doug and I didn't know what to do. Rachel had never acted like this before. We thought she might be experiencing some sort of trauma from when she went missing, but we figured she'd get over it, that all she needed was a little time.

"We tried to stay up the next night, hoping to catch Rachel as she was leaving the house, but we ended up falling asleep on the couch. We were so exhausted from the past few days, and it was only getting worse. I felt like we had to call someone, a child psychiatrist or something, but Doug convinced me to ride it out, that Rachel would snap out it.

"Then a few days later, Rachel came into our room in the middle of the night and woke us up. Her nightgown was even filthier than before, like she'd been rolling around in the mud this time. Then Doug turned on the bedside lamp and we saw it wasn't mud. Rachel was covered in blood.

"At first I thought she'd done something to herself, but when Doug and I checked her out, there wasn't a single mark on her. She was smiling at us the whole time in a way that really bothered me. When we figured out the blood wasn't hers, we asked her what happened, and Rachel said, 'I made a mess.'

"After we got her cleaned up, she told us she'd been out hunting. I don't know what Doug thought, but I remember thinking Rachel had gone out to the woods and killed an animal. A dog or a cat, maybe. I was so angry at Doug. I told him we should have taken her to a doctor. Then Rachel looked at me said, 'She was pretty, Mommy. Pretty like you.'

"It was Robin Endicott, wasn't it?"

Susan nodded. "Doug told Rachel to take us where she'd been that night. We got in the car and drove, following her directions. She was... proud. Almost excited to show us."

"The happy hunter."

"She took us to a house on the edge of town. It was miles away, even further than she had walked on the day she went missing, but that was the last thing on our minds at that moment. After we got out of the car, Rachel took us around to the side of the house where a window was open. The back door was wide open, too. We went inside..." She closed her eyes and swallowed. "...and we found her. She was lying on the kitchen floor. There was blood everywhere. At first, we told ourselves that Rachel must have found her like that. That she had gone out on one of her night-wanderings and simply happened upon the woman's body. But while we were standing there, looking around at all that blood, Rachel started telling us things."

"What kind of things?" I asked.

"Things that convinced us it was her who had... done this."

"And then you buried the body in the woods behind the house."

Susan lowered her head. "We were trying to protect our daughter."

"It sounds like it was other people who need to be protected from her."

Her head came back up and she looked at me with sad, tired eyes. "If you don't have children, Mr. Renn, then you can never understand. You'd do anything to keep your child safe."

"Does that include committing felonies?"

"Anything," she said in a small voice.

I could feel myself getting angry, so I tamped it down for the moment and pressed on.

"I assume she killed Paul Lindon and you buried his body, as well."

Susan shook her head, but I couldn't tell if it was in denial or because she was getting angry, too.

"The day after Doug and I buried the girl's body, we talked about what we should do. We knew something was wrong with Rachel and that it must have something to do with her disappearance. I remembered the flower she gave me — the one that didn't exist anywhere in our world. That was when Doug and I figured out what must have happened, that Rachel had stumbled upon a portal and gone to the Black Lands." Susan let out a choked sob. "You hear about it happening to people, but you never think it's going to happen to you or someone you know... someone you love. I knew we should've called the police, but we couldn't, we just couldn't. We knew what would happen. They'd tell the PIA and they'd come and take Rachel away. They'd lock her up and do tests on her and..." Tears were streaming down her cheeks now. "We couldn't let that happen. Not to our little girl. We knew we had to make a decision, and we had to make it fast. It was only a matter of time before the body was found, and we didn't know if there was any evidence that would lead to us... or to Rachel. We talked about leaving town, just packing up what we could carry, clearing out our bank accounts, and just going away." Her eyes drifted off to the corner — perhaps imagining the life that could have been, the path not taken — then they snapped back and locked onto mine.

"But before we could do anything, the nurse showed up."

I rose from the couch, took Susan's glass from her limp hands, and went over to the bar to pour her a refill.

I didn't want her drunk, but I wanted to keep her talking, and alcohol was the best lubricant for that. Not that she needed much prompting. Susan was info-dumping like a ship getting rid of ballast. I supposed that's what she was doing in a way, getting rid of all the things she'd been carrying for so long. The anger, the pain, the guilt.

I brought Susan her drink and sat back down on the couch.

"Tell me about her," I said. "The nurse who isn't a nurse."

Susan took a sip of scotch. "She showed up the morning after we buried Robin Endicott's body. Doug and I were sitting at the kitchen table, trying to figure out what we were going to do, when there was a knock at the door. We both went to answer it, and there was this woman standing on our doorstep. She was smiling in a way that made me think of the way Rachel had smiled at us when she came into our bedroom that night covered in blood. Like she had a secret.

"She cut straight to the chase and told us she knew everything that was going on. Doug asked if she was with the police, and she laughed at us. She said, 'I'm not the police and that isn't your daughter.' She pointed at Rachel, standing there behind us in the hallway. She kept pointing at her and said, 'She isn't even human.' Doug was about to slam the door in her face when she said, 'Is it easier to believe that your daughter is a murderer?' That's when I started to feel like I was losing my mind again. Not because what she was saying was crazy, but because a part of me knew it was true.

"The woman — she said her name was Nancy — came inside and proceeded to tell us that Rachel, or what we thought was Rachel, was actually a creature from the Black Lands — what she called a mimik. A shapeshifter that had taken the form of our daughter. If she'd said that to us even a day earlier, we would have thrown her right out of the house. But after the night we'd had, it wasn't so unbelievable. Still, Doug wasn't convinced. He said, 'Prove it,' and I'll always regret him speaking those two words."

Susan looked down at her hands. They were shaking, which caused the glass to shake, too. It made a small tinkling sound as it rattled against her wedding ring.

"What happened?" I asked. Those were another couple of words she'd probably regret hearing. I might, too.

"She changed," Susan said simply. "Nancy went over and started speaking to her in a low voice. There was a musical quality to it, like she was whispering and whistling at the same time. It's hard to describe because I'd never heard anything like it before. It was kind of like hearing a foreign language for the first time, which I guess is what it was.

"Rachel reacted immediately. The skin around her eyes began to darken, like she had two black eyes, but then it was happening to her entire body. The skin on her arms and legs went dark, like she was turning into one big bruise. She started making this horrible keening sound, like an animal in pain. I wanted to go to her, help her, but the woman, Nancy, said, 'Wait,' and Doug held me back. He was terrified, we both were, watching this thing that looked like our daughter turn into something else."

"What did it turn into?"

Susan closed her eyes and shook her head. "I can't."

"What happened? What did it do?"

"Nothing," Susan said. "It was crouched down on the floor, kind of hunched over, like it was cowering. Nancy got down in front of it and started whisper-whistling again. The thing… the mimik… made some sounds back at her, a sort of mewling like a cat. They were talking to each other. Nancy stood up and the mimik began to change. Soon it looked like Rachel again. Doug and I stood there watching, neither of us saying a word. It's like we were frozen. Nancy turned to us and said, 'Your daughter is in the Black Lands. She's still alive. And if you ever want to see her again, you're going to do everything I say.'"

Susan looked at me with bleary red eyes.

"And that's what we've been doing ever since."

NANCY TOOK the Weavers out to Burnside Road, where "Rachel" had been found. They drove down the dirt lane to the vacant lot, and Nancy got out of the car and started walking across the field with her arms spread wide. She wandered around like that for a while, Susan said, until she reached a spot at the far end of the lot, close to the treeline.

"The portal," I said.

Susan nodded. "Nancy said she could feel it. She said it was 'fresh'."

"Did she say how she knew Rachel had found it, or what had happened on the other side?"

Susan shook her head.

"What happened after that?"

"Nancy moved into our home," Susan said. "She said the mimik could act out again at any moment, so she needed to be close by to keep it calm. That's how she put it — 'acting out.' Like it was only having a temper tantrum when it killed that girl. If anyone asked, we were to say that Nancy was a nurse we'd hired to help Rachel work through some issues she was dealing with from her disappearance. That was the reason we used when we pulled Rachel out of school. She couldn't go back. Not... not like that."

"And the vacant lot..."

"Nancy arranged to buy it. She put the deed in our name so it wouldn't raise any suspicions if anyone found out about it. She had the Quonset hut shipped out there and placed on top of the portal so nobody else would find it. After that, Nancy said we were to go on with our lives like everything was normal." She gave a bitter snort. "Can you believe that? How were we supposed to act like things were normal when everything in our lives was a lie? But we didn't have a choice. Nancy had our daughter and she wouldn't give her back unless we did what she said. So Doug and I went back to work at the store, which turned out to be the best thing we could do. Neither of us wanted to be at home with that *thing* masquerading as our daughter. Not that we saw much of her, anyway. Nancy and the mimik spent most of their time in the apartment above the garage. But at some point Nancy must have started worrying about all the time we were spending away from the house, because she ended up putting someone at the store to keep an eye on us there."

"Haley."

"They were like a couple of prison guards, one of them watching us at home, the other at work."

"Did Nancy ever tell you who she was working for?"

"Never," Susan said. "We asked her. We screamed at her. We begged and pleaded with her. But she wouldn't tell us a thing. She wouldn't tell us how long we had to wait, or what we were even waiting for. We were living in limbo. And the whole time we were going crazy wondering what was happening to Rachel. The real Rachel."

"This has been going on for months?"

"Yes," Susan said. "It's been awful. Sometimes Nancy would take the mimik into the house and get her toys or food, acting like she was really our daughter. It was horrible and..." She searched for the right word. "... perverse. It was like she was making a mockery of our lives... the lives we'd been living until Rachel disappeared.

"But the worst times were when Nancy would go away for a few days. It didn't happen very often, but when it did we'd be left alone with the mimik.

Nancy told us to pretend like it was our daughter. Doug and I were so angry, but we were also scared out of our minds. It was like a sick joke, treating this thing like it was our Rachel. But we didn't have a choice. Doug and I spent those days walking on eggshells, always worried that something we'd do or say would set it off."

"Did it act like your daughter?"

Susan closed her eyes and nodded. "It was a mimic in every sense of the word. That's what made it so hard. We were afraid of making it *turn*, but because it looked and sounded just like Rachel, it was hard to believe it wasn't her." She gave a firm nod. "Those were the worst times. We thought if we could make it through those days, when we were alone with the mimik, then we could make it through anything. And then..."

"Paul Lindon was killed," I said. "The second victim."

"Yes. But we didn't find out about it until later on."

"It didn't happen during one of Nancy's absences?"

"No, she was there," Susan said. "She was the one who told us. She said the mimik was getting hard to control, so she had to 'let it off its leash' for the night. Those were her exact words. Nancy told us not to worry about the body. She said she'd cleaned up just like we did with Robin Endicott. She smiled at us when she said it, like we were all in on a big joke or something. This was in August. At that point, she and the mimik had been living with us for four months. *Four months*. That's when Doug started saying he didn't think we were ever gonna get Rachel back. He wasn't even sure she was still alive. I screamed at him, told him to never say that again. Of course she was still alive. Why would Nancy and the mimik still be here unless they needed something from us? Once they got it, whatever it was, they'd give Rachel back. That's what I told him back then. But now..." Her eyes seemed to shrink to small black dots. "...now I'm not so sure."

"Doug did something, didn't he?"

Susan gave a small nod.

"What did he do?" I had a pretty good idea, but I wanted to hear it from her.

Susan didn't say anything for a span of time. She started running the tip of her finger along the rim of her glass, as if to make it sing, but there was no sound. Eventually she began to speak again.

"Doug waited until Nancy was gone on one of her trips. She never told us where she went, but she was always gone for two or three days. One day he came home from the store and he just looked so tired. We were both exhausted, physically and emotionally, but that day it was like a dam had broke and all the stress of the past few months had come crashing down on him. He managed to coax the mimik into his truck, and then he drove away. I didn't even ask him where he was going with it. I think I knew."

"He was going to kill her."

Susan shook her head. "It," she said. "He was going to kill *it*."

"But he never came back."

Susan shook her head again, and this time it dislodged more tears in her eyes. They streaked down her reddened cheeks, cutting trails through the other tears she'd cried tonight.

"I knew," she said in a strained voice. "I knew he was dead. Just like I knew what he was planning to do with that thing when he drove off in his truck." She let out an anguished cry. "And then *it* showed up!"

"The mimik?"

Susan nodded. "Covered in blood, just like that night in our bedroom. I went out of my mind and grabbed it — even though I'd seen what it really looked like, what it really was. I grabbed it and shook it and screamed in its face — my daughter's face — *'What did you do? What did you do?'* Rachel… the mimik… smiled at me and said, 'Daddy was bad.' I slapped it across the face. Hard. I'd never hit anyone like that before in my entire life. I felt like I was going to throw up. Then I felt afraid. I thought this was it, now it would change and kill me. Part of me wanted it to because if Doug was dead, then I didn't want to be alive anymore, either. I started to think that he was right, that Rachel was never coming back, that she had died over there in the Black Lands, so there was no point in living. *Let it kill me*, I thought. I was tired of living a lie. I was tired of living."

"But it didn't kill you."

"No," Susan said. "It just kept on smiling at me. When Nancy came back, I told her what the mimik had done, and she gave it this frowning look like it had forgotten to pick up its toys or had tracked mud on the kitchen floor. She spoke to it with that whisper-whistling, and it spoke back to her with that awful mewling sound. When it was done, Nancy looked amused.

She shook her head and said, 'Well, this complicates things.' I told her this had all gone on long enough. Doug was dead, Rachel was gone, and I wanted her and her little pet monster out of my house. I told her I was going to call the police and tell them everything.

"Nancy waited until I was finished, then she told me I was right — the mimik had killed Doug, but it had only acted in self-defence. I told her I didn't care. I said this was over. Nancy told me it wasn't over until she said it was over. She said Doug's death was on him, and that it was a good thing he didn't succeed in killing the mimik, because if he did, then we would never see our daughter again. She said she was the only one who could bring Rachel back from the Black Lands. I wonder now if Nancy's monster-whispering also worked on humans, because the more she spoke to me, the more I was convinced there was no other choice."

She raised her glass and tossed back the rest of the scotch.

"She did want me to call the police, though. To report him missing."

"Nancy told you what to say?"

Susan nodded. "She always knew what to say."

"Then the murders started up again."

"I thought it was the mimik," Susan said. "I thought that Nancy had let it off its leash again. But when I asked her about it, she told me it was Doug who was killing those people. That's when I found out why she had looked so amused the night Doug had been killed. When she spoke to the mimik, it told her what it had done to Doug... and what it had done with his body."

"The mimik took it to the portal on Burnside Road," I said, "and buried it in the Black Lands."

"Yes," Susan said. "I asked her why it would do that, and Nancy said she wasn't sure, but that it might have been because Doug and I had buried Robin Endicott's body. She said that a mimik is capable of copying more than just its host's appearance. Sometimes it will also copy its behaviour. So if it saw us burying that girl's body..."

"It would do the same thing to Doug," I finished.

"Nancy called it an 'unforeseen wrinkle.' She said the soil in the Black Lands had the power to bring a dead person back to life. She said they were mindless creatures who didn't remember anything of their former lives. But

Doug was different. Something had made him… violent. She didn't know for certain, but she thought the mimik's bite might have done it."

The catalyst, I thought. The thing that made Doug go out and kill. How was I supposed to tell Susan that I'd seen her husband last night, that I had fought with him, and then helped someone chop off his head? I decided it could wait until later. Not knowing at the time that there wouldn't be a later.

"Soon after that, Nancy said it was time."

"Time?" I said.

"To call you," she said. "To bring you to Sycamore."

"They're up there right now?" I asked, turning to the window that looked out on the garage.

"Yes," Susan said. "I'm sorry. It's the only way I'll get Rachel back."

I looked at her and wondered if she still believed that, after all this time, after everything she'd been through. After her husband had been killed and brought back to life as a blood-thirsty monster. Did she really believe that Rachel would be returned to her? Did she believe her daughter was even still alive?

I didn't believe either of those things were true, but I wasn't the one to tell her that. Since she was my client, an argument could have been made that I was precisely the one to tell her. But even if that was true, this wasn't the time to do it. I had bigger problems right now. Two of them.

"Did Nancy say what she wants with me?"

Susan shook her head. "She never told me anything. She just said you were a private investigator from Toronto, and that I was supposed to hire you to find Doug."

I had a bit more information than Susan — I knew that Nancy and Haley worked for Mars, who worked for the Planets — but none of that would have helped her now. It would only have confused her, as it did me.

I took out my cell phone and held it in my lap. "Whatever happens, this ends tonight. You know that?"

Susan nodded and let out a long, deep breath. Maybe she was more aware of the truth than she let on.

"I have to make a call," I said, "and when I do, everything will come out."

"I know," Susan said solemnly.

I stood up and went over to the window. The light above the garage was like a beacon calling out to me. I didn't want to go up there, but a part of me felt like I had to, that it was inevitable.

What I really wanted to do was call Alice and tell her to send a STAR team out here so they could arrest Nancy and kill the mimik. But when I dialled her number, the call went immediately to voicemail.

With Susan watching me, I tried the PIA's 1-800 number, the line they used for tips on portals and sightings of supernatural creatures. I pressed buttons until I was patched through to a human being and spun it for them quick. I said that my name was Felix Renn, that I was a private investigator working on a case with Special Agent Alice Baffle, and that it was imperative she get back to me right away. I gave them the Weavers' address and said that time was of the essence (but in much more colourful language).

My next call was to the Sycamore police department. I asked for Detective Helton, but was told he'd gone home for the day. I didn't feel like going through the whole spiel again, so I said fuck it, then hung up and dialled 911.

"I'd like to report an impending crime," I said to the operator. "Someone's about to die."

I hoped it wasn't me.

CHAPTER 41

AFTER ENDING THE call, I gave serious thought to packing Susan into my car and driving away. That would have been the smart thing to do. Unfortunately, the smart thing isn't always the right thing. I could have let the local police and the PIA deal with things here. It was, after all, their jobs.

But it was also my job.

This was the reason I came to Sycamore. The reason Susan had hired me. Even though I'd been brought here under false pretenses, it didn't feel right to walk away when I was this close to the end. It was cowardly, for one thing, but that wasn't the part that bothered me. It had more to do with what was expected of me. Nancy — and by extension, Mars and the Planets — had been moving me around like a chess piece since the moment I'd arrived in town. Did they expect me to back out now that their plans had been exposed, or did they think I'd see it through to the end?

There was no way for me to know, so I had to do the thing I was prepared to live with.

Unfortunately, the thing I could live with was also the thing that could result in me no longer living. It was a paradox and a conundrum all rolled into one. Just like me. The paranormal PI who didn't like taking on supernatural cases — but who ended up doing it anyway. I couldn't decide if Fate had a great sense of humour, or was completely devoid of one altogether.

I put my phone away and took out my gun.

"Stay here," I said to Susan. "I'll be back."

I wondered if that was true.

I went out the front door and around the side of the house to the garage. At the foot of the stairs leading up to the apartment door, I stopped and tried to recall how much the steps had creaked the last time I was here. I decided it didn't matter. Nancy had probably seen my car when I drove up. She knew I was coming.

I climbed the stairs slowly with my gun held down along my leg. When I reached the landing, I opened the door with my free hand and stepped inside.

Nancy stood at the far end of the apartment, in the archway between the main living area and the bedroom. I didn't see any sign of the mimik, and there weren't a lot of places for it to hide. There was nothing in the small entry where I stood except an open closet to my left, and it was empty except for some wire hangers and a couple pairs of winter boots lined up on the floor.

I stepped into the living area and spun quickly to the left and right, checking the corners, but they were clear. The dollhouse Rachel had been playing with the other day was pushed up against the wall opposite the small kitchenette.

I pointed the gun back at Nancy, who was watching all of this with an amused look on her face. She stood at parade rest with her hands behind her back.

"She's not here."

"Don't you mean 'it'?" I tried to peer around her into the bedroom. It was more of a compartment than a room, and I didn't see how anyone, even a mimik in the form of an eight-year-old girl, could be hiding in there.

"Tomayto, tomahto," Nancy said. "It's been living as a she for several months now. I think she likes it." She chuckled. "*She* likes *it*. Pronoun humour."

"Hilarious," I said, raising the gun so it was pointed right at her head. "Where is she?"

"Close by," Nancy said. "But let's talk about you for a minute, Mr. Renn."

"What are you, a psychiatrist?"

"No, not exactly."

"And you're not exactly a nurse, either, are you?"

"No, I'm not a nurse, either."

"So what do you do for Mars?" I asked. "Are you his on-staff monster-whisperer?"

"I'm a facilitator," Nancy said. "I set things up for him. I align the stars when they won't align on their own."

"You've been in Sycamore for months. I guess the stars weren't very cooperative. I hope Mars pays overtime."

"He said you were funny. He very much enjoyed meeting you."

"Is that what this was all about?" I asked. "The mimik, the murders. All so Mars could meet me? He could've just come by my office. I'm in the yellow pages."

"We didn't plan for it to happen this way. We just took advantage of certain opportunities."

"The portal," I said. "How did you even find out about it in the first place?"

"We have our ways," Nancy said. "The PIA aren't the only ones listening."

"And the Weavers?"

"What happened to Doug was his own fault," Nancy said dismissively. "You mess with the bull, you get the horns. You mess with the Black Lands, you get killed. And that's only the start of your problems."

"What about Rachel?" I said. "Was it her fault, too?"

Nancy gave a small shrug. "If she hadn't wandered off that day, then none of this would have happened. She'd still be alive, her father would still be alive. Not to mention all those other people. Isn't it amazing how one small action can ripple outward with such devastating effects?"

"Are you saying Rachel is dead?" I'd already considered the possibility — more like the probability — but speaking the words aloud made it seem real.

Nancy frowned like she was disappointed in me. "Of course she is. She didn't go skipping across the street. *She went to the Black Lands.* What did you think would happen to her over there?" She let out an exaggerated sigh. "Well, she's not the first little girl to go wandering darkside." Her eyes locked onto mine and she grinned. "Is she, Felix?"

My finger tensed on the trigger. "You wanted me to find the portal. You led me right to it. Was that your master plan? To feed me to something in the Black Lands? You know there are easier ways to kill someone."

"You can't play chess until you know how the pieces move," Nancy said.

"Still seems like a waste of a perfectly good portal."

"How so?"

"Portals are rare," I said. "Especially an undocumented one. It would've been invaluable to an organization like the Planets, but it's worthless to you now that the PIA knows about it."

Nancy's grin faltered, and for the first time I felt like I had the upper hand.

"It was a calculated risk," she said. "What are the odds someone would survive a trip to the Black Lands?" She tried to reassert her smile, but it sat awkwardly on her face, like a mask that didn't quite fit. "I admit, you've turned out to be much more resourceful than we originally thought."

"Are you impressed or disappointed?" I asked.

"We expected you to contact the PIA. What we didn't count on was that they already had an operative in town." She hesitated. "That... complicated matters, and introduced an element we had not foreseen. We certainly didn't expect them to send Agent Baffle."

"You know her?"

"She is like you, alone in the darkness, but much more volatile and unpredictable. A veritable wild card in a situation such as this. But we have to play the hand we're dealt." She licked her lips. "We decided to proceed, thinking that two outsiders such as you and Agent Baffle might end up can-celling each other out. That your pride and your stubbornness would end up working in our favour."

"Kill two birds with one hand grenade, is that it?"

"If only it were that easy," Nancy said. "I thought if the portal didn't take care of you, then Doug Weaver would do the job. But look at what you've done!" Her grin returned, wide and radiant. "You killed the monster and saved the town. With a little help from your friend." Then, just as quickly, the grin fell from her face. "Only there's still one monster left, and Agent Baffle isn't here to help you this time."

I was suddenly struck by an intuition so strong I knew it was true.

"You can't control it anymore, can you?"

Nancy stared at me for so long I thought she wasn't going to answer. Then she said:

"No, I can't. I'm not sure if she's gotten stronger or if she just adapted. I don't suppose it matters now."

"What's stopping her from killing you?"

"Nothing," Nancy said. "But I'm beyond such concerns now."

"What does that mean?"

"It means I failed. And Mars doesn't accept failure. From anyone."

"Where is it?" I asked again.

"You'll find out soon enough," Nancy said. "Or it will find you. It's all part of the fun. Mimiks are such fascinating creatures. Especially to see them in the wild. Did you know they can shapeshift into other things besides living beings? Like a child's dollhouse for instance."

I didn't hesitate. I spun around and fired...

... and put three rounds into a perfectly ordinary wooden dollhouse.

By the time I turned back to Nancy, she had brought her hands out from behind her back. One of them held a gun. But it wasn't pointed at me. The muzzle was jammed under her chin.

"What are you doing?" I took a step forward. "Put down the gun."

"I'm glad we had this chance to talk," Nancy said. "I'll see you on the other side."

"Wait!" I shouted. "Why are you doing this?"

Nancy gave me the same disappointed frown, like I should already know the answer to this question.

"Because you have a shadow on you."

She smiled at me and pulled the trigger.

CHAPTER 42

I RAN OVER to her, but Nancy was dead before her body hit the ground. The ceiling overhead was splattered with a Rorschach of blood, bone, and brain tissue.

I checked under the bed, just in case the mimik was hiding under there, but it was clear.

So where was it? The answer was: anywhere. It could be lurking around somewhere outside, or in the woods, or it could have even gone back to the portal. Maybe it had finally gotten tired of living as an eight-year-old girl and decided to go home.

Either way, I felt like I had fulfilled my moral obligation by seeing this through... well, if not to the end, then pretty damn close to it. It was time to leave the hunting of the dangerous supernatural creature to the professionals. The police should be arriving any minute now, and if someone at the PIA managed to pass along my message, Alice and a STAR team would be close behind them.

I left the apartment and went back down the stairs, keenly aware of how dark it was outside. The mimik could have been watching me at that very moment. I dashed back to the house with my gun out in front of me, ready to fire on any shape that came darting out of the shadows.

The light was still on in the living room, and I only hoped that Susan hadn't passed out. I couldn't carry her to my car and cover us at the same time. But I couldn't leave her behind, either.

I came around the side of the house and heard a creaking sound. I pointed my gun at the front door, which stood a couple of inches ajar. I tried to remember if I had closed it when I left, but I couldn't remember.

Moving quietly and carefully, I pushed the door open with my foot and went inside. I debated closing it behind me, then decided to leave it open, and stepped through the foyer and into the living room.

Susan was still sitting in the wingback chair, but her scotch glass was lying on the rug. It seemed funny at the time that this was the first thing I noticed. The second was that her head was missing. Her neck was a mangled stump from which a heavy stream of blood had poured, painting her shirt a bright, livid red. Blood was pooled in her lap and crimson tendrils ran down the legs of her jeans. The back of the chair where her head had rested was stained with a gruesome dark smear.

The attack had been sudden and vicious — and it had come from behind. Susan didn't have time to stand much less put up any kind of struggle. The mimik had creeped up behind her, grabbed her head, and tore it off. It had accomplished this with speed and ease, as if it had simply ripped the head off one of Rachel Weaver's dolls. And it had happened recently. Very recently.

I retreated slowly out of the room, wondering why I wasn't hearing any police sirens. Was it possible they weren't coming? Did the 911 operator think my call was a practical joke? And what about Alice and the PIA? Was I suddenly the star of a Black Lands fable called The Boy Who Cried Mimik?

I decided it was time to leave, and with haste. Susan was dead and I was going to be next if I stuck around any longer.

Despite that, it required a herculean effort just to step across the threshold of the front door. It wasn't because of my nyctophobia, which was still there but more or less kept in check. No, what really scared me at that moment was the idea of the mimik lurking about — either inside the house or somewhere outside. I didn't know where to go, so my body decided it wasn't going anywhere.

As I stood there on the porch, my brain issuing commands that my muscles refused to carry out, I heard that low creaking sound again. It wasn't coming from the front door. And another thing: I recognized the sound. I'd heard it before. The first time I'd come here to meet Susan.

I finally got my legs to work and went around to the other side of the house, the one away from the garage. *The* dark *side of the house*, whispered an insidious little voice in my head.

All I could see was the tall silhouette of the oak tree set against the night sky. As my eyes began to adjust, I could make out the swing hanging from one of the branches… and someone sitting on the wooden seat. It had the shape of a little girl, but that's not what it was.

I shot a quick look over my shoulder. My car was only twenty yards away. Could I make it there before the mimik was on me? Maybe, but I didn't know how fast it was. The mimik wasn't making any move to attack me, but that could change at any moment, and a sudden movement on my part might provoke it. But then, I reminded myself, Susan Weaver had only been sitting in her chair nursing a glass of scotch when she was killed.

I raised my gun with one hand and used the other to fish out my cell phone. I turned on the flashlight app and shined it at the figure on the swing.

Rachel was sitting with her back to me, pushing herself slowly back and forth with the tips of her toes. She looked at me over her shoulder, and winced at the glare of the light.

"Too bright," she said, wrinkling her nose in distaste.

She didn't like the light, but she didn't seem afraid of it. So much for that idea.

She stood up and something fell out of her lap. It landed on the ground and rolled a little ways toward me… right into the path of the light.

It was Susan Weaver's head.

I swung the light and my gun back over to Rachel. Her clothes were splattered with gore. At a glance, she might have looked like any kid after a long, fun-filled day of playing outdoors. But these weren't mud or grass stains. It was blood and she was drenched in it. Staring at her I thought this was how she must have looked after killing Doug Weaver. I tried to picture what had happened afterwards, this small blood-covered girl carting a full-grown man's mangled body to a portal located miles away. How had she manage to do that? I wondered. And without being seen?

But of course that wasn't the way it had happened. Despite outward appearances, this was not an eight-year-old girl. It was a supernatural creature from the Black Lands, and it had been more than capable of carrying the body across such a distance. And no one had seen because it hadn't driven to the vacant lot on Burnside Road. It had taken a more direct route — through the woods. Helton had said something about a blood trail leading from Doug Weaver's truck into the park.

Rachel took a step toward me.

I pointed the gun and the light at her face. "Stop," I said. "Right now."

She stopped, which surprised me, and seemed to surprise her, too, if the look on her face was any indication. I wondered how much this thing understood of human speech. Maybe it responded to simple commands like a dog. Could I get it to stay? Play dead? Or be dead for real?

Another thought struck me, one I'd never even considered until now. What if this wasn't a supernatural creature? What if this actually was Rachel Weaver and something had been done to her in the Black Lands? Something that had made her like... this? If I shot her, I'd be murdering a child.

She took another step toward me.

"Stop!" I said again. "I'll shoot."

I wasn't so sure I would. And Rachel didn't seem sure, either. Her head was tilted down to avoid the light, her face concealed in a mask of shadow.

She took another step forward and raised her head. The light from my phone shined on her fully, but her face was still dark. As I watched, the darkness spilled down her neck to her shoulders. Her hands were turning black, too, like they'd been dipped in ink. That was all I could see of her exposed skin, but the darkness was no doubt spreading across her entire body.

She was changing. Her face narrowed and her cheeks sank in like her head was collapsing into itself. Her hair pulled back tight to her skull, then rose in a pair of horn-like ridges. Her mouth spread wide in a thin black line, while her arms and legs began to elongate into spindly sticks. Her hands stretched out and jagged nails sprouted from the tips of her fingers. There was a series of tearing sounds as her clothing stretched and ripped, unable to accommodate the new size and shape of the body inside them. The mimik's black skin was visible through the tears in the material, like black tar seeping out of cracks in the earth.

I found myself transfixed by the creature's metamorphosis. There was something darkly fascinating about watching a harmless young girl transform into a vicious supernatural monster. I might have stood there hypnotized until the creature eviscerated me if one of its feet hadn't snapped out involuntarily and kicked Susan Weaver's severed head like a soccer ball. It struck me in the shin and broke my reverie.

I raised my gun and fired three shots, striking the creature square in the chest and sending it flying backwards onto the lawn.

I'd actually pulled the trigger four times, but there had only been three bullets left in the gun. I'd used the first three to murder a perfectly innocent dollhouse, and I'd neglected to reload them after I left the garage. That was a mistake that could end up costing me my life.

I backed away from where the mimik lay unmoving on the ground. I wondered if I had managed to kill it, but wasn't about to go over there to check for a pulse. I didn't know if a mimik even had a heart.

What I needed to do was reload my gun, and I couldn't do that while I was holding it and my cell phone at the same time. I looked over at my car again, then at the front door of the Weavers' house, which was still standing open.

The house was closer, I decided, and easier to fortify, if it came to that. I could too easily picture myself locked in the car only to have the mimik smash through one of the windows.

I went through the open doorway, threw the door shut, and locked it. I slipped my phone into my pocket and pulled out my speedloader. I opened the cylinder on my Ruger, dumped the empties on the floor, then popped in the speedloader, turned it to slide in the fresh rounds, and dropped it on the floor, too. I managed to do all this in about four seconds, which was pretty good considering how badly my hands were shaking.

I stood there in the foyer for a long span of time, my head cocked at a listening angle. I started to think maybe I really had killed the mimik.

Then something heavy and pissed-off slammed into the door from the other side, causing me to jump back.

I glanced into the living room, where Susan Weaver's headless body was still reposing in the wingback chair. I wasn't going in there, so I backed down the central hallway toward a door at the far end, keeping my eyes — and my gun — trained on the front door that continued to bang and tremble in its wooden frame.

I bumped the door with my shoulder and discovered it was a swing door. I pushed through it into a kitchen that would have looked rustic and cozy with its dark-wood cabinets and butcher-block island if I wasn't currently being pursued by a blood-thirsty monster.

I put my gun down on the counter and started pushing a heavy maple table in front of the door. Out in the hallway, the steady, monotonous banging had changed to the much less pleasant sound of splintering wood.

I got the table wedged up against the swing door a split second before the mimik crashed into it from the other side. The table slid back a few inches, legs screeching on the tile floor, but it was a solid piece of furniture, and I managed to push it back against the door.

Apparently the mimik didn't like that and let out a wail so high-pitched it felt like someone had jammed a metal coat hanger through my eardrums.

I looked frantically around the room and spotted another door in the corner. It was a risk taking my weight off the table, but I didn't have a choice. I ran over and opened the door, then pawed around inside for a light switch. I knocked over a broom that had been propped against the wall, then tried the other side, found the light, and turned it on. It was a pantry. No escape there.

The mimik struck the door again. The table slid back with another harsh screech. I went over and pushed it back, then held it there while my gaze continued to rove around the room.

My eyes fell on the stove, and on a whim — maybe because it was close by, or maybe because I was starting to get the inkling of a plan — I reached out and turned on all of the burners. A couple of tea towels hung from the oven handle. I grabbed them and dropped them on top of the burners.

There was a back door leading out of the house. If I could find something to properly brace the swing door, I could make a run for it and get to my car without the mimik even realizing it.

Then my gaze drifted to the right — to the archway that led into the dining room. There was no door there, which meant there was nothing stopping the mimik from going back down the hallway to the living room, through the dining room, and into the kitchen. So why didn't it do that?

Another hard slam against the door, followed by another high-pitched wail, provided a possible answer.

Maybe the mimik was too angry to think clearly. Or maybe it didn't have those basic problem-solving skills we human beings take for granted. I didn't know anything about this type of creature, much less how smart it was. It might only have animal-level intelligence, or it could be smarter than I was. But the fact that it was throwing itself against the door over and over again rather than going around to the other side seemed to suggest the former.

We had reached a stalemate, at least until the mimik either broke down the door or figured out there was another way into the kitchen.

I reached out and dragged over one of the chairs that went with the table. I stacked it on top, then grabbed another chair and did the same thing.

The mimik hit the door again, and a long splinter of wood in the upper panel came flying out. A set of claws appeared in the narrow gap, long and dirty yellow, like blades of amber. They chopped at the hole in a mad frenzy, making it wider.

I reached over to the counter and picked up my gun. I pointed it at the hole, then pursed my lips and made a whistling sound like I was calling a dog.

The mimik stopped clawing at the door, and for a moment the hole was filled with a shifting blackness. I waited until I saw the creature's eye peering through — it was same dirty yellow as its claws, split with a narrow reptilian pupil — then I fired all six shots. The mimik howled in pain.

That's it, I thought. That has to be it. There's no way it—

The door came apart in an explosion of wood. The kitchen table slammed back into me and I was knocked to the floor. I lost my gun. I heard it clatter on the floor somewhere, but I didn't bother to look for it. It was empty, and I didn't have time to reload it again.

Climbing back to my feet, I once again considered making a run for it. But I didn't think I would make it. If I died tonight, it wasn't going to be while I was running and scared. If this really was the end, I would meet it on my own terms, standing and scared.

The mimik was clambering through the hole it had made in the door. It was still wearing the shredded remains of Rachel Weaver's clothes, which made me think of all the outfits the Incredible Hulk must have gone through. Strange things go through your mind when you think you're about to die.

Once it was through the door, the mimik crouched on the kitchen floor. At its full height it probably would've been close to six feet tall, but hunched down like it was, with its legs bent, it looked no bigger than the child it had been masquerading as these past months. It reached out with one of its long, sinewy arms and flipped the heavy maple table out of its path like it weighed next to nothing.

There was a knife block on the counter. I reached over and pulled one out. Bread knife. I tried again and got a large chef's knife. I brandished it at the mimik — a kind of stabby-stabby motion to get the point across to its dumb monster mind — but if it was scared it didn't show it.

I stared into the creature's eyes, looking for some indication that I could reason with this thing, or, failing that, maybe transmit my own sense of threat and superior dominance. But it was like looking into the eyes of a giant insect. I saw nothing in there but alien indifference.

Right at that moment, the tea towels on the stove went up in flames. The mimik snapped its head toward them, then recoiled from the flames. I couldn't tell if it was an instinctive response or one of actual fear.

It didn't matter. I had the distraction I needed.

With the mimik's attention momentarily diverted, I charged forward with the knife raised in both hands and brought it down in a flash of glinting steel. The blade sank into the creature's narrow chest with a solid *thunk*. If there was blood, I didn't see any. It was like stabbing a thick melon.

The mimik's head whipped around and screeched right in my face. It grabbed me by the upper arms, its taloned fingers biting painfully into my flesh, and slammed me into the side of the counter.

I grabbed onto the handle of the knife, as much to steady myself as to pull it out for another attack. I jerked it back and forth and side to side, but it was buried deep in the creature's chest. The mimik howled as I worked the blade around, making the wound larger. It shook me again, then threw its arms out wide, repelling me away.

I landed on my back and went sliding across the floor. My head slammed into the drawer under the stove with a loud, metallic bang. I groaned in pain and reached down to push myself up. My hand fell on something hard and narrow. It was the broom I'd knocked over earlier. I picked it up and climbed unsteadily to my feet.

The tea towels were burning merrily now; the flames were climbing the wall to lick the wooden cabinets above the stove. I reached over and stuck the head of the broom into the flames. The straw bristles immediately started to burn, and when I turned to face the mimik, I was holding a torch.

Only the mimik wasn't paying attention to me. It was turned slightly away, its attention focused on pulling the knife out of its chest. It was having some difficulty accomplishing this; it couldn't seem to get a grip on the handle with its long claws. Then, as I watched, its fingers seemed to melt and reshape themselves into narrower, more articulate digits. It wrapped its newly-formed hands around the handle of the knife and pulled it out with a powerful jerk. A geyser of black blood came out with it, the first indication I'd seen that this creature could incur physical damage.

Time to see if I could inflict some more.

While the mimik had its head down, examining the wound on its chest like it had never experienced such a thing before, I thrust out with the torch, jamming it right in the creature's face. It howled and batted the flaming broomhead away, stumbling back a few steps until it was in the corner of the room.

I moved forward and jabbed at it again. The mimik didn't have anywhere to go, so it tried to grab the torch with one hand while slashing at me with the other. I managed to hold onto the torch, but couldn't avoid the long reach of the creature's claws. They sliced up my left side, parting the material of my coat and shirt, and the skin underneath in a hot sizzle of pain.

I bit down on the cry that filled my throat and drove forward with the torch. It struck the mimik in the chest and the creature howled in pain. It made another grab for the broom and managed to latch onto it this time. We struggled for a moment, then it brought its other hand down in a powerful blow that snapped the wooden handle in two. The burning end fell to the floor, and I was left holding a broken stick.

I experienced a brief moment of déjà vu, remembering the other night when I'd attacked Doug Weaver with the shovel.

The mimik advanced on me.

I gripped the broken broom handle with both hands, and the moment it was within range, I swung a line-drive right at its head. The mimik didn't even try to move — either it didn't know what I was doing, or it didn't care — and the broom handle struck the side of its skull with a solid cracking sound. I might as well have hit it with a pillow for all the effect it had.

The mimik tilted its head from side to side, like it was working a kink out of its neck, then it continued toward me.

Now I was the one being backed into a corner.

As it approached, the mimik began jerking its head forward in strange birdlike movements, snapping its jaws at me in small nips. I knew it could move faster than that. It felt like it was playing with me, taunting me, daring me to run. Maybe it preferred the thrill of the hunt to attacking cornered prey.

During one of these darting head movements, I raised the broom handle and swung it down into the creature's face. The jagged end pierced one of mimik's amber-coloured eyes. It howled in pain and slashed out blindly with its claws. I skipped back out of its reach and my foot bumped the knife it had pulled out of its chest. I bent down to pick it up just as the mimik launched itself at me.

It crashed into me like a defensive tackle, driving us both to the floor. It started snapping at me with its needle teeth — faster attacks this time; it wasn't messing around now — with the broken broom handle protruding from its eye. I raised my hands to hold its head away and discovered I had managed to hold onto the knife. I swung it in an awkward sideways blow and drove half the blade into its other eye.

The mimik let out an ear-splitting shriek and flung itself away from me. It stumbled across the room on its sticklike legs, dripping spatters of blood on the floor that looked like hot tar.

Speaking of hot, the kitchen was getting very toasty. The fire that had started on the stove now engulfed half the room.

The mimik was staggering right toward it, which didn't make any sense until I realized it could no longer see where it was going with both of its eyes skewered. But it could still feel, and when it got too close to the flames it recoiled away, scurrying across the floor in search of escape. It stumbled toward a nearby doorway and, presumably thinking it was the swing door it had smashed through to get into the kitchen, it went scampering inside.

But it wasn't the swing door. It was the pantry. And there was no way out of there.

I jumped to my feet, wincing at the pain that ran down my entire left side, and ran over to the door, throwing it closed. Then I dragged the table over in front of it.

There was a hollow bang as the mimik threw itself against the other side of the door. The creature must have been seriously wounded because there wasn't much force behind the blow, and I was able to hold the table in place. I probably could have stayed there until the mimik bled to death, but the flames were spreading closer and the room was rapidly filling with thick black smoke. If I stayed much longer, all of my escape routes would be cut off.

There'd been nothing else from the mimik since that single feeble bump against the door. I thought it must be dead, or close to it. But what if it wasn't? What if it was waiting for me to leave so it could push the table away from the door and escape?

I managed to hold out for another couple of minutes before the flames and the smoke reached the point where I had to make a decision. I could stay here and make sure the mimik was dead, its body burned to a crisp, but I'd end up sharing the same fate. Or I could leave and risk setting the mimik free.

I decided I wanted to live more than I wanted the mimik dead.

Before I left, I stacked three of the kitchen chairs on top of the table, and wedged the fourth between the table and the island, making it so the mimik wouldn't be able to get the pantry door open. It was the best I could do.

As I scrambled toward the back door, bent over at the waist to stay clear of the smoke, I saw my gun lying on the floor in the corner. I picked it up on my way went out.

CHAPTER 43

THE FIRE DEPARTMENT showed up before the police, but it was too late for either of them. Everyone was dead and the house was a lost cause. I sat in my car on the other side of the road and watched it burn.

The flames reached out toward the oak tree at the side of the house, and it went up like an enormous matchhead. The fire devoured the old dry bark, blackening the limbs, and snapping the ropes of the swing. The garage was far enough away that it would probably survive the fire, although the police probably wouldn't know what to make of what they'd find inside. I doubted if there was anything to connect Nancy to Mars and the Planets except my word, and I wasn't sure yet if I was going to say anything about it.

Detective Helton showed up with a few other members of the task force. There was some confusion when he asked me what had happened. I did my best to explain that there had been two murderers operating in Sycamore, one of them a supernatural creature called a mimik, the other Doug Weaver, or at least a reanimated version of him created by the mimik. I think I lost him when I told him the creature had been living in the Weaver household these past few months under the guise of their daughter Rachel.

Fortunately it didn't matter because at that moment the PIA showed up in a couple of Crown Vics with government plates. They pulled in behind the ambulance where I was sitting in the back getting my side patched up. Helton went over to tell them they couldn't park there. Half a dozen agents emerged from the two cars and immediately began to ignore him. Alice was among them.

She came up to the ambulance and said, "You give them a statement?"

"I was trying," I said, "but I don't think they…"

"Good," she said. "Stop talking. That'll be hard for you, but do it anyway. This is now a PIA investigation and we don't want you speaking to anyone but us. Once the fire's out, the locals can get the hell out of my crime scene."

"I really missed you, Alice."

She nodded at the line of bandages taped to my side. "What was it?"

"A mimik," I said. "It had been masquerading as the Weavers' daughter."

Alice considered that, then said, "So what you're saying is that you got beat up by an eight-year-old girl."

"I shot her, several times, but it didn't seem to bother her much."

The EMT who was working on me stopped what she was doing and looked at us with wide, uncertain eyes.

"Can you give us a few minutes?" Alice said. "National security."

The EMT held up her latex-gloved hands in a sure-whatever gesture and went away. Alice climbed into the ambulance and sat next to me.

"What happened to the real girl?"

"Dead," I said. "She stumbled upon the portal a few months ago. That's what started this whole thing. She must've encountered the mimik over there and it took her form after it…" I trailed off.

"I'm sorry," Alice said. "The Black Lands takes. It doesn't borrow and it doesn't give back."

I nodded and we were silent for a time. A couple of PIA agents were having a loud, angry conversation with Helton and the Sycamore cops. The firefighters ignored them and continued their business of putting out the fire.

Eventually, Alice said, "I shouldn't have let you come out here by yourself."

I looked over at her.

"I knew you wanted to finish this on your own," she said, "and I thought you could."

"So did I."

"I thought it was the wife who killed the first two victims, not a supernatural. I guess we both messed up."

"The mimik killed Doug Weaver. There was something in its bite that made him more violent than the average undead."

Alice glanced down at my bandaged wounds. "Did it bite you?"

"No," I said, "but it clawed me up pretty good."

Alice looked away for a moment, then turned back and said: "It's probably nothing. Just don't die and get buried in the Black Lands and you should be fine."

"Thanks," I said with a laugh. "That makes me feel better."

"I could put you in quarantine again if you'd prefer."

"I think I'll take my chances."

"What are your plans now?"

"My plans?" I said. "I'm gonna go home and sleep for about a month. After that, I'm going to apply for a job at Home Depot, because even if the pay isn't great, at least it's regular." I looked at the smoldering ruin that was the Weavers' residence. "My last pay cheque just went up in flames along with my client."

"Oh, I almost forgot." Alice reached into her coat pocket and took out a small folded slip of paper. She passed it to me. "Diane wanted me to make sure I gave this to you."

I unfolded the paper. It was a cheque.

"What's this?" I asked.

"Think of it as a consultation fee," Alice said. "Along with some hazard pay."

I stared at the cheque for a long time. It was more than enough to cover my expenses and give Sandra the raise she had been asking for. With a little left over to blow the cobwebs out of my savings account. I let out a dry chuckle.

"I'm not sure I deserve this."

"Why's that?" Alice said.

"Well, besides the fact that it was *you* who saved *me* from the zombie Doug Weaver, I didn't do much in this case except stumble around until I eventually tripped over the truth. My client lied to me about her husband being missing. The woman working for her turned out to be an operative of a major crime syndicate. And the girl she was supposed to be taking care of was, in reality, a supernatural creature. I didn't find out about any of these things until they told me — and it very nearly got me killed. That doesn't exactly make me the world's greatest private detective."

Alice gave me a long, thoughtful stare. "There was a monster in this town. Two of them. They would have gone on killing people for who knows how long if you hadn't stopped them. Mars may have brought you here, but your actions are your own."

I lowered my head. "I still made mistakes. Big ones."

Alice pinched my chin between her thumb and index finger and raised my head until we locked eyes. "We lead dark, dangerous lives, Felix. We live, we learn. If we don't, we die. Simple as that."

She helped me out of the ambulance and we stood there looking at each other awkwardly — unsure whether to hug or shake hands or clap each other on the back. I decided on a small nod and headed for my car.

"We'll need to debrief you," Alice shouted after me. "We don't know much about mimiks."

"You know where to find me," I called back.

"You know something, Renn? I think I might be starting to like you."

I stopped and looked back at her. "Really?"

Alice shrugged. "I'm sure it'll pass," she said, and walked away.

I climbed into my car and started the engine. The radio came on with a news update about the portal in Boston. I turned it off.

I didn't need to listen to it. I already knew what it would say.

The portals would keep coming and people would keep disappearing into them. Sometimes they would come back, but most times they wouldn't, and the planet would keep right on spinning. Light side to dark, dark side to light.

The Black Lands only had a dark side. The time I spent there had changed me in ways I still didn't fully understand. Most human beings couldn't survive in a world of forever night, but I understood now that some people were meant to live part of their lives in darkness.

Alice was one of them.

So was I.

I couldn't deny it any longer. I knew it to be true.

There was a shadow on me.

ACKNOWLEDGMENTS

THIS BOOK HAS been a long time coming.

As some readers already know, I've been writing Black Lands stories for the past 15 years. They have appeared in various forms — chapbooks, anthologies, magazines — but I always knew there would be a novel that would truly kick off the series and (hopefully) draw in even more readers. *Sycamore* is that novel, and I feel it is both a culmination of all of the stories published to date, as well as an introduction to the series for those entering the Black Lands for very first time.

I'm not sure exactly when I came up with the idea for Felix Renn and the Black Lands, but I know *how* I came up with them. It happened because I wanted to combine two of my favourite types of stories — horror and crime.

I am by no means the first person to mix these two genres together. The occult detective character goes all the way back to Fitz James O'Brien in the 1850s, although the most memorable example from back in the day is probably Thomas Carnacki, created by the English fantasy writer William Hope Hodgson (there's also a good argument to be made on behalf of Dr. Abraham Van Helsing from Bram Stoker's *Dracula*).

There is something deeply compelling about combining paranormal fiction with the police procedural. Perhaps it's because they both deal with our innate curiosity of the natural (and supernatural) world, combined with our fascination for unsolved mysteries. Perhaps it's our almost pathological need to bring order to chaos — especially when it comes to the things that scare and disturb us.

I can't say for certain, only that I've been a lifelong fan of these types of stories. And I'm not alone. The occult detective character has become enormously popular over the years and has appeared in virtually every type of media. One of the most notable early examples, *Kolchak: The Night Stalker*, a cult TV show from the 1970s, was a direct influence on Chris Carter who ended up creating *The X-Files*. Mulder and Scully may be agents of the FBI rather than private investigators, but they both certainly qualify as occult detectives. Same goes for the blue-collar parapsychologists in *Ghostbusters*. To me they're no different than Felix Renn — just another group of ordinary folks trying to make their way in a world where paranormal has become the norm.

My favourite occult detective novel (I call them "supernoirturals") is William Hjortsberg's *Falling Angel* (later filmed as *Angel Heart*, which is also excellent). For me it's the perfect blend of horror and detective fiction, a story that owes as much to Raymond Chandler as it did Hodgson. I knew from the moment I first read it that these were the types of stories I wanted to write.

But first I needed to create a detective of my own.

I remember how I came up with his name. *Felix* is from the only two novels published by the late John Steakley — *Armor*, a military sci-fi tale, and *Vampire$*, an action-packed urban fantasy that received a very unfortunate (and very unfaithful) film adaptation by the otherwise excellent John Carpenter. The two books couldn't be more different from each other, but they both featured an enigmatic character named Felix (no last name). The surname *Renn* came from my favourite David Cronenberg film, *Videodrome*, whose protagonist, played by James Woods, is named Max Renn. Nothing terribly earthshattering there, but I've always enjoyed little easter eggs like that. (Want another one? Felix's ex-wife/assistant is named Sandra, after Sandra Dee — which is also Felix's nickname for her — in honour of *Gidget*, one of the very first surfing films ever made, and a personal favourite of mine.)

As a private-eye character Felix Renn is a bit of an odd duck. Even though my main influences include Ross Macdonald's Lew Archer books, Dashiell Hammett's Continent Op, and Robert B. Parker's Spenser series, Felix is a very different kind of detective. He isn't a former police officer, nor does he have a military background, as is often the case with other private investigators. He isn't a great fighter or a terribly deep thinker. And yet the more I write about him the more compelling he becomes to me. Felix is an ordinary guy who, despite his flaws, still manages to get the job done. After having written about him for 15 years, I've come to understand it's his flaws that make him interesting. It's part of the reason I enjoy writing scenes with Felix and his ex-wife Sandra. I created her because I wanted to take the popular detective story tropes and turn them on their head — in this case, the stereotypical assistant with the witty repartee and the sexual tension. I wondered, What would happen if the detective actually had a relationship with his assistant? Then I thought, What if I take it even further and they got married? *Then* I thought, What if I take it even further still and they got married, then got divorced, and now they're trying to find a way to become friends again because they're not quite done with each other yet? Now *that* was interesting to me. The rest of Felix's past has yet to be revealed, but I like to think this is part of the mystery of the series. For me these stories are as much about Felix's place in the world of the Black Lands as they are the supernatural cases he solves.

After I had my private detective character ready to go, my next task was to come up with a world to drop him into. Just like I knew from the get-go that my occult detective would be different from all the others, I also knew the world in which I set these stories would also need to be different. One thing I was tired of reading about or seeing in film and television were stories in which the detective spends an exhausting amount of time convincing the people around him that the supernatural is real, that ghosts and monsters actually exist. I find it to be a rather boring story trope, and one I was more than happy to ignore.

In order to do this, I created a setting for Felix in which the supernatural has been a part of everyday life for some time — all the way back to the late 1940s, to be exact. That's when the portals first started popping up, doorways to a world of perpetual night that was populated by every nightmarish monster you could imagine (and many more you couldn't). The timeline was intentional because I wanted the world to have been living for some time with the existence of the Black Lands, almost to the point where they've gotten used to its presence. And for Felix, I wanted a character who was born into this world. Someone whose existence has always been threatened by the reality of supernatural creatures lurking close by.

The first Felix Renn/Black Lands story was called "Temporary Monsters." It was published by Burning Effigy Press in September of 2009. "The Ash

Angels" followed a year later. Then "Black Eyed Kids," one of my most popular Black Lands stories to date, a year after that.

From there the series expanded to include other recurring characters — like Jerry Baldwin, who sells haunted houses for a living. I also started writing Black Lands stories that didn't include any recurring characters at all — it's a big world, after all, and I was curious to see how other people, from different walks of life, were getting along in this darkly dangerous world.

While there are story arcs and character arcs in the Black Lands series, I've always tried to write these stories in such a way that they all function as standalones. I learned this from my friend Jeffrey Thomas, who does something similar with his Punktown series. Stephen King does it too in much of his fiction, which is largely set in the same shared universe. I've always liked the idea of planting easter eggs in my stories, something that would enrich the experience for eagle-eyed fans without excluding the casual reader. It can be a challenge sometimes, but it's also part of the fun.

No one takes on an endeavour of this size without some serious help. So I'd like to take a moment to give a monster-sized shout-out to all of the folks who have helped me (and Felix) since the very beginning.

First and foremost, my thanks to Monica S. Kuebler, for being the first publisher to take a chance on the Black Lands. If it wasn't for you, this series probably would have died on the table and certainly wouldn't have a home today.

I also wanted to extend my thanks to Kevin Lucia, who picked up the baton and brought this series to Cemetery Dance Publications. My extreme gratitude to Dan Franklin and Richard Chizmar, as well, for believing in me and the Black Lands. And to Ben Baldwin (who I first worked with on the reissue of *Every House Is Haunted*, also from Cemetery Dance) for his phenomenal cover art.

Thanks to Mike Carey, who has been a big supporter of my Black Lands tales and wrote the introduction to my Felix Renn collection *SuperNOIRtural Tales* (which will be reprinted by Cemetery Dance in 2025). My childhood friend Kevin Drake, who lent me his expertise on police procedure; Daryl Foster, for helping me to keep my nose to the grindstone and my fingers on the keyboard; and Norman Partridge for his early support of the series and his bountiful kindness (I owe you big time, pard!).

My deepest thanks to Ray Cluley and Jess Jordan for their friendship and constant support (and all the cocktail recipes!). To Jake Witucki for his thoughtful feedback and keen eye for detail. Your Zen-like calm is the perfect antidote for my occasional bouts of writerly hysteria.

I also want to thank everyone who has been reading the Black Lands stories and supporting my work from the very beginning: Laird Barron, Craig Davidson, Gef Fox, Richard Gavin, Orrin Grey, Sadie Hartmann, Claire Horsnell, John Hornor Jacobs, Michael Kelly, John Langan, David Longhorn, Robert Shearman, Simon Strantzas, Jeffrey Thomas, Paul Tremblay, and Michael Wehunt.

Thanks are also in order to my agent Jack Gernert, who several years ago managed to bring me back from the dead without having to haul my rotting corpse through a portal and burying it the Black Lands. I couldn't have done any of this without his hard work and business expertise. Same goes for Peter Katz, who does the same thing for me on the film/TV side of things. I'm extremely fortunate to have you both on my team.

Much love and thanks to my family, especially my parents and my sister, who have been reading my stories since I was writing them with crayons (often with illustrations). Your love and support mean the world to me.

And finally, I want to thank my wife Kathryn, whose love and support has sustained me over the long years, especially during those times when I thought this book would never be written, much less published. Even when I doubted myself — and it happened often — she has never once wavered in her belief that I was meant to be a writer. She has always been my biggest fan, my strongest supporter, and my brightest light. I love you, Peaches.

ABOUT THE AUTHOR

IAN ROGERS IS the author of the award-winning collection, Every House Is Haunted. His novelette, "The House on Ashley Avenue," was a finalist for the Shirley Jackson Award and is currently being adapted into a feature film produced by Sam Raimi. His debut novel, Family, was published by Earthling Publications in Fall 2024. Ian lives with his wife and three cats in Peterborough, Ontario. For more information, visit ianrogers.ca.